"Methinks 'tis not my fearsome appearance you are afraid of, but my intimate touch." He smirked as she blanched white at the insinuation, knowing she feared her crew overhearing. He continued mercilessly, weeks of frustrated desire and unrelenting boredom making him harsh. "After all," he said silkily, "is it not true that only when you come too close to surrender in my arms do you run away? I'm sure," he said smoothly, seeing her face go from pure white to furious red and enjoying his newfound power over her emotions, "that were it not for our agreement, you would have locked me in that cell again for fear of your own lust! But then, you possess the key, so of course the temptation to steal in at night and ravish my poor body might prove too great. Not that I would have minded . . ."

"Bastard!" she screamed, flinging herself to her feet and heaving the table over at him. "You dare to speak such lies to me! Defend yourself!" With that, Lynnette whipped out her rapier and leveled it at Bradley. . . .

THE MAIDEN'S REVENGE

HILLARY FIELDS

St. Martin's Paperbacks

THE MAIDEN'S REVENGE

Copyright © 2000 by Hillary Fields.

All rights reserved. No part of this book may be used or reproduced in any manner whatsoever without written permission except in the case of brief quotations embodied in critical articles or reviews. For information address St. Martin's Press, 175 Fifth Avenue, New York, N.Y. 10010.

ISBN: 0-312-97282-2

Printed in the United States of America

St. Martin's Paperbacks edition / January 2000

St. Martin's Paperbacks are published by St. Martin's Press, 175 Fifth Avenue, New York, N.Y. 10010.

10 9 8 7 6 5 4 3 2 1

For Chris

THE MAIDEN'S REVENGE

PROLOGUE

*T*HE CABIN boy had fallen overboard again.

A shouted curse, followed by a resounding splash, jolted the captain from contemplative stillness to sudden action. Silhouetted against a vibrant blue sky, balancing at ease on the steeply canted deck of the port bow, the ship's commander had been idly tracking the path of a dapple-gray gull as it circled the topgallants high above. Gold-burnished red hair framed the hollow-cheeked face, and a billowing silk shirt fluttered in the sultry breeze, molding itself to a slender yet strongly muscled torso. Tight black breeches encased lean, perfectly formed legs, and a heavy sword belt was buckled low across slim hips. Power and grace fairly emanated from the captain's lithe figure.

A figure that had never, *ever* been mistaken for a man's.

Reacting instantly to the disturbance, the captain turned her attention down to the gently lapping waves below, where a quick scan of the situation told her all she needed to know. The ship's youngest crew member had slipped his tether, tumbling headlong into the aqua waters of the bay for an unexpected bath.

Lynnette swore she'd never met another human being quite so clumsy as young Davie, nor one so prone to making the same mistakes twice. She'd told the boy a hundred times to have someone else tie the knots on his makeshift sling when scraping the hull, or she'd make him do it the hard way—by keelhauling. Davie's own knots weren't worth the rope they were made from. This was the third time he'd fallen—and the last time she was going to save him.

She sighed, stripping off her high boots quickly. When they got back aboard, she was going to have someone teach the boy the correct way to tie a knot. She'd no time to mollycoddle her men.

"Damn," Lynnette swore. From all that splashing, it sounded like she'd better hurry, or he'd tire himself out before she could get to him.

She could have had one of the men aboard go after Davie, but in truth, she was the strongest swimmer on the *Maiden's Revenge,* and besides, she was their leader. It was *her* duty to protect her crew, and that, unfortunately, included fishing them out of the drink when necessary. Unbuckling her sword belt, Lynnette let it clatter to the deck. She leapt to the railing, balanced for a second, then dove cleanly into the crystal-clear waters of the Caribbean far below.

They weren't that far from the shore, reefed for the moment in a safe harbor on the north coast of Tortuga for repairs and a proper careening of the hull. The ship was pulled close to shore, and a system of weights, ropes, and pulleys held it slanted so that most of the port side was above water. That way, the sailors could get to work with their scrapers on the barnacles encrusting the hull, as well as check for possible weak spots in the seasoned wood.

Just above the waterline were several gaping holes that could only have been made by cannon fire. A couple of the men were repairing them with obvious skill and experience.

As she dove, Lynnette thought she heard someone snickering behind her on deck, but then she hit the water with a shock and, for a moment, could hear nothing as the water rushed past her. Surfacing with a gasp, she flung her long hair back impatiently out of her eyes. One of these days, she swore, she was going to cut it all off. But thoughts of shears and curls faded as she spotted Davie by the great splashes of water he was sending up. She made her way to the boy in short seconds, and had her arm beneath his shoulders before he could do more than blink.

"Easy, lad," Lynnette said calmly in his ear, "I've got you. No need to clutch me so tight; we've been through this before." She looked up to the rail of the ship, where her first mate stood ready with a rope and a grin. "Harry!" she called, and he tossed the line down before she could complete the order.

"All right, Davie-boy, up you go." The boy, a cheeky lad of thirteen, gave her a grateful, almost worshipful look and caught the end of the rope. With her support, he got a good grip and began ascending, his wiry arms more than equal to the task. When he was halfway up, Lynnette started up herself, and was soon aboard the sloping deck, dripping wet and ready to deliver a tongue-lashing the youthful cabin boy was unlikely to forget.

Before she even began, she noticed that the boy was directing his gaze somewhere below her own, and not toward the floor, either. Specifically, to her soaked white silk shirt, and what lay beneath, not at all hidden by the wet fabric. Lynnette's eyes narrowed. The coincidence was too much to be ignored. One simply did *not* fall overboard three times in a year, even in the worst weather, and the weather today was fine, sunny and hot. A perfect day, in fact, for a short dunk and a long look at the attributes of one's rescuer—especially if one was a young man just beginning to notice the fairer sex. She understood the meaning of that snicker now. Some member of her crew had figured out Davie's little scheme before she caught on to it herself.

Lynnette did not find the situation amusing.

"Don't ye think ye were a tad hard on th' boy, Cap'n?" asked Harry a little while later as they oversaw the repairs. "I mean, 'e was just havin' a little fun; nothin' any boy 'is age wouldn'a done. 'E didn' mean no harm."

Lynnette looked askance at her second-in-command. He was an older man, seamed and scarred by the weather, and other elements, to the texture of leather. He'd been her first mate as long as she'd captained the *Maiden's Revenge,* and her friend for twice that time.

"No, I do not think I was 'hard on the boy,' " she said sharply. "You know I don't tolerate that sort of insubordination from any member of my crew, not even from an imp like Davie. What do you think would happen to my authority if I let the men think of me as a woman rather than a captain? Nay." She shook her head. "Much as I like the scoundrel, he has to be punished. 'Twill serve as an example."

She spoke frankly with her first mate as she would not with anyone else. As far as Harry knew, he was the only person, the only man, at any rate, she trusted enough to do so. "Aye, Cap'n," he replied, knowing she was right. "Still, scrubbin' th' decks twice a day fer a month be a harsh punishment fer a little good-hearted deviltry."

"With any other captain," she reminded him, "it'd be a flogging."

"With any other captain," he said, grinning, "there wouldn't be a need."

"All the more reason, then, in my case." She returned her attention to the sailors below. The repairs were going well, but she was upset by the cannon-splintered wood on the port side. "That last encounter came too close to ending our lives," Lynnette remarked grimly. "As it is, we've been out of action too long. As soon as may be, we'll be shipping out. We shouldn't have had to make the repairs on Tortuga anyway. If we hadn't needed that new mast, I'd have waited until we could do it at our own base.

"Now we'll have to race to make our destination in time," she continued, voice filled with dark intent. "I wouldn't want to keep Lord Roger waiting. If the information the captain of that last vessel gave us is true, I'll face that son of a whore at last, and by God, when I'm done, there won't be enough pieces left of him to draw the sharks," she finished tightly.

"Cap'n—" Harry began, but she cut him off.

"If this is going to be another of your famous lectures on the perils of revenge, stow it. I've heard them often enough, and one more repetition won't change my mind. You know what he did to me, to Sarah. Lord Roger *will* pay."

"I wasn' gonna say no such thing, Cap'n," replied Harry doggedly. "I was merely goin' ta suggest—*suggest,* mind ye—that ye keep yer blood from boilin'. 'Taint goin' ta do no good ta stew 'pon it. Me 'n th' boys, we unnerstan' th' whys 'n wherefores of it. But as yer friend, Cap'n, I gotta tell you; this thing, 'tis eatin' at yer soul."

Before he could say more, Lynnette broke in, her voice harshly strained. "What do you expect of me, Harry? That I forget all about what that bastard did to my family? When I'm so close to final retribution?" She scowled blackly. "That I will not, cannot do."

"Nay, lass." He dared to put his hand on her arm, trying not to notice her flinching away from the gesture. "Not forget, but per'aps save it fer when it counts. In th' heat of battle." Harry sighed, wondering if he was reaching her with his words or if he was just blowing air for his own benefit. He tried again.

"This encounter's too important ta ye ta ruin by hasty action. Ye got ta keep yer head clear fer plannin' an' fightin' when th' time comes." He didn't dare say so, but he was worried for her. All that drove his captain was guts and a burning need for revenge, and he was afraid the flames of her dark ambition would consume her if she couldn't accomplish it soon. For that reason, he wanted to see Lord Roger dead almost as badly as did Lynnette.

His worries were eased a little by her next words.

"Aye, perhaps you're right," she sighed, flexing her shoulders to ease the tension Lord Roger's name invariably brought about. She glanced away abruptly to avoid seeing the unwanted sympathy in the first mate's eyes.

"Put some life in it, Jenkins!" she roared, to cover the emotions stirring within. The swab below, halfheartedly scraping at encrusted barnacles, looked up in surprise at her tone.

"Aye, aye, Cap'n!" he returned, and redoubled his work with good will.

Lynnette Blackthorne, known only as Captain Thorne to those whose misfortune it was to cross her path on the high seas, nodded approvingly. She ran a tight ship, and her crew was unfailingly loyal. Conditions aboard the *Maiden's Revenge* were better than most, as her sailors well knew, and woe to any man jack who laughed at the idea of them being captained by a woman. Men had died for doing just that.

Captain Thorne's men knew a good commander when they saw one, knew they were lucky to serve aboard a vessel with a record like hers, but their loyalty ran deeper than that. Crew and captain of the *Maiden* were family in a business full of cutthroats like no other.

Piracy was nasty work.

The *Maiden* was by no means the only ship at anchor off Tortuga that night. Vessels of every type lay off the coast, lighting the gloom with lanterns on bow and stern. Sounds of revelry could be heard from the nearby beach, along with the flaring snap of bonfires that illuminated the faces of drunken buccaneers. Islands such as this provided havens for pirates and other disreputable persons wishing to escape notice in more civilized climes. Lynnette knew all the faces well.

"Be ye goin' ta th' beach tonight, Cap'n?" asked Harry.

"Perhaps," responded Captain Thorne, not sounding enthusiastic about the prospect. The pirates' lively revels usually
served to relax her, to take her mind off more serious issues,
but tonight Lynnette wanted solitude and quiet more than an
evening spent drinking that would leave her surly and muddle-
headed on the morn. "But I doubt I shall stay long."

"Aye, lass," he acknowledged.

Lynnette shook her head ruefully. Only Harry would dare
call one of the most feared pirates of the Caribbean "lass."
Anyone else doing so would find himself on the wrong end
of a cutlass before he could do more than stammer out an
apology. "Be off with you, now. I can see you wish to join
the merrymaking." She looked suspiciously at her old friend.
"There's no need to stay just to keep me company," she said.
"I vow I'll not fade away merely from a lack of companionship. I don't *get* lonely, remember?"

Because ye don't need anyone, thought Harry, but he had
the grace to blush slightly at the reproof in her voice. "We-ll,
there is this tasty-lookin' wench I've had me eye on fer a time
now. Don't s'pose it could hurt none if I went an' made 'er
acquaintance."

That's not all he'd do, she knew, judging by the easy virtue
of most of the island's female inhabitants, and by the charm
the older man could exert when he chose. Lynnette waved him
off with an absent gesture, watching as he bypassed the longboats in favor of diving with a bloodcurdling yell from the
railing. *Really,* she thought. As if he were a youngster with a
fire in his gut at the mere mention of the word "wench," instead of a middle-aged pirate with the beginnings of a paunch
showing through the years of muscle he'd built up from a life
at sea. Snorting with amusement, she went down to her cabin
to don a fresh shirt. She was still wearing the salt-crusted one
from her unscheduled swim earlier in the day.

When Captain Thorne returned abovedecks a little while
later, all the crew had gone to join the revels—all except the
handful on watch, who never left their posts while on duty. It
was quiet and the ship creaked comfortingly in the rhythm of
the waves she loved. The sunset had left faint trails of lighter
blue against the evening's cobalt. A lilting breeze teased her

nostrils, smelling of land and sea conjoined. For a moment, Lynnette considered not going to the beach at all, but she knew she should put in an appearance for the sake of morale.

While Lynnette was careful about not flaunting her femininity among her crew, she also knew that they needed to see she was at least *human*. Holding herself aloof from her men would foster distrust and antagonism. If they thought she considered herself too good to share rum with them, they'd turn against her at the first sign of trouble. It was a tactical assessment of her motives, but not the only reason she decided to join the pirates. Lynnette's men were, with few exceptions, her friends and partners. They wanted her company, and she didn't like to disappoint them.

Rather than take Harry's method of disembarking and risk another transparent shirt, Lynnette lowered herself into the crudely fashioned dugout one of the islanders had earlier left tethered to her ship and paddled herself sedately across the night-black water to shore.

When she reached the circle of illumination created by the fires, she was hailed loudly by members of her crew and other pirates she knew, who waved bottles and wineskins and shouted her name. She smiled and accepted rum from a craggy buccaneer with a scar running vertically down the length of his left cheek. Swigging without a noticeable wince, she wiped her mouth with the back of her hand and looked around.

It was a scene most would be horrified by, but it frightened Captain Thorne not a whit. Women naked from the waist up lolled in the arms of dirty, dangerous-looking men who could not be mistaken for anything other than the outlaws they were. Some, more inebriated or more energetic than their fellows, were performing a swaying, impromptu dance to the tune of a fiddle played by a giant with tattoos covering every visible surface of his skin. Flickering light from the scattered driftwood fires made the figures seem demonic, like something out of a nightmare. Lynnette caught sight of an old friend.

"André, you scum-sucking worm, how the hell are you!"

"Captain Thorne, my favorite scourge," said a dry, French-accented voice. The man called André stood up, grinning. He was handsome in an angular, rakish way, with long, glossy chestnut hair and lean, hollowed cheeks. At six feet, he stood just a few inches taller than Lynnette. The two clapped shoulders congenially, then sat down together.

"I have not seen you in some time, *chérie,*" he said, surveying her slim body and the single red-gold braid that hung down her back to her hips. "But then, I hear you've been busy making a name for yourself. One cannot help but hear the tales of a female pirate with arms like tree trunks, teats that sag to the waist like goat udders, and a face that could curdle milk," he teased.

She threw a dirty look at him, so he hastened to add, "Not, of course, that I do not defend your honor to any who spread such vicious lies." With a look of naked lust, he said, "I deserve some reward for my loyalty, do I not?" His eyes roamed again with a practiced leer over her figure.

Lynnette looked at André coldly. "It *has* been a long time," she replied slowly. "Long enough so I'd forgotten how much I despise your crude attempts to get me into your bed. If you don't stop them," she said with soft menace, "I'll have no choice but to believe you want me to remove the organ causing you to behave so foolishly. I must," she mused, her hand reaching toward her boot, "have a dull blade somewhere about me with which to do the deed."

Wisely taking her attitude, if not her words, seriously, Captain André Bellairs quit that topic with a murmured apology. "I am distraught, *ma chérie,* if my ill-chosen words displeased your tender sensibilities," he said with such an obvious mockery of gallant groveling that she was forced to hold back a laugh, "but you have stolen my poor heart, and I cannot help myself when you are near!"

"Try," she advised dryly, but his words mollified her, and Lynnette could not stay angry with her old friend. His foppish manners and elaborate wit always improved her temper. "So," she continued, "from what I gather, you haven't been doing so badly yourself. I heard tell of your latest prize. A rich merchant with a cargo of silks to make the heart of any self-respecting buccaneer swell."

"Ah, that." He waved the victory away with a negligent gesture. "A trifle merely. A plump partridge that fairly begged to be plucked. A—"

"Enough," she laughed, amused by his backhanded boasts.

"I'm sure the tale of her capture has grown to the size of a blue whale by now."

André managed to look hurt. "But *non*," he denied with a twinkle in his eye. "The stories of my victories are never inflated—except when it comes to you!"

"Ah, André," she laughed. "It *is* good to see you."

"Good enough to prove it?" he asked slyly. "Everyone already thinks we are bed partners, so what harm—"

"Who thinks so?" Lynnette interrupted, skewering him with her cold emerald glare.

"Why, it is a common supposition, my dear *Capitaine*." He added, before she could accuse him, "I have never given them cause to believe it. It is simply that I am often seen in your company, and we of the Brethren are a filthy-minded lot . . ." André trailed off.

"And, I'll wager, you never denied the rumor."

Captain Bellairs spread his hands and shrugged. "Why should I ruin my reputation? Besides," he cajoled, "it does *your* reputation no harm to be named my lady."

"That's a matter of opinion!" she countered, then smiled to take the sting from her words because she knew he was right. André Bellairs was certainly cleaner than most buccaneers, if nothing else. Since rumors were bound to fly about a woman who wore breeches and carried a sword into battle with such great success, she supposed she was lucky the talk hadn't been worse.

One reason Lynnette was not entirely displeased with the rumor was that it provided protection. If everyone thought she bedded down with André, there would be fewer men attempting to get her in *their* beds. André Bellairs was a man to be reckoned with, and there were not many who desired to cross swords with him. Another thing: a woman not claimed by a man presented a challenge other men could not seem to ignore, whereas if she were spoken for, the challenge she represented was less. It was only Captain Thorne's reputation with a cutlass that prevented the invitations she received from becoming impossible to resist.

She'd had difficulties with such men when she first came to the islands, before it became known she was off limits to scum with rape on their minds, did they not want their balls cut off. Among the buccaneers it was told she kept the privates of men for trophies. When asked if it were true, she merely laughed and said, "Why would I want to *keep* them?"

Lynnette's good mood had been soured by the turn the conversation, along with her thoughts, had taken. After a few more pleasantries, she excused herself from André. He watched her go thoughtfully, marveling at her beauty—and her coldness.

For all their professed friendship, Bellairs knew only the side of Captain Thorne that she chose to reveal. Even in her cups, she was closemouthed about her past. It was common knowledge she showed a marked tendency to loot ships of a certain merchant company more often and more ruthlessly than any other, but none knew the reason behind her vendetta. Members of Thorne's crew were also remarkably reluctant to speak of it, though normally sailors were a garrulous, gossipy lot.

André was sensitive to the fact that many pirates and privateers had pasts they did not wish disclosed, but the identity of the young woman with the aristocratic face and cultured speech, the woman who raided ships for a living and wielded a sword better than any man he knew, including himself, was one mystery he dearly wished to uncover.

Such was not to be his fate.

After leaving André, Lynnette made the rounds of her acquaintances, greeting men she had not seen for months, drinking and exchanging loud conversation. For a while she sat among her crew, boasting with as much creativity as they about the ships they'd taken and the bounty that was their reward. Bellairs's crew and the men of yet another ship wagered with them as to the richness of their next prize. But Lynnette's heart wasn't in it, and when the party began to devolve into serious wenching, she got up quietly and walked into the darkness.

Captain Thorne tried not to hear the sounds of nearby fornication, the grunts and squeals of couples as they pleasured each other. The sounds brought only painful memories for her. Memories of her sister, brutally raped before her eyes . . .

She closed her ears to the not-so-discreet noises, turning her face upward. The moon was full, hanging large in the midnight sky. Silver rays framed her delicate face, glinted in her green eyes. It seemed all the stars in creation were shining tonight, spreading cold light and beauty upon the earth. Lynnette took refuge in their celestial radiance, wanting to forget the past, needing to forget—but never able to escape the images burned into her mind. She could not ignore the things that had made her what she was.

Lynnette curved her hands into hard fists, exhaling to relieve the tightness in her slender shoulders. *I shall avenge you, Sarah,* she swore, *no matter what the cost.*

CHAPTER ONE

CAPTAIN DANIEL Robert Bradley was pleased, proud, and excited. He stood on the quarterdeck of his merchant ship, feeling the sea spray and the wind whipping through his long blue-black hair. The ribbon that had held it in a neat club at the back of his neck was long gone, but he didn't care. It was appropriate, he thought, if one could place symbolism on such a small thing as a hair ribbon, for it seemed that for the first time in years he was unfettered, free.

A great sense of pride and accomplishment swept Daniel as his penetrating silver gaze surveyed the activity on deck. Everything was orderly, smooth; well oiled as though from long practice. Men completed their duties with no fuss or confusion. His orders were carried out without hesitation. No one would ever guess this was the *Empire*'s first trade mission, unless it was because of the newness of the vessel herself. The wood of deck and railing, mast and hatches, still shone without the scars of use; the brass fittings were undulled by time.

Daniel saw all of this and felt a fierce exultation. Below in the hold were the goods he meant to sell with great profit in the nearby Indies. The *Empire* carried silks and satins for the fashion-starved ladies who had followed their husbands to the colonies to become planters. There were also other less fine cloths that could not be manufactured in the Indies, as well as a variety of made and metal goods for the colonists. Ships like Daniel's were the lifeblood of the Indies. And in turn, the colonies supported England's thriving sugar and exotic goods trade.

Captain Bradley planned to buy with his profits the spices and sugar for which his native England hungered. In addition, of course, he would bring home the dark sweet rum that was one of the principal products of the sugar industry.

So far, this first mission of the Bradley–Richards Trading

Company had gone perfectly. Since the *Empire*'s christening mere months before, Lady Luck had been with him to an extraordinary extent. Not one storm had marred this maiden voyage, no problems that were not easily solvable had come up during the buying of trade goods or the provisioning of the ship. It was almost uncanny, but luck had not often favored Daniel over the years, and he figured he was just about due. In any case, he assumed his good fortune was attributable more to careful planning than any whim of fate.

Smiling, Captain Bradley recalled the day when he and his partner Simon Richards had stood on the pier to christen their new vessel.

It was early spring on the river Thames. The sun was shining for once, and a cool sea breeze fanned the faces of the two men standing shoulder to shoulder on the dock.

"By God," said Simon, reverently low-voiced. "She's beautiful. Absolutely the best-looking lady I've ever seen."

Daniel laughed. "If the marriage-minded misses of the *ton* could but hear you, they'd be green with jealousy. But you're right. She is a beauty." He looked fondly at the massive ship, which seemed impatient to be off, straining against the thick ropes holding her penned in the busy harbor. "I never thought this day would come, the day when our dreams became reality. All that work; convincing the investors, getting reliable contacts, building her. It's finally happening. I can hardly believe it."

"I know," Simon said quietly. "I scarce believe it myself. Yet here she is, and here we are, about to become successful businessmen."

Simon was a tall man, like Daniel, about two inches above six feet. His hair, in contrast to Daniel's pure black, was a bright blond. Both men had lean, hard physiques from years spent in the Royal Navy. Both men were startlingly handsome. They had served aboard the same ship, risen through the ranks together, and resigned within the same year when their captain was replaced with a doddering old aristocrat who had bought his way into the navy for a lark. Both had more than served their time in their country's service, and when the chance to strike out on their own had come, they'd taken it eagerly.

Now the future seemed to hold nothing but promise, and it

all depended on this first voyage. Nearly all their capital had gone into the building of the *Empire,* and the profits from her first journey to the islands would make the foundations of a reputation that Daniel hoped would secure their futures.

Of course, there was still the *Triumph,* a vessel the two had bought earlier that year, and were now nearly finished refitting for trade. She was a good old ship, but Daniel had a special place in his heart for the *Empire.* Still, if anything happened to it, he hoped the older vessel would save them from bankruptcy.

Daniel turned to Simon with a smile. "Not bad for a couple of second sons, hmm?" They both laughed, though Daniel's chuckle seemed a trifle forced.

"Indeed, my friend, not bad at all!" Simon clapped his friend on the shoulder. His voice was more serious than the occasion seemed to warrant, and his words took on a deeper meaning. "We do the best we can with what we have." Even, he thought, looking at his friend with troubled eyes, if some of us have less than we deserve.

"It's time we chose which of us will sail the first mission," said Daniel. "Shall we toss for it?"

"It seems the only way to decide the matter fairly," replied Simon with a glint in his eye. Each of the partners was qualified to captain the ship, but one had to stay behind and take care of the business side of things. They had decided to alternate roles, knowing that neither could stand be tied down to a desk position permanently. But both men wanted the first run.

"May the best man win." They shook hands, then clasped each other in a bone-crunching bear hug in a rare display of affection. Simon withdrew a guinea from his pocket. For a moment, as the coin left his fingers to sail into the air, it flashed brilliantly, blinding them both.

"Heads," cried the dark-haired man. It was his call. The gold coin descended as if in slow motion, and Simon caught it deftly, slapping it against the back of his other hand. When he lifted the concealing palm, both men let out their breaths, one in relief, the other in disappointment.

Daniel had won.

* * *

As the ship neared the Indies, the weather had grown warmer, the sea bluer, until it shone a clear, incredible aquamarine. The water was so light one could almost see the ocean floor, save for the blinding reflection caused by the ever-present sun. The balmy trade winds smelled exotic and new to Captain Bradley, who was seeing everything as an adventure today.

"Captain," cried the lookout. "Sail off to starboard!"

Everything except that.

Daniel called for his spyglass. The quartermaster brought it, coming to stand next to his commander. They were old friends from the navy, and they knew each other's minds from long association. "Captain," Quartermaster Jonas O'Neal queried, "can you see her colors?"

"Not yet," Daniel replied tersely.

"Any chance they be friendly?"

"Some."

They stood in silence for a moment. Then—

"Captain . . ."

"Not yet, damn it!"

Through both minds ran the possibility as they waited in nerve-racking silence for the ship to come close enough to identify. Pirates. In these waters, the scum abounded, and were a danger to any respectable merchant who dared to ply his trade. Larger, Crown-backed companies could afford warships to protect them, but small independent traders like Daniel did not have the influence or capital required to rate a warship. Men like Daniel took the risk, and prayed their luck held.

But Lady Luck had deserted Captain Bradley.

"Damn," he swore.

"Pirates?"

"Aye. They fly no flag." That was the signal to indicate there would be no debate—the pirates definitely meant to attack. "Damn their wretched souls to hell!"

"Can you tell who it is?"

"No—wait, yes." He squinted his silver eyes to see better. "The name on the vessel reads *Maiden's Revenge*." He turned to Jonas for information. "Have you heard of her?"

"*Heard* of her?" breathed O'Neal, going ashen. "You mean you haven't?" He looked at his captain as though he'd grown horns quite suddenly. At Daniel's quenching stare, he pulled himself together. "The *Maiden* is Captain Thorne's ship. She's one of the most bloodthirsty pirates on the Main," he said in a tone of fearful awe. The quartermaster returned his stare to the fast approaching ship with worried bemusement. "I thought she never attacked English ships!"

Daniel broke in impatiently. "Well, there's no doubt of it. Her lack of flying colors means that she can't be doing anything other than preparing for battle." He stopped, swung around to his friend. "Wait a minute. I thought I heard you refer to Captain Thorne as a 'she.' Tell me that was just a mistake," he said, hard-voiced. Jonas merely shook his head.

"You mean we're about to be attacked by a *woman*?"

"Not just any woman, Captain. That there is Captain Thorne. It's said," he whispered, "that she's never been bested in battle."

He'd never heard of this woman who aspired to piracy. No matter. No *woman,* no matter what her reputation was, could feasibly pose a threat to them. It was just too outlandish to contemplate. "Well, that's about to change," growled Daniel.

"Captain, don't you think we'd better try to run for it?"

"It's too late for that now. Their sloop is much faster than our frigate. We'd be captured before the hour was out. That time is better spent priming the ship for a fight." Captain Bradley turned away from the railing, turned to face his anxious crew. All had heard the cry of "sail," and all knew what that could mean. They were waiting for orders.

"Prepare to defend!" he shouted.

"Aye, aye, Captain!"

As the frigate was being maneuvered into a good defensive position, the cannons loaded, the guns and munitions handed out, Captain Bradley walked among his men, calling encouragement and orders alike. When at last the preparations were complete, the men gathered to hear their captain. There was fearful muttering among them. A great many of them had heard of the *Maiden's Revenge* and her history of being undefeated. Those who hadn't heard yet were quickly informed by their mates. None was anxious for a confrontation, but they would obey orders.

Daniel's raised hand silenced all conversation immediately. His eyes roamed the faces of the hard-bitten sailors ranged before him, proud of their discipline. "By God," he rallied them in a deep, carrying tone, "I could not wish for a better force, were we set against the whole Spanish Armada!" The men cheered loudly.

"But we are not asked to perform a task nearly so difficult," he went on when the cheering had died down. "In fact," Daniel shouted, "I almost hesitate to trouble you men with the battle at hand. Our foe, being merely a woman, will surrender easily, running away with her tail between her legs like the bitch dog she is, ere we are well and truly into the fight!"

More cheering as their manhoods were reasserted. Privately, Daniel wondered what his mother would have said could she have heard the slanderous words passing so easily from his lips. Yet his speech seemed to strike the right note with his anxious men, so he continued heartily. "Captain Thorne's men are naught but milksops, to be led by the nose into the fray by a *female*." Daniel's voice dripped derision, and the sailors laughed, roaring agreement and insulting opinions of such men. Daniel could almost hear his sainted grandmother rolling about in her grave, and he sent her a brief, wordless apology for his insults to her sex. Though he'd little doubt the pirates would prove a drunken, undisciplined bunch, and their female leader no better than a poxy dockside harlot, he harbored no great disdain for the fairer sex.

Of those who listened to their Captain's exhortations with such fierce courage, only a very few faces showed any reservations. They were those who had heard firsthand accounts from sailors who had actually *seen* Captain Thorne, or whose ships had been taken by her. They told stories of a giantess, strong as any two men together, who fought with a bloodthirstiness unequaled by any who sailed under the black flag. And they said there were particular portions of a man she liked to hack at first . . .

The captain gestured for silence once again. "Now," he yelled, "I would not have you waste your energies in this paltry encounter, but it seems the pirates leave us no choice. They are coming into position as we speak. So every man to his post, and when we've beaten these poor excuses for brigands, there'll be an extra ration of rum for all!"

The cheers reached the heavens this time. They were brave words.

* * *

"Goddamn their black souls to the lowest hell!" Lynnette fairly screamed. "I was so sure I had them!" She glared unseeing at an inoffensive spot on the aft deck. Her body was trembling with near uncontrollable rage. Harry, behind her, spoke soothingly.

"Cap'n, there was nothin' ye could do! How were ye ta know there'd be two warships trailing Lord Roger's frigate? Not even ye could face such odds an' come out th' victor. Ye had ta let 'em pass."

"But he's never had warships before! There was no news of this from the other captain. Unless . . ." Her green eyes narrowed.

"Unless it was a trap," concluded the first mate, only seconds behind her.

"Of course! Lord Roger knew I was getting information on his trading schedule from his captains, so he fed me lies through them! I should have killed them to ensure they couldn't report back," she muttered.

"I'll bet the bastard wasn't even aboard," Harry said slowly, visibly thinking it through.

"You're probably right. The man has never deigned to oversee his shipping personally before this, so why should he start now? I wager he thought the rumor of his presence would flush me out right quick; straight into the arms of the warships."

" 'E almost succeeded, Cap'n," said Harry. "It were plain luck we spotted th' first man-o'-war, an' that we were able ta flee 'fore th' other got us pinned b'tween 'em, I'm thinkin'."

"Hardly luck alone, Harry," replied Captain Thorne, slightly stung. "It was our superior speed and agility that saved us."

"An' a good leader as well," he said soothingly.

Lynnette accepted the compliment absently. Her mind was still fixed angrily upon her nemesis. "Lord Roger has more up his sleeve, it seems, than an embroidered handkerchief. We will have to tread more cautiously in future."

She thought about their close call. Lately, destroying Lord Roger's shipping trade had been growing harder. As Lynnette ruined his business, the man grew more and more desperate to get rid of the threat she posed. The last ship of Lord Roger's she'd attacked had turned out to be a decoy ship, heavily loaded with weaponry instead of merchant goods. When the pirates from the *Maiden's Revenge* attacked, they had not encountered a quick surrender as they'd expected, but a prolonged sea battle, which they'd won only by a narrow margin.

As it was, they'd had to sink Lord Roger's vessel instead of taking the precious munitions, and the *Maiden* had been forced to limp into port without a prize. Lynnette's men were as loyal as any crew, but even they were beginning to grumble about the length of time since last they'd seen rich rewards for their efforts. Captain Thorne knew she would have to procure a fat ship full of plunder for her crew, and do it soon. She herself was in no wise reluctant.

"I'm going to my cabin," she said to Harry. "Take over. Tell the men I'm not to be disturbed."

"Aye, aye, Captain."

Still furious and frustrated, she stalked belowdecks to her cabin. Hours later, her mood had not been one whit lightened by a prolonged and solitary bout of sulking. Thus, when the knock came on her door, followed by Davie's tentative, "Cap'n?," Lynnette was hardly pleased. Yanking open the door, she scowled down at the young boy's timid face.

"Didn't I leave word I was not to be disturbed?" she snapped.

"Aye, Captain. But—"

"So what, I wonder, could be so important that you would go against my express orders and do that very thing?" she mused in a tone of silky menace.

The boy swallowed audibly, and Lynnette suppressed a surge of guilt. She knew she should not be taking her anger out on Davie, who was probably still shaking from her previous wrath on the day he'd played his little joke. The boy was half finished now with his punishment, and in his eyes she saw the fear that his captain would add another month to his sentence. Sighing, Lynnette raked her hands through her long hair and smiled encouragingly at the lad.

"Since you've already disturbed me, you might as well tell me what brought you here."

Davie spoke excitedly. "A ship, Captain! A fat merchant, by the look of her! She's riding so low in the water she can barely sail."

Captain Thorne could feel her blood heating at the prospect. A prize! It would bring morale on the *Maiden* back to its usual high level, as well as serve a personal purpose for her. The idea of a good fight was welcome, indeed. Lynnette needed a battle to get over the disappointment of missing her long-awaited confrontation with Lord Roger earlier that day. "Whose flag does she sail under?" she asked shortly.

Davie sounded a bit downcast as he replied. "England's, Cap'n." Then he added in a wheedling tone, "Shall we take her anyrate, Cap'n?"

They would, indeed. Lynnette couldn't afford to remember her heritage on a day like today, not when she was accountable to a crew full of pirates who'd already done some fancy sailing this morning avoiding Lord Roger's trap. They deserved this reward. Instead of replying to Davie, she turned away and began to buckle on her sword belt. It was a clear indication of the captain's intent, so when she waved him away, the cabin boy scurried abovedecks excitedly with the word. They were going into battle!

Lynnette quickly braided her hair into a rope as thick as her wrist, then pinned it up in a coronet around her head. In a fight, she could not afford to let it hang down where it could impede her vision or be grabbed by an enemy. Then she tucked a knife into her boot, and two flintlocks into her belt. They could only be fired once each before reloading, so she'd have to make the shots count. Captain Thorne, now prepared for any occasion, smiled a feral smile. Quickly, she left her cabin and ran up the ladder to meet her crew. Perhaps this day would not entirely go to waste after all.

Daniel could not believe the speed with which the *Maiden's Revenge* had overtaken his ship. He'd known the other ship was faster, so he'd counted on his superior skill as a captain to outmaneuver her. But all his attempts to gain the upper hand and a better firing angle had failed. Each time he moved, the *Maiden* moved faster, cutting off his advantage before he could make use of it. It was as though Captain Thorne had read his mind. Now he was about to be boarded, and he hadn't even been able to get off a single successful shot. The *Empire,* however, had sustained several disabling blows from the other's cannon.

Daniel had noticed early on that the gunners aboard the pirate ship were taking extraordinary care with the placement of their shots, and he knew that could only mean one thing. They meant to take his ship as part of their booty. It was a fine new ship; it would bring a high price if they decided to sell it. The pirates would not want to damage their spoils.

Captain Bradley did not mean to accede gracefully to their plan—not at the expense of his future, his hopes and dreams.

"To arms!" he shouted as the grappling hooks began to fly. "We'll defend the ship to the last man!" There was a great flash of steel as the men drew forth their cutlasses. Seconds later they were engulfed in a tide of pirates howling blood-curdling war cries and grinning with fierce battle madness.

All thoughts fled for Daniel except parry and thrust, attack and defend. Sweat poured from his body and the faces of the dirty buccaneers before him blurred. All around he could hear the sounds of screaming, dying men; the grunts and shouts as the battle raged. It was utter chaos.

Daniel brought down one man with a thrust that went clean through his heart. He caught a glimpse of the man behind him, about to skewer him with a wicked-looking knife, just in time to pull his sword from the dead man and block the blow. In minutes that man was dead, too.

He was squaring off with a third when he became of aware of a queer silence pervading the ship. The man in front of him was huge, at least six and a half feet tall, and he wore a grin over his ugly tattooed features that showed his confidence of the outcome of their duel. Daniel, panting, cast his glance about recklessly for signs that one of his men could come to his aid.

What he saw stopped him cold. He was the only member of his crew still fighting. The rest had all been captured or killed.

A strange sort of madness overtook Daniel. Everything that mattered to him had just been stripped away. His business, his future, his ship, *everything*. Without the *Empire,* he had no livelihood, and no reason to go on. He resolved to go out fighting. Captain Bradley had just raised his sword to the giant before him when he heard a piercing voice cry halt. A woman's voice.

*   *   *

Lynnette had been amazed by the fight the little merchant vessel put up. Usually, when they saw the name *Maiden's Revenge* on the side of her ship, sailors struck their colors with such haste it was comical. But not this one. The captain of the *Empire* was obviously a man worthy of her respect. The fact that she'd had difficulty countering his moves proved that. And the fight they'd had while boarding had come as a not entirely unwelcome surprise. Because of the reputation the crew of the *Maiden's Revenge* enjoyed, and because of Captain Thorne's own notoriety, they almost never encountered a ship willing to fight anymore. This little exercise had given the men more excitement than they'd seen in nearly a year.

She surveyed the outcome with pride. A knot of the trader's men stood to one side of the deck, disarmed and guarded by her own men. The vessel itself was minimally damaged, which was fortunate since she intended to sell it at the first opportunity. Members of her crew were at this moment ransacking the hold for the goodies sure to be within. There was only one thing about the situation that did not please her.

Across the deck from where she stood, one man still put up a defense. The brave but foolish captain, she surmised. Lynnette guessed astutely that he planned to waste his life with his ship. She shook her head with disgusted wonder for anyone with that much misdirected honor. A man like that could be dangerous when cornered, as he surely knew he was. He'd already laid low two of her men, and although she didn't think he'd manage to harm the gargantuan Charlie, she didn't want to take the chance. She started over to where the tableau was playing out.

Daniel blinked sweat from his eyes, wishing he dared lift his aching arm to wipe the moisture off his forehead, but he couldn't let down his guard. The ugly man with the tattoos was backing away, his grin even wider as he listened to something the woman was saying. "Well, sure, Cap'n, 'e's all yers if'n ye want 'im."

"Thank you, Charlie, that will be all for now."

Captain? That woman's voice was the *captain's*? It didn't sound at all the way he'd imagined it would. No, it was not in the least like the shrilling tones of a witch, nor was it the hoarse bellow normally associated with large, uncouth barbarians. In fact, the tone was cultured, softly resonant, quite like the voice of a lady addressing a servant. Very slowly, Daniel lifted his head to see the fabled Captain Thorne.

And gaped. Boggled. Was struck with uttermost shock. She was the most beautiful woman he'd ever seen.

Autumn-golden hair formed a coronet around sweet, delicately youthful features that, although liberally smudged with black powder from the fight, were still fair beyond comparison. High cheekbones formed the perfect accent for eyes that gleamed brighter than the best quality emeralds. A nose reminiscent of the Roman sculptural ideal was saved from haughtiness by a slight, intriguing uptilt at the end. Her lips were lush and red as cherries, while her small chin looked surprisingly stubborn. It was a face artists would kill to paint.

His eyes followed the line of her body to the next obvious stopping point. Her breasts, under the thin white silk of her skirt, were high, full, and impudent. Daniel could tell she wore nothing beneath the billowing material, and his fertile imagination provided the details so nearly disclosed by her manner of dress. The nipples, he decided, would be rosy, hard-pebbled to invite a man's touch.

Dragging his heated gaze with some difficulty from her chest, he saw that her waist was tiny, and below that, the tight black breeches she wore hid absolutely nothing of her lower limbs. Her hips flared softly down to the longest, most delightful pair of legs Daniel had ever been privileged to behold. They were strong, slim, firmly muscled and divinely shaped. Captain Thorne was altogether gorgeous.

He felt an insane, unconquerable desire to laugh.

CHAPTER TWO

AS DANIEL'S guffaws wound down to chuckles, then to mere gasps of hilarity, Lynnette continued to stare. Was he mad? He didn't *look* insane, although his actions this day would not be reason to deny such an affliction. After all, attacking pirates wasn't the most rational thing a person could choose to do. Still, in his place, with so much to lose, she might have done the same. Trying to fathom the tall man standing before her, his forgotten sword pointed toward the deck, Lynnette spoke.

"I'm glad you find me so amusing," she said dryly. "Or is it only your present circumstance you find mirth in? I confess, capture at sea does not seem much cause for levity to me." It was a pointed reminder of his defeat, and one that caused Daniel to sober immediately.

With labored aplomb, he pulled his scattered wits together. Bowing, Captain Bradley said, "Indeed not, milady. I apologize for my appalling breach of etiquette. Quite simply, it was your appearance that set me to laughing." Instantly, he saw that this was not the thing to have said. Captain Thorne frowned and several sailors behind her muttered and drew their blades. He rushed to explain his words.

"What I meant was, I had not expected you to be so beauteous." Swords and knives returned to their sheaths and the murmurs stopped, but if anything, the captain's frown grew deeper. He went on hurriedly. "My crew told of a woman so hideous none could bear to look at her . . ." Appalled at the manner in which he seemed determined to swallow his foot whole, Daniel ceased speaking and stared in confusion at the author of his misery. Her frown had now disappeared. Incredibly, she seemed to be laughing at his faux pas.

"Peacock," she chuckled, "you amuse me greatly. Perhaps I shall not kill you after all, but keep you so I may watch you writhe in embarrassment and blush like a maid when you misspeak!" The sailors laughed, but Daniel stiffened. Her words had recalled him to the pitiful situation he was in. Captured— and by a woman, no less. Simon would laugh himself sick to hear of it. *If* Daniel survived to tell his friend the humiliating tale.

"What *do* you plan to do with me?" he asked sullenly.

Good question. Lynnette was wondering that very thing. Carefully, she looked him over. The man's clothes were of a fine cut and material, obviously made for him by an expensive tailor. Bond Street, no doubt. Naught but the best for this man, from the dove-gray knee breeches that molded his muscular thighs, to the fine white linen of his ruffle-edged shirt. His long, split-sided jacket, now torn and sweat-stained, had recently been an eminently fashionable black velvet shot with silver brocade—not too ostentatious, but clearly chosen with his unusual coloring in mind. The boots were new, tall jack-boots like her own. But it was the man himself that caught her attention, more than his rich attire.

Breeding was evident on every inch of his aristocratic face, from a high, intelligent forehead and slashing dark brows, to eyes that were deep-set and stunning in their impact. Thickly lashed, a startling shade of stormy silver ringed in slate-gray that set off his long, blue-black hair to perfection, they glowed almost unnaturally. His lips were firmly chiseled and sensuous, his nose regally straight. His body, she couldn't help noting, was utterly magnificent. The man was so large Lynnette had to tilt her head back to see into his eyes, and she was quite tall herself. He was obviously fit, muscles outlining a figure to set any woman's heart fluttering. Except, she thought cynically, for herself. She was not some innocent maid to be thrown into a swoon by the first handsome man to come her way. Still, she had to admit, he was a fine specimen of male beauty.

What concerned Captain Thorne most was not his attire or his looks but what they represented. Money. A man with clothing like his and breeding undeniably stamped on every feature had to have coin and a family back home in England. A family who would pay dearly for his return. Lynnette could smell an aristocrat a league away.

"What is your name?" she asked abruptly.

The man before her, sizing her up as she had him, remained silent. He knew the purpose behind her question, and was clearly not going to cooperate. Protecting his wealthy relations, no doubt. "Oh, come now, Captain," she said in an exasperated tone, "it's all very well and good to care for the welfare of your family, but this *is* your life we're talking about. Do you think they'd rather wonder for the rest of their lives if you're dead, or pay a little to see you again?" She was no longer amused by his disproportionate sense of honor, and her impatient tone showed it. "A man like you has connections, perhaps a wife or children back home. I can see you're not a pauper, and, I assure you, my rates are very reasonable. So I ask you once more: *What is your name?*"

He did not say a word.

"Oh, hell, not that it matters. We'll find out soon enough

who you are. Charlie," she called to the burly giant, dismissing
the need to question Daniel, "go fetch His Highness's papers
from the captain's cabin." Daniel's eyes flickered briefly in
that direction, and Lynnette smirked. "Didn't think to destroy
your identification, did you? Lesson number one, my fine
friend: when attacked by pirates, always ditch your personal
papers at the first sign of trouble." Daniel flushed with deep
chagrin at this rebuke. He knew she was right, but it rankled
him sorely. To hear a woman reprove him for something that
was elementary procedure for ships' captains in distress was
unbearable. Roiling in humiliation and fury, he almost didn't
catch her next words.

Captain Throne was speaking to a grizzled old sailor at her
side. ". . . set the crew off in the longboats with food and water
for a week, and directions to the nearest island. In this area,
they shouldn't have trouble making their way to safety. But
first, search them for valuables. You never know what they
might be hiding from us. We wouldn't want to lose any of
our booty to these pathetic wretches." She gestured to the huddled seamen standing miserably within a ring of well-armed
pirates.

The older man laughed in response. "Aye, Cap'n. Like th'
time we caught that yella-bellied priest tryin' ta make off with
'is weight in jewels, remember? We sure made 'im change 'is
mind quick enough!" He chortled heartily again.

"We did at that. I wouldn't have this pretty bauble if we
hadn't, would I?" She fingered the gorgeous gold links about
her throat in memory. Flat, an inch wide, and studded with
giant square-cut emeralds that matched her eyes perfectly, the
necklace was worth a king's ransom. To see it about this heathen pirate wench's neck made Daniel feel ill. He wondered
what she'd done to the poor man who had tried to keep it from
her, then decided he didn't want to know.

Calling herself back to the task at hand, Lynnette swiftly
decided the disposition of the rest of the stolen goods. "We'll
put a skeleton crew aboard our new ship with instructions to
bring her to the base. We'll accomplish whatever repairs and
refitting need to be done there. As for him"—she indicated
Daniel, fuming impotently nearby—"I think he'll bring a right
good ransom for us all."

Hearing them talk about him as if he were no more than a

piece of property, Daniel lifted his head, glaring fit to kill. No shred of amusement colored his tone now. "Nay!" he shouted. "You'll have naught more of me than you've taken already! Put me in with my crew or kill me now, but I shall not let this ransom plot be undertaken." He raised his sword in blind wrath, ready to kill anyone who tried to capture him.

Captain Throne held up her hands in a placating gesture. "Now, now, there's no need for all that," she began, then her eyes focused on something above Captain Bradley's head. "Ah, Charlie," she said in a warm voice just before all went black for Daniel and he collapsed to the deck, "you have excellent timing, as usual."

She surveyed the figure crumpled lifelessly upon the blood-stippled planking, and the man standing over him, belaying pin held like a club in his massive hand. "I just hope you haven't hit him too hard and damaged our spoils. Take him to the hold and lock him in. Have you got the papers? Good. Everything else is in order, I trust. Marvelous! Commend the crew for their fine work and give them an extra ration of grog tonight," she added to Harry. "We'll have funeral services for Harlon and Old Jake later this evening. They were good men."

Harry nodded and set to work. Charlie, none too gently, hefted Daniel over one shoulder and climbed the space between the ships. Once aboard the *Maiden,* he crossed the shifting deck easily and carried his burden to the hold, where he carelessly dumped him in with the rest of the cargo, securing the hatchway in his wake.

When Daniel awoke, it was an unpleasant experience, to say the least. The darkness of the enclosed space surrounding him was absolute, stifling hot, and smelled terrible. Other than that, he had no clue as to where he was or what had happened to put him there. His head hurt; he thought that might have something to do with it. Daniel put a hand up and gingerly felt the sore spot above his right ear, discovering that the blow he must have been dealt had only barely broken the skin.

Suddenly, as though touching the lump on his head had triggered his memory, the events of the past day came surging back to fill his fogged recollection. The pirates, the defeat, his humiliation. He wished he hadn't woken up at all.

Since he couldn't do much about the state of his consciousness, he tried to discover his location. From the heat and pitchy blackness, as well as the muted sounds of rats scurrying, he guessed he was locked in the hold of the pirate ship.

"Shit," he swore, quietly and succinctly.

He knew there was little he could do to change what had happened. He was stuck here on this filthy floating den of iniquity, and he'd lost his beloved ship to the pirates who had captured him. They played the pipes and he must dance to their tune, no matter how galling he found it. That was why, he supposed, it was better to be the cap*tor* than the cap*tive*. Thinking this only served to remind Daniel of his jailer. His beautiful jailer. He still couldn't believe it. That a woman of such undeniable comeliness could be sailing the seas under a buccaneer's flag strained the limits of his imagination and sent him reeling emotionally, confused and angry for reasons he couldn't define. Had she been as grotesque as the tales made her out to be, he thought, her existence might have been easier to swallow somehow.

But a woman like Captain Throne, a woman of beauty and delicacy; well, he simply could not get over his shock at the sight of her wearing breeches and carrying a sword. Women like her served refreshments in fine manor houses in the country, cared for husbands and children and stitched embroidered cushions. Or entertained guests at London soirées, covered in jewels and without a thought in their heads beyond the design of their newest gown.

Pretty females simply should not be going about bedecked with weaponry, attacking respectable men and consorting with ruffians of the lowest sort. It wasn't *done*. Never mind that Daniel had never cared for flighty, frivolous women; something in his sense of the world had been knocked out of balance by his encounter with the pirate, and the feeling wasn't pleasant.

Daniel was appalled, and if there was the smallest spark of admiration in him for the woman who had brought him low, it was buried beneath a tidal wave of anger. She'd taken away his life's dream when she'd stolen the *Empire*. Beyond the galling fact that a mere female had so easily ruined his first chance for success was the wrenching sorrow Daniel felt for the loss of his prized frigate. No, he didn't admire Captain Thorne, he told himself determinedly, he hated her.

And this was the person with whom he was going to have to negotiate. Daniel reluctantly accepted the idea of paying out a ransom, if it came to that. He was fairly confident of his ability to escape the pirates and their outrageous leader, but he knew that, on the slim chance that he failed, he must be prepared to pay for his freedom.

For now, he would appear to go along docilely with the wench's demands, in order to lull her and her men into thinking he'd accepted his lot. Daniel would bide his time until he found the perfect opportunity to slip from beneath their watch, rather than indulging in foolhardy heroics. A little forethought and planning would serve him twice as well as a headlong leap into the fray, he decided.

All he had to do when the time came was convince the captain of his paucity, so her ransom demand would be relatively low. Otherwise, all he'd worked for in the last year would be ruined. The Bradley-Richards Trading Company, so newly opened, could easily fold if Simon had to withdraw a large amount of cash to pay for his partner's safe return. The loss of the *Empire* was bad enough to set them back a year as it was—not to mention the fact that future investors would be spooked by the line's obvious bad luck. The situation was bad, but Captain Bradley felt sure he could survive the experience intact both physically and financially. He'd never encountered a threat he hadn't conquered, and no half-sized pirate wench was going to break his record of victory.

The hatch above creaked open, jolting Daniel out of his ruminations. For a moment, a shaft of dusty sunlight blinded him. Blinking his eyes to adjust them to the sudden source of light, he saw one of the buccaneers outlined by the glare, waving a flintlock pistol at him in a distinctly unfriendly manner. Daniel decided to come quietly when the laconic seaman jerked his head for him to follow. The grunt the sailor gave was enough in the way of explanation. Captain Thorne wanted to see him.

He *thought* he'd gotten a handle on his anger, but when he saw the woman, oh-so casually perched on a high-backed chair, one leg resting on the top of a scarred mahogany table, and, of all things, paring her nails with an evil-looking little dagger, he found out differently. Her braid had been released from its tight coronet and hung straight and thick down her back. Gold and emeralds gleamed from her neck-cuff, peeking through her partly opened shirt. A hint of cleavage was just visible.

The pirate queen looked cool and unruffled, in contrast to Daniel's perspiring dishevelment. Animosity hit Daniel like a punch at the sight of her. Reconciling the loss of his ship and his pride would not be nearly as easy as he'd assumed, particularly when the thief sat before him so unrepentantly, so calmly. Daniel did not feel calm; he felt furious, and he also felt a great desire to kiss the smug look from the wench's face, which only made him more furious. At himself this time.

To cover the conflicting emotions sure to be plain on his face, Daniel looked around with studied casualness at the furnishings of the room. The cabin surrounding her was large and sparsely decorated. Maps covered the wall behind the captain's chair, and to the left, at a right angle, thick leaded-glass windows let in light but little in the way of a view. Another chair like the one she sat on (one of a set originally meant for some planter's home, no doubt) was positioned across the table from the slim buccaneer.

An armoire was placed next to the one extravagance in the otherwise spartan cabin. The bed. Huge, canopied, a velvet and feather-stuffed monstrosity, it caught the eye and only reluctantly let it go again afterward. Even so, Daniel couldn't resist looking at it once more. What use could a slender thing like Captain Thorne have for such a bed? . . . The answer was obvious. So, she liked her bedsport, did she? Well, perhaps Daniel could accommodate her. He knew he would like to. Reassured, he looked back at the woman, who was industriously rubbing her nails against the leather vest she wore in an effort to smooth them. He was growing annoyed with her long silence.

The brusque pirate had left them alone and closed the door behind him, much to Daniel's surprise. Obviously, they did not consider him a threat to their leader's safety. He didn't know what to think of that. Either Captain Thorne's men had a very high opinion of her ability to defend herself, or they thought that Daniel, unarmed, was not foolish enough to try anything with a boatload of cutthroats but a shout away. On that last count, they were correct. He had no heroics in mind, at least not until he had a better chance of success with them. The idea of taking Thorne hostage had occurred to him and he'd dismissed it instantly as a less-than-realistic plan. Daniel knew he wouldn't get more than a step outside the door before her men cut him down.

Thorne still had not spoken, hadn't looked up from the fingernails she was meticulously shortening. The knife she used was menacing, throwing reflections every which way as she turned it. She looked like some sort of exotic barbarian. An Amazon, Daniel thought, recalling the myths he'd read of the ancient warrior women.

Finally, curtly, just as he felt he would explode, she spoke. Barely looking up from her task, she said politely, "Have a seat, Captain Bradley."

The witch was telling him she knew his name now. Daniel remembered the papers. Well, at least there was nothing very personal about them, merely a letter of introduction to a planter on St. Eustatius who was distantly related to Simon, and with whom Daniel had planned to stay during the sale of his goods. His registration as captain of the *Empire* was among the documents, along with a few other papers and certifications. In other words, nothing of very much use to her, aside from his name. Warily, Daniel sat in the chair across from her. "Thank you," he said, equally polite.

"Well, then, let's get down to business," Captain Thorne said briskly. She swung her leg down from the table and sheathed her dagger smoothly in her boot, satisfied with her handiwork. She took up a sheaf of parchments, shuffling the papers into a neat pile. "It says here that you are a merchant out of London, carrying goods to the Indies. That much is obvious." She waved the information away dismissively. "What it doesn't say is who your people are. Once we've established that, the proceedings should move swiftly. So, if you'll just cooperate . . ."

"I'm surprised you can read," he interrupted, his tone pleasant, mildly inquiring; belying the insult implicit in the words.

"Oh, aye, I can read. Not all of us pirates are illiterate, you know," she said cordially, not at all insulted.

"So I see." His curiosity was not appeased. Daniel was finding this unusual woman fascinating. She sat there so coolly, discussing ransom demands as easily as though the conversation were no more than a debate over the weather. In spite of himself, he was impressed. She parried his barbed words with ease, unflustered. Captain Thorne, it seemed, was no ignorant cretin. In fact, nothing could be further from the truth. Daniel wondered what events of the past had created the woman before him.

She was nothing like the highborn ladies he knew in England, and nothing like the dockside wenches who sold their wares so blatantly in every port of call. As far as Daniel had been aware, there was no in-between, although sometimes, he thought sardonically, there was little difference in the behavior of the two types. The rich, titled noblewomen merely sold themselves for a higher price. But this woman was neither of those things. She would never be bought—or sold. He doubted there was another like her in the world, and he found himself intensely curious to understand the enigma she represented. He found his anger fading again beneath his admiration, and in the back of his mind, he knew this should worry him—he must not fall under the witch's spell.

The pirate's voice interrupted his musing, bringing him back to the important business at hand. "As I was saying," Lynnette declared, "with your cooperation, we should be able to get this unpleasant business done with quickly, with as little annoyance to both parties as possible." She sounded like a governess coaxing her charge to take his medicine without a fuss, and Daniel was mildly amused by her no-nonsense attitude. "You seem to be in a more reasonable frame of mind than when I last saw you." She smiled wryly because she knew that being knocked silly and tossed in a stinking hot hold was likely to subdue anyone. "And I only want to know one thing—to whom I should write the ransom note." She picked out a clean parchment sheet and poised a pen over it, one winged brow cocked, mutely saying: Well?

"I don't have any family," he said simply.

Her look said she didn't believe that for one minute. "No, truly, I don't. I'm perfectly willing to help expedite this disagreeable business, but I simply *have* no relations. My father died ten years ago, my mother long before that. I have no wife," he continued, as though making a list, "no grandparents, aunts, uncles, or cousins to speak of; if I have any children, their mothers never thought to notify me—"

"I get the point, Peacock," she interrupted sharply. Lynnette was not at all sure she believed him, but she could detect no guile in those silver eyes, and his voice held the ring of truth. It was certainly *possible* that the man didn't have any family, though unlikely. Damn, this complicated things.

Daniel saw the suspicion in her beautiful eyes, and unwillingly decided he would have to add an unpleasant fact to his story to make it more plausible. "I do have a half brother. But," he continued before she could ask for more information, "we are completely estranged." His voice was unwittingly bitter, and that, more than anything else, told Lynnette what she needed to know. "I have not spoken to him since before my father's death, and I can tell you in all honesty that if he received a ransom note for my hide, he'd throw it in the trash and pretend it never arrived."

"Give me a reason to believe your story," she said softly, leaning forward across the desk. The note in Daniel's voice as he told of his half brother had almost entirely convinced her he wasn't lying, but she wanted to be one hundred percent sure.

"One very good reason, milady. We are bargaining with my life, as you so eloquently informed me earlier today. I have a very high regard for my skin."

"Don't call me 'milady.' It's Captain Thorne."

"My apologies, *Captain* Thorne." Only a slight emphasis on the words indicated his sarcasm. "As I was about to say, there *is* a way for you to collect your ransom, and for me to escape with my hide intact." Daniel spoke ruefully, not liking the fact that he must give her the information in order to survive. There was no doubt in his mind that Captain Thorne would have him killed if he did not prove useful. Much as he was coming to respect the beautiful pirate wench across from him, he was sure she felt no such feeling in response. She seemed so cold and disinterested he couldn't envision her reacting to him at all, for better or for worse.

He was wrong.

Lynnette had been greatly and pleasantly surprised by the man called Captain Bradley. His composure at this second meeting was admirable. Most men would either have gone for her throat in anger, or decided their superiority immediately, treating her with condescension. Men doing the first would have been brought up short by Lynnette's knife, and if that didn't work, she was no slouch at hand-to-hand combat. She had learned early on that it wasn't enough to be better with a sword. Anyone, even the best swordsman, could be disarmed or caught unaware without a blade. So Lynnette had learned how to fight with her body, how to defeat an opponent twice her size, and had remained unmolested since that time. Thus, being alone with Captain Bradley hadn't worried her overly much. Still, she was pleased he'd proved smart enough not to attempt violence, doomed as his effort would be.

It was even more of a pleasure to find he didn't assume her wits were inferior to his. A man who patronized her would have found his ransom doubled within seconds, and tripled if that didn't give him pause. Lynnette hated men who thought they were more powerful or smarter than she, merely because they possessed a piece of flesh between their legs that she, thankfully, lacked. But Daniel had done neither. She'd seen his fury when he entered the cabin, and she'd seen the way he clamped down on it, not letting his emotions get in his way. It showed he had control and intelligence. Any threatening move Captain Bradley made would have been countered with swiftness and a great deal of pain on his part. Obviously, he'd been smart enough to think his situation through, and had kept himself in check.

Another thing. Although she called him "Peacock," Lynnette could see the man was no languid fop: useless, but given a position of authority because of his wealth. No, she sensed in Captain Bradley an aura of strength and barely leashed energy, and for some reason, it interested her.

The fight he'd given her for the merchant ship had been impressive. He had courage, she'd give him that. He wasn't bad as a strategist, either, although Lynnette was better. His tactics were well planned, but in her seven years as captain of the *Maiden's Revenge,* she had had a great deal of practice in outmaneuvering skilled enemies, which gave her the edge. Still, with a bit more experience behind him, Captain Bradley would undoubtedly be able to give her a good run for her money, and possibly even best her. There were not many men Lynnette could give that honor, even in the private confines of her mind.

He was nothing like the men Lynnette usually had contact with—filthy, bloodthirsty scum, or fat, stupid merchants with an eye only for their profits. Or lusty pirate captains like André, who wanted to get into her breeches to the exception of all other considerations.

She'd seen Captain Bradley staring at her, and he'd been quite plain with his admiration during their initial encounter, but that was nothing new. All men stared at her, and it had ceased to bother Lynnette once she stopped wondering why. At least Captain Bradley was more discreet than most about it. Despite that, Lynnette felt hot when he stared at her, not cold and disgusted as most men left her. Daniel intrigued her. Why, she wondered, was he different from other men? Why should his scrutiny affect her when the looks from other males made her feel nothing but emptiness?

His looks were extraordinary, that was certain. But appearances had never affected Lynnette before as they did now. She felt a strange warmth when she looked at his tall, masculine form . . . Angrily, she squelched the train of thought in order to listen to his words. He'd been talking of an alternative contact for ransom, had he not?

". . . You may contact my partner, Simon Richards, for the payment," said Daniel. "But I warn you, he is not a rich man, and the company we represent together is small."

"In other words, do not couch the demand too high," she said cynically. Lynnette spoke harshly to counter the unreasonable liking she'd felt for the man a moment ago. "Well, Peacock, you aren't worth quite as much to me as I had thought. What a disappointment." Lynnette gave a mock pout. "Still, it will have to do." She took down the information Daniel gave her, and he was relieved to see that the demand, though higher than he'd hoped, was not going to send them into bankruptcy.

Efficiently, Captain Thorne dripped wax on the missive to seal it, then set the folded parchment carefully aside. "When we reach our destination, I'll have it sent to England on the next ship."

"And until then . . . ?" he questioned.

"Well, I suppose I *should* let you know your fate," she said with a slight smile.

"Are you a seeress as well, Captain?" Daniel dared to tease.

"Nay." She scowled. "I meant but your fate aboard the *Maiden*." A knock interrupted them. "Come," she called curtly. It was apparent to Daniel that Captain Thorne was not one to appreciate a jest.

Davie entered, spoke hesitantly, his eyes darting to the prisoner frequently. "Yer supper is ready, Cap'n."

"Good. Bring it in. Oh, and set two places." She swung to face Daniel. "Unless you'd prefer not to dine with me?" It was an invitation, and he was extremely surprised to hear her offer it. He'd assumed that he'd be sent back to the hold straightaway. But he was also very pleased. Supper with the pirate queen, as he'd begun to call her inwardly, would give Daniel a good opportunity to study her.

Lynnette was not far behind him in amazement. Why, 'fore God, had she asked Captain Bradley to eat with her? Certainly, there was no need to do so. He could be fed as easily by the cabin boy from his secure position in the hold. Lynnette had all the information she required, and need have no dealings with her prisoner at all until the time for the ransom exchange came. The thought was strangely disheartening. This man who remained urbane through circumstances that would have had most frothing with rage, whose intelligent, long-lashed silver eyes seemed to burn through her clothes, this man held her interest as none other had. She did not wish to end their encounter quite yet. And that frightened Lynnette as nothing else could.

"No, no, I'd be pleased to sup with you. Honored, really."

"Save your flattery, Captain, for someone who'll appreciate it more than I." Abruptly, she was angry again. "We need to discuss the terms of your stay, and I am hungry. Why not combine the two? Did you think that because we're pirates, we did not intend to feed you?"

The note in her voice was a shade defensive, and he wondered why. "In truth, Captain Thorne, I did not know what to expect." His eyes roamed quite thoroughly over her ripe figure, making it plain as day Daniel didn't mean only the conditions of his captivity.

Pewter plates were set in front of the two, and leather tankards of ale as well. The fare was simple, as ship's fare must needs be, for spoilage was commonplace at sea when food could not be replaced often. Hardtack, salted beef, and a thick soup Daniel could not readily recognize were set on the table. Daniel held his breath, waiting to see the sort of abominable table manners the woman was sure to have, cultured voice or no. But again, she surprised him.

Lynnette broke open a hard ship's biscuit daintily, and dipped it in the soup to soften it. She did not cram it into her mouth all at once, as a woman of the lower classes would have. She ate it slowly, and did not lick her fingers afterward. Daniel wished, somewhat contrarily, that she had. He would have enjoyed the sight of her pink tongue bathing those slim fingers.

The bread was stale, but no vermin had managed to invade it yet, proving the *Maiden* had not been at sea long. Daniel, during his sojourn in the navy, had tasted biscuit that was so hard it could be used to prime cannon; had experienced the joys of banging hardtack against a table to shake free the weevils that infested it, and he found nothing to complain about here. Dipping one's bread was acceptable at sea.

Cautiously, Daniel dipped his own. He discovered that the soup, which turned out to be a kind of seafood chowder, was not nearly as bad as he'd been dreading. Obviously, the cook knew his trade, which was more than Daniel could say for his own aboard the *Empire*.

Lynnette sliced neatly into her salted beef. Without preamble, she said, "You will be taken to our island base nearby. I have a house on the isle where you will stay until the ransom arrives. I'll deliver the note when we put in at St. Eustatius to sell the goods."

That hurt. The pirates would sell his cargo on the very same island that had been Captain Bradley's original destination. Now, a bunch of murderous thieves would divvy the profits while Daniel rotted on some dismal islet, waiting to be ransomed. He said nothing. There was nothing he *could* say without upsetting his precarious hold on safety by angering the pirate wench. He promised himself, right then and there, that he would have retribution. Daniel didn't care at that moment that the object of his fury was female. Captain Thorne had shown clearly that she didn't desire to be treated as a woman, and he resolved that he would not do so.

"I must warn you," he said pleasantly, "that I do not intend to do nothing but twiddle my thumbs while you proceed with this plan."

Lynnette laughed, took a swallow of ale. "I expected nothing less."

"I will escape."

"You can try." It was a challenge. "Your attempts will keep my men amused while we're ashore. They could use the distraction."

Daniel bristled at her plain assessment of his abilities. Captain Thorne did not believe he had an iceberg's chance in hell. Well, the wench would find out her mistake soon enough. He hadn't spent his life in near-constant activity to meekly acquiesce to whatever the pirates had in store for him without a fight.

Angered, Daniel said calculatingly, "Tell me, Captain, how did you ever get into this savage business? A woman like you"—he gestured, indicating her obvious youth and beauty— "a woman like you ought not to have need of such an undignified, not to mention dangerous, profession in order to earn her living. You could make more, I'll wager, from a year's work as a courtesan."

His tone was light, friendly. Purposely insulting. Daniel didn't ask out of curiosity, although his interest in Thorne's mystery was still high, but as a way of paying her back, slight for slight. He was rewarded by seeing an angry flush color the creamy skin of Lynnette's face and neck.

Her eyes glinted furiously, but she spoke blandly, saying only, "You'd be surprised at how much I make a year as a pirate." Food was forgotten as she leaned back in her chair, glaring with narrowed eyes across the table at Daniel.

Frustrated again, he could only marvel at this slip of a girl, who probably couldn't claim a day over twenty years of age, who yet managed to best him at every turn. He'd thought sure to get a rise out of her with that last statement. And then, as Lynnette could no longer control her fury, it seemed he had.

Unable to stop herself, she hissed, "*Why* is it that you men seem to think a woman is better served to be a whore and live off the bounty of men than to fend for herself?"

"And as a pirate, you do not 'live off the bounty of men'?" he asked shrewdly. "What else would you name it?"

"At least I may choose when and where to distribute my 'favors'! I take what I wish, and need never be at the mercy of some man's whims." The timbre of her voice was harsh, black. "And I'm damn good at what I do. Your presence here is proof of that."

"Indeed," Daniel murmured. He wondered at her vehemence. In truth, he wondered at everything concerning this woman. Deciding not to antagonize her any further, he said softly, "I am sorry if I've offended you by prying. It was not my intent." But it had been.

She apparently knew that. "Was it not?" she said sarcastically. It was the second time Captain Bradley had apologized to her. Obviously, it discomfited him not at all to admit his wrongs, sincerely or otherwise. Which was unusual in a man, or at least in the men of Lynnette's experience. To quell her rising curiosity about her prisoner, she quaffed down half her tankard in one swallow.

Daniel's eyebrow rose; then he followed suit, draining his mug to the dregs. Lynnette poured more for both of them, an entirely unconscious gesture of graciousness. Silence stretched between the two for long minutes as they sipped slowly this time.

Finally, the pirate captain spoke, and her voice was bemused. "Peacock," she said, "I'm not sure whether to like you or to *dis*like you intensely."

Daniel laughed aloud. He felt exactly the same way.

CHAPTER THREE

ANIEL AWOKE again to a dank, cramped hold. He assumed it was daylight, though he couldn't be sure. Three days had passed according to his reckoning, but here in the dark, it was damned hard to tell. Omar, the swarthy pirate who, as far as he knew, never spoke except in grunts, had tossed him food twice a day, the light streaming through the open hatch showing it was noon and then evening on each successive day. The food he was given did not compare to Captain Thorne's fare, but it was mostly edible, so he had no fear of starving.

He was bored and stiff. The noises from the deck told him nothing except that there was smooth sailing above. Daniel was experienced enough in seamanship to know that the days had been fair, even though he could see nothing of them. At least had there been a storm, he thought, it would have brought some excitement to his confinement. His legs were sore from being bent for long periods of time, for there was little room to stretch them in the crowded hold, and they were quite long.

But his treatment hadn't been as bad as Daniel had anticipated. The buccaneers had done nothing to add to his comfort, but on the other hand, they hadn't made his imprisonment horrible either, as they easily could have. Captain Bradley shuddered at the images his mind called up in reference to possible piratical brutalities. Thank God the scum had so far left him unmolested. In truth, they'd simply left him here, and seemingly forgotten his presence except to feed him.

Which left Daniel a lot of time to think—a practice that, right now, he would rather forgo. Because his thoughts kept coming back to the same subject, no matter what direction he tried to cast them in. Captain Thorne. He envisioned himself in the same scenario a thousand times a day, his hands wrapped around her neck to strangle her . . . but each time he squeezed, the vision changed. His hands would loosen their grip, turning it to a caress. He would lean close to kiss her, aching to touch her sweetness, but each time before he reached that honeyed nectar, her lips would curl in that mocking sneer, and Daniel's daydream would come to a jarring end. Her face swam before him again and again in the darkness, laughing at him, infuriatingly clear.

Red lips pouted at him, taunted him to take up their luscious provocation. Autumn-toned hair framed a face of unrivaled sweetness; her apparent innocence belied by wary, ancient eyes of deepest green that lured him in to drown in their mysterious depths. He saw again the long, slim legs that went on forever, the breasts that stood up so impudently, seeming to challenge a man to taste them.

Her graceful carriage—queenly, Daniel thought—and athletic stride conjured a vision of a tigress in bed. He could imagine that strong, nubile body wrapped around his own, pleasuring him better than any soft, overfed society lady could. Daniel felt himself hardening, thickening, and cursed vilely. Damn the wench for taking over his mind, haunting him with her perfect features, when she went totally unaffected by him. How could she be so cold while he burned for her? She must be a witch, to enchant him so fully. He cursed again.

But Lynnette was not entirely unaffected. She had been in a foul mood for the past three days, and her men walked lightly when they had to pass her for fear she would find fault with them. And, indeed, she had snapped at sailors for the smallest infractions, taking her anger out on her crew since she could not very well face the source of her fury. What would she say to him anyway? "Stop invading my thoughts, damn you," she muttered.

Harry, who alone dared to stand beside her in her blackest moods, turned to look questioningly at his captain.

"Wha'd ye say, Cap'n?"

"Nothing!" she snapped, flushing slightly at being caught talking to herself.

"Uh-huh." He smiled knowingly.

Lynnette gritted her teeth and ignored the first mate. Harry had teased her unmercifully about the "prettyboy" captive they'd taken. He thought she'd "taken a shine ta 'im." In no uncertain terms, Captain Thorne had assured him that such was the furthest thing from the truth she could imagine. Now, relieved, she squinted into the hot Caribbean sun. Very soon, they would make port. She looked forward to it as a way to take her mind off unsuitable things like silver eyes and masculine beauty personified in the form of her prisoner.

The island was tiny, nameless, and perfectly suited to the needs of pirates such as the crew of the *Maiden* were. A natural deep harbor, hidden in a fold of the land, provided a good place to anchor, while abundant fruit trees, wild boar, and goat meat gave them ample food. A freshwater spring was located in the interior, which let the buccaneers refill their casks easily. The sea itself promised an unending bounty of fish, tortoise, and shellfish for any who sought them. That the island was idyllic, a paradise, was a gift most of Captain Thorne's men did not appear to appreciate. But she did. While No-name Island, as it was ingenuously called, was only one of dozens of hidden pirate sanctuaries, it was home to Lynnette.

Her house stood there, build at substantial cost by captured Spanish artisans working to pay their own ransoms. It was not overly large, containing only two bedrooms, a dining room, a study, and a kitchen, but to Lynnette it was the equivalent of a palace. Because it was hers.

Many of the pirates, she knew, thought their captain was out of her mind to spend her wealth on building materials for a house when she would likely end up stretching her neck in a noose before too many years were out. They preferred to squander their booty on liquor and women and fancy baubles, and that was fine with her.

But Lynnette had small use for rum save for the occasional swallow or two, and none whatsoever for whores. Baubles were pretty, but unnecessary. Revenge mattered. Nothing else.

While she plotted for her vengeance to come to its fruition, she might as well have a permanent place to sleep, a place to think and plan and be alone. But now she must allow Captain Bradley to share that place—under lock and key, of course—for a matter of several months. No place else on the island could as easily be made secure. Lynnette planned to be gone for as much of that time as possible.

She swung to face Harry. "We'll reach No-name by afternoon." Relief colored her remark.

"Aye, Cap'n. I reckon th' boys'll want ta raise a ruckus when we drop anchor," he commented casually.

"That's fine with me; so long as they report back to start repairs on the frigate in the morn."

"That they will. They know th' value of a ship like that as well as any man. Not even th' comeliest o' wenches will keep 'em dallyin' *that* long."

The island sported several inhabitants other than the pirates. Escaped slaves mostly, Indian and African alike. Lynnette, who could not abide slavery in any form, harbored them and promised harsh penalties for any man of hers who tried to return them to the bigger islands for the reward their capture would bring. In turn, the escaped slaves had made the island more of a home than most pirate havens.

They had set up huts, a village; eking out a living by raising pigs and goats, selling fruit and fish, which they traded to the buccaneers in return for flour and other goods that had to be imported to the tiny isle. A couple of the village girls came and cleaned her house. Others made their living as whores. It was not much of a life, but undeniably better than slavery had been. No few of the men had joined her crew, and would guard her back to the death. It was more than a fair trade.

"We'll get a bundle for the prettyboy's cargo," Harry ventured. He had been surprised, then tickled pink, at hearing his captain had invited Captain Bradley to sup with her. Never before had she done so with a captive, and he marveled at the charm the tall, black-haired man must have exerted to wrangle the concession from this steel-hearted woman. Harry slid his glance to watch her profile.

Silhouetted against the bright sun, Lynnette was breathtaking. But her expression was grim. "Aye," she replied absently.

"He's one ta watch, 'e is. 'E might try ta escape."

"I've no doubt of that. He said as much."

"Did 'e now? That's innerestin'."

"Why?" she asked sharply.

"Oh, no reason. I wuz just a'thinkin'. 'E might just make it, ye know."

"Harry! You sound as if you admire that—that popinjay!" she sputtered disbelievingly. Her first mate was not one to give what was tantamount to a compliment to just any man. That he rated Captain Bradley's chance for escape as within the realm of the feasible was a sign of Harry's high regard. "I assure you," she said darkly, recovering herself, "he's no match for me."

" 'E's th' perfect match fer ye," muttered Harry, so she couldn't hear, "an' that's why ye hate 'im." He felt a surge of pure glee welling up. These next months should prove interesting.

When Daniel was brought, blinking, into the sunlight, the sight of No-name Island took his breath away. From where he stood, he could see the protected cove and the gentle waters drawing his eye to the beach. The sand was—well, pink. A lovely coral hue, ranging from mauve to nearly white, it blended beautifully into the aquamarine ocean. Sea grape and palm trees shaded the interior. Above the line of trees, a low, sheer cliff arose, framing the whole picture perfectly. Daniel, whose experience with Caribbean islands was as yet small, felt overwhelmed with the panoramic vista. Still stunned by the beauty of the place, he responded blindly to Omar's prodding and climbed down the ladder to the waiting longboat.

Once seated in the rocking boat, Daniel forgot the beauty

he had just witnessed, for there was a vision even more lovely seated across from him. Thorne. He thought it an appropriate name for a woman who bristled with as much as weaponry as she did. Was her first name Thistle? Certainly not Rose, although it would describe her physical appearance well. But he doubted Thorne was her true surname anyway. Didn't most pirates take on new names to make themselves sound more terrifying on the lips of fearful travelers? If not for that reason, then to hide their true identities, and he was sure the woman facing him had many secrets to protect.

To keep himself from staring overlong at the luscious figure, Daniel glanced around him. He noted that there were seven other buccaneers manning the oars in the longboat, not including his guard, and that all of them kept hands conspicuously near knife or sword hilts, all of them glaring suspiciously at Daniel. One of them, he recalled, was named Harry, and he was apparently the first mate. He sat close to his captain, in the first row of straining oarsmen. Omar had taken his slot just in front of Daniel.

Harry, it seemed, was not as eager as his fellows to gut their captive, even going so far as to wink at the bound man's unfriendly predicament. Captain Bradley wondered at the gesture. What made the grizzled first mate so jolly and welcoming when his compatriots were nothing of the sort? Daniel dismissed his curiosity impatiently. Perhaps old Harry had merely been out in the Caribbean sun too long. Certainly, the man would be of no help to him, loyal as he obviously was to his slim captain.

He spread his bound hands as far as they would reach to show the pirates he wasn't about to try anything, and offered a sheepish grin. Several of the men relaxed at his gesture, but Lynnette kept her hand casually close to the sword at her side.

"What do you think of my island?" she asked when the silence and the slapping of wavelets on the wooden boat grew tedious.

Daniel narrowed his eyes against the sun glare framing and shadowing her from behind. He spoke over the shoulders of the rowing pirates from the tail end of the boat. His voice had to carry to reach Lynnette in the prow. "Truly, I have never seen a place more lovely." He hadn't expected to be impressed by the island. Surely, he'd thought, a pirate's base would be squalid and filthy, not a wonder of nature.

The peacock's words pleased her well enough. She smiled slightly. "I thank you." They were nearing shore. Her earlier conversation with Harry on her mind, she said, "You'll find No-name Island has many other qualities as well as beauty. It's quite defensible; nearly impossible to escape from."

"Only time will reveal the veracity of your belief." He was quite relaxed, and Lynnette was amused by his attitude.

"Oh, indeed. You are entirely correct. It will be helpful, for future reference, to see if you can find a weak spot in our defenses. I would not want our guardianship to be lax in any respect." She grinned tauntingly. "I will welcome any ideas you have for improvements in our precautions." Snickers from several of the rowing pirates told Daniel that her men were paying close attention to their repartee, and he flushed a little under his tan.

"Certainly, Captain Thorne," he managed to reply gracefully. "But I may have to post my opinions a long distance— from England." That silenced them.

He had seen the outline of another island in the distance, and he figured all he needed was a map and a small boat to make his escape. He would watch carefully for his opportunity, for he doubted there would be many.

Then the bottom of the small craft ground against the sandy shore, and men leapt out to drag it further ashore. Lynnette went with them, helping to pull it in and directing the landing party to unload the boat after they had secured it.

Daniel clambered out as best he could with tied hands, and stood waiting to see what came next. He did not feel particularly happy about the situation. Then Captain Thorne came striding up to him and gestured that he should precede her up the beach. For a moment, Daniel couldn't move. He'd had enough of abetting these scoundrels, and he could not force himself to comply, even as he realized it would be the intelligent thing to do. She seemed to understand that.

Sighing, Lynnette drew her sword. "Let's make this easier for both of us," she said. "I have a sword, and I'm not averse to the use of it. You are bound and have no weapons." She waved the sword descriptively. "So, would you care to walk in front of me on that path you see before you? The other available option is less favorable."

Somehow, this made acquiescence much less disagreeable, and promptly, Daniel was headed along the jungle-bordered path. It led him higher and higher, curving around the left side of the cliff face, where the ground was not as steep. The cliff itself seemed to have been formed by a landslide, or a falling away of the low mountainside of which it was comprised. It rose nearly a hundred feet straight up from the beach, and looked as though it had been chopped clean from the side of the mountain by a giant hand. To the top of this ridge they headed, sharp steel pressing into Daniel's back when he walked too slowly.

At the summit of the shelled pathway, they came out of the trees and into a large clearing. The lush jungle had been cut back for fifty feet around the house—which looked nothing like the dilapidated shack he'd envisioned, even to the most critical of eyes. Of Spanish design, it was not overly large, but exquisitely crafted down to the smallest detail.

Pastel pink paint gave the house its color, and a verandah wrapped itself around the entire structure. The dull red-tiled roof sloped down to cover the verandah, and arches every few feet brought breezes to its shadowed interior. The windows were not glassed, but had shutters that could be opened to catch the slightest cooling wind.

Many planters in the colonies refused to bow to the hot climes, so different from their native countries, and had built just as they would have had they been in Europe. Which meant hot, stuffy, gloomy residences completely unsuited to the Caribbean. But not Lynnette. Her home was built for the terrain, and remained several degrees cooler inside than outside. Daniel was once again happily surprised.

Bougainvillea and hibiscus surrounded the front entrance, lending their sweet fragrance to the salt-tinged air. As they climbed the few steps to the entrance, he noticed lime and lemon trees lined the villa on two sides. The far end was bordered by the cliff-top. Not only was it as beautiful, it was also as defensible as Captain Thorne had said. With his eye for strategy, Daniel had seen the careful landscaping that characterized the place. It was built on high ground, and all the foliage nearby had been cut away, so that any attackers would

be seen in time to protect the villa. Then there was no more
time for sight-seeing as Lynnette prodded Daniel inside.

"Welcome to my home, Captain Bradley," she said, her
courtesy exaggerated considering the circumstances.

After the brilliant sunlight outside, it was hard to see immediately, and she didn't give him time to linger. He was
marched through the house, getting only the impression of
spare, tasteful furnishings before they came to a door with a
large bolt on it. "I see you are no stranger to keeping prisoners," he commented.

" 'Tis true, and lest you get cocky, let me inform you that
not one of them ever managed to get away from me."

Had they even desired to? With such as she keeping them,
no man could be faulted for enjoying his captivity unreason-
ably. He wondered if she ever shared her favors with her male
prisoners. But he wasn't to find out, not today.

Lynnette pushed wide the door and made a sweeping bow.
"Please. Enter." Steel reinforced her honeyed tones. "I hope
you will be comfortable for the rest of your stay," she said.
She stepped close to him, the scent of her elusive, spicy per-
fume tangling in Daniel's senses. Then she drew a dagger and
sliced cleanly through his bonds. Before he could respond to
her nearness she had already backed away, knife in one hand,
sword in the other. She smiled mockingly. "I regret that there
will be no special conveniences today to refresh you, no
change of clothes or bathwater to wash with . . ." She was
teasing him, and her obvious belief that Daniel was a London
dandy grated on his nerves.

"I'll manage," he said through gritted teeth, stepping inside.

"No doubt," she replied sweetly, "as you have little choice."
The door closed behind her, and bolted audibly. He stood staring at the thick planks of wood, stewing angrily, hating the
uppity wench who thought herself the equal of men.

CHAPTER FOUR

*H*E WAS still stewing several hours later when he heard
the sounds of distant revelry. After launching himself
furiously at the solid oak barrier of the barred door with no
result aside from a sore shoulder, he'd paced the modest con-

fines of his room—or cell, if one wanted to be brutally honest—a thousand times already. Reluctantly, he'd come to the
discouraging conclusion that there was no way to escape unless the door were to be unlocked. Still, as prisons went, it
wasn't the worst he could have suffered.

A four-poster bed stood to one side of the room, with a
washstand adjacent. A sea chest containing nothing more interesting than spare linens was set in one corner, and a desk
was to the left of the locked door, with one chair to sit on.
The best feature of his cell, Daniel decided, were the French
doors leading to the balcony. He had looked out a couple hours
ago and discovered that his room faced the cliff, the doors
opening directly onto a section of the wraparound verandah.

Unfortunately, the verandah was blocked off on either side
of Daniel's room, forming a sort of overhanging terrace. Its
walls on either side were smooth, with nothing to grasp onto
should he attempt the dizzying climb around the edge and back
to the solid ground at the side of the house. He could go
nowhere but straight down, which would surely kill him if he
tried to sneak away in that direction. The pirate wench was
no fool. This had to be the only room in the villa so well-nigh
impregnable.

Now the noise of happy, soused buccaneers letting loose
came faintly to his ears from the direction of the beach. He
opened the doors and stepped out on the terrace to see. One
thing he could say; he had a terrific view from this fortress of
hers. He could see the whole of the beach and the cove, and
the trees just below, as well as a magnificent span of aqua-
colored ocean. With twilight beginning its descent, the western
sky was filled with all the colors of the spectrum, from fiery
reds to deepest violet, with orange, pink, and blue in between.
It was simply gorgeous, but he did not feel like appreciating
things like sunsets just now. Not when the pirates lay sprawled
on the beach, torches and cook fires burning, carousing loudly
and with a vengeance. Probably toasting his downfall. He
wanted to kill them, one and all, for being happy at a time
like this.

Disgusting people, he thought, debauching themselves day
and night like animals. He saw a man grab one of the island
women, and while she shrieked with laughter, pull her down
to the sand with him. The man delved his hands into the

woman's bodice, baring her breasts for all to see. She did not seem to mind. Disgusting, Daniel repeated in his mind. And where was Captain Thorne in the midst of all this? She had not come into view as yet.

He realized he was waiting to catch a glimpse of her and cursed himself, but did not move. For a good while there was no trace of her, but then a shout went up. The pirates were calling her name with great gusto. Daniel told himself he was merely waiting to see if the wench would take one of her men to her bed; to see if her morals were as loose as he suspected they must be, but when Captain Thorne came into sight, his breath caught in his throat for a long moment.

Arriving from the pathway down the beach, her stride was long and graceful. Her braided hair swung jauntily down her back to her hips and caught the firelight, gleaming like burnished copper. She wore the full-sleeved shirt well, he thought, its collarless design showing off her long neck to good advantage. And those breeches—had he thought them shameful? What better way to view unimpeded the longest, shapeliest legs this side of anywhere? No, they weren't shameful, they were a crime to let loose.

Of course, she was utterly without morals, unbelievably brazen to wear what she wore and be what she so blatantly *was,* but somehow, Daniel felt all of his scorn for Captain Thorne melting away. She was absolutely radiant. And he wanted, suddenly, to be down on that beach with her. All his years of cultured upbringing seemed to dissipate in a scant second, and he longed to forget society and propriety and carouse with the rest—or better yet, with Thorne alone.

He watched as she seated herself with a group of pirates who were dicing enthusiastically and joined their play. From this distance, he couldn't tell who was winning, but from the congratulatory slaps on the back that Thorne received, he guessed she played knucklebones as well as she did everything else. Daniel saw a bottle passed among the rowdy group; rum, most likely, since it was produced in the island colonies and sailors had a tradition of favoring it. When it reached the woman, she took it unhesitatingly, downed a large swig, and he had to hold back a sympathetic wince for the burning it must cause her throat. But she apparently felt no ill effects, for she took another gulp before passing it to the next man.

Seeing her so comfortable with the bloodthirsty bunch, drinking and barbarously shouting boasts, should have caused Captain Bradley to feel revolted. But he did not. He could only imagine the kind of life she must have had to bring her to this, and began to appreciate the scope of her determination to hold the respect of such men under her command. For a man, it would be a full-time occupation—and a dangerous one, what with the nature of pirates. A backstabbing lot, if there ever was one. For a woman, it was almost inconceivable. Such strength those narrow shoulders must have, to hold such a weight of responsibility. A sea captain himself, Daniel knew how much nerve, how much sheer charisma, it took to bend hard-bitten sailors to one's will. It took guts, and that the woman had in plenty. He could not but admire her.

He imagined Thorne's struggle. Most men thought that to have a woman *aboard* ship was to invite calamity, but to get them to accept one as a leader, well, that was a feat not undertaken lightly. Yet she'd done it. Not for the first time, Daniel wondered why she had. It was not a dream little girls usually harbored, to grow up to be a buccaneer leader. And he doubted she had grown up among such ruffians, not with her fine manners and mannerisms.

From the way Captain Thorne taunted him with politeness, the way she seemed to laugh at his breeding, it was clear that she was not unfamiliar with the behavior of the gentry. It was more as if she knew exactly what his upbringing had been like, and scorned it anyway.

What was he thinking? Captain Thorne, a recalcitrant aristocrat? Not bloody likely. The idea was laughable. Highborn ladies didn't run off to become notorious criminals.

He scrubbed a lean hand across his face, feeling three days' worth of beard growth, and wishing he had a razor. But, of course, they hadn't left him one. A razor could be used as a weapon against his keepers. He decided he must be going out of his head. First he found himself wanting his jailer's sweet little body, and now he was entertaining notions that she was some long-lost noblewoman. And feeling admiration for her. Aye, he was definitely a case for Bedlam.

Daniel blew air through his sculpted lips in a heartfelt sigh, then his sensual mouth twisted in a wry grin. Nothing was the same as it had been mere days ago, and now he was not even sure he regretted the change. He wanted the chance to know this pirate woman, to find out what made her who she was. And he knew she would do her best to stop him from figuring it out.

He turned his gaze again to the beach and the merrymaking in progress there. Thorne had engaged one of her men in a mock sword fight, and with much laughter and cheering, the men called out encouragement to the two facing off. Mostly to the hapless sailor. She was beating the breeches off him, and Daniel could tell she wasn't half trying. Chalk up another point for the vixen, he thought with a smile as he watched her disarm her opponent easily. The man, laughing uproariously, threw himself to his knees in front of her, begging playfully for "mercy." The other pirates suggested rudely that she not grant it, but she merely laughed and raised the man to his feet with a strong right arm.

Down on the beach, Lynnette was enjoying herself immensely. The men were flushed with victory, as, to tell the truth, was she. The mock battle just ended had exhilarated her, causing her blood to sing, although she was not out of breath from such a small exercise. The rum she'd consumed was making her feel warm, and she grabbed a passing bottle for another drink.

Here on No-name, she and her men were as safe as they were ever likely to get, so she felt that a couple of victory toasts would not get her into trouble. It was rare for Lynnette to allow her guard to drop even a little, for one slip on her part could bring death and destruction to all of her men. Again, she did not like to be incapacitated when among large groups where other pirates gathered, for there was always someone who thought it would be a good job to make her his bedmate for the evening. She was very cautious in such matters. But these men, the crew of the *Maiden's Revenge*, were as close to a family as Lynnette could have anymore. She trusted each and every one of her men as far as she dared trust anyone. If she wanted to imbibe tonight, no one on her little island would harm her.

She preferred to trust herself *only* to herself, having learned long ago that no one, not even the most reliable-seeming person, could keep her as safe as she herself could do. Even with

her crew, Lynnette held a part of herself back. In her line of
work, she could not afford to trust unequivocally. It was all a
matter of taking things into her own hands. But to get a mite
foxed once in a great while was not too far to let things go,
she judged. Even intoxicated, she could best any assailant with
a sword.

All of Lynnette's decisions were her own, and that was the
way she liked it. She almost never found it necessary to
second-guess her choices, but right now, the decision to keep
Captain Bradley in her house was plaguing her mightily. Log-
ically, she knew that there was no other place where he could
reasonably be held for a period of months, but still, she felt
uneasy. The thought of sharing a roof with that silver-eyed
man sent a frisson of sensation threading through her being,
and though she wasn't quite sure what the feeling was, she
knew she didn't like it.

Contrary to the impression she had given her prisoner when
she'd left him earlier, there had been only one other captive
before Captain Bradley to stay in her home—the others, including the artisans who had built her house, had always been
quartered in a barracks guarded by her crew. Sharing the villa
with the timid little Spanish heiress, however, had not made
Lynnette at all uncomfortable. She doubted Bradley would
cause her as few troubles as Maria had.

The diminutive, frightened young girl had not left her room
once in the entire time she had spent on No-name, though
Lynnette had invited her several times to take some exercise.
The girl had shrunk away from her as though she carried the
plague, which annoyed Captain Thorne no end. She had never
threatened the chit in any way, but the stupid shivering thing
had persisted in her demonstration of wide-eyed terror until
Lynnette had given up on trying to be nice, and kept her
locked up as she seemed to desire.

She did not entertain the notion, even for a minute, that
Captain Bradley would be as easy to control. He was no whimpering milksop, afraid of his own shadow. But that was precisely what was causing her unease. It was his overwhelming
masculinity, his total lack of intimidation concerning her, and
damn him, his eyes that made her stomach flip-flop nervously.
Without volition, Lynnette saw them again as he gazed steadily at her in her memory. Pure silver, with slate-colored rims

around the irises, outrageously long black lashes framing all. They made her shiver with a strange premonition of doom.

But she was being ridiculous. So he was handsome. She knew men nearly as attractive as the blasted Captain Bradley, and none had ever caused her to feel oddly before this. So why was she wasting her thoughts on *him*? The night was young, and there was food and drink to be had! Tearing her thoughts from the disturbing captive, Lynnette determinedly threw herself into the fun.

He was still there, long after his tired body told him he should make use of the oh-so-inviting bed. He couldn't tear his gaze from her. Laughing, eating, relaxed, Captain Thorne was a vision to behold, and he couldn't control himself. He wanted her more than any woman he'd ever seen before. Unbidden, images of her naked, writhing in his bed, kept coming to torture him. Daniel's blood raced in his veins, raced to a spot that caused his tight breeches to become extremely uncomfortable. How could he survive the coming months, with her so close, and yet so unbearably unattainable?

He watched her sprinting across the sands, weaving just a little, to chase a squealing pig. She corralled it into the arms of another pirate, laughing all the while. The unfortunate porker was destined for roasting, and it must have guessed its fate, for it swerved away just in time, tossing the man to the sand in its wake. She laughed so hard, she fell over as well, and Daniel felt an answering smile come to his lips.

She enchanted him in this playful, carefree mood. He doubted, sadly, that that blinding smile would ever be turned his way. The thought hurt him strangely, and he resolutely dismissed it as absurd. Why should he care if some strumpet—beautiful beyond all reckoning though she might be—turned her smiles upon him? He did not need her affections, he needed her negligence, so that he could get off this blasted island and make his way to England before he lost everything to her. But even telling himself this did not help. He still wanted her. Finally, as he looked on, she and the other pirate gave up the chase as unfairly biased in the desperate pig's favor and let it go.

After a long while, during which Daniel watched anxiously to see who she would take to her bed, the woman rose to leave.

Alone. He felt relief sweep him as she headed for the path. He left the terrace, the object of his interest having departed, and stripped to his breeches for sleep.

As he was settling on the bed, he heard her footsteps in the corridor. They paused at his door, and Daniel's heart pounded for an instant, and then he heard her.

"Good night, Peacock," she called airily. The footsteps crossed the hall, and a door creaked open. God's balls, Captain Thorne's quarters were just across the hall from his! To know she slept scant feet from where he languished in painful desire was cruel, indeed.

He cursed and reached for the rum bottle the servant girl had brought in earlier with his food. He did not put it down until it was empty.

CHAPTER FIVE

*T*HE SUN sent streaks of light through the chamber where Daniel slept, causing him, still deeply asleep, to throw a well-muscled arm up to shield his eyes. He mumbled incoherently at the bright intrusion, not wanting to rise and face the day. In an effort to deny the sun, he flipped over onto his stomach and buried his head under the feather pillow, but his body, accustomed to waking at first light, would not allow it. Finally, with profound reluctance, Daniel gave up. Levering himself to one elbow, he surveyed his surroundings. *Different,* he thought muzzily, then slowly recalled the events of the previous day. He was in Captain Thorne's villa, in the "guest" chamber. And he had one hell of a hangover.

The night before, knowledge of the pirate queen's close accommodations had sent him racing to the rum bottle in an effort to cool down. He'd had to reach oblivion before he could manage the slightest cessation of the burning ache her presence caused. This morning, it was easier not to care.

Daniel's head was pounding unmercifully, but worse than that was the twisting sensation in his stomach. He felt as if he'd been poisoned, and he supposed he was not far wrong. That swill the pirates called drink tasted more like horse piss than spirits. Give him a good brandy any day over that wretched brew. Gazing about, he wondered why he'd bothered to get up. He had nowhere to go.

"Blah," said Daniel to the room at large. Not even knowing why he did it, he swung himself out of bed and picked up his shirt from the wood floor where he'd left it the night before. Habit, probably. He was used to waking early and being active all day. Donning the rumpled linen quickly, he went to the door. He knew it would be locked, but could not resist trying it anyhow.

The handle turned easily under his hand, opening with nary a sound. What was this? Daniel searched his foggy memory, but he was sure the door had been locked yesterday. This was tantamount to an invitation. Never one to refuse an invitation, he cautiously stepped out into the corridor.

Retracing his steps, Daniel found his way to the front of the house. No one was about, it seemed, and he heard no voices calling for him to stop. He reached the front room decorated with thick, jewel-toned carpets and blue brocaded settees. A couple of quite decent landscape paintings, removed from some captured ship no doubt, hung from the cream-and-gold fabric-covered walls. Curtains of the same dark blue as the couches fluttered in the open windows. It was then that he noticed the half-open door to the verandah.

Curious, for he heard the sound of cutlery being rattled outside, he made his way to the doorway. Hesitating just this side of it, he saw a table set up on the sun-drenched porch, and the woman his dreams could not shake seated at it. Daniel must have made some sound, for she looked up at that moment.

Daniel caught his breath in his throat. He would have to stop reacting in this adolescent manner every time he was faced with the wench or he would surely suffocate, he thought with a scowl. But faced with the pirate's autumn-hued hair shining that way in its coronet and her golden skin glowing so brightly with health, not to mention her beautiful body so slightly clad, controlling his breathing was a task Hercules would have shied from.

This morning, the shirt Captain Thorne wore was of fine white lawn, almost sheer. A black leather vest, loosely laced at the sides, went over it and saved it from total immodesty.

He had noticed that, though her manner of dress was enough to catch any man's eye with its very unusualness, she never left her shirts open too far, nor did she flaunt her body in any way. All of her sensuality was unconscious. He wondered what she would look like if she tried to be seductive, perhaps if she donned skirts like other women, and decided he liked her appearance well enough in its natural state. Artifice would not suit a woman like Captain Thorne.

Looking at him with her head slightly tilted, he could tell she was assessing his somewhat disheveled state, his hand-combed hair and wrinkled clothing. Daniel felt his face heat, but reminded himself that the disarray of his wardrobe was entirely her fault, so he had nothing to be ashamed of. But Thorne was so fresh-looking, he had to take a second look. Daniel had personally seen her guzzle enough rum to down a small army, yet she seemed to suffer no ill effects whatsoever. Instead, she was smiling as she said, "Have a seat, Captain Bradley. I was just about to break my fast. You are welcome to join me, if you will."

She said nothing of the unlocked door, and he was not about to question it. So he sat, nodding his thanks curtly, though he knew that, for the sake of his continued sanity, he should probably stay away from her.

Lynnette lifted the silver covers from the servers on the table before her, inhaling appreciatively the steaming fragrance of scrambled eggs and ham, pork chops and rolls and fresh butter. Daniel turned slightly green.

She started in with a will, eating heartily. He watched her, envy and nausea warring with admiration. After a moment, she looked up at him, surveying his still-empty plate. "You do not eat." It was a question. "Is the fare not to your liking? My cook is very good, truly. If there is something else you would prefer—"

"No," he interrupted quickly, rudely. "I'm quite sure the food is fine, but I—I have no appetite this morn, is all." He was acutely embarrassed and striving hard not to show it. He did not want to give this wench more reason to think him a green boy.

Her eyes were twinkling. She knew, damn her. She was purposely torturing him! "Are you sure? Mayhap some kippers, or liver, or buttermilk?" She was hard put not to break into gales of laughter at the appalled look on his face, the tightening of jaw muscles as he strained to keep himself from being ill right there and then. She could not help herself, though, for having never experienced the fabled "morning after" herself, Lynnette had little sympathy for those who were afflicted. Besides, although she had authorized the bottle to be placed on his tray last night, she had not expected him to drink as much as he obviously *had*. It was not her fault if the man overimbibed.

"No, thank you!" He was sure of it, now. The heartless witch knew of his predicament, and was using it against him. He hated her. He really did. How could she drink like that and *not* have a hangover? It wasn't fair, damn it! By chance, their eyes met at that moment, and the mutual realization was in both sets.

Suddenly, the whole situation struck Daniel as immensely funny. The corners of Lynnette's lips curled up at the same time, and soon, both were shaking helplessly with mirth, holding their aching sides and gasping for air as they roared with laughter.

When finally Daniel managed to get his breath back, he studied her covertly from under lowered lashes. Captain Thorne was still chuckling softly, her slim arm about her waist as though to hold more laughter at bay. He decided she had a beautiful laugh. Unlike the ladies he knew in London, she did not simper or giggle falsely, but laughed with real amusement. The throaty sounds were very arousing . . . But he would not think that now.

She looked happy today. When they had first met, Daniel had had an impression of anger above and beyond what could be laid down to battle fever. He had sensed too that it was directed elsewhere, at someone far away. Today she seemed calmer, less hard-edged, although he saw something deep and raw in her eyes that did not leave even when she smiled. That which had made her into a renegade? Knowing something about soul-deep pain himself, Daniel believed it was so.

Lynnette *was* happy today. Being home always made her feel so, which was perhaps why she had magnanimously decided to allow Captain Bradley the freedom of the island— under the watchful eyes of her men, of course. After all, what was the harm? With so many of her men around, there was no way he could escape unnoticed. And she hated to think of anyone locked up when it was such a beautiful day. Not that they had anything other than beautiful days here in the Indies. The weather was always mild, balmy, and exquisitely sunny. Except during hurricane season, of course, which was not for another month or so. Still, she need not have invited the man to breakfast, especially not after the disquieting dream she'd had about him last night. But to see the look on his face when she mentioned liver . . . It was worth it.

More kindly, she asked, "Some coffee?"

Looking mightily relieved, he nodded. "Thank you," he said gratefully as he took the cup from her. Their fingers brushed, and both jumped a little. Fortunately, the coffee did not spill onto the fine linen tablecloth. But the streak of sensation caused by the brief touch caused both captor and captive to sober abruptly.

Covering her reaction, she said brightly, "We'll be making repairs to the *Empire* today. The bowsprit needs work, and the aft gun ports."

"Because of you," he growled. Mention of his ship and the damage she had caused it brought back all his resentment.

"Aye, well, that's a fact. I can't take it back now, nor would I care to," Lynnette said evenly. "All's fair in love and war . . ." She faltered, suddenly distressed by the word "love." *Not,* she told herself, *the most apt axiom I could have chosen.*

He knew it. The gleam that came to his eyes told her that. "Indeed, and one may take any measure necessary to succeed in either." He certainly planned to.

"Aye," Lynnette said shortly, closing off the subject before it could get out of hand. She was uncomfortable with his sudden sharp, intense stare.

Daniel sipped his coffee reflectively. His headache was easing, and his stomach began to protest its emptiness. In short, he had begun to feel human again. A good thing, since he would need all his wits to keep up with Captain Thorne. Buttering a roll, he asked sarcastically, "What, no maiming and pillaging to do today?"

"No," she replied flippantly, not at all put out. "I've taken the day off. Besides, my men and I only pillage on alternate Wednesdays. We've another week and a half to go yet."

"I see. So you restrict your robbing and killing of innocents to certain days." He had not forgotten that the buccaneers had injured several of his crew, and it showed in his voice.

"Come, now, Captain Bradley. You did not expect me to order my men to harm none of yours while they went out for blood themselves? You yourself laid two men low. No matter how I may feel about that, I do not lay the blame at your feet. You did what you had to do."

Daniel was incredulous. "As you did merely what you had to? You had no need to take my ship!"

"Had you surrendered as you should have, there would have been no need for bloodshed."

"So now I'm supposed to just hand over my vessel without a murmur! Captain, you go beyond all bounds of sanity!" He stared at her, furious. What kind of man did she take him for? A fool, certainly.

"I had need of your ship," she said coolly. "The seas belong to whomsoever can rule them. The strongest always win."

"You think yourself more powerful than I?" He laughed. "Captain, one look will prove that I am the stronger."

"Perhaps bodily," she replied, eyeing him up and down, noting the hard muscles of his lean body, the way his broad shoulders tapered to a tight, firm waist and slim hips. "But I have no doubt I could best you by other means. And I have proved it by taking your ship."

He said nothing, merely looked scornful. "The question is moot," Lynnette continued. "What's done is done, yet, if it will make you feel better, I regret the loss of life involved. I am not fond of killing."

As apologies went, he had heard better. Still, he supposed it was as much as he could hope for, and she was right. It was no use railing at the author of his miseries whilst he remained in her power. Later, perhaps, he could do something to even the score. For now, he would let it lie.

Silence reigned for a long moment.

"I suppose," said Daniel resignedly, "that you'll have me locked up again anon."

"Why, no. I see no reason that you shouldn't have a look at your surroundings. You had little chance yesterday to see the island. Wander about at your leisure, enjoy the beaches, explore a little." The pirate's tone was relaxed, magnanimous.

Daniel arched one winged black brow. "You don't fear that

I might simply disappear out from under your nose if you set me at liberty?"

She laughed. "I think you'll find there's little hope of that. One of my men will be watching over you at all times, and this *is* a small island. You make one foolish move and ten men will know of it before you can blink. They may not be as civil as I would be in stopping you."

He reined in his temper with an effort. Of all the arrogant . . . But her underestimation of his skills and determination could only work in his favor. If she thought he couldn't handle a few pirates, she'd be more careless when it counted. Best to let the wench think him a popinjay, much as it galled him. When he made his move, she'd never know what hit her. So instead of biting her head off, he merely pasted on a pleasant, harmless smile.

Lynnette nodded equably. "Good. I'm glad you're being so reasonable about all of this. When you've toured the island a bit, you're welcome to come and watch the repairs we're doing on the *Empire*." She rose from the table, tossed her napkin down absently, and gestured him toward the shell-lined cove path.

As he got to his feet, Daniel smiled wider. "Ladies first," he said, because he knew it would gall her.

CHAPTER SIX

*L*YNNETTE DIDN'T know what had come over her where Daniel was concerned. She gave him freedom, all the while knowing he was dangerous. She shared meals with the man, which, Lord knew, was totally unnecessary. Worse, he had begun to creep into her mind. At odd times the past few days Lynnette had found herself wondering what the prisoner was doing, and now that he was here on her island, she felt his presence everywhere—even in her rum-soaked dreams. She blushed to think of it.

In the night, Lynnette had woken—or thought she woke— to feel a delicate, delicious pressure on her mouth, arousing her senses to center on the touch. She slowly recognized the sensations for what they were. The lightest kisses imaginable fluttered upon her lips like the wings of butterflies. Again and again, hot, soft lips descended to hers, and she did not shy away or attempt to stop them. It felt too right, too natural, for her to ever want it to cease.

Then they pulled away oh, so gently, and she saw the face of her fantasy lover. It was he. Long, silky raven hair framed his sensual face, and dark-rimmed silver eyes stared heatedly down at her in the moonlight. And her dream-self did not think it strange.

Captain Bradley smiled slowly, and she reached up to touch his jaw in wonderment. The skin she touched was so smooth underneath the beard stubble, yet it was firm, and she felt the underlying strength at the unyielding core of him. He ducked his head once more to meet her lips with his, and now the kiss was hard, sure; demanding and possessing her very soul. He tilted his head to take her lips more fully, deepening the searing kiss until she was shaking from the intensity of it. His tongue mated with hers in an erotic dance, lush and heady, pleasuring her voluptuously.

Those long, lean hands moved to touch her throat, her collarbone, stroking lightly across her silken skin. Then, in a sudden rush of desire, his arms came around her, crushing her close, and she felt the length of his entire strong, hot body. His naked body.

But she was naked, too, Lynnette realized hazily, and it was *right*. She reached eagerly for him, in the dream perfectly sure of herself. She wrapped one long, slim leg around his, needing to feel his hard flesh against hers. And she begged—dear God, had she truly begged?—for him to touch her more fully, to make her his. He obeyed instantly.

Callused hands molded her breasts, caressing boldly, palming the hard peaks that burned so sweetly for him. She gasped at the shooting pleasure and said his name as if in prayer. Then his wet mouth replaced his hands, and she could not think, it felt so good. A hot ache flared to life deep inside her as he drew first one nipple and then the other in to be laved and licked and suckled. He tongued the pebble-hard tips without respite until she pleaded for mercy from the fiery sensations he caused.

But he was relentless. His right hand stroked her taut belly;

moving slowly, slowly lower. He caressed her hips, the insides of her creamy thighs, easing his way closer to the place where the flames burned highest. Lynnette held her breath, she couldn't stand it; she knew she would die if she could not have him. Then his searching fingers invaded her damp, swollen petals, and she let out her long-held breath in a scream of ecstasy.

And woke from the dream, trembling with unfulfilled passion.

Desire turned to horror as she realized what she had done. She'd dreamed of him; touching her as no other ever had or ever would. How could she have? It was inconceivable! For fully half an hour she lay in shock in her empty bed, unable to stop shaking with a nameless dread. That he should invade her sleep with his image, that Lynnette could envision her captive in such a fashion; it was wrong, incredibly wrong, not natural as it had seemed in her dream! What was happening to her? Never before had she felt these feelings of desire, had never wanted to, and she did not now.

At last, as the dream faded a little, her fear started to seem silly. It *was* only a dream, a nightmare, really. It foretold nothing, and no one but she would ever have to know about it. Besides, she reasoned, it had to be merely the result of her overindulgence last night, because, as everyone knew, strong spirits produced bizarre imaginings. The dream had been a fluke, and, she told herself sternly, it would not occur again. Seeing it so, Lynnette swore off drink forever, just in case. She also decided that in order to prove to herself that he didn't *really* affect her, she should face him. Accordingly, on her way to breakfast, she unlocked her prisoner's door.

Still, it had taken all her will to remain impassive when Captain Bradley appeared in the doorway that morning, looking tall and handsome and altogether too masculine for her comfort. The urge to blush was enormous. She forced it down with sheer determination, and greeted him as though she had not recently been dreaming of his searing, enraptured touch.

Lynnette had a strong will, and no hint of her agitated state had reached him. Once she was sure of it, she had begun to relax and forget her restless night. Soon, it was as if it had never passed, and she began to feel more like her normal self. She'd been right to face both him and her fear of his touch.

Even so, at odd times, flashes of the dream and her fantasy lover returned to haunt her. As the afternoon wore on, her concentration frayed and she had to shake herself frequently out of daydreams when her advice was needed on repairs for the captured ship. It didn't help that Captain Bradley had wandered into the sheltered cove where the ship was anchored and was watching the proceedings with hooded eyes.

Lynnette told herself it was common courtesy that compelled her to treat their "guest" with cordiality, even when he had such a profound effect on her unconscious mind. Not that their conversation this morning had been exactly cordial. Truly, it more resembled a verbal battle for the most part. But she remembered their laughter and was no little shaken. The effect his deep chuckles had on her spine was extraordinary, she thought. A chill, not unpleasant, had coursed through her nerves at the sound. And gazing at his face during such a careless moment was dramatically disturbing to her peace of mind, she'd found. With tiny laugh lines crinkling the corners of those ungodly steel-colored orbs, he had been breathtakingly handsome.

She felt his regard; she had felt it these three hours past, burning into her back like a flaming brand. It made Captain Thorne—one of the most feared buccaneers ever yet to sail the crystal-clear waters of the Caribbean—distinctly uncomfortable. With a great effort, Lynnette forced her eyes to remain fixed on the men working just beneath her. But the feeling persisted. Finally, she could stand it no longer; she turned.

Of course, he was watching her, just as he had been the other half-dozen times she'd swung about, feeling eyes upon her. But this time, she noticed that Captain Bradley was not alone. Harry sat with him, enjoying a respite from the hot sun.

It did not bode well for her. The first mate would always be foremost among the men Lynnette chose to have beside her in a fight, for despite his advancing age, he was crafty and strong, but he could be a tad loose-tongued when he took a liking to a man.

Harry would never betray his captain, not for any price or in any circumstance. If tortured, he'd die rather than let her secrets be wrested from his lips, but he had ideas of his own when it came to her well-being. Harry tended to be a trifle proprietary concerning Lynnette. He could almost be her father, and was most certainly a better one than the man who had spawned her, she thought with a surge of bitterness, but Harry believed he knew what was best for her, which she could not accept. For his own reasons, he might tell the peacock something she did not desire him to hear. Especially as he so obviously liked the man more than Lynnette thought was warranted.

Nay, she could trust Harry, she told herself sternly, berating her suspicious nature for its lack of trust. He would be discreet. Lynnette had known him nearly all her life, and no matter what out-of-character affection he felt for her prisoner, he would not betray her confidence. Just to be sure, though, she sent him a fulminating glare, warning him to keep his trap shut.

The mate pretended not to notice, but Lynnette knew full well he had gotten the point. She turned back, satisfied, and tried to return her wayward mind to her work.

But images from her dream kept returning to haunt her, images of that shadow kiss, Daniel's hard, muscled body atop her own, and the pleasure! Dear God, that she should create a fantasy, even unwillingly, of ecstasy between them, when she knew nonesuch could be the case in reality . . .

Lynnette understood the pleasure men received from fornicating. Too, she recognized the fact that certain women enjoyed the act as well. But *she* could never, of that she was sure. Not after what she had seen . . . her sister, brutally raped by two men, as she stood by, helpless to prevent it. And then not so helpless. She had killed one of the men that very night. The other she continued to hunt with a vengeance none could deny.

Now, years later, she felt naught but a faint disgust for the mating act, her initial fear and misconceptions having disappeared. After being in the licentious company of buccaneers for more than seven years, she had witnessed a great deal and knew that sex was not always a violent thing. Lynnette had been forcibly educated to the point where nothing shocked her anymore, both by sight, and by the bawdy talk of sailors. One could not close one's eyes or ears to the realities of pirate life, not if one wished to stay alive. Still, she felt no desire to make forays of her own into the sensual world and discover for herself the truth of the matter.

The dream was mere foolishness, she assured herself, induced by too much drink and too much sun. She would not worry the issue further. And she would work herself to exhaustion tonight to ensure a dreamless stupor when she fell into bed. Lynnette had done the same countless times when plagued by the other dream she still occasionally suffered through, and it nearly always worked. Much heartened by her resolve, Captain Thorne turned her attention fully to the repairs once more.

Splintered wood on the aft gun ports was replaced carefully by men who had seen to such tasks many times before, and Daniel had no complaints. The ruined bowsprit was dismantled altogether to be used as firewood since it could not be salvaged. Even now, a gang of men were fashioning a new one on the beach close by; the long, thin frontispiece of the frigate was carved from a tall cottonwood, since there was no oak to be had. The vessel had been minimally damaged because of Captain Thorne's fancy maneuvering, and he estimated the repairs would take no more than a few days to complete.

Over the sounds of hammering and sawing, Daniel did not at first hear the footsteps heading toward him. When he looked up from the bare, horny-toed feet that had stopped in his line of sight, the *Maiden's* first mate was standing beside him. He was curious, for the man—Harry, wasn't it?—had seemed sympathetic and kindly toward him in a rough sort of way. He raised a questioning eyebrow.

"Mind if I join ye fer a spate? 'Tis mighty hot, I'm thinkin', an' this little bit o' shade be about as welcomin' as a whore on a Sunday morn." He laughed wheezily, displaying blackened teeth. "In case yer fancyship don't know, 'tis th' least busy time o' th' week fer a doxy."

"I am aware of that," Daniel replied dryly. "Be welcome; sit. If the ship were yet mine, I'd offer you refreshment aboard her, but as she is not, I can only offer a cool place to rest in her shadow."

"Ain't ye th' p'lite one! They don't call ye 'Peacock' fer naught, now do they! I'll take what ye offer an' gladly." Harry seated himself with a grunt.

Captain Bradley winced at the moniker. He hardly looked the part now, clad in sweat-stained shirt and breeches, having discarded his heavy jacket once they reached the island. He had a feeling that the name was here to stay, however, and attempted with limited success to take the jibe in good humor. Harry, he knew, meant nothing by it.

Captain Thorne was another case entirely.

Once again, Daniel's eyes strayed to watch her figure as the two men settled into a companionable silence. She moved with such purpose, unlike the other women of his acquaintance. Probably, he thought, because she *had* a purpose, while those ladies had none besides their newest bedroom conquest. Their mien was languid, practiced; hers was nothing if not unstudied. Captain Thorne seemed as unaware of her beauty as a creature of the jungle.

A lioness, he thought her, stalking back and forth before her pride with energy to spare, fluid in her grace and strong as the regal feline he'd just compared her to. His eyes grew a shade brighter with hunger.

"I seen ye starin' at my lassie a time er two afore, with a look in them silver eyes like ye got jest now. Ye want her, I kin tell." There was a smirk in Harry's tone.

Daniel started at the older man's voice, jarred from his acute study. He turned his head to look piercingly at the man, but answered lightly. "Who would not?" *My lassie? Just what sort of relationship did the two have?* Then he shook himself in disgust. Of course there was nothing between them; Harry was old enough to be the wench's grandsire! No doubt she preferred younger bedmates. Besides, his tone had been nearly paternal in its nature. Daniel told himself he'd been out in the sun too long. Jealous of this old man? Jealous—at all? *Hardly,* he scoffed privately. He did not care whom the wench bedded. It was no concern of his! He listened again to the first mate.

"Aye, all th' men be wantin' a piece o' th' captain. But none gets more than a prick from 'er sword fer 'is pains, I tell ye! My lassie won't have none o' those ruffians."

Captain Bradley had serious doubts as to the veracity of that, even as he was relieved to hear that the pirate queen was not indiscriminate with her favors. He could not believe, as Harry implied, that Captain Thorne had no lovers. Still, the man would not say it if she were *easily* had. So, very likely, she picked her bedmates discreetly and did not flaunt them in front of her crew. *Smart of her,* he thought. He could well imagine there'd be a riot if she paraded her chosen lover in the other men's faces.

Each member of the crew would want to kill the man and take her for himself if the wench displayed her sexuality so blatantly. It would be like waving a red cape in front of a bull. Not that it was any of his affair, he reminded himself.

"From the familiar way you speak of her, I assume you have known Captain Thorne for quite some time?"

"Oh, aye, from th' beginnin'. Ye should'a seen th' way she took Tortuga by storm! Walked right inta th' meanest, dirtiest, lowest tavern on th' whole damned island, plunked 'erself down at a table with six o' th' most notorious renegades this side o' hell, all playin' cards, an' said, 'Deal me in,' like 'twas a card room in London!" Harry shook his head with fond remembrance.

"Well, they all laughed, an' pretty quick they was doin' their best ta' get 'er on 'er back, but th' captain wasn' havin' none o' that! Cut them bastards, one an' all, so's not a one of 'em was left unbloodied, an' while they's moanin' an' clutchin' their hurts, she turns an' says ta th' tavern in gen'ral, 'So, who else would like to lose some flesh?'" He mimicked her throaty, cultured voice roughly. "An' then she says, 'My name is Captain Thorne. And I don't like being mauled. So, if you'd kindly remember that, I think we'll get on nicely.' An' then she goes on ta put every single buccaneer in th' Indies ta shame with 'er record o' prizes. What do ye think o' that, my friend?"

Daniel could envision the scene well. Thorne, surrounded by scum on all sides, holding them at bay with cold steel and even colder words. She must have been magnificent, and he devoutly wished he had been there to see it.

"I think your captain takes too many risks for her continued health," was all he said.

Harry merely laughed. "Ye wouldn't say that had ye seen her in action. See, 'twas the only way ta make 'erself known ta th' Brethren. We ran th' risk o' bein' attacked, else. E'en so, there were no few buckos who tried it. But once word got round that th' captain was no one ta be trifled with, our place in th' pirate kingdom was secured."

He knew the first mate was right, but his curiosity made him incautious, so enthralled was he with the older sailor's narrative. He forgot that Harry was Thorne's man, and that he had no reason to trust Daniel, so he asked the question that had been burning on his mind since first he'd seen the woman. Before he could stop himself, he found the words pouring out that would surely recall the talkative pirate to his wits.

"What was she like—before, I mean? Before she was Captain Thorne." As soon as the words left his mouth, he wished to call them back, but he could not. So he waited, breath unconsciously held, to hear what Harry would say.

" 'Tis not fer me ta say," answered Harry after a pause, sighing heavily. " 'Twould be wrong fer me ta tell ye what be not yer business, an' th' lassie wouldn' thank me fer it. But this much I may say, as I like ye, boy." He stopped for a second, thinking. When he continued, his voice was soft. "She was different. Aye, very different. None so hard, not like she be now . . ." At this moment the subject of their discussion turned to glare at Harry, who quickly averted his gaze and stopped talking.

"But surely," said Daniel, who could not prevent himself from pushing, "there is something more you can tell me!" Desperation tinged his voice, to learn so much and be stopped short of what he really wanted to know.

"Nay, I'll not say more," returned the older man, staring doggedly into the distance. He became as a rock, impervious to all of the younger man's pleading questions. At last, Daniel, sensing that the first mate would leave if badgered further, lapsed into silence. He thought for a minute.

"You've told me this much for a purpose, haven't you? For some reason, you wanted me to know more of this woman." It wasn't a question. He stared sharply at the man for an instant, until Harry turned his head aside, muttering under his breath.

"Nay, boy, ye have it wrong. 'Twas no more than idle chatter." Getting up, he stretched. "I'm gettin' ta be an auld woman, gossipin' at every turn. I oughta watch meself, afore I wake up in th' mornin' an' put on a skirt instead o' me britches! Now, I gotta be goin' or I'll catch all hell fer laziness." With that, he ambled off. But Daniel had seen the truth in his eyes.

* * *

The remainder of the afternoon passed slowly for Captain Bradley, with nothing more to do. He'd been over the island that morning, but in the presence of his pirate shadow, a man he'd not seen before but with much the same taciturn attitude as his former guard Omar, he'd been reluctant to investigate possible escape routes too closely. Seemingly idle, in reality keeping a sharp eye on anything that might be of later use to him, Daniel had strolled across the idyllic pink sand beaches and wandered into the tiny village. There was nothing to see there besides a few thatched huts and a dirt track leading to the water's edge. A few women busied themselves with domestic chores, hanging laundry, watching their children. The menfolk were nowhere to be seen, and Daniel supposed they were all out with the fishing boats.

The guard had stopped him from entering the jungle composing most of the interior of No-name Island without explanation. The loaded pistol in the man's hand had been enough of an incentive for the merchant to obey. Instead, he'd wandered the beaches for a time, till the pirate's surly presence at his back began to spoil his pleasure in the sun-washed sand and surf. Finally, he'd headed to the center of activity, the cove where Captain Thorne and her men were refitting his ship.

He watched the pirates at work for a while, seeing how they interacted with the ease of long association, but soon enough that became tedious. The men were a lively lot, full of salty curses and good-natured jibes. Once or twice, they broke into bawdy song, and Captain Bradley found it hard not to hum along. But as the sun crawled infinitesimally toward the western horizon, he found that he was restless. Watching them work on what *had* been his prized ship was painful, to say the least. Watching their captain stride about in those tight breeches of hers was agonizing.

He turned Harry's words over in his mind again and again, but he could not guess why the old man had been so garrulous. Perhaps, as the mate had said, it was merely gossip, but he doubted it. He was sure he had seen a flash of hidden intent in the man's clear eyes. So, why would he tell Daniel about Thorne's supposed celibacy, and her early days on Tortuga, unless . . .

Unless, somehow, he wanted what Daniel wanted. For the two to be together. But that was impossible! Still, it rang true. Captain Bradley had the ability to judge people, to know their purpose with a glance, and his intuition told him Harry was an honest man with a devious ambition.

But it made no sense, and at last, with an impatient shrug, he told his instincts to go sod off. This was getting him nowhere. What he should be thinking about was escaping, and here he was, wondering what some old man who, for all he knew, could be mad as a Bedlamite, had meant by some passing remarks. Instead, he should be studying the pirates' habits, trying to determine their weaknesses. Perhaps he could divine which of the crewmen seemed dissatisfied, or who was inattentive by nature.

It did not occur to him to attempt persuasion or bribery with Harry. For all his willingness to tell what must be common lore, the man would never, he was positive, sell out his captain.

As the hours passed, he watched the pirates, and, by sunset, was extremely discouraged. They never relaxed their discreet vigilance. He knew they were keeping an eye on him, although no one said anything about it. And they were not lazy workers, as sailors often were. Daniel knew the signs of good captaincy: willing, well-fed crew members, a clean ship, and a general sense of order. All of these were present. None of the buccaneers would be anxious to cross their leader by helping him escape, nor would they wish to incur her wrath and lose their share of the booty his ransom would bring by allowing him to slip free.

His best hope, or so he figured, was to escape when the pirates left No-name Island to sell the *Empire*. Until then, he would simply have to bide his time. It was not so bad a prospect as he'd originally thought, for it gave him a chance to be near Captain Thorne. As soon as might be, Daniel would escape. Until that time, what harm in exploring his fascination with the pirate wench?

He did not get a chance to indulge his fancy anytime in the next four days. That night, he was escorted to his chamber by Omar, whom he was beginning to hate, and the door was locked. Even though he had assumed there would be no summons to sup with the captain, he found that he was yet gravely disappointed when hours passed and the door stayed locked. Much later, a sleepy-looking island woman, the same who had fed him the previous evening, brought a tray. He ate without even checking to see what it was. It didn't matter that the food was delicious, prepared by Lynnette's French chef. It could have been sawdust, he would not have noticed.

Daniel was consumed by three things. Thorne, escape, and his chagrin that these things were categorized in order of their importance by his foolish brain. Escape should be first and foremost, but all his plans stubbornly refused to stay firm in his head, maddeningly dissolving time and again into pictures of that damned seductive witch.

He slept restlessly, and awoke to find the door still locked. Obviously, she thought it had been a mistake to let him out yesterday. But it left him with nothing to do. The native woman came in to feed him, murmuring incomprehensibly in what he presumed must be the Arawak Indian tongue spoken by many West Indian islanders. He saw that she was eyeing him with interest, but felt no response stirring within. The girl was pretty, but she was not her mistress. He ignored her, and soon she left, pouting slightly.

The following days were much the same, with boredom becoming Daniel's constant companion. A few books, mostly nautical texts, had been left on the desk, and he tried to read them, but he couldn't concentrate. From outside, he could hear the sounds of the repairs his former ship was undergoing, and it made him sick to realize they were going to sell it, and there was absolutely nothing he could do to stop them. Caught between desire and fury, he spent hours on the terrace, trying to catch a glimpse of Captain Thorne. But it did no good to see her.

The woman was a fever in his blood, causing him to alternately crave the feel of her neck beneath his wringing hands, or under his caressing mouth. He desired her with an intensity that made all other women pale by comparison. And he wanted to kill her nearly as much. Daniel Bradley was not a happy man.

Four days had gone by, and Lynnette judged that the prisoner must be stewing in his own juices by now. Left for so long with nothing to do, a man such as he would surely be going mad. She felt a twinge of guilt, then shoved it down. She'd had no choice but to keep him locked up, for she couldn't spare the men to watch him, as their slow progress on the repairs, and her own distraction that first day, had shown.

They'd be leaving tomorrow to sell the *Empire,* and Captain Bradley would have to remain under lock and key again whilst the buccaneers were gone. Therefore, she would have to let him out of his prison tonight. To do else would be cruel, she told herself, and that was the sole reason behind her clemency. It was not that she wanted to see him. She did not care if she ever saw his too-handsome visage again. But she didn't want the man to suffer unduly. Now, while her crew were still on the island to guard him, she would give Bradley one night of semifreedom.

Thus resolved, Captain Thorne inhaled deeply of the flower-scented night air and turned to leave the verandah. Supper was over, and the day's chores had been completed long ago. She'd been enjoying the cool evening breeze and contemplating the stars. The sky was exceptionally clear, and a full moon presided over all the brilliant constellations. Hibiscus and frangipani nodded in the breeze, lending their sweet fragrance to the night. From her vantage point, Lynnette could see the lush jungle and a hint of the beach that ringed No-name Island all around. The path to the cove was picked out with shining white shells, and to her right, on the other side of the tiny island, was the faint beginning of a freshwater stream. It quickly hid itself, plunging into the dense foliage of the interior.

Only five miles wide, No-name Island was heavily covered with jungle. A man could get lost in there, if he didn't know where he was going, as her men had discovered when they first claimed it for their own. There were wild pigs in the interior, among other deadly creatures, and Lynnette never entered without a pistol. It was a wild, ungodly paradise of hidden dangers and hidden delights. Her thoughts turned to her captive again as she pondered the idea of unknown pleasures— and risks. Suddenly the pirate could no longer enjoy the scenery, for she knew how her captive must feel, cooped up and unable to take pleasure in the night.

She should warn him about the jungle. If she exaggerated the dangers a bit, she might even have a hope that her prisoner would stay out of the interior if he tried to escape. *When* he tried to escape, she amended. There was little doubt that a man as intrepid as Captain Bradley would make a bid for freedom. The thought was sobering. Bradley would cause her a great deal of trouble before he was ransomed, she was sure. Striding indoors, she reminded herself that she was in charge of everything that went on on this island, and she had absolutely no cause to feel the fluttering her insides were just now experiencing.

At the door across from her own, she did not hesitate but threw the latch and pushed open the wooden panel.

Daniel looked up, and she sucked in her breath. Naked from the waist up in the candlelight, he was magnificent. Hard bands of muscle corded his chest and ribs, defining every ridge and valley. His arms were like steel, the biceps big and rock-like, the forearms sinewy. He was stronger than she'd expected. The sight of him threw her into confusion. It was not so simple a thing to just waltz into her captive's room as the pirate queen had hoped. Not when the mere sight of him started her blood racing.

Recovering herself, she saw that he was just as discomposed by her entrance as she had been. Daniel had seen no one but the servant girl for four days, and he had clearly long since given up hope that his captor would again take an interest in his welfare. Now, his eyes kindled, and Lynnette wished she had not chosen today to wear the snug-fitting black breeches, the tightest pair she owned.

When she spoke, her words were curt. "I'll allow you to take the air tonight, for you'll not get another chance in the next week or more. We go to sell the frigate tomorrow at dawn."

"You're extremely gracious," he said sarcastically, angry at being kept in his cell for so long. Daniel got up from the bed, tossing aside the book he'd been trying to read. Shrugging on his one shirt, he quickly tucked it in without a thought for modesty.

She watched his hands dip into the waistband of his gray breeches in an odd state of fascination. She was flustered by his nearness, having forgotten his effect on her in the intervening days. Being so close to the man was more than unsettling, it was torturous. It made her skin feel suddenly hot, as if she had contracted a fever, and her nerves, normally steadier than rock, were wired as tightly as a harp string.

Recovering her wits, she said spitefully, "God's wounds, Peacock, in the time it takes you to put on a shirt, I could have taken your ship all over again!" It was an unfair accusation, but she felt provoked and out of sorts with herself for allowing her body to be affected by the man, and lashing out gave her back her equilibrium. It put her back in control of the situation, and Lynnette would have it no other way.

"If I'm not fast enough for you," he suggested mildly, with just a hint of mischief, "you could help me tuck it in."

"Ha! I'll see you in hell first!" It was a halfhearted threat at best, because, despite herself, she felt an answering pull of amusement. It was hard not to laugh when he had such merry eyes and a wicked tongue to match. The composed, jocular manner he had of responding to her rudeness had the effect of dousing her anger better than a splash of cold water. Moreover, although she was not one to joke frequently herself, she appreciated humor in others.

"Mayhap. But I will be devoutly praying the day you wish to slide those pretty little fingers of yours into my breeches will come sooner than that."

Her eyes became slits. "If my hands come near your breeches, 'twill not be for the reason you desire, but to add your puny balls to my collection!"

Daniel placed his hands over his heart, feigning an attitude of deep offense. "Milady, I assure you, my balls are nowhere near 'puny.' If you would care to investigate, you will see for yourself that I do not lie." He looked hopeful. Then he asked curiously, "Do you really have a collection?"

He seemed so sincere in his foolery, she had to laugh. "No, I would not care to investigate, and no, though rumor has it otherwise, I do not have a collection of men's privates. How disgusting." She shuddered. "Men may prize their balls above all else, but *I* do not!

"Now, do you want to leave this chamber, or not? I don't have all night to spend bandying foolishness about with you." She indicated the open door.

"Certainly I wish to leave. It's just that your presence is more to me than any fleeting moment of freedom. I wonder, will you walk outside with me, milady?"

She told herself she should not. But a wheedling voice in her head said, it was only for one night, a few hours, and there could be no danger in it. She *wanted* his company, she realized. She was mad. He was her prisoner, by God! Not some colleague, not like Harry or André or her men. But none of those men made her feel the way this one did. It had to be the full moon making her contemplate such an unwise course of action. After all, it was common knowledge that people did crazy things under its influence. But who was she to fight it?

"I will come," she heard herself say. More in her normal manner, she added, "But don't *ever* call me 'milady' again."

"Your pardon: Captain," Daniel corrected himself, hardly able to believe his ears. "Shall we?" He held the door for her in true gentlemanly fashion. She shot him a look that said she did not appreciate the gesture and preceded him out the door.

As they strolled down to the cove, not touching, Lynnette warned him about the jungle. "If, when we return, you should be given the freedom of the island—and I am not saying you will—do not enter the jungle alone. There are wild boar and snakes, and you have no weapon." Quite seriously, she said, "You will be of little use to us if you die."

"I'm touched that you should care for my safety so," he replied with an edge of sarcasm to his voice.

"Why should I?" she asked frankly. "To me, you are a profitable venture, naught more." But it wasn't precisely true, not anymore. Captain Bradley, with his outrageous sense of humor, had caught her admiration. None dared to make so free with her as he did, jesting about things that had caused her to take a knife to other men. Perhaps he did not know of her reputation. He had seemed surprised to hear of her supposed inclination for grisly trophies just now, and anyone who knew about Captain Thorne would have heard that particular erroneous tale. Perhaps he knew no more than his crew had told him before she took his ship.

Still, she was amazed at Captain Bradley's audacity. Then she laughed at herself. Not everyone had heard of Captain Thorne. It was the height of arrogance to assume that all men knew of her. Lynnette was notorious, but not *that* notorious.

She supposed she had gotten used to fear from the men she met, bothersome though it was. They cringed at the sight of her anger, and were disgustingly obsequious when they had dealings with her. Pirates, merchants, nearly everyone she met, feared and respected her. But not him.

Why should she care, indeed? wondered Daniel. Because he did? 'Twas laughable. While Daniel had fallen beneath the spell of her laughter and her honesty, it appeared that she felt no ill effects herself. She did not care if he lived or died.

They stopped at the base of the cliff a little away from the well-used walkway, next to an old palm tree with hoary branches. Lynnette leaned her back against it, crossing her arms over her breasts. He merely stared, hopelessly enthralled. Her hair hung down in that single braid over her chest, shining softly against the black silk of her shirt in the moonlight, and her face was framed with a soft light. Emerald eyes glowed, and he wondered what secrets they held. She was tall, he realized, for standing in front of him, the crown of her head was level with his chin. He decided he liked tall women.

"Tell me something, Captain Bradley. Before I took your ship, had you ever heard of me?"

A strange question. "No, I am afraid not," Daniel answered cautiously. "Had I known of your beauty, I would have surrendered myself to you immediately," he joked.

It seemed to answer something for her. Nodding, she murmured to herself, "Well, that explains it."

He heard. "That explains what, Captain?"

"Why you were not afraid to join battle with me, I assume," Lynnette replied unwillingly. She had not meant for him to overhear her mumbled statement and did not wish to bring the subject up.

He just laughed. "I would not have feared you, Captain Thorne, had I heard a hundred tales of your exploits." He shrugged. "These tales are always overblown, and I would wait to see for myself what threat lay before me, instead of assuming that my foe was stronger than I."

"I believe you speak truly," she said with wonder. She stared up into his silver eyes. Not many men could say the same without being liars or braggarts, but she believed him to be neither. Nay. Here was a man with true courage. The thought warmed her all over, although she did not know why it should.

Perhaps it was simply because Lynnette had had so few positive encounters with men that she found it surprising to encounter a genuinely brave, decent man. Or perhaps it was his incredible good looks. Whatever it was, she discovered that she could not look away. With the whispering breeze rustling through the dry leaves of the palm tree, and the sound of nearby waves crashing on the beach just out of sight, it seemed the night was enchanted. Feeling the wash of unfamiliar sensations, Lynnette swallowed anxiously. And yet her eyes remained glued to his face.

"Captain," he said in an abruptly ragged voice, "it might be better if you did not stare up at me with those big green eyes of yours."

Misunderstanding his meaning, for she had been called a witch for the unusual color of her eyes in the past, her wide-eyed stare became challenging. She felt a spirit of mischief enter her, and a tiny, buried portion of her mind cursed the full moon. But she would not retreat to common sense now. She knew it was too late. "And why is that, Captain?"

"Because," he grated, "I might have to do *this*." Hot, demanding lips swooped down on hers, and he dragged her bodily into his arms. Stunned, she did nothing for a moment while his mouth slanted over hers fiercely. The dream flooded back to her, and she remembered his kisses in the night, but they were nothing compared to the reality.

His left arm around her waist held her still, and his right cradled her nape as he took possession of her mouth. Pleasure swept her body, making her go limp in his arms, allowing the kiss to go on, at first passively, then with growing response.

Her hands came up to rest on his shoulders, then burrowed in his thick, shining hair. She turned her head to better receive his plundering, gasping as she did so. She had wondered, oh, she'd wondered, what it would be like for him to truly hold her as he had in her restless dreams. His lips were so firm, yet velvety, turning her body to flame with the slightest caress. And he knew what he was doing. Skill was evident in each long taste he stole from her lips.

Daniel drew her lower lip into his mouth, sucking gently, and she moaned. Then his tongue shaped the contours of her lips, dipping in at the corners and flicking lightly at the center of the top lip, where it formed a tiny vee. He pulled her closer, whispering encouragement, and she lost all reason. His tongue thrust into her mouth, and she opened for him, feeling the sweep of it spreading rapture inside her.

Lynnette had never been kissed this way before, and the ache his touch created was entirely new. She had no defense against it, did not want to defend herself, only to feel more of his pleasuring. "Don't hold back," he whispered against her mouth, and her tongue tentatively touched his in response. It sent flames up Daniel's spine, and down to his groin. He grew thick and hard, pressing against her belly uncontrollably.

At first, she did not recognize through the haze of passion what it was, with their tongues dueling and all of her concentration centered on his mouth. But when he cupped her buttocks, pulling her up to feel his hard shaft against her mound through the insufficient cover of their breeches, Lynnette felt as though she had been dashed with icy water.

What in God's name was she doing? Allowing a man to touch her, responding to him? Nay, it would not continue! Stiffening, she tore her mouth from his. "Stop!" she cried. "Damn you, let me go!" For a moment, she feared she had been wrong about him, and that Captain Bradley would not let her go. A rush of fear swamped her, as she recalled that terrible incident so long ago. Would the same now happen to her? *Oh, stupid, stupid Lynnette!* she cried to herself. *You know better, or you did when you swore never to allow a man's touch!* But his arms were already loosening around her slim waist.

Her words penetrated Daniel's passion-fogged brain slowly. Somehow, the fiery beauty in his arms had turned to ice betwixt one heartbeat and the next. Automatically, his arms loosened, and she pulled free, panting. He stared at her, dazed at the hissing viper she had suddenly become.

"You bastard!" she yelled hysterically. "I swear, if you try that again I'll carve your liver to ribbons!"

"Try what, dear Captain?" he asked, regaining control of his labored breathing. Anger ripped through him as swiftly as passion had done a moment before. How dare she kiss him like that and then threaten his life? It was beyond bearing. "I do not recall forcing you to do anything against your will. In fact," he said smoothly, dripping disdain, "I seem to remember you clutching me rather tightly just a moment ago." Daniel was furious at her for accusing him of molesting her, when it had been a mutual embrace. He might have started it, but she had responded eagerly after the first few moments. "What's your game? Take a man to heaven's door, then leave him stranded without the key?"

"I have no game, Captain Bradley," she bit off. "And I do not like being pawed by the likes of you."

"Do you not?" he sneered.

"Nay, I do not, and you would do well to remember it!" She drew the sword that had remained by her side as always, and leveled it menacingly at him. "I do not make idle threats." Lynnette took a deep breath to calm herself, then waved the weapon toward the path. "Your freedom is at an end. Move!"

Daniel saw that she was just angry enough to use it, and stiffly began to walk up the cliffside. He could not understand what had just happened. One minute, they were flying high enough to touch the clouds, the next she was brandishing a sword and crying foul play. In a virgin, he might understand such baffling behavior, but Captain Thorne was no untried maiden. Her kiss had told him that much. No innocent had that much fire. An innocent could not possibly have responded with such sweet uninhibited passion.

Innocents did not point swords at men they had just kissed into near insensibility. As he was forcibly marched up the cliffside, Daniel grew steadily more furious. He had gained some of his desire by tasting the lush red lips of the pirate queen, but the greater portion remained unfulfilled. She had, he became sure, left him panting intentionally.

When Captain Thorne had agreed to come outside with him, his hopes had soared, thinking perhaps she found him as intriguing as he found her. In great detail, he now recalled her estimation of him. *A profitable venture,* nothing more or less. But when she'd looked up at him with those mesmerizing green eyes, he'd thought there was something more in them than just shrewd calculation. Obviously, he'd been wrong. He was only her plaything, to be kept for a time and then sold for a sizable sum. And used.

With the advantage of being armed, and with a shipload of loyal men a shout away, Captain Thorne held all the cards, and he knew she orchestrated things to be that way. It was one of the qualities he admired in her, but just now, he wished *he* had the advantage. He would teach her it wasn't safe to play with fire.

They reached the villa, and without a word, she prompted him toward his room. He went quietly, knowing that he could probably disarm her, but that one threatening move on his part would bring her crew down on his head like the wrath of God. All she had to do was shout, and he would be dead in an instant. And it did not matter to her if he were killed. The pirate wench would likely just rack it up to bad luck, her only regret for the ransom she would not now be getting.

She thought to use him for her own pleasure, to toy with him, but if *he* had anything to say about it. Thorne's ploys would backfire on her. Just let her try her wiles on him once more, and he would give her more than she bargained for. Shooting the teasing wench one last venomous glare, he retreated to his cell.

Lynnette slammed the door behind him and locked it with a vicious twist. Leaning against the far wall of the corridor, she finally allowed the nearly uncontrollable tremors to overcome her. Close to panicked tears, she put one shaking hand to her forehead in despair. She was lost.

Before she could come completely unglued, she sheathed the sword that still dangled from one limp hand and quickly entered her own room. She had to get some sleep, she thought dizzily, for they would leave at first light. Unable to put two thoughts together in her state of horrified shock, she automatically undressed and fell into her bed. She had just enough wits to blow out the candle Mari, the native girl, had left burning by her bedside.

But sleep was as far away as the dawn. Lynnette realized it was still quite early. That was not why she tossed and turned and punched the pillow, however. She could not escape what she had just done, try as she might.

Letting the man kiss her had been possibly the greatest mistake of her life. She could not afford to allow Daniel to distract her from her purpose. She was sure that if she didn't nip this crazed infatuation in the bud, he would interfere with her carefully ordered plans, interfere with her concentration, and possibly ruin everything.

She knew that only one concern could occupy her if she was to succeed in her chosen course. The destruction of Lord

Roger of Pennsworth and all he loved was her goal, and she could not achieve it if she were rolling about in the proverbial hay with her prisoner. In the past, she had easily been able to dispatch other matters from her thoughts in order to pursue her revenge. Emotions, a normal life, the search for happiness, all had been discarded so that she might follow Lord Roger to the ends of the earth and, hopefully, kill him.

Now her plans threatened to be destroyed, and all because she could not control her own base urges. Contrary to her spoken words, Lynnette knew that the kiss had not solely been Captain Bradley's doing, but she would never admit it. It was a craven defense, to suggest that he'd forced her, and she knew it. There had been no coercion involved, but her shame could not permit that to be said aloud. Better to make the whole fiasco his fault and keep him at bay with her misdirected fury than to admit she liked his touch and invite more of it.

She had never felt the things he'd shown her how to feel before tonight, and she vowed never to allow herself to feel them again. She would not betray her sister by failing to avenge her. Nothing must get in her way, not even a glib-tongued, silver-eyed rogue with the power to make her tremble. *I will not fail you, Sarah,* she said silently to the tortured spirit whose presence she felt always in the back of her mind.

I will simply ignore him as I do all the others, she decided. *He will be as the ground beneath my feet, to be forgotten as soon as passed.* But until he was gone, she'd keep a tight rein on her contrary emotions. She would *not* succumb to the madness of passion again!

CHAPTER SEVEN

A S DAWN arrived trailing streamers of rose-colored light, Daniel heard sounds of departure from the beach. Getting up stiffly from the bed where he had passed a sleepless night, he moved to the terrace. The buccaneers, he saw, were boarding both ships, his own and the *Maiden's Revenge.* They would sell his vessel and return aboard their own, richer at his expense. He could not prevent the tight knot of rage that lodged in his throat or the snarl that twisted his sculpted lips.

It was all *her* fault. The witch who tormented him with heated kisses and brandished a wicked Toledo blade had caused all of his troubles. Well, now she was leaving the island, and he would escape. Once he had reached England and his partner, Simon, Captain Bradley swore he would pursue revenge on her for her degradations. But first, he had to get out of this infernal cell.

He watched as the pirates left with hope rising in his heart. He saw Thorne's bright head among the others taking a long-boat out to the ships and sighed with satisfaction. Now was his chance, if only he could find a way to use it. From the number of men he'd seen leaving, at most there could be only one or two men left behind to guard him. That was, if any were left at all. Captain Thorne's arrogance in underestimating him might have led her to believe he could not so much as get out of his cell without assistance. Well, she would find out the magnitude of her mistake soon enough.

The door rattled, jolting him to awareness. It had to be Mari with his breakfast, from all the clattering on going on outside. She was having trouble juggling the heavy silver tray and unlocking the door at the same time. At last, the door swung open, and the pretty young girl entered, heavily laden. "For you," she said softly in her thickly accented voice. Daniel's eyes took on a hard gleam. Escape was indeed possible.

The girl simpered at him, and unlike the previous times she had made advances, he smiled back welcomingly. Mari giggled a little at the unexpected attention. But he knew it would have to wait till later. It was too soon after the pirates' leave-taking to implement his plan. So he made no further encouraging moves, and the bold wench soon left without what she so obviously desired. Daniel set himself to waiting till afternoon.

He expected that somewhere in the villa there must be maps of the area, and hopefully a boat of some kind to be had someplace on the island. If these things were to be found, then nothing would stop Daniel from simply removing himself from under the pirates' neglectful supervision. Stupid of them to have left him here with so little policing, after all their boasts that he could not get away. Why, it would be an effortless adventure for a man who had sailed seagoing vessels ranging in size and diversity from dinghies to galleons. A little luck and any form of small craft was all he'd need to pilot his way to freedom. His guards, if there were any, would be dealt with as they came.

These islands, he knew, were as numerous and closely scattered as pebbles on a beach. A week's provisions from the kitchens or filched from one of the islanders at the village nearby, and he would be on his way. Meanwhile, getting out of his cell would pose no problem.

When Mari returned bearing his noon repast, Daniel smiled winningly at her. He fingered the lengths of cloth he had torn to make bindings for her, hidden in his pocket. "Come," he said, crooking his index finger to beckon her. "Sit, talk to me." When she hesitated, unsure of his changed attitude, he added pitiably, gracing her with a charming grin, "Will you make me bear another lonely meal? I vow I've not had a word with a pretty maid like yourself in so long I'm fair wasting away for lack of companionship. Join me, please," he finished in a cajoling tone.

Mari blushed becomingly, nodding agreement. She had not understood all of the man's words, but she liked the way he spoke; all soft and deep. And his smile! It sent shivers down her back. Oh, how she wanted this one! Ever since she had been assigned to feed the prisoner, her heart had soared each time she neared his chamber. She was sure that he would take her to his bed, though he had shown disappointingly little interest in her before today. It must be the loss of his fine ship that had caused him not to notice her abundant charms until now, she thought smugly. No man without a great deal on his mind could ignore her. Now, it appeared that her initial impression of the captive, namely, that he was an exceedingly virile man, had been correct.

Soon she had joined him, setting aside the tray on the desk absently as she crossed the room. She had forgotten to close the door in her haste to reach the object of her desires, and the key was still in the lock where she usually left it. Sitting on the bed and leaning forward to give Daniel a better view of her chemise-clad figure, she flashed him a sensuous smile, licking her lower lip in a blatant invitation for him to touch her.

His eyes lowered deliberately to examine what she offered.

The gaping shift hid almost nothing, revealing her full breasts clear to the nipples. And she did indeed have fine breasts, he thought, tracing a teasing line across the ample swells with one finger. She cooed excitedly, asking in broken English, "You—you like what you see, yes?"

"Oh, very much," he drawled, throwing a surreptitious glance at the door, which was still slightly ajar. There was no one in the hallway, no guard posted to witness the little scene being enacted in his room. There had always been a guard waiting in the hall whenever Mari served him in the past, but there was no such evidence of his jailer today. Daniel figured the man had gotten drunk seeing off his shipmates last night and was now happily sleeping off his grog somewhere on the compound. Good enough, he thought. When the guard did show up, he would be in for a nasty surprise.

Meanwhile, the seduction was going perfectly. The girl no more suspected him of treachery than she would her own mother. Of course, with a buxom figure like hers, Mari had no reason to believe a man could want anything *other* than her body. But Daniel did. He wanted his freedom, and the remorse he felt over what he was doing was nothing to his desire for escape.

He drew forward, kissing her lightly at first, then deeply, skillfully feigning passion until she was totally limp and complaint in his arms. Her eyes shone dazed with desire, and he smiled into them knowingly. "Open your mouth for me, sweetheart," he murmured. She complied breathlessly. And before she knew what he was about, he whipped a strip of cloth from his pocket and stuffed it between her ripe red lips, wrapping another around her head to secure it. She squawked in surprise, but the sound didn't carry through the wad of linen, and Daniel was already working on her wrists. In no time, she was trussed head to toe and helpless on the bed. "Sorry, darling," he said to the furious Mari as she glared impotently at him. "Perhaps some other time."

Then he gathered up his jacket and quit the chamber, locking the door behind him and pocketing the key. When the others thought to search for Mari, they would waste valuable time breaking down the door before they discovered his disappearance.

The hallway was yet empty, and Daniel heard no sounds

from the rest of the house, but even so, he trod lightly over the creaking wooden floorboards. Swiftly crossing the hall, he tried the door to Captain Thorne's quarters. It opened without protest, so he pushed inside. A small antechamber greeted him, and he crossed it impatiently, not bothering to notice the furnishings. On the other side of the second door, which led to the bedchamber, however, he was brought up short. Another one of those gargantuan beds took up fully half the space in the room! Reminding himself that he had no time to ponder his captor's sleeping habits, he contented himself with a wondering shake of his head. A thought wandered through his mind all the same. *Where did she get such large beds?*

The room was much like her cabin aboard the *Maiden*, spare with the one exception, utilitarian in its decoration. By the large window stood a scarred desk, strewn with papers. His best guess placed her maps there, and he was correct. Quickly rifling through the various piles of documents, Daniel soon found what he sought. Several maps lay about, a compass, sextant, and other tools of navigation weighting them against the breeze that came in from the unshuttered window. He brushed the devices aside, wincing when the compass fell off the desk with a loud metallic crash. He stood utterly still for a minute, waiting tensely, but when no uproar was raised he continued his search.

A detailed navigator's chart of No-name Island and the surrounding English colonies yielded to his questing fingers after a short search, and he tucked it into his belt with great alacrity. It wasn't safe to stay in the house much longer, he knew, for when Mari's prolonged absence was noted by the other servants, they would come looking for her. At any moment, someone might walk in and spot him, and his escape attempt would turn out to be a lot shorter than he'd planned.

He could exit through the window, but that didn't solve the problem of provisions for his journey. Without food, and especially water, he would die on the open ocean. A glance at his pilfered map had told him that St. Thomas was the best chance he had, and it would take a him a while to reach that island. It too was a haven for pirates with stolen goods, but legitimate traders flourished there right alongside them, and in any case, he had little choice in the matter. No other port of call was as close or as promising. From St. Thomas he could contact the colonial governor, and, he prayed, secure a passage back to England. The journey to St. Thomas should take no more than a couple of days in a skiff, if he kept up his strength and steered a true course. But first, supplies.

Tiptoeing stealthily, Captain Bradley made his way back to the corridor and listened for the sound of footsteps. Nothing. Cautiously, he crept forward, heading toward the kitchen. It was off the front parlor, if he remembered aright. He strained his ears for the sounds that would tell him if the servants were within, but again, he heard nothing, no pots being rattled, no gossip floating through the humid air. Sweat trickled from his brow as he waited an excruciating moment before gathering his courage and pushing wide the swinging door.

Inside, the kitchen was deserted. Bundles of onions hung from the ceiling, along with pitchers and spices and peppers slowly drying in the heat. The area where food was prepared was neatly kept, utensils and chopping board gleaming with good scrubbing. All this he noticed in his first sweeping glance; then, sure no one was inside, he decided to waste no more time on sightseeing. The servants might be away now, but that could change any second. Being caught meant a fight.

Daniel did not want to have to injure servants in order to escape. They weren't responsible for their mistress's actions, and should not be made to pay. Tying up the gullible, lusty girl who brought his meals had been bad enough, though unavoidable. He didn't want to compound his sins if it was at all possible to avoid it. Besides, he didn't know where the pirates who had been left behind to guard him were located, and if one of the kitchen staff gave the alert, it would likely bring an armed buccaneer on the run. Better to get out of here fast. He found waterskins, biscuit, and bacon with no trouble, quickly wrapping them in his once-fine black and silver brocaded jacket. Then, as a precaution against capture, he slipped a sharp meat knife into his belt alongside the precious chart.

A jabber of voices drifting in from the parlor reached his ears suddenly, and he swiveled to face the danger, every muscle alert. The servants were returning! In a flash Daniel was out the back door, leaving behind no trace of his brief occupation. He now crouched underneath the kitchen window, listening carefully for some indication that they would follow. When no alarm was sounded, he took a quick look around.

He was in a neat vegetable garden, and looking beyond, he saw the interior of No-name Island. It too seemed utterly deserted! Was it possible that Captain Thorne had left no one to guard him? Nay, the thought was ridiculous. From what he had seen of the pirate queen, she took no chances. The sentries had to be somewhere, and he would have to be careful. Still, while the coast was clear, he would make his move and pray he remained unseen.

As he set off away from the house, Captain Bradley recalled the pirate's words and carefully skirted the jungle. He did not want to spend hours wandering in circles, lost, or have to fight off feral animals armed only with a kitchen knife. He spied the freshwater spring that gave the tiny island its reason for habitation, and, spearing his gaze far and wide, was relieved to see no one else in the area. He filled his waterskins, doubled over among the trees that surrounded the stream to make himself less visible to prying eyes. Then he looked around him uncertainly.

He needed to find some seaworthy craft. Which way to go? Not to the cove, they'd search there first. But he knew almost nothing of his environs and could not guess which direction would serve his needs best. Following the stream was not an option, for it led straight into the steamy foliage, and besides, it would take too much precious time to traverse the interior. Any moment now they would discover Mari tied up on his bed, and him escaped. But there had been no better opportunity to make the attempt, and he doubted there would be one later. He could not afford to foul this one up by standing indecisively only a few steps from the house, for surely they would keep a tighter guard on him in future if once they recaptured him. So, sending up a fervent prayer for luck, Daniel struck out in the direction opposite from the villa.

After walking fast for half an hour, cautiously following a dirt track, sometimes ducking in and out of the thick undergrowth that characterized the island in order to avoid being seen, he came to the village. Perfect. The men here had a small fishing fleet, didn't they? Perhaps he'd find a skiff here, if he could make his way around the shantytown and to the shore. Daniel looked around cautiously for the best way to do so.

The village was little more than a row of shabby huts settled in a clear space, but people were congregated there.

Women carried loads of laundry in baskets on their heads, managing a graceful sway to their hips despite the heavy burden. Men herded goats through the one street, ogling the young women. Old folk rested from the noonday heat on shaded stoops in front of the shacks. In spite of the obvious poverty of the village, there was a spirit of joy in the people that showed clearly in their faces. Daniel suspected they were escaped slaves, as many of them were African, and some of those whose features bore the stamp of Caribbean natives had hideous whip scars upon their backs.

He wondered what they were doing here, for most pirates would be happy to make fast money by turning in an escaped slave, yet these people seemed to coexist with the buccaneers in harmony. But it was not important now, he reminded himself irritably. Who cared about the origins of a shantytown at a time like this? What mattered was getting around it unseen. Up to now, his escape had been almost *too* easy, but now he faced his first real challenge. No pirates had stopped him yet, but some villager, spotting him, could raise the alarm and alert them to his presence. By this time, he was beginning to doubt there even *were* guards, but he was taking no chances. He had to get around the village.

This he accomplished by dint of crawling, running, and ducking under the shelter of the fringe of trees at the edge of the jungle until he had passed the place. It seemed to take forever. To ensure that he remained hidden, he had to stop every few yards and wait in silence, eyes darting in all directions to scope out danger. It was taxing, anxious work, the stress as draining as the physical effort. At one point in his slow, agonizing journey, Daniel tied his jacket with the provisions inside it into a bundle and knotted the sleeves together to make a sort of sling. This he carried over his shoulder. It made toting the bundle much easier, as he could now use both hands to push aside tangled growth.

He stumbled suddenly onto a beaten earth track, one he remembered was used by the villagers to reach the sea. Not daring to walk in plain sight on the track, he followed it from the cover of the thick foliage, catching himself several times on giant thorns and exposed roots. Branches stung his perspiring face, but Daniel kept his curses behind his tongue, endeavoring to be silent. The heat was oppressive.

At last the trees opened up to a sparkling pink beach, and he was dazzled for a second by the switch from shady gloom created by overhanging branches to bright sunshine in the open space. But he saw clearly a sight that gladdened his heart. A short way across the hot sands lay a skiff, small, yet perfect for his needs. It had a sail, a rudder, and was seemingly in good repair. He needed nothing else, not with the addition of his stolen supplies. No doubt some islander had been using it for fishing or island-hopping. Too bad for him, thought Captain Bradley exultantly. The skiff was about to be commandeered.

An ominous clicking noise pulled him up short just as he reached the boat. Ah, damn, he knew that sound . . .

A second later, he felt the cold hard muzzle of a pistol against his neck.

"Congratulations, Captain Bradley," Lynnette murmured from behind him. "You almost made it." The stress on "almost" was plain.

Daniel spat out a foul curse, swinging to face his nemesis. Damn, he'd known it was too easy! But how could she be here? He had seen her leave with the rest of the buccaneers not seven hours ago! Was she indeed a witch? He'd called her so before, in his mind, but never had he believed she might have powers beyond those of a normal, albeit strong-willed, woman. Now it seemed the only answer to the mystery of her sudden appearance. Had it been any other buccaneer, he could have explained it easily. He wouldn't have known the exact number of the crew, and someone could have been left behind without his knowledge. But he had seen the pirate queen go aboard the *Maiden* himself! There was no mistaking her!

She saw what he was thinking, and smiled thinly, emerald eyes as cold as the stone they resembled. "No, I do not have supernatural abilities. I simply have common sense. It stood to reason that you would try to escape whilst we were gone, so I left Harry in charge of selling off the frigate, and returned via longboat. And I was right. Here you are, nearly to the skiff already." She *tsked* her tongue reprovingly.

"How can I trust you now, Captain, when you have shown such a penchant for departing without farewells? You break a lady's heart with your insensitivity. Don't you know you should always make your excuses to the hostess before you take your leave?" She laughed mockingly, making him burn with the desire to strangle her.

"Perhaps if my hostess *were* a lady," he bit off, "my manners would be better." Damn her! He had been so close! How could he bear to be meekly led back to his cell now that he'd tasted the sweet flavor of freedom? Even now the ocean breeze fanned his sweating skin, and he thought furiously.

The knife! He still had it in his belt. If he could reach it before she blew his head off, he had a chance. But could he kill the wench? There was no other way to make sure he got away cleanly. Leaving her tied up was too chancy. Captain Thorne would not be as easily subdued as the kitchen girl had been. She might free herself and somehow overtake him, or ruin his plans in any number of other ways. But he had never even dreamed of killing a woman, never once entertained the notion before he'd met Captain Thorne. Could he bear the sin on his conscience? Daniel didn't think so. It was a most extraordinary circumstance.

But she must have sensed his quandary, for she reached over and withdrew the knife from his belt, shaking her head as though he were some naughty child she was rebuking for muddying his clothes. He was angered by her patronizing attitude and relieved at the same time to be divested of his means of killing her. Now, there was no choice.

Of course, he could take the gun away from her with one well-placed kick, but now he realized that he would not do that. The idea of harming this woman was anathema to him. One did not deface a beautiful statue. The same way, he could not bear to think of the pirate queen lying in a pool of blood of his doing. Or anyone else's doing, for that matter. The realization shook Daniel from head to toe, and he stared at her, bemusement and fury combined in his light eyes.

"I really hate this, you know," he said casually, both to ease the tension between them and to fill the silence.

"I understand perfectly. Were I in your position, I would feel just as you do. But," she continued cheerfully, "I am not, and I feel splendid. Shall we go back to the villa, Captain Bradley?"

She didn't look splendid, thought Daniel honestly. Oh, she was still the most incredibly gorgeous woman he'd ever encountered, but she seemed a little gray around the edges today.

Her eyes were shaded purple about the lids, and she was just a trifle drawn. In fact, she looked much like he did, he realized. As though she had not slept.

Had last night's events disturbed her as much as they had him? Was she less than immune to him, his kisses, his nearness? He had thought their love play no more than a game for the pirate queen, but now he was unsure. Why else would she spend the night sleepless? No other man had entered her bed after she had left him. He knew, for he had heard her door close only seconds after his was locked. And because he had not slept, he knew no one had entered later on that evening. There was no other reason he could think of for her restless night except their encounter.

And she appeared uneasy in his company now, he observed. Walking beside him up the beach, she held her body stiffly, uncomfortably, as though she were wary of his touch. For all her scornful tone, she seemed less in control of the situation than before, and less sure of herself.

"This won't be my last attempt," he said warningly. Now, when she was more shaken than he'd ever seen her before, seemed a good time to impress his seriousness upon her. "I'll keep trying until I win free of you and your nefarious plans for me."

"Nefarious, Captain? Don't you think that's a little harsh? Ransoming captives is a common practice. I don't see how this is a particularly vicious act on my part, or on the part of my men." She cast him a look that made him feel like a penny actor for his melodramatic statement. "As to your continuing escape attempts, you may *try,* certainly. That is your right. But you won't have much success, I promise you.

"I am impressed with your near getaway," she complimented, "but I shall take measures to ensure it won't happen again. I do not wish more harm to come to my servants than you have already caused them," she finished pointedly.

Seeing poor Mari trussed like a hog on the bed had sent a shaft of guilt through Lynnette. She should not have left the girl in a position of danger. Even though Daniel had done no real harm, she should have prevented the possibility from occurring. Not every man had scruples as fine as Captain Bradley's.

Her servants were loyal, and deserved better from her. Ah,

well, the only thing hurt on the wench was her pride, and that would recover soon enough. Thank God Bradley had done no worse. She did not blame him for his actions, however. In his place, she would have done far more if necessary in order to free herself. But she had gained a new respect for the man, even as she knew his ruthless deception should put her further on guard against him. She had not suspected he could be so determined, and she knew she would have to watch the man more closely from here on out.

But he hadn't tried anything on the beach, when she knew he had been pushed to the limits of his control. He had not endeavored to wrest the gun from her, though he could have, and she had seen the desire to do it in his eyes. Why had he stopped himself? She wouldn't have. It made no matter, Lynnette told herself, irritated by these inward questions; grabbing for the pistol would not have availed him anything. Even if he'd somehow managed to get it away from her, she would have taken him down in the struggle. There were other ways to fight than with weapons, and she knew them well.

Daniel flushed at the reminder of his deviousness. He felt bad enough without her snide jabs to salt the wound. "What will you do, chain me to the wall?" he asked.

She pretended to think about it. "Mayhap, but I usually reserve that punishment for men with roving hands, not roving feet." Her eyes narrowed. "But then, you are guilty of both those offenses, are you not? Perhaps I should take your suggestion, after all." Now she was angry.

"Not unless you chain yourself up next to me," he taunted. "As I remember, you did some roving of your own last night. Or are you still denying all responsibility?"

His words struck deep. "Shut your mouth, Bradley, unless you want me to shut it for you! Remember, *I* have the pistol, not you." She prodded him with the muzzle to make her point. Lynnette did not want the truth of their evening thrown back in her face again. She had a gut full of shame as it was.

"That is quite evident, Captain Thorne," Daniel replied bitingly. "You need not remind me twice." Without another word, he strode back along the path. The rest of the journey to the house was made in bitter silence.

CHAPTER EIGHT

ANIEL PACED back and forth in his cell (well appointed though it was, he refused to think of it as anything else) consumed with frustration. Every few steps he stopped to curse the name of Captain Thorne—her name, and her damned quick thinking. How could she have caught him so easily? Since his arrival on No-name Island, he'd been bested more often than he cared to think about by this unnatural female in breeches. This was an intolerable situation. What had happened to the civilized, masterful Captain Bradley he was accustomed to seeing in the mirror every morning? Completely gone. Everything was turned upside down. Even his appearance had suffered; several days wearing the same set of clothing had seen to that! He was rumpled, disgruntled, and near to tearing his hair out in great fistfuls because of it.

He flung himself about in an ecstasy of exasperation and began to pace the good-sized room with faster strides. He wasn't sure he could stand this anymore. No longer did he wish to match wits with the pirate captain; no, all Daniel wanted now was to get off this benighted strip of land 'ere he ran mad with a cleaver! Or without a cleaver, as the case was. Either way, he felt his grip on calm rationality sliding under the morass of roiling emotions the devil-wench caused. He needed to leave the witch behind, forget her and her unwomanly ways, go back to what he knew. In England there were no bloodthirsty, sword-toting women. Ah, for the peace of it! There Daniel could conduct his life as a respectable ship captain with a new-fledged, growing business, not race through hot, sticky jungles with cutlass-carrying Amazons on his trail!

And just how had she managed to sneak up behind him with no betraying sound? Not one twig had snapped to give away her presence. He had been extremely careful listening for just such noises. No chance she had been following him directly, unless she was part ghost.

But Captain Thorne, he thought with an instant rush of heat to his loins, was all flesh and blood. Holding her so close last night had proved that beyond a doubt. More passionate than most women she might be, but definitely of human origin. She had kissed him so deeply, tasting of honey and wine, making him dizzy from the drug of her hot, sweet mouth! Just the thought of it made Daniel groan with renewed frustration. Why had she pulled away, when it had been so good between them?

Captain Bradley was not vain of his looks, but he knew that his face was more than passably appealing to the ladies. Hadn't that been proved time and again by the women who threw themselves into his path, practically begging for him to take them to his bed? On no few occasions, he had complied (most willingly), and not one had ever complained of a lack of expertise on his part. Quite the contrary, in fact. So it couldn't be his looks or the quality of his embraces that were at fault. There had to be another reason.

Daniel recalled the incident by the beach and studied his memory of each separate moment to figure out what might have gone wrong. It was very important to him to figure this out, for he had decided that his first impression of the situation, namely that Captain Thorne was playing with him like a cat with a trapped mouse, was incorrect. Her wariness toward him today showed that clearly; what had happened last night by the light of the full moon was no casual amusement for her. If it had been a game she routinely played, her attitude would surely have been more relaxed, comfortable. Instead, she'd been taut, hair-triggered, upset.

Going over the scene repeatedly, intently, Daniel realized that only when he had tried to deepen their contact had Thorne stiffened and demanded her release from his arms. While the love play was still light, while parting would still be easy, she had made no protest, but when he had taken their kisses and caresses one step further, she had seemed to panic. Perhaps, he thought with wonder, the brave, fearless captain of the dreaded pirate ship *Maiden's Revenge,* a woman who defied convention, danger, and the law with one bold act, had been afraid of greater intimacy. He still didn't entertain the notion she might be a virgin, but he suspected that the situation between them had gotten out of hand for her, made her leery of continuing.

Maybe the pirate queen only bedded men whom she could

control, men who allowed her to dominate their lovemaking. It was possible, and it fit in with what he knew of her. Always, Captain Thorne took the advantage, strictly maintaining the upper hand with almost fanatical single-mindedness.

Daniel couldn't truly blame the wench; for a woman to wield the power Thorne did, she had to keep full control of her men and her surroundings at all times. He imagined what she would be like if once she let go that control. After holding herself guarded for so long, she would be wild, uninhibited, if she allowed herself to simply let things happen. In his bed, she would be magnificent.

He knew somehow that beneath her ultrawary exterior, she was full of life and passion just waiting to be set free. He could see it in her stride, the way she paced like a caged panther. Her expressive eyes told him of pain that had made her careful—but also that there was more inside her than just reined-in hate. Much more. He wanted to free it for her, but of her own accord he doubted she would ever let go. Nay, she'd hold to her anger and her mantle of command with each breath, and count them dear as the air she breathed.

It explained, at least, why she had thrown harsh words at him last night, and why she had put an end to their embrace so abruptly. She had not initiated the contact of their bodies, and when desire raged out of control in the heat between them, she'd been frightened that their love play would go too far.

If the wench had been affected even half so much as he, then the frantic urges compelling her to submit to lust would have been enough to send her flying out of his arms, he reasoned. If control mattered so much to her, no wonder she'd been furious. But not, he realized, furious at *him*. No, Captain Thorne was angry at herself for losing her head during their drugging kisses. Daniel himself had been more than a little shaken by the force of his desire for her; the wench was only shaken to a greater degree, because she had not been planning for such an incident. He of course had, if only in his fevered imaginings. And he had nothing to lose. Obviously, she felt she did.

He had a measure of understanding for her now, on further reflection, seeing her actions as mere self-defense. Understanding, but no pity. Mercilessly he would pursue her, trying again and again to break down the walls around her heart, for he sensed that it was indeed possible to do so. The first mate's oblique encouragement fueled his own feeling that he was just the man to pierce Captain Thorne's thick hide. Nothing would stop him from making the pirate queen his. Subtly, he would win her hard-earned trust, then, with heated kisses, steal her reason, until she gave up her body to his touch.

But it would have to be a gentle campaign, one of wooing and seduction; else, pushed too far by his eager suit, his captor might be driven to do something drastic. Something he would not enjoy. After all, she held his fate in her slender hands, and she was more than half wild. Unflappable though she seemed, Daniel sensed her restraint was no more than a thin veneer covering an untamed spirit, capable of most anything.

He wanted her to give up her control over him, but knew that if he backed her against a wall, she would protect herself at his expense. Captain Bradley walked a thin line between love and death, held in the hands of a powerful woman. It was a strange sensation for a man used to controlling his own destiny. He was forced to consider a mere woman as a real threat to his safety. He knew that not to do so would be a major mistake. He was not about to underestimate the pirate. It was strange, possibly laughable under other circumstances. Yet it was exhilarating, too. Had he thought that he desired to leave No-name Island forthwith? Nay, he would not leave now for the world! Soon enough to make his escape through the slackened fingers of a love-sated woman, when he had made her his and had his fill of her luscious body.

With the beautiful Captain Thorne as his lover, Daniel would fulfill all his desires. His passion glutted, he was sure this insane obsession for the brazen pirate queen would quickly die. Then he would slip away from her watchdogs without difficulty. Thorne, thinking more of his body's abilities than of his mind's, would not guard him sufficiently, and he would simply walk out from under her gaze and into an escape craft.

Nothing could be easier. He'd be back in England with no more thought of her than of a serving wench tumbled at a coaching inn on a long journey. It had been good enough for Odysseus with Calypso, he rationalized. He'd read once that that hero of ancient legend had been held forcibly by a nymph for years upon an island, and when the time came for Odysseus to escape, he never once looked back to the lovely creature who had detained him there for so long. He merely took his leave, and sailed on to other adventures. So it would be for Daniel.

But before all he planned could come to pass, he had to get close to his nymph. With him locked up tight in this lonely cell, and her away about her own business elsewhere, none of it could happen. That must not be. So, what to do? The door was locked once more and, plainly, Thorne would not be sending Mari with his food any longer. So who would be bringing his meals? Would he be able to evade that person and go in search of the captain?

He did not have long to wait for the answers.

When dusk dimmed the daylight to violet shadows and locusts began their song in earnest, the answer came, but not in the form that the prisoner had expected. The object of his desire and of his fervent scheming pushed open the door to his room, so surprising the unprepared man that, for a moment, his mouth hung open foolishly. Of all the things she could have chosen to do—starving him in punishment for his escape attempt, or getting a strong man from the village to guard him, or merely having his tray shoved inside the room and slamming the door behind it, Captain Thorne's coming for him in person was the one alternative he hadn't planned for.

She stood with arms crossed defensively over her breasts, leaning against the door frame in a pose of feigned casualness. A long jacket of emerald with silver threads embroidered into a design of vines hung loosely about her slight frame and whispered about the backs of her shapely thighs. Probably taken from some unlucky passenger whose ship she'd raided, he thought. The fit wasn't too bad for all that.

About her neck the priceless neck-cuff of gold and emeralds glinted through her fine cambric shirt, opened in a vee to expose her lovely golden skin all the way to the dusky shadow of her cleavage. A tiny mole graced the flesh between her full, rounded breasts, and Daniel had a sudden, overpowering desire to taste her silken skin there. Only with great determination did he resist the urge, telling himself that it did not serve his new-fledged purpose to seize the pirate queen bodily and maul her at the very entrance to his cell. How then could she ever begin to trust him if he proved himself unable to contain his passion at the first opportunity?

But, by damn, she was breathtaking! The coming weeks were going to be hell, with restraint as his byword. He would have to be careful not to touch her, and by so doing, inflame his senses with the feel of her smooth, satiny skin. But he could still look, couldn't he? His silver gaze moved lower to trace the lines of her long, shapely legs, so perfectly contoured by the tight breeches she wore. Of a darker shade of forest-green, they complemented the brocaded jacket well, and the plain blouse did nothing to detract from her appearance. Only the long strawberry braid that caressed her buttocks teasingly belied the masculine outfit. He was getting used to seeing the woman in men's clothing, and the notion of it no longer offended his sensibilities as it had at first. In fact, he thought she looked well in the outlandish garb.

He wondered if she had chosen the breeches and jacket to match one another. Certainly, the colors looked good on her, with her bright green eyes and red-blond hair. Yet somehow the idea of the indomitable Captain Thorne dithering over which items of clothing coordinated well with each other and with her eyes seemed extremely unlikely.

The heavy necklace, he'd noticed, was seldom far from her, and he thought it was more of a symbol to her than a bauble worn for the sake of vanity. He wondered what she would look like wearing the jewel-studded gold links and nothing else. The image was so enticing that he had to force it from his mind abruptly, lest the swelling in his breeches become embarrassingly prominent. Still, the question rose. *Why was she here?* It was not for the purpose of enticing him, he was sure.

"An unexpected pleasure, Captain," said Daniel, since she seemed unready, or unwilling, to speak as yet. He nodded politely to her. "What can I do for you? Perhaps," he said—not entirely jokingly—"I could provide a target for you to practice your swordplay or pistolry upon? I am, of course, at your disposal."

Lynnette merely scowled. She still wasn't sure what she was doing here. All she knew was, a strange urge had come over her to see her prisoner face-to-face. She told herself it was only caution. After all, he had nearly escaped today. It was not unnatural for her to want to reassure herself that he was still under her control and where she wanted him. Trouble was, she didn't know just *where* she wanted him, but it wasn't here in this cell. All day she had wandered her island aimlessly. There was nothing for her to do, no one to talk to once she had recaptured Captain Bradley, since preventing his escape had been the sole reason for her return.

The villagers had asylum under her protection, but she had not exerted much effort to get to know them personally. Excluding, of course, those men who had joined her crew years earlier. It was not her way to open her heart to people, trustworthy or otherwise, and she had steered clear of most everyone except her crew. She was close with them mostly because on shipboard there was not much room for privacy. One could not keep secrets from one's mates at sea—indeed, a swab locking his sea chest against prying eyes was likely to find both chest and lock tossed overboard for his troubles. Privately, Lynnette was glad that sailing conditions prevented holding oneself aloof from others, for the close environment had allowed her to form friendships she otherwise would not have permitted herself.

Captain Thorne's heart had been scarred to such a degree that letting anyone in was almost an impossibility. And she believed, as she had told Harry, that she did not care. No, she never felt lonely.

So why was she standing at the door to her captive's chamber, feeling like a complete and utter ass? It could not be because she had spent the entire day pacing directionlessly about the sandy shoreline, trying to think of something that could occupy her for a whole week. Her bookkeeping was all up to date, and there were no internal disputes among the islanders for her to settle, as she sometimes did. Her maids did all her sewing, and her efficiency in everything she touched had left her with no leftover chores.

Normally, a week's worth of privacy would have been her greatest wish, and so she had thought the case would be earlier today. But merely hours after her ridiculously easing snaring of Captain Bradley, she began to feel unpleasantly isolated from the world, and the knowledge that another human being lay in her house, apart from her, made her feel hunted. She wasn't alone, not with *him* on the island with her. And his presence had continued to burn a hole in the back of her mind until, finally, Lynnette gave in and went to him.

Now, after letting the silence stretch to the breaking point after his joking comment, she finally spoke. "Well, come on then," she said crossly. "Since you're so hot to get out of this room—though, I might add, you insult my accommodations with your eagerness to leave—you might as well come with me. Supper is being served on the verandah." Without another word to him, the beautiful pirate turned on one booted heel and stalked out of the room.

He had seen a faint blush stain her cheeks in the second before she turned, and, mutely wondering, followed after her fading footsteps. The woman herself had provided the means to her own downfall, and he, for one, was not about to question his good luck!

Daniel surreptitiously tried to brush the wrinkles out of his clothes as he trailed after her. He had little success, but he assumed that would not be too much of a problem in what he was about to attempt. Although he would have preferred to look his best in this campaign, he doubted Thorne put much stock in appearances. For the slow seduction and wooing he planned, words and deeds would be of much more importance than the state of his apparel. And starting tonight, Captain Daniel Robert Bradley would be exerting so much charm it would be a wonder if birds did not come to roost on his fingertips when he called them. Captain Thorne didn't stand a chance.

They traversed the length of the house in silence until they came to the verandah. She went out first, but he, close behind, moved to pull back her chair in a show of gentlemanly manners. She sent him a suspicious glare, but sat peaceably enough. He sat down opposite her, waiting, knowing there were things she wanted to say to him. Weighing the air between them were memories of heated passion and angry words, and Daniel guessed that Thorne did not want the strife to continue. Likely she would prefer to blot the memory of last night from her mind permanently, and she could not do that while they were still liable to throw nasty reminders at each other in the heat of argument. Much easier for her to pretend nothing had happened if they made their peace. Her next words proved him right.

Cautiously, she began by stating the obvious. "We are not on the best terms we could possibly be on at this moment. For various reasons—which," she added hastily, "we need not discuss right now. Suffice it that the both of us have reason not to trust one another." She stopped, waiting for his reaction.

He merely nodded, saying, "Go on. I would hear what you propose to do about it."

Taking a deep breath, she went on determinedly. "We will by needs be spending a great deal of time together, and I don't see why that time has to be unpleasant. I understand that the nature of our acquaintance is . . . unusual, to say the least," and here Lynnette grinned wryly, "but we might as well make the best of it. I hate to see a man restricted to one small area in which to live. I would rather give you the freedom of the island. Unfortunately, you persist in these futile attempts to get away, and this forces me to curtail your freedoms."

She stretched out a slim hand in a gesture that said, "*What else can I do*?" and Daniel smothered an angry response to her warped sense of fairness. Forced, indeed! She could let him go, that was what she could do! But he tamped down hard on his temper, knowing that that was the one thing she would never do. Besides, knocking his head against the stone wall of her will wasn't going to get him what he wanted. Nay, he'd better listen to the wench and privately continue to work with his new agenda.

"I propose," she concluded, "that we strike a bargain."

"I'm all ears." He smiled falsely. "What is this bargain you speak of?"

"Good." She sighed with relief. "You will listen to terms. I propose this: if you will swear not to make any more escape attempts, I will in turn allow you the run of the island. Escape, as you have seen, is impossible, so you have nothing to lose, really. There will be no locked doors for the duration of your stay. But," Lynnette added warningly, her tone dark, "I will need your oath to abide by my wishes—there will be no repeats of last night. Do you understand? You may explore the island, roam here at your leisure, but if you try anything on me—either escaping *or otherwise*—these freedoms will be immediately revoked and the matter dealt with as I see fit. Now, what say you?"

Daniel pretended to consider her offer. Inwardly, his heart

was singing with duplicitous joy. If he complied, he would have the chance to implement his plan, plus a much greater range of freedom. Instead of stewing in this cell, he could be exploring the island for a better means of leaving, and while he mentally mapped the terrain, he would have all the time and opportunity he could ask for to make the pirate queen his, body and soul. There was no question of his acceptance. But he should not appear too eager, or she would suspect him of treachery. Thorne, he knew, was as quick to spot a lie as a hawk to sight its prey. Her keen eyes missed nothing.

Slowly, pretending reluctance, he answered the waiting woman. "It seems I have no choice but to accept your proposal. Even a little liberty is worth more than none at all, and since you have clearly proven that you will not allow me to leave until the ransom is paid, I would rather abide by your rules than waste away in a cell while we wait for it." He managed to look rueful. "Therefore, I give you my word not to attempt escape—or," he added meaningfully, "anything else. Unless you ask it of me."

The last words were muttered under his breath, and Lynnette, in her relief at resolving the troublesome issue, paid no heed to them. "Excellent!" she cried. "I do believe," she said sincerely, "that things between us will be much simpler now." Then, picking up the serving fork, she daintily offered him a slice of roast chicken from one of the silver platters set on the table before them.

As he accepted the juicy meat. Daniel reflected that things between them were likely to be anything but simple from this day forth. Captain Thorne was in for one hell of a surprise if she thought her troubles were over.

CHAPTER NINE

S THEY ate, an uncomfortable silence stretched itself between the two. Lynnette picked at her food, searching her mind for something unexceptional to say, something that would not rouse anger on the part of her captive. She did not want to lose the ground they had just gained by saying something like, "I'm sure your ship will fetch a good price on St. Eustatius," and thereby remind the *Empire*'s erstwhile captain of his unenviable position. But polite conversation had never been her specialty, and she could think of nothing. Fortunately, Daniel was more socially adept.

"This food is delicious," he remarked casually. "I've been meaning to ask you about that. Wherever did you come by such a remarkable chef in this part of the world?" He waved his hand to indicate the untamed, nearly untouched landscape visible from the open verandah. "I know of several peers in London who would sell their grandmothers to acquire a cook of this caliber."

She smiled in remembrance, eager to talk now that they had hit on a subject that was unlikely to cause dissension between them. "Well, now, that's a story!" She leaned back in her chair, more comfortable now. "You see, my crew and I were just on our way back home from a lucrative trading mission in Barbados, when along came this French vessel, a merchantman. The crew was all fired up to take her, but I thought it best to leave her be. Normally," she explained, "we leave the French—and the English—to their own devices, and concentrate on trading vessels from Spain, Portugal, or the American colonies for prey."

Lynnette neglected to mention her *other* quarry, since her hunt was a personal matter, and she didn't think it any concern of his. Very few people even realized that all—excepting the most recent—of her English prizes came from the same shipping company, and she preferred to keep it that way. No need to reveal personal details to this virtual stranger! "Many of my crew are of French or English origin, though they tend to forget that when there's a fat prize for the picking." She chuckled. "I sometimes find it necessary to remind them of their nationality at such times."

"Yet you seemed to have no qualms about taking *my* ship, and she flew the Union Jack," he reminded her mildly.

She studied his face for traces of anger, but he appeared to be merely interested rather than challenging in his statement. "A slight divergence from normal practice," she said. "We needed a prize badly, and the lure of that shiny new frigate was too much for my crew to ignore. And, of course," she added hastily, "for me as well."

He wondered. Could the piratess truly be in it only for the gold? Something told him no. All the evidence showed him that this woman was not greedy for the things money could buy, but for something else entirely. She dressed plainly, her quarters were spare, and she didn't seem the sort to hoard her coins jealously in some hidden cache as did some of the rich misers he knew. The usual brand of rough sailor spent his earnings on drink and women, but *this* sailor wasn't the type to drink her money away, and she certainly had no use for whores. What reason could she have for piracy, then, if it wasn't for gold or what it bought? "If you attack only the enemies of the Crown—mostly," he stuck in wryly, "why are you not a privateer, with a letter of marque to protect you from the noose?"

Lynnette smiled cynically. "And who, pray tell, would issue a letter of marque to a woman? One of our fine colonial governors? Not hardly! Nay, they'd laugh me right out of their offices, with a pat on the head for my efforts, if it wasn't a pinch on the ass!" She spoke crudely, her anger at the situation obvious. But she kept silent about the real reason for her unsanctioned acts. All that she'd said was true, but secondary to other considerations. Captain Bradley, never having heard of the infamous pirate queen before he had actually met her, could not know that she did, indeed, attack England's ships.

Her letter of marque, even had she been able to obtain one, would have been revoked as soon as the news of her betrayal got back to the colonial authorities. She did not plan to give up her sworn quest simply for the safety of tacit Crown backing. If she had accepted the terms of being a privateer—namely, that she attack only the enemies of England and share her profits with the Crown—there would be no reason for her dangerous profession at all. Nay, she was not in the dangerous business of marauding simply for money, but for revenge.

In fact, Lynnette hardly cared for her share of the booty that the *Maiden*'s crew, under her leadership, took in such plentiful quantities. For herself, she didn't care for any reward at all, but her crew would not sail with no recompense for their trouble. Of course, she wasn't stupid enough to actually refuse her share, being a practical woman, but it meant nothing to her except as a means to an end. But Captain Bradley was not to know that.

"I think I understand you," said Daniel slowly. "You had no choice but to become an outlaw once you had chosen your course, for you could not gain your country's sanction." Yes, he could see the scene she'd just put before him quite clearly. The proud Captain Thorne scorned and laughed at by the bunch of aging warhorses who'd been put out to pasture in the Indies by a government who had no further use for their failing skills at home. Her petition would be taken as the rarest form of jest, and the woman herself treated like a witless child. The thought angered him, knowing Thorne for what she was: a strong, intelligent woman who deserved respect.

Had he gone completely mad? Now he was empathizing with the very woman who had taken him prisoner, ordered the death of no few of his men in battle, and was at this moment in the process of selling his prized frigate! She was unscrupulous, amoral, and worthy only of his contempt. Simply being unable to gain a letter of marque did not give the wench the right to prowl the seas uninhibited, scuttling ships of every nationality!

The only question that plagued him now was why she had had to take to the seas in the first place. That, he could not imagine being necessary for *any* woman. But she must have had some reason, and he meant to find out what it was before he escaped. No telling what use he might have for the information in the future. Learning her motivations might help him devise an escape, for he might discover something he could use as a weapon. And he hated to admit it, but he was intensely curious to know her story for his own personal satisfaction. But to accomplish his goal, he must have a clear mind and a sure purpose, not vacillate between hatred and desire, as he was doing now.

Throughout all these reflections, he kept his face impassive, allowing no outward sign of the conflicting emotions raging in his mind to show on his features. Only his eyes narrowed a fraction, changing in hue from pure silver to smoky gray. Daniel thought his feelings through, for he needed to resolve the conflict before he could proceed with any success. Captain Thorne *did* deserve respect, for, as he had discovered personally, she was a worthy adversary. She was powerful, quick, and ruthless. She would soon learn that he too was not lacking in these qualities.

It was not wrong to admire one's adversary, he thought to himself. In fact, it was useful to have a healthy respect for his—or her—abilities. Underestimating Thorne's intelligence was not a mistake Daniel wanted to make, for it could cost him much. And when he had her in his arms, begging for his touch, his possession, he would count it a great victory to have subdued the wench to his will. It would be no easy task. Until then, he would keep his own counsel, while forcing her to divulge her secrets to his waiting ears.

Charm, he decided. Charm was the key to all that he wanted. Whatever the wench said, he would control his temper and shower her with enchantment until she could no longer resist him. This course of action, designed to allow him to escape with both of them unscathed, was perhaps dishonorable, yet certainly kinder than brute force would have been. And infinitely more satisfying for both parties involved.

"But continue your tale of the acquisition of your cook," he requested with that in mind, changing the subject smoothly. "I am sorry to have interrupted it with my questions, yet, I pray you, tell me the rest. I vow I will keep quiet now."

"Ah, yes. I was talking about that, wasn't I?" She was confused by his quick switch from topic to topic, but not entirely displeased by it. It was safer to talk about inconsequentials than serious matters. "Well, as I was saying, we came upon a French merchant ship. I expected her to run when she saw us, but apparently, the crew was too occupied with other things to even notice the *Maiden* approaching off her starboard.

"*We* thought she was readying for a fight, since she didn't change course, and we decided to investigate to see what sort of cargo could make them stand their ground before us. But when my men and I came close enough, we saw that they were not even aware of our presence! A great shouting and commotion was coming from the deck of the vessel, and at first we thought it might be a mutiny. Just then, the lookout on the French ship spotted us, for we *were* no more than a hundred yards away by that time, and all the yelling stopped as they took heed of the danger." Lynnette laughed softly.

"And then the strangest thing happened. A man, clothed all in white, who seemed to be at the center of the disturbance, took one look at us and jumped ship. Swam straight for us, too! I, for one, was amazed. No sane man swims *toward* a pirate ship! But on he came, and we hauled him aboard out of pure curiosity. He was big and fat—a huge man—and it took four men to bring him up. Soaking wet from head to toe, he made his way to me. 'I cannot stand zat woman one second more!' he said, and then he kissed my hand." She imitated the French accent perfectly, and Daniel had to laugh along with her.

"What happened next?" he asked, absorbed in her story. Even had she been describing the best way to gut a fish, he would have been rapt. With her eyes shining vivid green in the lamplight, and her whole posture radiating relaxed content, she was more beautiful than ever. He listened more to her throaty voice than what it depicted.

"It turned out that Georges—that is his name—had been commissioned by a terrible, rich old harridan to cook for her aboard the ship for the duration of her voyage to see her planter son. I suppose she believed she could not survive without good food even for the time it took her to reach the Indies." Lynnette shook her head in disgust for people with so little tolerance for hardship. "But the ship's galley was not up to his standards, and the old lady was displeased with everything he prepared, to boot. Now, Georges, who claims to have cooked for royalty, did not take this abuse of his talents kindly. He was in the middle of giving the old biddy a piece of his mind when we showed up, and he says, 'Somezing just snapped in me, *Capitaine*, and I could not take eet anymore. So I jumped over, and here I am! I swear, I weel cook you zee best meals zis side of heaven, only, *don't send me back to zat crazy old beetch!*' " She laughed heartily, remembering how Georges had looked that day, with his normally neat fringe of gray hair wild about his head, and water dripping off his long, bulbous nose. He'd impressed her with his offbeat brand of courage as well as with the fact that he had immediately recognized her captaincy.

"Well, all the crew were bowled over with gales of laughter at hearing this speech. Imagine a pirate ship looking a better prospect than another day spent with one old lady! Our own cook was so bad that we couldn't tell the laundry water from the stew, so we took Georges in. And a better prize I've never taken, gold or otherwise," she declared, finishing with a smile.

"A fine tale," Daniel complimented, still grinning.

"Thank you, Captain Bradley."

They resumed their meal after a moment, no other conversation coming to mind. Finally, he put his fork down. Something niggled at his brain, something he wanted to ask her about, and he had to have the answer.

"Captain," he said in a sudden rush, "there is something I'm burning to know. How did you creep up behind me this afternoon, without a sound? And why did you delegate yourself as the one to stay behind and be my guard, instead of a man from your crew?"

Lynnette replaced her mug on the table carefully. "Easy enough to answer, I suppose. For the first, I didn't come from behind. I circled about through the jungle and came from the side. The interior really isn't as dangerous as I had led you to believe, you know," she confessed unrepentantly.

She gave him a sweet, superior smile, and he wanted very much to kiss it off her smug face, but he merely inclined his head in salute to her duplicity. "I congratulate you on guessing that my knowledge of the tropics would be slight. And my other question?"

"Simple. I knew that you were resourceful, and I wasn't taking any chances with someone as valuable to me as you are. I prefer to watch over my own investments, rather than leaving their care to others who may not be as thorough as I am."

"Very sensible of you, Captain Thorne. And I suppose I should be flattered that you consider me valuable, if only as an investment." Not for long. Soon she would think of him as more than just a quick way of making money.

"Tell me more of your thoroughness, Captain," he asked suavely. Keep her talking, keep her guard down! he told himself. "I am curious to know what a pirate's life is like."

"Thinking of changing businesses?" she quipped.

"It's not out of the question," he returned, although, of course, it was. Piracy was a capital offense, and one that, as a reputable trader, he must needs despise.

"I do not know exactly what you are asking, Captain Bradley. What is it you want to know?"

How you got into this deadly business, he thought, but said nothing of the sort. Questions like that would shut her beautiful mouth up tighter than the legs of an unpaid whore.

"Merely what it is like to be on the other side of those cannon, I suppose. I freely admit to admiring your competence at sea, and I simply wondered how it feels to do what you do. Remember, I'd never spoken to a pirate before we met, and my curiosity is boundless, I assure you." There, just the right amount of flattery, mixed judiciously with honest feeling, to get her talking.

Lynnette was cautious. Why, all of a sudden, was the man being so amiable? One might even call his manner charming. He had never exerted any effort to behave in front of her previously, but now he acted as though he were a perfect gentleman, and she a lady he was entertaining. Appealing to her interests as though he truly cared—treating her respectfully as if she were a gently born girl he was becoming acquainted with. Or even courting ...

Ridiculous, she scoffed. He had not made any moves toward her tonight, and besides, he'd given his sworn word not to try anything on her. Still, something told her to be wary. Why this change in attitude? He'd seemed so opposed to piracy, plainly displaying his contempt for her trade, and now he wanted to know more about it! Instinct told her to keep her senses alert for trickery.

And something else told her that the first feeling ought to shove a stocking in it. She was usually overcautious, and she knew it. No reason to mistrust him, now that they had made peace. And if he did try anything, well, she'd put an end to it right smart! She was in no danger from her captive that she couldn't easily handle. Not for naught had she gained her hard reputation. Captain Thorne could take care of herself.

She had seen no dishonesty in his eyes during his last speech, only real curiosity. And there was no reason she could not talk to him about *this*. Her exploits were common lore across the Caribbean, and she need tell him nothing that he couldn't hear from someone he met in any settlement from Barbados to the Carolinas. Or even in the seaports of England, for rumor had it her name had reached even so far.

Soon, Lynnette found herself telling a fascinated Captain Bradley some of her more notable shipboard experiences, of storms that had almost destroyed them, and of battles that had made her famous. It felt good to talk, to boast even, to this rapt, willing audience. What made it better was his complete ignorance of her notorious escapades, which made him all the more eager for her tales.

And Daniel was a good listener. He didn't interrupt or judge her actions as she'd thought he might. In fact, he showed no abhorrence for her profession at all, instead seeming to appreciate her valor for itself, no matter that they were on different sides. He even got her to talk about the rigors of command. When she spoke once of being caught in a gale that lasted a full three days, he commented that he had had a similar experience, and commiserated with her on the difficulty of holding together a crew's morale under the force of such driving elements.

His careful questions nearly brought her to disaster. They talked freely of all manner of things related to sailing, and as they talked, Lynnette grew less and less cautious of her words. "It was hard to hold the crew's loyalty," she said at last, ruminatingly. "Being a woman, whenever there was a storm or a bad run of luck, I'd hear whispers. 'Bad luck to have a woman aboard,' they'd say. Or, 'This is her fault that we're having no success.' Especially at first . . ."

Abruptly, she shut her mouth, her fine white teeth clicking together sharply. Dear God, how could she have run on like that! In another minute, he'd have had the whole story of her entrance into piracy, with no more prodding than a little flattery! He had cast a spell over her tongue, surely, to make it flap so long. Well, no more! He'd not gain any more information about her, not if he plied her with hot irons.

She grabbed her goblet of wine and drained it furiously, wishing herself and him to perdition for this night's work. She should never have struck that bargain with the man. Too dangerous by far, considering his most unusual effect on her senses. Even now the sight of him, one dark, slashing eyebrow raised at her sudden silence, created a queer shivering sensation down her back. His handsome face, seemingly chiseled from marble by the loving hand of a master sculptor, made her feel a queer warmth that had nothing to do with the wine. He must be a devil, to have her talking so freely.

Captain Thorne was not a woman who confided in *anyone,* least of all a dark, sensual stranger with reason to hate her! Yet somehow his quiet, intent face as he listened to her ramble on had muddled her senses. Instead of remaining her usual closemouthed self, she had conversed with him as though he were a long-lost friend. She should have left him in that room to rot, damn his cunning soul! But it was too late now to go back on her word. She would just have to watch her mouth from now on.

She wasn't sure, but she had the feeling that it had been his intention to keep her talking. But to what end? Why was the man so all-fired curious about her? She couldn't guess, but she knew she wouldn't like the reason, whatever it might be. *Careful, girl!* she berated herself. *You know this man is tricky. Don't let him under your skin, and for God's sake, don't ever trust him!*

Daniel, meanwhile, was both mesmerized by the tale the wench wove and disappointed by its precipitous end. He knew she'd been close to revealing something important when she'd quit talking so suddenly, but he couldn't feel *too* badly about it. After all, look at everything she'd already revealed in one night! It was only the first day of his campaign to seduce and bemuse his captor, and things were working out splendidly so far. At this rate, he would know everything Thorne had to tell long before the ransom demand was to be paid. With her trust gained, it would be but a simple matter to take it one step further . . . into bed. And he wanted her now more than ever.

Listening to Captain Thorne talk, he had felt his budding admiration bloom into something bigger. She truly was the most incredible woman he'd ever met. And the challenge she represented had grown with every minute she spoke. Though she was no braggart and did not stress her exploits above those of others, her words told him that she was a veritable legend. Daniel doubted that there was—or ever had been—a woman to equal her. For that reason too he wanted to tame her. A woman like Captain Thorne would be a true virago in his bed; one night with her would be worth a thousand nights with the most experienced courtesan in England. If he could make her his . . . Sweet ecstasy to last a lifetime!

Although he tacitly disapproved of her activities, he was careful to show nothing of his censure. She would sense it in a minute, and the progress he'd made would be ruined. As it was, she sat across from him now with her arms crossed defensively, her eyes hard and distrustful. A tense hush had fallen over the table, with only the humming of cicadas to disturb it. He had no real hope, he knew, of persuading her to continue where she had left off, but he felt he had to try.

"You were saying?" he prompted, letting his voice trail off.

"Nothing!" snapped Lynnette. In a calmer tone, she continued. "It's late, and I've quite talked you to faintness by now, I'm sure. Furthermore, supper is long over." She started to rise, tossing her napkin to the tabletop. His voice arrested her.

"One more thing—"

"What is it?" she asked warily.

"I would know your given name, if you do not think me too forward in requesting it."

"Why do you want to know?" she asked bluntly.

"If you want the truth," he said, offering her a lopsided grin, "I grow tired of calling you Pirate Wench in my thoughts."

For a long moment, she stared at him unresponsively. Finally, she said coolly, "I am called Lynnette. But"—she paused for emphasis—"I do not give you leave to use that name." Then she rose and walked into the villa, leaving him alone on the verandah to face the night.

He awoke shortly after dawn with her name on his lips, still tasting the flavor of her in his dreams. "Lynnette," he murmured to the room at large, trying it out on his tongue. It sounded very good to him. Such a feminine name, but then, what had he been expecting? She could not very well have been called Blade or Lance as some men were. And, of course, at her birth her parents could have had no idea that their child would become a notorious criminal, and would not have thought to baptize her accordingly.

Which only reminded Daniel that, at some point in her life, Lynnette must have *had* a family. How had she come so far from a normal life? Had she no father or brothers to protect her? But somewhere, the wench had acquired polish, manners. These could not have been learned in the gutter! She was as much of a mystery now as she had ever been. Last night he might have learned something of her bravery and her unyielding character, but he still knew nothing of her past. That would come, he assured himself. Just now, his stomach reminded him rather impolitely in the form of a loud grumble that breakfast would not go amiss.

Would she be there this morning? Last night she had invited him to join her for supper, but that was no indication of whether she chose to eat with him today, or even that she had not gone back on her word and locked him in while he slept. Only one way to find out, he told himself as he got out of bed, tossing aside the thin sheet that was his only cover in the tropical heat.

Normally, he slept entirely nude, but since he could not be sure when someone might choose to enter his room unexpectedly, he had taken to sleeping in his breeches for the sake of modesty. Now they were wrinkled beyond redemption, a disgrace to his tailor. And damn, but he needed a shave! Rubbing one hand over the dense growth of stubble on his chin, Daniel reflected that a bath would be nice as well. Perhaps the wench would grant him these small favors. A change of attire would also help, he thought, not daring to hope for so much, however.

He found her on the terrace, looking fresh and lovely as ever in a white silk shirt and fawn-colored breeches. High boots of plain black leather encased her slim legs past her knees, and he found them unbelievably sexy on her shapely, feminine form. Her hair was worn in a braided coronet again this morning, but already wisps had begun to work loose, framing her heart-shaped face in red-gold tendrils. What a woman to wake up to! he thought, desire heating his blood.

"Good morning, Captain Bradley," she said pleasantly enough, but there was a guarded sheen in her emerald eyes.

He returned the greeting, seating himself at her gesture to do so.

She initiated the conversation. "Perhaps this morning you will tell me something of your experiences, since I seem to have dominated the conversation last night with talk of myself. I vow I know nothing at all about you—except, of course, that you are almost entirely without relations." Her tone was slightly cynical, even sarcastic. "I think today it would be best if you were to describe something of *your* life, for I would not want to bore you with endless chatter of my own."

He demurred. "You have not bored me at all, Captain." An almost imperceptible stress on the last word told her that he remembered last night's cool parting shot. "I believe I could listen to your fascinating stories forever, and never grow tired

of hearing them. Besides, you have not told me so very much."
His voice was light and urbane, in keeping with his plan. He
would not openly argue with the wench, but he would do his
best to pry away at her wall of mystery.

Nor will I! she thought, but all she said was, "Just the same,
sir, I would like to hear more of you, for I too am curious."
A note of steel had crept into her voice.

Was that a command? he wondered. No matter. If she
wanted to know about his past, then she would indeed hear!
Perhaps if he told her something of himself, she would begin
to trust him more. After all, he was still a virtual stranger to
this highly suspicious woman . . .

"There's really not much to tell," he began. "My life has
not been filled with the stuff of legend as yours has." Was it
his imagination, or did a faint blush creep to her cheeks at his
compliment? "I grew up in the countryside and in London,
the second son of noble parents. My mother died when I was
very young, and I barely remember her."

Lynnette winced in sympathy, but he did not seem to notice. His silver eyes had darkened, and he seemed not to gaze
at her but *through* her. Some unpleasant memory? She waited
while he halted for a moment.

"At age sixteen, after my father died, I joined the Royal
Navy and remained there for over ten years. It was only in
this past year that I left to start my own shipping company.
Which," he finished, "you may well have put a premature end
to."

She did not apologize. To her mind, it was merely the luck
of the draw that had sent him into her hands, and she refused
to feel guilty now that the deed was done. "So, that's where
you gained your knowledge of seamanship," she mused. "But
why did you join the navy?" she asked. "I mean, it's a career
not many would choose—but then, I forgot, you are a younger
son. You mentioned you had a brother, as I recall."

His voice was harder than she had ever heard it before.
"Half brother. And yes, that is why I signed up with the navy.
I needed to make my fortune somehow, and it seemed the best
way at the time. Eventually I worked through the ranks and
became first officer, a post I left in order to go into business
for myself."

Daniel was not being entirely truthful. He *had* joined the

navy, but not purposely. He had been given to a press-gang by his half brother, drugged and gagged, so that they were well at sea before he could do more than shout for help. But Captain Bradley did not want to tell the piratess about *that*. It was not something he told even to his closest friends.

He had started out as a lowly cabin boy, taunted and teased by the crew for his overfine manners and cultured mode of speaking. No one treated their newest crew member any better because he was a member of the nobility, for it had been made clear that his family did not want him—had, in fact, paid to have him removed. Daniel's "haughty" mannerisms had made him the best bet for a laugh among the crew, who took pleasure in performing cruel practical jokes and the like upon him.

Eventually, though, when they saw that the youth was not going to give up or give in, the men had begun to gain respect for the gently bred boy who fought so hard to keep up. For, once he had ascertained that there would be no rescue, Daniel had decided to make the best of it, until such time as he could face his powerful older half brother with some status of his own. In time, he discovered that the sea was in his blood and that he loved sailing. Within three years, he had made ensign, his captain promoting him because of his extraordinary gifts as a sailor and leader above other youths who had paid their way into the navy. In five years he'd made lieutenant. Bradley had been first officer when their captain had retired.

"I might have stayed on, but after seeing the incompetent man given the captaincy merely because he had connections within the Admiralty, I became disillusioned with the whole corrupt system and only wanted a chance to get out of it."

She nodded, knowing what the navy was like. Men were often promoted on the strength of their bribes to the Admiralty instead of their ability to handle a ship. Corruption was rife in His Majesty's Royal Navy. "And your half brother, why do you not mention him?"

Daniel spoke tightly. "I believe I told you that we are estranged. There is naught more to it."

Lynnette's eyes narrowed. There was assuredly a great deal he was not telling her. Mayhap it was all a lie? Indeed, perhaps the man was merely protecting this brother of his by telling her that they no longer spoke. But, no, his very manner told her that there was bad blood between the two, unless he was a better dissembler than she believed possible. And besides, why would he have given her his partner's name for the ransom if he had a relative who would pay instead? Nay, she believed him. Mostly.

Since she was sure she would get nothing more out of him on that subject, she concentrated on her food instead. Long neglected while he told his story, the ham and fluffy scrambled eggs had grown cold, and the scones were no longer steaming, but she ate with good appetite anyway. As did he. When they had finished, she sat back with a sigh.

"Do you fish?" she asked abruptly.

Taken aback, Daniel merely nodded.

"Good, then. I had thought to have fresh fish for supper tonight. You are welcome to come along, if you would like." She drew in her breath at her own audacity, for the words of invitation had seemed to emerge from her throat of their own volition, without the will of her mind. Maybe this wasn't such a good idea, on second thought. The notion of spending the bulk of the day on a small boat with that much overwhelming male was disconcerting, to say the very least! They might have a truce, but honestly! This was beyond necessary. She had to stop inviting him into her company like this!

Fishing was a pastime Lynnette usually enjoyed, but with that silver-eyed rogue so close to her, she doubted she would get much pleasure out of it today. Nay, she'd be watching her back the whole time. But she couldn't retract the offer now, for he was already agreeing.

"I would indeed enjoy that, Captain. Thank you."

She nodded curtly, still amazed at that perverse side of herself that appeared to relish finding ways of bringing the two together. "Fine, then. Meet me at the cove in twenty minutes. And don't be late, or I'll leave without you." Lord, but she hoped he would be late!

CHAPTER TEN

$\mathscr{B}$UT DANIEL had no intention of giving the wench an excuse to leave without him by being tardy. Such a grand opportunity was not to be wasted! In fact, he arrived at the sunlit cove only fifteen minutes later, and found that the curvaceous buccaneer had yet to arrive, although there was a small skiff similar to the one he had tried to escape with the day before pulled up high on the pink sand beach. His eyes scanned the beach, but it was deserted at the moment. Oddly, he did not even consider taking off with the craft then and there. He had too much else on his mind.

Soon Lynnette arrived down the shell-lined path from the villa, her stride long and graceful, swinging a straw basket in one slim hand. "Fishing gear," she announced in response to his questioning glance as she came up beside him.

That was not all she had brought with her, he noticed. Peeking out of the top of her high boot was the hilt of a dagger, and tucked into her black leather belt was the same pistol she had threatened him with yesterday. The sword she carried incessantly was missing, however, but he knew that was merely because the long-bladed weapon would be useless in the confines of a boat like the one they were about to board.

"Is all that really necessary?" he asked skeptically, the direction of his gaze telling her that he did *not* mean the fishing equipment. "I have given you my word of honor not to attempt an escape, and I do not mean to break it now. Unless," he added humorously, "you plan to shoot or stab our dinner instead of catching it in the traditional manner."

Her face flushed at the lightly spoken reproof. "Merely a precaution, Captain Bradley," she said coolly. "I would not want the lure of this tempting boat to cause you to break an oath."

"Ah, I see. You are simply protecting my honor by draping yourself on this hot day with enough weaponry to send the entire Spanish Armada scuttling back home to Castille, quaking in their boots." One dark brow rose mockingly, and he shook his head at her distrust. "Well, then, I suppose I must thank you for looking out for my interests, Captain Thorne."

Her blush grew deeper, and she turned her face away so that he would not see the damning color. God rot him, he made her feel like the greatest of fools for mistrusting him, when she knew bloody well he bore watching! No matter, she would keep the weapons, and so what if he mocked her for being overly cautious. Better to be safe than dead.

"Just help me get the boat in the water, will you?" she snapped gruffly.

When they had reached the open ocean Lynnette furled the sail and pulled the basket from under the plank board that served her as a seat, where she had stowed it to keep the contents from the hot sun. She handed Captain Bradley line and bait, and took the same for herself. Then she dropped the small anchor overboard. All that time, she was careful not to touch him, staying as far to her end of the craft as possible, while he sat in the front, legs stretched out as if he had not a care in the world.

Once or twice, his bare foot brushed her leg, for he had removed his boots as soon as they dropped the anchor on the tiny boat. Did he allow their limbs to touch purposely? she wondered as his elegantly shaped foot touched her calf again. Nay, it was only the close confines of the skiff that forced them into contact, she reassured herself. She should not be so skittish. Trying to relax, she inhaled deeply of the salt-tinged air and forced her tense muscles to loosen up.

Waves lapped at the hull, providing the only sound on the open water. Occasional seabirds circled overhead. The downed sail flapped a little in the breeze and they rocked idly. The motion of the boat was very soothing. So soothing, in fact, that once Lynnette had become somewhat accustomed to Bradley's presence aboard her private skiff, she was able to relax and turn her face up to the bright, hot sun, basking in the golden rays.

Daniel watched her through heavy-lidded eyes masked by incredibly long lashes, leaning his arms against the sides of the boat and his head against the prow. By God, Thorne was a beauty! The sun gilded her smooth, satinlike skin, making her appear as if she had just stepped down from heaven as an angel without wings. In temperament, the wench might be better compared to a Fury, he knew, but she seemed like one of the Graces in her form. Unlike the fashionably pale ladies in London, Thorne had allowed her skin to tan to a golden color that gave her a healthy glow.

Was she tan everywhere? he wondered with a sudden rush of desire. She was so close, and yet if he made one move, she'd not hesitate to blow a hole in him large enough to see straight through.

"I could take that pistol from you, you know," he said pleasantly, causing Lynnette to turn her head sharply in his direction. "Don't worry, I won't," he added hastily.

"I highly doubt you could, Captain, for two very good reasons!" Her voice was hard with quick anger. "First: you could *try* to wrest this gun from me, but I would never allow you to take it—I'd kill you first. Second: this is a very small craft, my friend, and any sudden movement could cause it to capsize, which would not make it easy for you to engage in a struggle with any success. I am a very good swimmer, and could easily make it to shore, but you might not have such luck, what with the sharks and all. Even if you managed to reach the beach, I'd be there waiting with my knife. And I'd have to kill you for being more trouble than you're worth after that, sorry to say." She didn't sound even one tiny bit remorseful. "Therefore, I am glad you have decided that you will not attempt to do any such foolish thing."

After a moment's hesitation, she asked in a calmer voice, "Why do you say you wouldn't try it anyway? I know *I* would, regardless of my chances or my captor."

Daniel, trying to control his temper at being dressed down so thoroughly by this mere female, did not hear her question at first. Did she truly think him so damnably ineffectual that he couldn't manage to wrest a gun from her slight fingers without falling out of the bloody boat? Especially when she knew he had been at sea for a great portion of his life. And that she thought she could possibly win in a contest of strength with him was patently absurd. Why, anyone could see that he was by far the stronger, standing as he did nearly a foot taller and outweighing her nearly twice over! What overweening arrogance! It was almost funny, and would have been if the wench had not been so deadly serious.

When her query did manage to penetrate his humiliation, it only made him scowl harder. He did not want to admit his reasons for remaining placidly in her trap; it might make him seem like a coward in her eyes. Finally, though, he told her the truth, not being able to come up with a facile lie.

"I don't want to see you harmed," he mumbled, "not at my hands."

Her keen ears caught his nearly inaudible words, and she laughed outwardly at his naïve chivalry, even as, inwardly, something that had been coiled in her gut relaxed. "Because I am a woman?" she asked.

At his acknowledging nod, she shook her head disgustedly at him, as if to say, "There's just no hope for you." "You are a fool, then," she said incredulously, "not to take this chance—slim though it is—while you have it. I assure you, were our roles reversed, I would have no such scruples about taking the advantage over you."

"Ah, but Captain," he replied, unperturbed, "we have already established that you have no scruples."

"True." Lynnette chuckled. "Touché, Peacock." She sat back to regard his handsome features with no little amazement. She could hardly believe what he had said a moment earlier. The men she normally associated with, the members of the Brethren of the Coast, would have had no such moral compunctions about sticking a knife in her back the second she turned around, if they thought it would gain them something. God, how long had it been since she had known men who were gallant, who abided by the rules of chivalry?

"I had forgotten the mores and niceties of the gentry," she said unthinkingly. "Where I make my living these days, men do not feel themselves constrained to behave gently toward women." But then, Lynnette recalled bitterly, that terrible night that had determined her fate had occurred in London, and the man who had caused it all had been a so-called gentleman, so she estimated cynically that men were probably the same wherever they came from. Only some of them hid their callous cruelty behind masks of civilization, while others, the men she had dealings with in the Caribbean, were simply more open about it.

But this man seemed to truly believe in protecting the "fairer sex" from violence—or at least, in not being the cause of it. Still, he'd had no compunctions about trussing up Mari, so perhaps his profession of squeamishness was no more than a ruse to gain her trust. She must remember his duplicity, or she might soon find herself in the same position as the young serving wench.

But Daniel was wondering about something else. Thorne had said that she'd *forgotten* the ways of the gentry. But how could she have ever known them in the first place? Who *was* she, damn it? That slip told him something, but he'd be damned if he knew what! Still, if he wanted to question her, he'd have to do it subtly.

"Where did you acquire your manner of speech?" he asked. "That is to say, I cannot imagine that your cultured tones are the product of a childhood spent in the streets." He waited anxiously for her response.

Wouldn't you like to know, she thought. "Oh, I was raised in a convent school and planned to take holy vows," she replied with mocking glibness. "The good sisters are rather insistent on a thorough education of their charges, you know." The wench was quite clearly lying; she knew it and he knew it, but her bright green eyes dared him to call her bluff. Captain Thorne had never been cut out for a life devoted to the veil.

Obviously, Lynnette didn't plan to reveal anything to him that easily. His frustration was growing all over again, for today the wench was closemouthed as a clam, and he had made barely any progress in ferreting out her secrets. She was on guard, her mocking, ready answers to his careful questions telling him that her tongue would not be so easily loosened now as it had been yesterday.

Perhaps this seduction was going to take longer than he'd thought. But how was he going to restrain himself to wait if she could not be persuaded to come to his bed soon? He could be patient only so long in the face of temptation. His vow to leave her alone and unmolested was not going to be easy to keep, not when all he wanted to do was pull her beneath him to taste and touch that sweet, wanton body of hers.

Just then, Lynnette's gaze traveled to the side of the boat, where he had one leg thrown over the side to dangle just above the water. And, unbelievably, she saw that he had tied the fishing line around his largest toe. "What do you think you're doing?" she cried in surprise.

Daniel, thinking that she had somehow read his mind, did not at first understand. "Doing, Captain?" he asked cautiously.

She indicated his unorthodox manner of fishing, and he relaxed. "Oh, that." But, eyes wide with dawning horror, she cut off whatever else he had been about to add.

"Oh, *shit!*" she yelled, leaping up and drawing her dagger from her boot.

For Christ's sake, was she going to kill him for fishing with his feet? But before he could do more than stare in confusion, she had sliced quickly through the line between his toe and the water, tossing the cord away from the boat. He gaped foolishly at her, completely bewildered.

She saw his reaction. "Damn it, man, there was a barracuda coming straight for your bait! Do you know what might have happened if he took it? You could lose a toe, or worse! One of those bastards could drag this boat quite a distance, I tell you! Jesus, and what if you'd caught some other fish, and a shark had decided to make a meal of it? *What* were you thinking of?"

"I always fish that way. It's much more comfortable. Besides, I usually carry a knife for just such emergencies."

"You didn't have a knife this time!"

"But *you* did, my dear Captain, and I trust you to watch out for your—how did you phrase it?—ah, yes: investments. And you have proved me correct, just this very minute. So why should I worry? I feel very safe with you, you know." Daniel let his eyes roam over her slim, armed figure. "It's a bit of a change, I'll admit, to be protected by a woman, but I find I rather like it." With that, he subsided back against the prow in pure satisfaction at having bested the wench, closing his eyes and crossing his arms over his chest.

Lynnette fumed, speechless at his audacity, and silence crept over the open boat while they fished—correctly, this time.

Later that day, when the two had gutted and cleaned their catch—for they had caught a goodly number of fish once they'd managed to settle down—Daniel asked for and received soap, a change of clothing, and, surprisingly, a razor for his beard. The piratess had merely shrugged at his request, and, reminding him caustically of his oath, sent her plump Dutch housekeeper, whose name, he'd discovered, was Inga, to fetch the things he'd need.

Now the beautiful buccaneer led him to a secluded place, a fantastically gorgeous pool where the water was churned into white froth by the grace of a low waterfall. It was about a quarter of a mile into the densely vegetated interior of the island, and the pirate told him that the pool was a part of the system of freshwater springs strewn about No-name Island, some of which had come together to form a stream.

Sea grape and cottonwood and palm surrounded the small,

deep pool, shading it and providing shelter from prying eyes. Thickly blooming layers of hibiscus bushes, frangipani, and many other sweet-smelling flowers he could not begin to name crowded around the water's edge in a riot of colors: red, yellow, pink, and purple. It was a truly lovely spot. Here Lynnette led him, and then disappeared into the jungle without a word. Her eyes seemed troubled to the acute man, but he shrugged it off in order to enjoy the pleasures that bathing would provide.

The clothes he had been given to replace his own filthy ones were by no means new, but at least they were clean, and hopefully, of a size to fit his rangy body. There were black breeches and a white cotton shirt—plain attire, to be sure— but Daniel was not about to complain, for after more than a week he would have climbed into anything, even the pirate queen's clothing, rather than remain in his own. Then again . . . wasn't getting into Captain Thorne's breeches the whole idea?

He stripped quickly, striding into the clear, cool water with a sigh. Oh, to be clean again! He, unlike many of his peers, did not have a great tolerance for his own body's odor, and while they might go for months without washing, he defied convention and bathed whenever possible. Thank goodness Captain Thorne appeared to subscribe to the same philosophy!

Now, taking up the thick cake of strong soap, Daniel scrubbed at his body fiercely, thoroughly, ducking underwater to rinse the suds off his strongly muscled frame. He washed his hair and then swam for a while, luxuriating in the opportunity to get some exercise and refresh himself at the same time. When he was done, he washed his own clothes and lay down naked alongside them on a flat, sun-drenched rock to dry.

What he did not know was that during this entire interlude, he had been watched.

For reasons unknown to her, Lynnette had been unable to simply leave once she'd shown Daniel the pool that she herself was used to bathing in. Just knowing that this enigmatic, unpredictable, and above all, *handsome* male was at this very moment stripping to wash in the private haven she came to

every morning was enough to send shivers of trepidation—
and curiosity—running down her back.

What would he look like nude? she wondered, ashamedly
realizing she had taken but a few steps away from the enclosed
spring. She'd seen him shirtless before, and, much to her
pleased surprise, the man had firm, hard muscles, clearly delineated against his lightly bronzed skin. She would have
thought a city-bred dandy like the peacock would be flabby—
all lily-white flesh and no muscle—but the opposite was true.
His biceps and pectorals were well developed, and his stomach
was like a washboard, ridged and hard over his ribs. Not one
ounce of extra fat was visible on his spare, lean torso. But
what would the rest of him look like?

Before she knew it, the pirate queen's feet were making
their noiseless way through the jungle—in the direction opposite the one her mind wished them to take her. Sincerely
believing she had completely lost her wits, Lynnette nevertheless peeped through the screen of trees and flowering vines to
see. Time enough later to think about what she was doing;
now she would brazenly play the voyeur.

A gasp escaped her rosy lips as she took in the magnificent
vision in front of her. Captain Bradley was naked as Adam in
the garden of Eden, his clothes strewn about his feet, just
stepping into the water. And he was beautiful. His long, raven-
black hair hung unconfined to his broad shoulders in glossy
abandon, giving him a wild, savage appeal, while below, he
was even more splendidly uncivilized. She had to resist the
urge to emit a low, appreciative whistle as she gazed shamelessly at her captive.

From his head straight to his perfectly formed feet, the man
was all lean tendons and hard muscle, whipcord and bone,
with little to mar the deep, even tan that covered every single
inch of his six-foot-two-inch frame except a few nasty-looking
scars. Gained, she speculated, from his years in the navy. Perhaps his life had been more adventurous than he'd modestly
declaimed. But where, she wondered, did he sunbathe to get
such a tan all over his body? From his wide shoulders to his
waist his torso tapered to lean, fine hips. His legs were strong
and straight, thick muscle groups clearly defined under the
hair-roughened skin.

His buttocks were small, rounded, and firm-looking, muscles bunching under the skin as he waded, Lynnette noted with a blush. But when he turned around in the shallow water, the blush went even deeper, suffusing her slender throat and all the way up to her hairline with rosy color. She didn't look away, but only because she sternly forced herself not to. "You've seen nude men before, girl!" she told herself. "What's one more—handsomely built thought he be?"

If she didn't look, she was a coward: to come so far and then back away at the sight of a man's organ—nothing new when one lived aboard a ship with a crew of nearly twenty men and no necessary facilities except over the railing! What in heaven's name was she suddenly so timid about? It wasn't as if she were some innocent, sheltered maid who swooned at the mere thought of bared ankles! Yet, when she forced herself to boldly stare at the thick shaft nestled in its thatch of curling black hair, her breath arrested in her lungs with a jolt of sizzling sensation.

Her mind, of its own volition, sent images to torment her. How would that strong, blatantly male shaft feel inside her body . . . ? "Horrible—unthinkable!" she mentally shouted. "Don't even *consider* it!" But even when Daniel had waded a little farther into the pool, relieving her of the sight of his rampant maleness, her thoughts continued in their heated path relentlessly.

Watching him as he ran the bar of soap across his sleek, wet flesh, Lynnette felt her temperature rise several degrees. He looked so good, like Adonis rising from a fragrant bath. Feelings she hadn't known existed within herself began to uncoil lazily, bringing a strange heat to her belly—and then lower. She found herself wishing she could switch places with the soap, to be run lovingly across that smooth skin all over his body. Her breathing quickened. How would it feel to caress his strong chest, to run her palms along the length of his straight back? Or lower, to grasp those slim hips or firm buttocks as he . . .

"Dear God," she murmured, "what am I *thinking*?" She wanted Bradley, the peacock—her prisoner! Never had a man appealed to her senses in the manner this one did—his kisses and her response to them had proved it, and now, the aching desire in her blood reaffirmed the dreadful news.

As he ducked beneath the water to rinse off, Lynnette stared fixedly at the place where he had been, no longer even seeing the secluded grotto. What was he doing to her? Even now her loins ached in a strange new way—feeling empty and on fire at the same time—and she knew perfectly well what was wrong despite her pained mental query. She desired Daniel as a woman desires a man—in that way that she had never thought she would feel for *any* man, least of all a captured, dangerous man under her power being held for ransom.

Oh, no. She was in deep trouble now. The one emotion she had thought would never be in her way—passion—was now a factor to be dealt with. And deal with it she would, the pirate resolved darkly. She might desire the man, but that fact was entirely irrelevant. If she wanted to keep to her quest for vengeance, she must not let her inappropriate passion hinder her. She simply wasn't going to do anything to feed her newly awakened feelings—and neither was *he,* if he knew what was good for him. Lynnette would just ignore the force of desire— of pure lust, really, she thought cynically; exactly as she had ignored all other emotions detrimental to her plan.

Hate, anger, and impatience she nurtured to help her stay on her course; but happiness, love, and trust she pushed away, for she feared they would make her weak. Desire too would eat away at her resolve, making her complaisant and greedy for the touch of a man when she should have been hard and cold and scornful of any advances. She would steel herself against its stirrings and proceed as usual.

With this in mind, the pirate captain watched her prisoner surface, shaking water everywhere, with a steady eye and an *almost* steady heartbeat. When he began to swim laps across the small water hole, she forced her gaze and then her feet around, and quietly left him alone. She had seen more than enough.

Over the next week, while the rest of the pirates were away, Daniel and Lynnette discovered much about each other. At dinner every night, and during the occasional breakfast the two spent together, they talked about everything from the spice trade to the atrocity of slavery. Lynnette grew to like her captive, if grudgingly, and Daniel learned to deal with frustration. Although they spoke on topics that interested both, the wench refused to ever reveal anything personal about herself.

Even so, the two in such divergent positions began to see a common ground in their views. When Daniel outlined his plans for the great shipping empire he wanted to build, Lynnette surprisingly approved. He'd expected that a pirate would have scorned legitimate trade, believing that merchants were no more than prey for stronger foes to take advantage of. But she gave him encouragement and advice—not that he needed it, but he listened politely all the same—and in turn she provided an enthusiastic listener to all his dreams.

He tried to extend her the same courtesy, forcing himself not to condemn Thorne's unlawful actions even when they involved himself. And in doing so, he found that he could not feel very much disapproval for the pirate any longer. As he came to know her better, he became more and more positive that she had a specific reason quite unrelated to greed for marauding the seas.

Captain Thorne quite obviously knew the difference between right and wrong, and he suspected that she had simply overruled her natural code of ethics in order to accomplish something that, to her mind at least, would justify her piracy. He desperately wanted to know what the reason was, and not simply because the knowledge might be of use to him in escaping. The longer he spent with the beautiful, extraordinary woman, the more he yearned to know everything about her. He didn't dare question himself as to why.

He didn't make any more overt attempts to seduce her, although he was most certainly trying to charm his way subtly into her confidence. Daniel knew that any rash move would destroy his hopes of eventual success, and he was, if not content with his restraint, at least managing to hold on to it. Still, he entertained the notion more than once of giving up his guileful campaign in favor of seizing his quarry in his arms and kissing the breath out of her.

Lynnette found that her hours with Daniel were by far the most pleasant she'd ever spent, and she learned to respect him more and more as the days passed. She relaxed in his presence, made comfortable by the fact that he had made no further amorous advances since their agreement. Even so, when they sat down together at dinner, there was a strange sort of anticipation in her every time he held out her chair for her to be seated. She wondered if his fingers would chance to brush her shoulders as she sat, and when once they did, caught her breath with the sudden rush of heat in her blood.

She also discovered disappointment when he removed his hand politely and without hesitation. His chivalry was exactly what she had required of him, yet now she secretly wished, although she tamped it down each time the shameful feeling occurred, that he would be just a little *less* honorable. These feelings rocked the pirate queen to the bones. Firstly, she was growing lax in her guardianship, tending to believe that the peacock would be true to his word—she, who *never* let down her guard! Secondly, she feared that she might be losing her control over the situation, finding herself in a morass of not-entirely-sexual feelings for a very wily, extremely sensual man.

Why was he being so cordial? Was it a natural trait for Bradley, or was he purposely using charm to lull her into a state of complaisance? Questions like these plagued the back of Lynnette's mind, even as she perversely continued to spend time with the man.

Their discussions became a sort of ritual wherein each reveled in having found a person of intellect to share observations and beliefs with. For Lynnette especially it was a wonderful experience to talk to someone who cared about something other than plunder or wenching exclusively. Thoughts of revenge and escape were put on hold while they waited for the *Maiden*'s crew to return and disrupt their idyll, for each was painfully aware that this strange, pleasant interlude in time must end soon.

After seven days had passed and the pirate had begun to look toward the cove for a glimpse of her returning shipmates more and more often, it happened that in the evening, after their supper, both decided separately that a quiet night in their rooms reading would not suffice to still the restless nerves brought on by their proximity.

Daniel snapped shut the text on navigation he had been blindly staring at for an hour and tossed it away from him. Damn it, but the crew of the *Maiden's Revenge* would be returning any time now, and he still had not remotely begun to accomplish his purpose. With the men back on the island, Thorne was sure to change her behavior toward him. At least, she would if she didn't want rumors to start about their unusual relationship. He didn't want to lie here in his small room and stew about it anymore, however. The night wind beckoned, drawing him out of the chamber and through the front door in search of some peace for his roiling emotions.

Down to the beach he walked, trying to reconcile himself to the fact that he might have to wait out the ransom instead of the more pleasant alternative he had envisioned. He thought about how stupid his moral compunctions about hurting Lynnette probably were, especially when his own captor told him she didn't believe in such niceties. But he knew as surely as he knew his own name that there was nothing he could do to change his feelings. It was frustrating, this conflict of interests.

Instead of the acceptance he was searching for, he found the source of his troubles on a tiny stretch of pale shimmering sand adjacent to the main harbor.

Picking his way through the pitchy darkness, Daniel didn't see the slender figure of the captain until he stumbled right into her. Lynnette, who had been deeply absorbed in her own disturbed thoughts and totally unaware of his quiet invasion, gasped and nearly fell over from spinning so quickly to face the threat. A wickedly sharp knife, blade flashing in the fitful moonlight, was in her hand before he could blink.

Grasping the pirate's arm to help her regain her balance, he felt an intense frisson of desire sweep him at the sight of her, clad only in a fawn-colored leather vest closed by three thong ties and a pair of skintight dark brown breeches. For once without the high boots, her legs were bare from below the knees, and her toes dug into the sand for balance. Her feral posture, crouched and ready to spring, dagger held ready, clearly showed her magnificent form. The waning moon chose that moment to fully emerge from behind the shifting pattern of cloud cover, and Daniel, staring into Lynnette's sparkling emerald eyes, scarcely managed to get out an apology for bumping into her. He fell silent a second later, dazed by the untamed beauty before him.

Lynnette relaxed, but only slightly. She did not sheathe the dagger, feeling the abrupt and profound tension that had entered the air between herself and the tall, handsome man and desiring to protect herself from it in a purely instinctive way. She continued to stare at the magnificent man standing so very close, her blood racing with overwhelming feelings. Fear took second place to desire. Her arm lowered, bringing the knife out of its threatening posture.

Something was going to happen; she knew it and he knew it, and suddenly the pirate was deathly tired of pretending she could deny it. The last week of careful civility had worn her out; trying to maintain a polite demeanor when in the back of her mind a little voice said, *You'll never have a better chance than this. Take him and be done with it. No one will ever know.* Now their time alone was almost over, and she had failed to stay away from his enchantment, for she could not resist anymore. *I'm sorry, Sarah,* she mentally anguished, *I've failed you.* And she swayed helplessly toward her charismatic captive.

Daniel met her halfway. He knew it was premature to his plan—she wasn't ready yet and would hate him for it later—but he could no more stop what was compelling them than he could sprout wings and fly off No-name Island. *Lust,* he told himself, *that's all it is,* just before their lips met in a kiss so hot it scorched the air between them.

She let the dagger fall from her fingertips to the sand with a soft *plunk* as his arms came tightly around her, dragging her flush with his hard-muscled body. She made no protest, having given herself up to the forces of passion that now ruled her completely for the first time in her life. His lips seared a hole in her tightly guarded soul, plundering with more than simple skill. His tongue swept her lips, seeking and receiving entrance, then seeming to swallow her breath with its force. No gentleness characterized this kiss; they'd gone far beyond that patient stage.

Daniel's hand slid to the back of her waist, pulling her even tighter to him so that their lower bodies fused into one hot being. She could feel his arousal—huge and hard and insistent against her lower belly. Gasping with sudden urgency, she rocked her hips forward to meet his, rubbing shamelessly against his throbbing shaft.

Now it was Daniel's turn to gasp. He swept his hands up to cup her face, kissing her even more deeply in response to her action. Some part of his mind wondered at her abrupt change of heart, but most of it was busy singing with triumphant pleasure. From her smooth cheeks, his callused hands slid downward till he reached the ties on her leather vest. Obviously, she had not meant to be seen wearing the garment; it was indecent the way it revealed her impressive cleavage, and the pirate had never showed herself to be indecent previously. Probably it was the unusually hot night that caused her to wear it. No matter, it was coming *off* now! His shaking fingers nearly tore the thongs off the vest, but she didn't seem to mind, whimpering low in her throat and pressing wild kisses all over his face.

Her hands too raced over his body, pulling at his shirt, tugging it out of his breeches while she gave a little mutter of frustration at the difficulty. Just as he managed to untie the last of her laces, she got the shirt out and they mutually divested each other of their top coverings, barely breaking the kiss to do it. When they rejoined the embrace, the shock of naked skin against skin was enough to raise the temperature in both to the boiling point. Daniel slid his fingers up to cup her smooth, full breasts; Lynnette stroked his slick, muscled chest with much the same motion.

She felt his hands like a brand on her sensitive breasts and could not prevent a groan of ecstasy from welling up. As he expertly fondled the high-tipped globes, she arched her back for easier access, their lips breaking contact as she threw her head back. She'd given up thinking; now she was just a body, an aching, needing, glorying *body*. And it was beautiful. Minor considerations like a lifelong quest for revenge, a dangerous game being played between Bradley and herself, and, of course, her virginity, were washed away in the heat of the moment. Nothing else mattered save Daniel's touch; his kiss, his hands, his long, lean body pressed to hers.

Her exposed neck drew his seeking lips downward, nuzzling and licking his way to her bare shoulders, shining in the moonlight like alabaster. His tongue laved her collarbones, then slid to trace the vee between her upthrust, rosy-crested breasts. Then, fiercely he claimed them one after the other, drawing the nipples in to be suckled and tantalized until she moaned helplessly under his searing torment.

"Please," she gasped weakly, the first word spoken between them. It was the only word she could think of at the moment, and he understood perfectly. Wrapping his strong arms around her, he pulled them both off balance so that they fell onto the sand—he made sure that he took the brunt of the impact by

twisting so she landed on top. Very naturally, Lynnette strad-
dled his hips and brought her lips back to his. She kissed him
until his head swam with passion, and all he could think of
was the consummation of their desire, right there on the sand
and out in the open.

"Damn," he managed. "This—is not the best place—we
could have chosen to do this." Sand was scratching his back
raw with their untamed movements, and it had somehow gotten on his hands, so that when he stroked the pirate's silky
skin, he could feel its gritty texture on his palms. Surely she
felt it too.

"I don't care!" she sobbed, engrossed in the pleasure of his
loving and mindless to all else. "I don't care about *anything*
but this! Just touch me, take me, now!" Wildly, she writhed
upon him, grinding her loins against his. It was all he needed
to make him forget the circumstances. As they kissed, his
hands slid down her silky back until they reached the waistband of her breeches. He slid his fingers inside until he
grasped her firm buttocks in his lean hands, pressing her hard
against him.

Little gasps escaped her throat as Lynnette felt her body
drowning in need of him. This closeness was not enough to
satisfy the raging passions that knifed through her belly.
"More!" she demanded hoarsely, and he, as lost as she, complied. Her breeches were unlaced in a heartbeat, and Daniel
twisted so that she lay on the sand on her back, and he beside
her, his hand dipping beneath the loosened garment to stroke
between her thighs.

No subtlety accompanied their movements, just pleasure
that bordered on agony, and the direct satisfaction of it. His
long fingers delved into her slick, swollen folds, rubbing and
teasing, then suddenly, thrusting hard into her depths. She
cried out with the sharp, unexpected ecstasy of the touch, arching her hips instinctively to meet his demanding strokes. She
tossed her head back and forth in the sand, bright copper-gold
tresses, loosened from the braid she'd woven them into, flying
across her face. The pirate was no more, there was only Lynnette, as she might have been had not cruel fortune stripped
her of the freedom to let go and simply *feel*.

Daniel's fingers stroked in and out of her heated body,
catching her rhythm and accommodating it. He marveled

dimly at her tightness, her incredible heat, sure that no other woman had ever felt so good to him. All he knew was that he had to have her, and that, miraculously, she needed him just as much. His body felt nigh to bursting with the strain of holding back, and he shook slightly, overwhelmed with desire for his pirate woman. And from the looks of it, he would not have long to wait. Her face was flushed and her eyes glazed with passion, unseeing. She raised her head for his kiss as soon as she realized he was watching her, pulling his head down with one hand to get what she wanted more quickly. He sensed that she was about to climax, and tugged urgently at her clothes. He was pulling the breeches to her knees and moving to cover her with his hard body, when a noise he'd hoped never to hear again stopped everything abruptly.

The clanking of heavy chains as the anchor of the *Maiden's Revenge* dropped, and the splashing and cursing of her sailors as they lowered the longboats to the sea froze Captain Bradley for an instant. "No," he muttered hoarsely, "we're too damned close!" And he turned back to Lynnette, determined to ignore the pirates' untimely arrival. But it was already too late. The creature beneath him was transformed.

Cold, completely lucid green eyes stared up at him without recognition for what had passed, without affection of any sort at all, and her body was stiff as a corpse. For a moment he simply stared desperately at her, silently willing his hot, unreasoning Lynnette to return to him. He got nothing from the pirate.

"Get off," she said very, very quietly. "Right now."

For a second or two, he could not even do that much. But, as her gaze continued to stare frigidly into his, almost as if she understood his struggle and would wait, but would not compromise, he slowly returned to sanity. He had lost. The pirate captain was back to stay. "Damn you!" he swore, hating the fact that her control was so much better than his. He rolled abruptly away from her, curling into a sitting position with his back to the site of their near bliss. Raking a shaking hand through his thick raven hair, he breathed deeply several times, hoping futilely to regain a semblance of composure. He heard the pirate queen righting her clothes, and then, as her footsteps retreated, he heard her pause and turned to face her, wondering what there was left to say.

"Don't ever do this to me again, Bradley," she said softly, with a tremor in her voice that spoke of deep emotion. "Not *ever,* do you hear? Just stay the hell away from me!" She spun and ran through the trees to the main harbor, so close to their trysting place.

Soon he heard her voice ringing out along with those of her crew, laughing loudly as though nothing had ever happened. But was it his imagination, or was there an hysterical edge to her overloud mirth? Was that strain he heard in her voice as she greeted her sailors, or was he merely wishing the pirate could not have forgotten already what had happened between them scant moments before? He wondered if anything really had, for it was nearly inconceivable that Captain Thorne would have allowed anyone to be so close to her, to see her so abandoned.

Daniel got up, finally, still wondering whether their passionate encounter was all just some heat-induced delusion his mind had come up with to torment him. Then he noticed that his shirt was missing. The wench had obviously stolen it to preserve her modesty, since she could not very well appear in just a vest with ties that likely were broken in front of her lewd sailors. But as he returned to his barren, lonely room, he wondered why she even cared about appearances. What had she to lose, after all?

CHAPTER ELEVEN

ANIEL, STANDING on the balcony of his small chamber to let the fragrant night breeze cool his heated blood, felt as if he were about to explode. He was more frustrated than he'd ever been in his life. Nothing was within his control on this stinking little island, and it was all the fault of that thrice-damned unnatural woman, that siren in breeches, that, that . . . He ran out of words to describe how he hated her power over him. She'd ruined his life, and yet all he wanted to do was tumble the woman and make love to her until she begged for more.

But of course, she would never beg. Not the notorious Captain Thorne. Nay, even though she'd wanted him every bit as much as he'd wanted her, she would not give in again as she almost had tonight. She'd never allow herself to be so wild and unashamed with him again; he'd seen that much in her eyes when she'd turned from him.

Why not? he wanted to howl, his body singing with unfulfilled desire. What had she to lose, after all? It wasn't as though she were saving her favors for marriage. Indeed, he scoffed at the very notion. The infamous lady pirate, a virgin. Not bloody likely! He was sure that she was quite experienced, in fact, for her unbridled response to him tonight was more than any maid could live up to. Her kisses, her hands on his body—definitely not those of a chaste woman. Her demanding, wanton urging, her brazen love words, too hot and explicit for an innocent by any stretch of the imagination! So why, for God's sake, would she not just surrender and let what both of them wanted so badly happen?

Perhaps, in his use of the word "surrender," he had hit on just the reason why. Captain Thorne never surrendered, not to *anyone*. He was her adversary; she knew she couldn't trust him, so would naturally never give her body up to him—her body, or anything else. Had Daniel been a different man in a different position—another pirate perhaps, a nonthreatening crewman with whom she could always retain her control—he was positive she would have had no such scruples.

He remembered the emotion in Lynnette's voice as she told him to stay away, and knew that emotion betrayed her. At least, he consoled himself, he'd had *some* effect on her. Problem was, that effect was the opposite of the one he'd hoped to have. He'd pushed her too far, pressed his advantage too soon, and from now on the pirate would be doubly on her guard. Daniel knew he'd lost all the ground he had gained this past week in a single night, and he was sure he'd not be able to regain it in the time he had left before Simon came to deliver his ransom. She distrusted him too much now, and, if he knew the wench at all, she'd be as cold as the depths of winter from now on.

Daniel stared out into the night at the dwindling fires of the returned pirates and sighed heavily. His plan was ruined, and he did not have another.

*   *   *

Lynnette was outwardly composed as she greeted her crew with the amount of enthusiasm they expected her to show. Soon she was listening to their ribald stories of their week on St. Eustatius, and receiving the latest news. It seemed two more pirates had been caught in the last three months, and been hanged. Luckily, neither captain was a man she knew personally. By reputation they were low-life scum whose vessels were little more than floating dung heaps, and whose record of prizes were nothing compared to hers. Still, although her men discounted the ramifications of the hangings, saying loudly and often that with a captain as good as theirs, such would never be their fate, Lynnette herself was disquieted. She wanted to complete her mission and get out of this dangerous business before the same happened to her.

But it wasn't really the deaths of two members of the Brethren that bothered her, nor was it the reminder—a reminder that she was not at all in need of—that pirating was hardly risk-free, but her loss of control with her captive. Even though her men noticed nothing, she knew her hands trembled slightly, she held her body too stiffly, and she was certainly not feeling herself. She hadn't since that damned Captain Bradley had come into her life. He wasn't worth the trouble he caused, and she knew it, but disposing of him at this point was out of the question.

The merchant was no longer just some handsome figure to admire distantly, nor simply a prize she'd won, but a flesh-and-blood man. This last week, they'd talked like old friends, and she had learned a great deal about what went into this man. And what he wouldn't tell her intrigued her even more because he *was* so forthcoming on so many subjects. He talked about his gently bred childhood easily, about his naval experience and his ideas concerning shipping with no trouble, but of the time between the two, of the reasons behind the sudden changes in his life, he was evasive. She didn't think he realized that she sensed his reluctance to speak, and that was just fine with her. If Bradley underestimated her perceptiveness, that was all to the good. *Any* advantage she could get over the man was just fine with her. Especially as she was so peculiarly vulnerable to his brand of charm . . .

How was it possible for him to so easily rob her of her very wits? No one in her life had ever been to affect her emotions even *half* so powerfully as Daniel did with such seeming ease. And tonight, dear God in heaven, she'd been within a scant breath of lying with him! If her men had not arrived at the exact moment they had, she would never, she admitted to herself with utter shame and horror, have been able to stop the act herself.

Seven years ago she'd sworn never to lie with any man, never to allow a man that much control over her senses and her mind, and tonight she would have tossed that blood-soaked vow into the sea like the slops thrown over the side of a ship.

And for what? To experience Bradley's kisses, his body's loving? Loving, hah! There was no love connected with his touch; merely what every other man she'd met seemed to feel for her—lust, plain and simple. Yet *his* lust caused her long-dormant body to awaken as no other's could. There was no logical reason for it, Lynnette anguished. Her body was finally betraying her when for so long she had believed it was the only thing she could count on to remain hers. It had most definitely chosen an inopportune time—and an inopportune man—to do it with.

Lynnette ran a shaking hand across her sweating forehead. She was standing too close to the bonfire, and the fire in her blood was having a hard time cooling with these real flames to keep them alight. Backing off, she saw that her men had forgotten her presence by now, since she'd stood silent so long. They were all seriously involved in getting drunk and eating of the pigs that roasted over the open fires—not to mention in reacquainting themselves with the village women. Even Davie had a bottle in the crook of one arm and a pretty little wench in the other. At merely thirteen, she realized, he had more experience with the opposite sex than she at three-and-twenty. Well, the captain told herself crossly, that was just fine! And that was the way things were going to stay if she had any say in the matter.

If . . . Did she have a say? she wondered. Whenever her troubling prisoner was around, everything Lynnette had striven to become came unglued. She went soft and allowed him too many privileges. She could not maintain her icy control—indeed, she became just the opposite! All fire and wild abandon at that thrice-damned merchant's slightest caress! It wasn't right, and it shook her to the core. She didn't even know this

brazen side of herself—the side that had recklessly told her
enemy she didn't care about anything but his possession. Suddenly the renewed shame as she recalled her own words to the
peacock filled Lynnette with mortification. She couldn't stand
herself, couldn't deal with all these warring emotions. She
knew she was no longer in control and it frightened her as
nothing ever had before.

Making sure no one saw her, the pirate edged out of the
circle of firelight. When she was secure in the sheltering darkness, she took to her heels and simply ran, driving her feet
down the pink sand beach at breakneck speed, tears she refused to let fall stinging her eyes and blinding her.

Hours later Lynnette returned to her room, dripping sweat and
totally exhausted, but with a clearer mind. She'd run for miles,
outracing the wind, yet unable to outdistance her confused
thoughts. She pounded the sand until her feet ached and her
breath came in harsh gasps, and still she ran, collapsing at last
on a stretch of shoreline where moonlight shining on the foam
painted the waves white in the night's blackness. Lynnette beat
the encroaching water with her fists like a spoiled child having
a tantrum, cursing herself and Captain Bradley equally; cursing fate also for not letting her life be simple. If life had gone
as it was *supposed* to, she'd not now be struggling to keep
aloof from all feeling, trying to keep control of men who
barely knew what civilization *was*, trying to destroy an enemy
who by rights should have been kissing her hand gallantly . . .

Still, the slim pirate reminded herself, had life proceeded
as her birth and breeding had indicated, by now she'd have a
babe at her breast and two more hanging on her skirts, and
she'd never have tasted the freedom of salt-sprayed wind on
her lips, never have stood in command at the bow of a ship
as she crested the waves, never have experienced *anything* like
the adventures she'd had over the years.

Lynnette had not chosen her course willingly, would not
have wished for circumstances to create her existence as they
had, but she did revel in the independence her unusual position
had given her. Not one woman in a thousand ever got the
opportunity to control her destiny as the pirate Lynnette Blackthorne had become did now; nor had they the privilege of

bowing to no one as she did . . . And by damn, no silver-eyed *merchant* was going to take that away from her!

The pirate arranged to be wherever *he* was not for the whole of the next month. How she managed it, Daniel was never quite sure. Oh, he caught glimpses of her as she went from this task to that, but she so skillfully avoided him that he got no more of a chance to speak to her than to utter a curt word of greeting before she breezed past him with barely a nod. She left the house very early and returned very late.

What jobs occupied the pirate he did not know, but wherever he searched for her, she was busy somewhere else. If he looked in the village, she was at the cove; if he sought her out at the pool, she was off inspecting the goods stockpiled in the warehouse on the opposite end of the island. She ate before or after he did, although at the same table, and he never caught up with the wench.

Daniel tried to accept the situation as it was. Escape was impossible with the rest of the pirates back on No-name Island, dogging his very step, watching him night and day. His plan had hinged on Lynnette's being his primary guard, and his own charm lulling her into laxity. But she was having no part of him, that was clear. He tried valiantly to accept that his plan had failed, that he would never taste Lynnette's sighs as she writhed under him, would never discover what demons possessed the woman who had come to obsess his every thought. It was well nigh impossible. All day long he had nothing to occupy him save fantasies of her lissome body and fierce tongue, and his nights were much, much worse.

He listened for the sound of her footsteps across the hall, and when they finally came—usually in the wee hours of the morning—he drove himself into a frenzy imagining her stripping for bed. Did she sleep naked? he wondered heatedly. How would she look standing nude in the candlelight, her fiery hair loose all the way down to her sweet round buttocks? Would her smooth, golden skin reflect the light? Would her rosy-tipped breasts point eagerly upward as she stretched lazily? He could almost see them, the hard nubs just begging for his mouth to suckle . . . Daniel's pillow became flattened from repeated frustrated pounding.

He thought of marching into her room—breaking in the

door if he had to—and tossing her onto that great huge bed
of hers for a night of bliss the haughty pirate would not soon
forget. How many other lovers had shared that bed with her?
he fumed. Why should he be excluded from the list (a long
one, he was sure) of men who were granted Mistress Thorne's
favors? He took no notice of the fact that during his enforced
stay on No-name, no other, heavier, footsteps had ever accompanied hers to her chambers.

He thought too of the day Simon would arrive, bringing
the ransom with him. Daniel had gambled on successfully seducing the pirate queen before that day came, but he had lost.
Of course, he had never dreamed that the pirate's will would
prove so strong in the face of his renowned charm. By damn,
to have so little effect on a woman when he was going all out
in his efforts to woo her was no little blow to his confidence.
It seemed he might never taste the full measure of Lynnette's
fiery passion, since he couldn't even get her alone long enough
to blink, let alone kiss.

Daniel had tried many times to catch her, but always she
eluded him. It seemed to him sometimes as though she were
not even on the island, except for the occasional flash of her
red-gold braid he caught out of the corner of his eye as she
disappeared into the jungle. It was crazy, but her luck in avoiding him on the five-mile-long island was uncanny.

That luck ran out at the end of the next month, even as the
wait for Daniel's ransom to arrive neared its close. Some of
the pirates were clearing out patches of undergrowth that had
crept up toward the house when Daniel returned for the noon
meal. Georges always left platters out on a table on the verandah for his pirate employer and her captive; a new practice
since she'd begun to avoid the young man and one that upset
the cook, for now his fine creations frequently became cold
before either sat down to eat.

Personally, the chef did not care why Captain Thorne refused to entertain her prisoner as she had in the beginning, but
it angered him that his talents were being ignored in favor of
indulging petty emotional disputes. In fact, several times in
the past weeks he'd seen Thorne heading toward the verandah
as he was setting out the dishes, only to stop and abruptly turn

away into the foliage when she caught sight of the tall merchant captain.

It was so childish! Georges clucked his tongue with disapproval. This was not what he had come to expect of the woman who had taken him on as ship's cook so casually and decisively. To run from one's own table, simply to keep from having to speak to one man, especially a man whom she could simply order from her sight if she wished to dine alone! *Bon Dieu!* And that man took his own sweet time, the cook noticed. As though he were waiting for her patience to run out . . . When he finally gave up and left, soon enough there would come the pirate, striding along as though she had planned to eat dinner at three o'clock when it had been waiting since twelve. Georges could swear he'd heard her stomach rumbling all the way from the jungle fifty feet away. Stupid and wasteful, that's what this whole business was, if you asked him, which of course nobody did.

But Lynnette couldn't lock Bradley up as she wished to because she'd promised him the run of the island, and, hard though it might be on *her* freedom, she would both avoid him and keep to that bargain. Well, she sighed to herself, at least today she'd gotten to table first. She knew he was trying everything in his power to encounter her, and also knew that since she'd come late and he early yesterday, today he would likely try late. So she was free to eat—not just grab some cold meat and a slab of bread and leave as she had been doing for the last few days. With a small sound of pleasure, she sat down and tucked into her food. Thank God it was still warm.

Daniel had given up on trying to guess her movements. Now he was just going to eat and then maybe roam a bit on the island. Not that he hadn't already seen all there was to see a hundred times over, but what else was there to do? His tan had deepened to a deep, rich golden hue from basking on the sun-drenched beaches, and he'd swum and explored until he couldn't muster even an iota of enthusiasm for either activity anymore. He'd tried tracking his pirate a hundred times, too, until he realized that as long as she didn't want to be found, he'd not find her.

She'd had help in that department, or he was sure he'd have pinned her down long ago. Whenever he felt he was close, one of the other pirates blocked his path, coming out of the jungle silently to encounter him, some with idle banter and feral smiles, some with less subtle warnings to stay away. He'd spent some time with the first mate, who seemed at least willing to speak to him, but even Harry would not go against the express orders of his captain and help the peacock find her. He chatted with the merchant in a friendly yet guarded fashion, but felt obviously constrained not to interfere.

Harry, as it turned out, was quite sure nature would do the job for him, and was enjoying watching the scene unfold in the meanwhile. His captain jumped at every sound, fled her captive as though *he* were the guard and she the escaped prisoner, and generally scowled at everyone. It was quite amusing. The lad, on the other hand, looked murderous. The mate could see immense frustration written on his every feature. But he was not about to sit his captain down and explain that though he didn't know what had happened while the crew was gone, he had a pretty damn good idea, and it was plain as sin that you couldn't tease a man like Bradley and not eventually face the consequences. Nay, it was too much fun to play innocent spectator instead.

Harry very much wanted to see the two together—oh, aye, that he did indeed!—but he'd begun to fear the situation would not reach the boiling point before Bradley's ransom came and the merchant was set free. Today, however, as he supervised the men clearing out the growth from the open space around Thorne's villa, he felt in his bones something would happen.

He glanced at Lynnette, eating dinner with a calm aspect that was so clearly forced that he wondered how she could remain still in her chair from nerves, and then at the doorway behind her that led into the house. And at Captain Bradley filling that doorway. Smothering a chuckle, he turned back to his task.

Lynnette felt the sudden hush descend over her men and let her knife clatter to the table, overcome with foreboding. Slowly she turned her head to see what they were all looking at—something behind her, although she already knew what (or rather *who*) it was. And then she saw him, dark and handsome in the doorway, a surprised look on his face that no doubt mirrored the one she knew she wore on her own. Sudden fear, desire, and fury welled up all together, and the pirate half rose from her chair to flee before she realized what she was doing.

Running away? Her? A woman who'd never known fear in her life—never avoided a fight when she could take it up? Nay! It was enough. This was her table, devil take it, her house, and *her* damned island! No foppish peacock was going to make her forget that fact again, especially with most of her men avidly looking on! Anger won decisively, and she plopped back down into her seat and glared at the man who'd forced her to sneak around her own home base like a recalcitrant child awaiting punishment. She'd been a fool, but she'd not be one any longer. She could handle this, she told herself, no matter that her blood raced at the very sight of his magnificent physique. God rot it, did he have to look so good?

She cursed herself for not anticipating the possibility that he wouldn't follow the schedule she'd blithely assumed he would. If she hadn't been so preoccupied with the news Harry had gleaned, she'd never have been so stupidly careless. But one of their informers had sailed over from the mainland with vital information a week ago, and the knowledge of what was coming up had occupied most of her thoughts since then. The fact was that one of Lord Roger's ships was due to sail into nearby West Indian waters in two days' time, and her attention had been focused on plans for the taking of the ship, instead of, for once, her captive. Now all thought of anything *but* the disturbing, infuriating man fled.

As Daniel came toward her, Lynnette saw that the Caribbean sun had done wonders for his complexion. Clean shaven, wearing his dark breeches and a thin white cotton shirt that was unbuttoned halfway down his smooth, muscled chest, he had grown darkly bronzed and appeared more fit than she'd yet seen him. His hair had grown a bit, coming down past his shoulders in shiny black waves that ate the sunlight, and his stance was tall and proud. She tensed, feeling herself grow unwontedly warm.

Uninvited, Captain Bradley sat down across from the woman he'd tried so hard to find for an entire month. What luck to catch her now! He could see that she wanted to escape, could sense it in the way she sat so stiffly and challenged him with her eyes to say aught of her avoidance. He met that challenge; as angry at her frustrating games as she was to be caught in them.

"Well met, Captain Thorne," he greeted with heavy sarcasm. "I hope now that our paths have finally crossed, you will give up this silly pretension of hiding from me. I know there is nothing so urgent here on No-name that takes up so much of your time that you cannot even spare a moment to speak with your prisoner."

His words were a goad she could not resist, prickly as she was in his presence. "Hiding!" she fairly shrieked. "Hiding from you? I? As though I feared you!" She forced a scathing laugh. "Oh, Peacock, you flatter your terrible aspect too much!"

"Methinks 'tis not my fearsome appearance you are afraid of, but my intimate touch." He smirked as she blanched white at the insinuation, knowing she feared her crew overhearing. He continued mercilessly, weeks of frustrated desire and unrelenting boredom making him harsh. "After all," he said silkily, "is it not true that only when you come too close to surrender in my arms do you run away? I'm sure," he said smoothly, seeing her face go from pure white to furious red and enjoying his newfound power over her emotions, "that were it not for our agreement, you would have locked me in that cell again for fear of your own lust! But then, you possess the key, so of course the temptation to steal in at night and ravish my poor body might prove too great. Not that I would have minded—"

"Bastard!" she screamed, flinging herself to her feet and heaving the table over at him. "You dare speak such lies to me! Defend yourself!" With that, Lynnette whipped out her rapier and leveled it at Bradley, who sat, quite calmly, wiping his breeches with a linen napkin. He seemed most fascinated with the dark water stain slowly spreading across his leg.

"You must be jesting, Captain," he said mildly, not even looking up from what he was doing.

He wasn't even taking her seriously! All the while he'd been taunting her, he'd spoken in a relaxed, casual tone that was calculated to infuriate, and now the bastard wouldn't even fight! Her rage mounted till she could barely see. "Damn you, draw your sword! Captain Thorne bears no such insult without reprisal!"

"Captain," he chided, still without lifting his face to meet her white-hot glare, "may I remind you that I *have* no sword? And, you know, you are causing quite a scene. Your men"— and he waved at the pirates staring unabashedly at the confrontation—"are all agape at your regrettable theatricality."

Unable to help it, Lynnette glanced over the verandah railing. Her men were indeed intent upon her every action. They'd heard her challenge; she couldn't back down now. Nor did she want to. Never had she been so insulted and angered by any man! Bradley had never shown this side of himself to her before—he was definitely nearing the end of his patience— dangerous in spite of his deceptively lazy posture. In the past, he'd always been easygoing and relaxed, even if his jests were too racy to be acceptable. But now, masked behind his quiet tone and averted eyes, she saw a resurgence of the man she'd first seen furiously challenging overwhelming odds for the possession of his ship . . . He might be handling it differently, but the anger was plain to see. And Lynnette, reckless and angered herself, didn't care.

"Harry," she called loudly. "Fetch my other rapier for the prisoner. We shall have a duel." Turning to her enraging opponent, she growled, "Unless you prefer a different choice of weapon. It is, of course, your prerogative to choose since 'twas I that challenged you. But you *will* fight. For the sake of honor, I demand satisfaction."

Only then did Daniel look in her direction, and nearly swallowed his tongue in surprise, for he saw that the pirate's legs were almost entirely bare! The remnants of black breeches clung closely to her hips and buttocks, but they had been cut off at the tops of her slim, shapely thighs. He gulped, his groin receiving such a rush of hot blood that he thought he would split the laces of his breeches—if he didn't split *hers* first. And then he knew he would fight—for a price.

"If your pride demands it," he said slowly, finally meeting her smoldering emerald eyes as she received her sword, "I will fight you, but only on certain conditions."

"And what might those be?" she demanded sharply.

"One: that the duel be only to first blood—I doubt I could force myself to commit such a crime against my own eyes as to permanently mar your lovely flesh." He raked her scantily clad from deliberately up and down with his hot eyes. "In the unlikely event that you manage to best me, you must realize that it would not be to your advantage to ransom a corpse. My partner would not take kindly to receiving a dead man in return for his hard-won gold. As I see it, there is no advantage to senselessly killing one another when honor can be satisfied with less."

Lynnette wanted to laugh in his face. He, best *her*? No man had ever come close! But the ransom—she'd gone through much trouble to secure it, and it would truly be a shame to lose it now. Honor would indeed be satisfied at first blood. "Agreed. Are there more of your 'conditions,' or is that all?" She was clearly sneering at his prevarication.

"Yes, as a matter of fact, there are," he replied, unperturbed. "I would wager on the outcome. If you win, you may collect the boon of your choice—if I win, the same."

Anything? she mused. Her original anger was cooling, but Lynnette still wanted the fight just as much as she had in the first flash of rage. 'Twould finally and irrevocably cement her control over her prisoner—for once she bested him she was sure he'd not be a worry to her anymore. Having proven to herself that he was no match for her prowess with steel, she would prove herself strong enough to withstand the intriguing man in *every* respect. And having firmly commanded his admiration for her abilities, he would be impudent no longer.

Well, why not wager? But what could she possibly want from him? Then it came to her in a sudden flash—something that had been niggling at the back of her mind since their first shipboard encounter. "I want the name of your half brother," she said aloud.

"Fine," he agreed, "although I have told you it will avail you naught. My request too is simple. I want a kiss. A real, full-on-the-lips kiss freely given from you to me—with no false accusations to follow it afterward."

"Fine," she assented recklessly, for she'd fought with similar stakes before. Certainly if she'd lost any of those long-ago battles in her first days on Tortuga, she'd have been tossed on her back in a trice. But she had never lost. "Take up your sword and follow me."

And Captain Bradley, equally sure that he would be the victor in this decidedly unequal contest, did as he was bidden.

CHAPTER TWELVE

*T*HEY FACED each other across a sandy stretch of beach near the main harbor. It was a perfect place to duel, for there were no rocks to trip over, nor high ground to give one the edge over the other. Daniel had removed his boots for better traction. Lynnette had already been barefoot—and bare-legged—because of the heat of the day. The combat area was marked by one of the pirates by means of a large rectangle drawn with sword point in the sand. The sun shone down equally on both of them. He had to admit the pirate was fair, for when she'd stepped into the ring, he'd seen her calculate the angle of the sunlight, then position herself so that when he entered opposite her, neither caught the light in their eyes. As he tested the balance of the rapier Harry had handed him, finding it suitable to his reach and finely tempered, he wondered what other tricks the pirate wench knew, and which she *would* use.

He looked at her in the shimmering August heat. A braid filled with roses and gold hung down her back, a white silk shirt open at the throat and tied at her small waist outlined her torso, and tight black cut-off breeches molded hips that men would kill to press against their own. Her legs, long and slim and firmly muscled down to her finely turned ankles, revealed the fact that she'd spent her life in exercise—and that she'd gone bare-limbed before was evident from the golden tan color that graced them. He scanned her perfect body for a place to blood her that would not leave a permanent mark.

Whether or not he *could* cut his opponent he never doubted, and at this moment his anger with her was such that he no longer cared that he might have to hurt the woman. Of course, he wouldn't wound her severely, or even really painfully, but Daniel reasoned that a little nick might be considered no more than proper reprisal for her constant tormenting behavior.

Besides, had she been a *normal* woman, playing by the rules that women usually did, this ridiculous situation would never have come up. After all, hadn't it been Thorne herself who had goaded him into this fight? Well, though she be female, she was going to learn that if she wanted to play at men's games, she'd best be prepared to take her licks like a man. He was perfectly sure she'd soon regret her foolish decision to try to fight him.

Lynnette was reminding herself to pull her blows so as not to kill the peacock. She'd not much practice in these mock duels that ended before their natural conclusion came; namely when one of the combatants no longer posed any sort of threat at all. But she'd promised this time to go according to his rules, and that was what she'd do.

The crew of the *Maiden's Revenge* crowded around the tense figures who stood so still, staring at one another assessingly. The men, totally without shame, began sizing up the duelists and wagering among themselves with cheerful bloodthirstiness as to the outcome. They'd all overheard the terms the two captains had practically shouted at each other, and so it was merely with relaxed curiosity that they placed their bets. After all, no one was going to end up bleeding their life away on the hot sand today, so there was no need for them to be concerned about what was really just one more fight.

The men indulged in such bouts frequently, both to keep their skill with steel honed sharp while they were on land and to settle disputes, for their captain forbade them to kill each other over petty issues, and supervised the matches strictly. More than once Thorne had been forced to intervene when tempers grew too hot, but on the whole the method she'd imposed on them to keep relative peace was quite satisfactory.

The only titillation the men received from this match, in fact, came from the knowledge that there was definitely something out of the ordinary going on in their captain's relations with this particular prisoner. The topic of Captain Bradley and his strange effect on their mistress's behavior had indeed been of great interest to them of late when they got together in the evenings over mugs of grog and ale. There was not a sailor aboard the pirate vessel who hadn't noticed how tightly wound up the captain was. She'd snapped at men for no reason at all, stalked off suddenly in the middle of conversations, and, on the whole, been more distracted than could be accounted for merely by her quest for revenge. They were used to their leader being a woman of sharp temper and grim moods, but lately she had become even more so than before. It was obvious to even the meanest intellect that most of her darkling looks were directed toward her captive. Perhaps, they thought, the outcome of this fight would shed some light on the situation.

Harry, standing close to the ring in his capacity as referee, was the only one of them to place his wager on Bradley, a fact that caused no few of the others to stare incredulously at him. The rest of the buccaneers were betting only on how long it would take their captain to defeat the merchant, feeling the outcome to be a foregone conclusion. What had gotten into the first mate? Betting against his own captain! Damned lucky Thorne hadn't heard him playing traitor—she'd have his balls for it, she would! But indeed the captain was too engrossed in taking the measure of her opponent to pay attention to their wagering. So deep was her concentration that they might not even have been there for all the notice she took of them.

Daniel, having the odd sensation that the world had truly gone topsy-turvy to place him in this bizarre situation, felt obliged to note the circumstances as the tension grew. "This is not exactly the most proper duel procedure I've ever seen," he said dryly.

"I suppose you are distressed by the lack of a surgeon and seconds?" she asked mockingly. The pirates snickered at her wit. "Harry will officiate, but we need no seconds, and the terms of our match—if both of us have the skill to abide by them—" and here her voice suggested that she was confident that *she* did, but not nearly so sure of him, "make it unnecessary for a leech to be present. *I* do not cheat, and if *you* do, my men will immediately have you killed. Besides, would you choose your second from among men loyal to me?" She grinned tauntingly. "There is no other kind of man here, and although no one will interfere if you play by those rules you are so worried about, stray but a little from form and, I assure you, you won't last long."

Daniel was getting damned tired of her endless threats. "Understood," he said through gritted teeth, wanting to wring the wench's neck. He could hardly believe his situation; here he was quibbling over niceties with people for whom the sword was the only form of justice, standing barefoot and tousled on a pink sand beach in the Caribbean with filthy pirates on all sides, and he was about to fight a duel with the most beautiful woman he'd ever met. And everyone expected her to win.

He heard the command to stand ready. By reflex, he went into position. The woman across from him nodded curtly, saluted him with raised blade. He returned the gesture, inwardly fighting the urge to laugh at the mental image of his partner Simon finding out about this little episode. The whole situation was farcical. His reach was far longer, his muscles *much* stronger, and his skill, gained from years of exhaustive drills and actual battles in His Majesty's Royal Navy, surely greater than this mere *girl's*. He had no doubt that the extremely unbalanced match would be over in seconds.

Ten minutes later as he panted for breath and blinked the sweat out of his eyes, Daniel's belief had changed dramatically. He hadn't been able to *touch* the virago who fought with such swift and deadly skill. She fought silently, determinedly, and totally unconventionally. Oh, it wasn't as if she played dirty—not in the least—but he could swear that the moves she pulled, the thrusts she nearly speared him with, were not the type learned in a gentlemen's book of fencing etiquette—nor in the navy. He was hard put to figure out how to block her strikes in time to save his skin. What Thorne lacked in height and mass, she more than made up for in speed and agility. Yet truly, her blows were no lightweight's; they rang from his blade time and again, drawing sparks.

Had they fought with cutlass instead of rapier, he would have had the edge, for skill was of little importance in bouts with the heavy, crude weapon. Made with a thick, curving blade, cutlass fights usually involved two-handed swings and mere brute strength. The wench would never have had the endurance to keep bashing at him and still keep her guard up in that case, whereas with the slim, strong Toledo steel rapiers, skill was the most important factor.

After the first few feinting strikes they'd exchanged in testing one another, Lynnette had taken the offensive. Daniel, when it came down to it, found himself reluctant after a lifetime of being drilled into protecting the fairer sex to actively attempt the opposite. He also wanted the opportunity to see what sort of fight she'd offer, so that he could then plan his own accordingly. There was no use humiliating the wench too much, was there? But within the first moments he discovered that he'd vastly misjudged Thorne's skill, and he realized that, hard as it was to believe, she was every bit as good with a sword as she'd claimed. He found himself barely able to parry her lightning thrusts in his bemusement.

Damn. This was not amusing anymore. He was, if not losing, at least doing poorly by his own standards. Always in the past he had easily overcome his opponents within a few minutes, for he favored the sport of fencing even above and beyond what had been required of him in his long stint in the military, and had devoted himself to mastering it. To lose now, to a *woman*, was unthinkable. He decided to get serious, and took the offensive for himself.

Steel rang off steel as he thrust suddenly, causing Lynnette's eyes to light with fire and approval. "Ah, good, Peacock!" she said, a little short of breath. "I see you've decided to fight after all."

"It seems, Captain, that I have again underestimated you," he replied ruefully.

Again, she was surprised by his willingness to alter his preconceived notions, once he'd been shown why he ought to. But she wasn't about to let that change anything. "Yes," she smiled nastily, "you have." And lunged—only to draw back when she was immediately countered.

"Perhaps, my pretty merchant, I have done the same."

Lynnette really was impressed by his skill—for no other man had ever yet lasted this long against her, and though she concealed it well, she was beginning to tire. That he gave a better fight than she'd been offered in years exhilarated her in spite of—or possibly because of—the fact that it scared her a great deal. But cold sense told her to end this quickly, in spite of her unexpected enjoyment of the bout, before he could wear her down further. If she lost . . .

Daniel began to think he might even lose this match, unbelievable as it sounded to reason and all that he'd ever been taught. For though they circled and clashed and spun and blocked, and neither had yet lowered their guard long enough for the other to be able to draw blood, he had begun to believe she was just slightly better than he—more controlled, more accurate, faster. But he wasn't about to lose—not when the prize for winning was so great.

She came at him, and instead of simply deflecting her sword, he met her head-on, blades screeching as his ran the length of hers to lock at the hilt. They were a mere foot from touching with more than steel. She braced herself with legs spread to keep her balance, for now, unless she was careful, his superior strength would overcome her skill and he would simply bend her over until she fell backward into the sand.

She felt a tremor of anxiety. They were too close—eye to eye and mouths so near that their gasping breath mingled. It reminded her of the last time they'd been this close—and of how different the circumstances had been . . . Lynnette suddenly knew that if she didn't break the bind of their weapons, she was going to lose her composure *and* the duel.

She realized, and wondered if he did too, that this battle was about more than mere insults. It was about who was going to win the war of wills that had raged since the cursed moment she'd first laid eyes on him, fighting alone on the deck of a smoking ship for his life and his livelihood.

Taking a great chance just as she saw Daniel's eyes darken with intent to finish it, Lynnette jumped back suddenly, pushing off with her sword. She dropped into a roll, crossing the sand in a tangle of arms, legs, and hair to lengthen the distance between them. Coming to her feet a yard away, she reassessed the situation. What she had just done was not precisely legal in fencing, and certainly not a move she would have used unless it was completely necessary—which, she judged, it had been.

In close encounters, she had a definite disadvantage, for both his strength *and* his presence could overset her, and she was positive he knew it. She had seen his intense stare, and knew he was controlling his reaction to her a great deal better than she restrained her own to him. It galled her that he should pick just now to be immune to her charms, when, up until this point, it had been he who, with his damned randiness, had caused all the trouble that created their present stand-off. If he was as savvy as she thought he was, he'd take every advantage her difficulty both in keeping up with him and keeping away from him offered . . .

He did. The pirate was made to give ground again and again as he repeatedly attempted to close with her, forcing her to give up the offensive in the process. She fended off his thrusts and crab-stepped back and forth, straining to find a way to change the situation. Now she was not above attempting to maneuver him into facing the sun, nor any number of other distracting little tricks she normally kept in reserve for untenable situations, for this, she judged, was about as bad a circumstance as she ever wanted to be in. No matter that this wasn't a fight to the death—her crew's respect was in the balance. Worse, her self-respect, not to mention her very control over what happened in her life, seemed to depend on the outcome of this match. Because if he won, she could no longer force him to do her will except by threat of the pirates backing her. Captain Thorne needed no bodyguards to enforce her wishes, for that was how she'd built her reputation—not on the strength of those who stood behind her, but on her own skill and strength of both body and will.

Her men, she noticed, had grown silent. They'd been cheering her on, but as the duel became drawn out and she didn't fulfill their expectations by soundly defeating the peacock, a profound hush fell over the discomfited men. One or two fingered knives, but at a sharp glare from the first mate, reluctantly subsided.

And then she saw it. The peacock's guard was just slightly lowered, and it seemed he hadn't noticed he was vulnerable. If she could only . . . Lynnette moved in, realizing only too late that she had been tricked as he whipped up his sword at the last second, taking advantage of her surprise to close with her. She was trapped for the moment. She couldn't pull off the same evasive maneuver she'd used last time, for without the element of surprise, it was a simple move to block. They faced each other, arms locked as they struggled. She felt her forearms tremble.

She knew ways to get out of this—if only he didn't detect her purpose in time to prevent her. The eyes gave away intent all too often. Unable to resist the urge, she looked up anyway, telling herself she wanted to see what *he* would do—and was caught by those burning silver orbs, darkened to tarnished pewter. But not with anger.

Her breath, labored as it was, stuck in her chest. She felt paralyzed as he slowly ran his searing gaze along the contours of her figure, one corner of his chiseled mouth quirked in an approving smile. It was as if his glance were hypnotic, for she could not seem to do aught but stand there idiotically as he continued his insulting perusal. All thoughts of countermoves flew from her mind, and it was all she could do to maintain hold of her blade against his.

He didn't give an inch. Still not breaking the pressure of his rapier against hers, he glanced down again and then back up into her emerald eyes a bare foot from his own. And then he spoke. "You have exquisite legs, Captain," he murmured low so that only she could hear, all the while increasing the pressure on her tired arms to keep his blade from biting into her flesh. "I can't wait to feel them wrapped around my waist when I take you and make you mine."

It was a dirty move, but one he didn't regret for a moment, for the shock of his blatantly crude words, as well as the flood of erotic images they brought forth, made her loosen her hold for an instant. It was only a slight lessening, but enough for him. Daniel wrenched his arm sideways, jerking the pirate's sword out of her hand and letting it spin away onto the sand out of her reach. Then, knowing she'd not concede defeat unless he left nothing to chance, he quickly brought his sword back on its controlled arc and whipped the very tip of the blade across the fleshy part of her upper arm. A few beads of deep crimson sprang to light against the white of her torn shirt.

Lynnette stood still in shock, her breath coming out of her lungs in short gasps. It was impossible—the peacock could not have bested her! But he had, as the sting of her arm told her, and the sight of his unmarred body before her grinning in satisfaction. That he'd won by foul means she discounted—men always tried to distract her with crude insinuations when she fought them—but that she'd allowed his words to *affect* her, that she had even fleetingly entertained the image of doing as he said . . .

Harry stepped into the ring, years of guarding his captain's back drawing him forward instinctively. The look on his lass's face made him worry if perhaps he'd been too flippant in thinking all would come out right between her and the merchant if he let nature take its course. She was pale and had a look of dazed shock about her that caused all his protective instincts to come to the fore. He had not seen her look that lost since she'd first come to him, begging for his aid seven years ago.

But Lynnette was not that far gone this time. She waved him back, her brain functioning enough to realize that interference at this point would qualify as reneging on her bet. She continued to watch her captive steadily. He stared back impassively, his expression of triumph wiped clear of his features as he realized the gravity of the loss she'd suffered. Finally, she could stand the tension no longer. "You have won," she said heavily. "Take your wager, then, and be done with it." She straightened her back proudly, wrapping the shreds of her dignity about her like a mantle. He could almost see the wall of ice return to shroud her after the brief glimpse he'd had of her vulnerability. It struck his heart unexpectedly, and almost, he wished that he had not defeated her, that he had left her untouched as she had been before. Almost.

"Not here, I think," he said. "A bit of privacy would be more appropriate to the nature of our bet." He glanced meaningfully at the pirates milling about them. "Will you not accompany me to the villa?" His steely voice left no room for debate. She must do as he asked, or lose her honor. Yet for a moment she wasn't sure that was too heavy a price to pay. She feared to be alone with him now nearly more than she feared the condemning stares her men would give her if she did not fulfill her bargain. But she'd never expected to lose! Too, what would her men think if she went inside with him now? She'd never be able to command their respect in the future—or her own—if she blatantly went to kiss her prisoner in the dimness of the house. Irresolute, Lynnette simply looked helplessly at him.

Daniel seemed to understand, though whether he felt any sympathy for her plight was debatable. He went to her, and before she knew what he planned to do, he had scooped her over his shoulder and started off toward the villa. She barely had time to shout her rage before she was carried out of sight of her men. Captain Thorne's last sight of her crew was their faces as they doubled over with mirth at her embarrassing predicament.

CHAPTER THIRTEEN

*T*HEY REACHED the house. Lynnette had given up on struggling with Daniel, realizing that it was even more undignified to do so than not. Just inside the door, he bent over, putting her back on her feet. She swayed, dizzy for a moment as the blood rushed back out of her head. He caught her by her upper arms, making her hiss as his hand brushed her cut.

"Have you any bandages?" he asked quietly.

"Any what?" she questioned absently, her mind on other, more immediate issues.

"Bandages," he repeated patiently. "Your arm is still bleeding a little, though I don't think it will scar."

"Aye, in there." She indicated his room with a distracted wave. "In the linen chest." She was torn between fury and fear: fury because of the humiliation he had caused her in front of her men by carrying her off with her bottom in the air, and fear because he'd had the right as victor. She'd been bested, and now she had no choice but to accept that, or lose her honor by reneging. And, truly, the only way she *could* stop him from taking what he'd won from her was to call for aid. He'd proven himself stronger than she, if not in sword-fighting, then in keeping his emotions under lock and key.

For, as Lynnette reasoned it, it had not been superior skill with a blade that had won the bout for Daniel (indeed, she conceded only that they were about evenly matched) but his ability to play mental games and win. In that, he was the undisputed master. And, to her mind, such a skill was far more dangerous than simple strength. There were ways to get around an opponent stronger than oneself, as she well knew. What she didn't know was how to deal with one who held the upper hand when it came to a battle of wills.

And now, however briefly, she must surrender to him. Worse than that, she must *kiss* him. It would have been better if he had merely asked to claim a kiss from her. In that case, passivity on her part would clearly show him that he'd won nothing in truth. Her soul would remain her own, untouched. But he had specifically stipulated that *she* kiss *him*. The pirate couldn't imagine how she would bring herself to do it.

As these thoughts raced through Lynnette's troubled mind, Daniel had been leading her toward his chamber. They stood now in the doorway. He ushered her in, then pressed her to sit on the edge of the bed. Mentally, she prepared herself to face his gloating expression, and turned her head to see him. But he had turned from her to the chest across the room, and was rummaging through the contents. Relief, confusion, and a strange sort of disappointment speared through her in quick confusion. Relief, for the delay of the inevitable. Confusion because he was not acting as she had expected, was instead obviously going to tend her slight wound before he came to take his reward.

Why should *he* care that she was bleeding? Hadn't he caused the hurt in the first place? Most men would be demanding payment right now, instead of ripping clean linens to bandage the loser's arm. But the peacock (who looked anything *but* a vain peacock in his plain white shirt and black breeches) was definitely not most men. Her disappointment was something she refused to think about. It could *not* be because Daniel didn't seem eager to claim his forfeit!

She scrutinized his face for signs of smugness but found none, seeing only intent concentration as he bent close to examine her arm. His hair brushed her shoulder as he came up close, and she could smell the clean masculine scent of his sweat. "You don't have to do this," she said between clenched teeth as he peeled her sleeve away. "I've suffered far worse than this puny scratch and lived to tell of it."

"But I have never wounded one so fair before, and I would see it taken care of so it will not leave another scar on your sweet flesh," he returned. "In this climate, the wound could fester and become serious quickly."

She emitted a noise that sounded like a snort of disgust, but made no other comment as he went to the washbowl and wetted a cloth to wash off the blood that streaked her arm. She was tense, nervous, waiting for the ax to fall. And he wasn't helping by sitting so close. Daniel had come back to her side almost instantly, and perched so near their thighs touched. She remembered the last time they'd touched. She hissed, not entirely from pain, grabbing at the cloth as he tried gently to wipe away the blood that concealed the extent of the cut. "I can do it!"

"I'm sorry I hurt you, Lynnette. It was not my wish to do so," he murmured. She wasn't sure if he meant now or during their fight, but she didn't answer, remaining stubbornly silent in the face of his contrition. He let her take the cloth, watched as she tried to reach the affected spot with her other hand. Since it was high up, near her shoulder, she couldn't see it properly. She muttered a curse, craning her neck. "Let me," he said. "It's easier this way." His voice was oddly gentle, his hand steady as he held it out for the linen square. She angrily slapped it back into his palm, not looking in his eyes.

Daniel worked quietly, his own rangy frame as taut with pent-up feeling as the woman he tended. At this distance, her presence was like a brand thrown on the ready timber of his desire. He could smell her, touch her, almost taste her luscious musky womanly flavor on his tongue. Wisps of her red-gold hair that had worked loose from her braid tickled his face. Her firm, naked thigh was pressed close to his own. The urge to pull her down on the bed and make love to her until she begged for more was almost irresistible. But he continued to concentrate on the task at hand by sheer willpower. It wasn't easy. Her breasts rose and fell rapidly, outlined by the thin white shirt she wore, bare inches from his seeking fingertips. Was she feeling the same anticipation as he, or was her quick breathing only a result of her hatred for him?

Whatever Lynnette was feeling, it wasn't hate. As before during their duel, the cursedly virile merchant's nearness was playing havoc with her senses. She couldn't allow that to continue. He'd won the duel, but she swore she wasn't going to give him another victory! While he finished cleaning the wound and tied a clean strip of linen around her upper arm, the beginnings of a smile turned up the corners of her mouth as a scheme formed in her mind. Captain Bradley no doubt expected her to be grudging about giving up her due to him. Well, she'd show him who was in control here. She'd give him such a kiss as would unravel all his stitches, then coolly back off and claim them even. Yes! she thought excitedly, it would work, and it would give her back the ground she'd lost by coming unglued during their bout. She'd show him she had more tricks up her sleeve than he could counter. *If* her hastily concocted plan didn't backfire on her . . .

Turning to face the tall rogue, she took a deep breath and offered him a dazzling smile. "I'm ready, Peacock. Are you?" She spoke with a false confidence, pretending to be completely unaffected by the feel of the gentle fingers that lingered caressingly on her skin.

"More than ready." He was bemused by the sudden resurgence of the pirate's confidence, as well as by the power of her smile. What had made her change so suddenly? He didn't think he really cared when she leaned over, bringing her lips close. "But your neck will get a crick in it if you lean over like that," he said huskily. "Why don't you sit here instead?" He patted his lap.

For an instant, Lynnette hesitated, but she quickly recovered, realizing the position would render him even more vulnerable to her untested charms. She might not have much personal experience with the art of love, but certainly she'd *seen* enough to last a lifetime. Didn't the doxies in the taverns usually seat themselves on their customers' laps? She sent what she hoped was a seductive glance in Bradley's direction, excited and nervous because of what she was about to do. Playing with fire was a dangerous game.

She was right about the look. Daniel could barely get a breath after she sent those emerald eyes roaming across his hard body, heating a flaming response in him. He could hardly believe this ice woman had suddenly turned to molten lava right before his eyes. But he wasn't about to question it. And when she sat herself down on his lap, he feared he'd never be able to question anything again, for his brain had turned to mush.

Lynnette placed her hands on either side of his head and plunged right in. Her kiss was deep, powerful, and full-blown, as he'd requested. Her lips molded to his fiercely, her tongue boldly outlining the shape of his sensual lips, then dipping inside his surprised but more than willing mouth. She kissed him with pent-up emotion, whether of rage or fear or passionate longing he could not guess, and the kiss went straight to Daniel's head like the rum the pirates drank so freely. She tasted of honey and sweetness and desire, and he felt nigh to drowning in the maelstrom. He returned the caress with equal fervor, his arms coming around her waist and neck to hold her firmly right where she was. His tongue forayed out to meet hers, greedily devouring all she was offering and more. His head spun and his mind could not reconcile the confusing images his pirate woman was sending. One minute she was cold as an iceberg, the next she was kissing him with enough fire to incinerate his control instantly. That, however, was his last thought for some time, as desire swept him into its stormy arms.

Lynnette realized dimly that her plan had, indeed, backfired. She'd intended to kiss her captive only until his victory turned to ashes in his mouth, losing all savor when she coldly pulled back and announced her debt paid in full. Now she knew with a sense of despair that she had only proved him the winner twice in the same day, for she could not seem to break away from the ecstasy of drinking in his kisses. He'd taken control of the kiss just as he had the duel, silently proving that she was not immune to the temptation he represented. But the realization did not help her any, for as his hand stroked its way up her neck to cradle her by the nape and pull her yet closer, she could do nothing to prevent it. Indeed, she found herself pushing her fingers into his thick black hair to tangle in the glossy locks and keep him anchored to her aching mouth.

She needed. As his tongue dueled fiercely with her own, that was all the pirate could think. She moaned softly, sucking his lower lip between her teeth to nibble and worship with her teeth and tongue. He responded with a soul-devouring kiss, slanting his mouth to cover hers more fully.

"God, Lynn, I want you more than any woman I've ever known!" groaned Daniel, breaking the fusion of their lips for a gasping moment. Then he pulled her left leg across his lap so that she was straddling him. His arms about her were all that kept her from tumbling off the bed when she arched her back so that he could sear her neck with his fiery lips and tongue. All she could think of was his touch, the feel of his hard muscles beneath her thighs as she rode him. His passionate words too provided a goad to her already overwhelmed senses. He wanted her as much as she wanted him. Lynnette wasn't even sure when the tables had turned, but she no longer cared.

Daniel's hands came up in a sliding caress to her shoulders, massaging them gently; then he ran his palms up and down her arms. Goose bumps followed the path of his fingers, and her spine tingled with the heated messages it was receiving. Then his hands were on her breasts, cupping and molding them through the thin material of her shirt. Lynnette gasped and pressed herself closer to his touch, reveling mindlessly in his loving. Her own hands stroked down his strong neck to his chest, dipping into his shirt to feel the hard, hot muscle underneath. He felt so good to her sensitive, seeking fingers.

Before she even realized what he was doing, Daniel had opened the laces of her billowy white shirt, untied the knot at her waist, and pushed it over her head to fall to the floor in a soft heap. She was bare to the waist, with only a thin layer of clothing below between her naked flesh and his. Lynnette felt the sultry breeze caress her tightening breasts, then the heat of his tongue replaced the air in a very satisfying manner. He traced the curves of her high, rounded breasts with just the tip of his tongue, teasing her aching flesh with promises of further exploration, while never quite touching the aching center of her desires. Her nipples contracted, becoming hard rosy nubs that fairly begged to be kissed. He licked the tiny mole that nestled between the creamy twin globes, drew a line across the tops of her breasts, then outlined them in an inward-turning spiral. He ran his wet mouth across her collarbone, nipped at her shoulders, carefully avoiding the white bandage tied around her arm, then spread kisses down the slope of her breasts.

Finally Daniel gave in to the call, sweeping his tongue across the eager points, giving them the individual attention they deserved. He laved them with long, hot sweeps, then bit gently, kissing and suckling them to soothe the tiny stings. He drew in strongly, tasting her exquisite flavor in his mouth as he filled it with satiny smooth flesh, hearing Lynnette gasp and feeling her arch closer for more of the same. She was wild in his arms, yanking compulsively at his shirt until she got it off, then stroking her hands up and down his naked chest. He settled her closer to him, grasping her hips and pulling them to his until they were fused into one. Her legs were spread on either side of his slim hips as she knelt above him, writhing slightly to torment them both, brushing her loins against his without conscious volition.

This time *he* groaned, stroking his hands down her breasts to her taut belly, sliding up her back and down again to cup her buttocks in a tight grip. He ground his hard shaft against her through their clothes, pressing insistently and hearing the woman astride him moan and beg for more. He drew his skilled fingers up and down her bare legs, hearing her hiss with drawn-in breath as he tickled the insides of her golden thighs. Before returning his hands to cup her tight, firm buttocks, he teased her unmercifully with the touch of his hands on her upper thighs, tantalizingly close to the hot, molten core of her desires.

Then, knowing she was more than ready, Daniel slid his fingers inside her tight breeches and down her buttocks to stroke her between her legs from behind. She was hot, wet, ready for him. He stroked her skillfully, passionately, making the embers inside her burst into fire when he thrust his long fingers inside her heated body to pleasure her. Wantonly, she writhed against him, moaning and gasping from the unbearable pleasure. God, it felt so right! Lynnette pulled his head up to hers to administer a deep, drugging kiss that drove Daniel wild. He let go all control, kissing and fondling her with savage delight. She wasn't afraid, nay, she was anything but! She wanted him fiercely, mindlessly, more than anything she'd ever wanted—even revenge. And that was what finally stopped her.

Cold, shaking, aghast at the betrayal she was capable of, Lynnette came up for air, gasping as though she'd been drowning; as indeed, she felt she had. Drowning in primitive desire. She thought of her poor, dead sister, her sister whose young life had been cut off so cruelly before it could really begin. And of how she was dishonoring Sarah's memory by her act. To think, even momentarily, that one's base urges of lust were more important than avenging the death of a kinswoman was something Lynnette had never even imagined being capable of. But now she knew better, to her everlasting shame. One taste of that silver-eyed sorcerer's kisses and she forgot her honor—even if it had only been for honor that she had consented to the embrace in the beginning!

She ripped herself from Daniel's startled grasp, almost falling backward in her haste to get away from the man. Scooping up her discarded shirt, the pirate had it tied about her waist, not bothering to lace it, before the befuddled merchant could do more than blink. "You devil!" she hissed. "Our wager was for *one* kiss! One kiss only! But you—you cast your sorcery on me and would take it all. Well, I say you nay! You will not so easily steal my wits and bind them to your will." She paused for breath, then continued raging. "I told you once to stay away from me, but this time, I swear, I will kill you if you do not! Do not dare try more of your enchantment on me, or you'll rue the day you met Captain Thorne!" And she slammed out of the room, locking the door behind her.

"I already do, Captain. *Believe* me, I already do," was Daniel's only response to the empty room.

The next morning when Daniel tried the door he discovered that it was locked. Somehow, he didn't find that fact terribly surprising. Still, he fumed impotently. It was a dirty trick to pull, and one that broke the agreement they'd come to. Because of yesterday's turbulent events, the pirate wench had obviously changed her mind. *Well, that really corks it!* he thought in a rage. A sleepless night coming right after the most frustrating afternoon in the history of mankind was not improving his mood any. If Captain Thorne wanted to break the rules, he thought viciously, then he certainly had no obligation to abide by them, either. No holds were going to be barred in *this* fight! The beauteous witch wasn't going to torment him any longer. He'd had enough of her teasing games. It was just plain mean, what she'd done to him. It was not enough for Lynnette to take his ship, his money, and his livelihood from him; no, she wanted his *sanity*, too.

For Daniel could think of no good reason for the pirate to tempt him with her lush body, then leave him at the brink of ecstasy, not once, but three times! He was damn tired of thinking up excuses for her baffling behavior. His previous rationalization that it must be her fear of losing control simply didn't hold water anymore. Oh, he knew control was important to the strong-willed woman, but hadn't she already lost the duel to him? What more decisive display did she want in order to prove that he was every inch her equal? She already knew it, and whether she surrendered her body to him now or not, she couldn't change that fact. So why had she not simply given in to her passions?

Daniel knew well that the pirate had wanted him every bit as much as he'd wanted her. Passion like hers could not have been feigned! And surely she was experienced enough in the ways of love to need the fulfillment of their desires as much as he had. Why then deny both of them, if not out of pure maliciousness? Perhaps he could have understood behavior such as hers from an untried girl, but Captain Thorne was no such thing. There was just no way that an inexperienced woman could kiss a man as Lynnette had kissed Daniel yesterday. It was impossible. And again, there was no reason to think a woman who'd spent her share of years aboard a pirate vessel could remain relatively untested. Not a woman who looked like Captain Thorne. She knew all the ways to set fire to a man's blood. Nay, the only question in his mind was why she had chosen to torment *him,* in particular.

Perhaps she was laughing at him at this very moment for putting up with her cruel sexual tactics. Maybe she considered him weak, someone to be manipulated for her pleasure, he thought with mounting rage, simply because he had acted in a chivalrous manner toward her. Because he had admitted he didn't want to hurt her, she took that as a signal to play whatever mental games she wished upon her captive. The notorious Captain Thorne was a wanton tease.

This was going to end. No longer was Captain Bradley going to meekly go along with whatever his captor wanted from him! Breaking their truce had canceled any civilities left between them. He began to beat furiously on the door of his cell, calling out and demanding a response as he silently vowed Captain Thorne would soon regret her actions.

Lynnette was far too pleased with herself the next day to bother regretting anything. She stood aboard a ship that had recently belonged to Lord Roger of Pennsworth. It was now hers, the cargo safely stowed aboard the *Maiden,* the crew set afloat in longboats with enough food and water to last them until they reached land. The captain of the *Invincible,* after much heated debate between Lynnette and her first mate, had been allowed to remain with his crew, but not before they had questioned him closely for information about further shipping dates and routes. He didn't have much to offer, for because of the heavy losses Lord Roger's company had suffered in recent years, the man had taken to keeping his shipping schedules strictly secret, not allowing his captains to fraternize or exchange gossip about their runs.

Still, there were ways to discover any sort of information one wanted if one had the money to pay for it, as Lynnette knew. The informer who'd come in answer to her discreetly worded request for any news about Lord Roger's plans had been a good one. Whores, the captain reflected, probably knew more secrets than anyone in any other form of business. The details of how the girl had discovered just when the next ship was due, Lynnette did not particularly want to know.

Still, it was dangerous for so many who knew of her interest in Lord Roger to be walking about freely. She'd paid the whore well to keep her mouth shut. The captain of the ship they'd just taken was a different matter. Lynnette hadn't wanted to kill the poor slobbering sot, while Harry had argued that it had been the captain of the last ship who had given them false information and almost got them killed, plainly on his boss's orders. And, by letting this one go, they were assuring that Lord Roger would get back word of their doings.

Lynnette knew all that, but she considered the danger to be slight. Lord Roger would find out soon enough anyway what had happened to his ship, and since there were not very many female pirates about, the identity of his attacker would become known quickly, even if most of the crew chose to scatter rather than return to work for such an unlucky employer. Short of sinking the ship with all hands, there was no way to quell the rumors that would surely reach her enemy's ears. And she would not countenance having the cold-blooded murder of innocents on her hands, no matter that letting them go might cause her trouble later. Harry would have to accept that, shake his head as he might at her foolishness. She knew that if the final decision were his, the first mate would probably do the same.

The pirate turned to her trusted right hand. "We're close to the end of this business, my friend. That captain might not have been able to give us much information about future sailing dates, but he's helped us in other ways."

"Why, what d'ye mean, lass?"

"Weren't you listening, Harry? Once we put the fear of the fishes into him, I'd say he told us a great deal." At the mate's still uncomprehending expression, she explained impatiently. "Remember his description of the warehouses our enemy owns? He told us that there was little left in the storehouses, and no indication that Roger was planning to buy more cargo to fill the spaces. He also said one more interesting thing. To the captain's knowledge, Lord Roger only has one other ship left in his fleet. The others have all been sold to pay for his losses or taken by us.

"Seems to me," she mused happily, "that my nemesis is having difficulty convincing potential investors to use his company. He's operating under heavy losses rather than the huge profits he used to enjoy. And you know how easy it is to go bankrupt after even a few losses. Lord Roger has had more than a few." Briefly she recalled that Captain Bradley had received many of the same uncomfortable setbacks at her hands, but she shoved the guilty feelings out of her mind with a frown of annoyance. He'd recover; Lord Roger would not.

Returning her thoughts to the conversation, she continued. "I'd say that our favorite peer of the realm will not be able to sustain even one more attack to his business before being financially ruined. But he's in a bind, my friend." Harry looked at her blankly.

"He has to send that last ship out, no matter how great the danger is that we'll attack. At this point, he can't afford *not* to. The last of the cargo in Roger's warehouses has to be shipped, sold, or left to rot, and he'll not get a profit unless the stuff is sold in the Indies where 'tis needed. If he tries to sell the cargo or his ship to another shipping company, he'll lose a great deal of money. 'Tis common knowledge by now he's in dire straits financially. Those bloodthirsty merchants in London would love to get rid of the competition, and they'll have him exactly where they want him if he tries to sell—at a disadvantage. He'd be lucky to get a fraction of the vessel's worth." Lynnette was grinning broadly. "Nay, the swine will sail his usual route, and right smartly if he wants to keep his business afloat. All we have to do is wait."

"An' then ye reckon that's it?" Harry squinted dubiously. "We'll catch 'im, sink th' ship, an' 'e'll be done fer?" The first mate brightened as he thought it through. "Aye, yer right, lass. He hasn't much choice in the matter, does he, the swine! With his goods suited only fer trade in th' Indies, he 'as ta enter our waters. With th' spies we 'ave about, we'll hear o' it soon enough ta catch 'im."

"Indeed. I estimate no more than a month or so before the ship enters the Leeward Chain. With luck, we'll find her soon after, and I'll have my revenge at last."

Harry gazed into her blazing eyes, fearing for his dearest lass; the woman he thought of as a daughter; the only person he'd ever call "Captain." The unholy light in her eyes needed quenching. 'Twasn't natural to burn so bright with hate. He'd secretly hoped her association with Captain Bradley might teach her there were more important things than revenge. Yet she hadn't softened at all under Bradley's influence. Worried, he dared to ask the question he'd never asked before. "And when he's ruined, lassie? Is that th' end o' this fer ye? No more pirating, no more hatred burnin' ye up?"

Lynnette avoided giving him a direct answer, knowing he wouldn't like what she had to say. Harry didn't know about some of the things she'd done over the years in pursuit of her vengeance, and she preferred he never find out about the nasty little gifts she'd sent her nemesis, some of the horrible tricks and hauntings she'd paid to have performed on the man. Nor did the ship's mate truly understand how deep her hatred went, what it would take to satisfy the burning in her gut. She didn't want to shock her old friend, or concern him unnecessarily. "When his fortunes are ruined, he'll do one of two things, or I don't know him at all." And she knew him, knew the bastard all too well. She remembered the small eyes with dark circles ringing them, the evil, dissipated face as he leered at her, his foul breath . . . She closed off that unhappy line of thought quickly, not wanting to spoil her triumphant mood. "Either he'll be forced into hiding to avoid going to debtor's prison for the rest of his miserable life, or he'll come after us. I rather hope he does the latter. That way"—she smiled with malicious relish—"I can be sure of killing the bastard myself."

"But will it be enough if 'e don't?" Harry asked urgently. "I mean, can ye let th' matter rest at mere ruination?" He feared that until the man was cold in his unmarked grave, his captain would never be at peace.

"I know what makes that bastard tick. Without his fortune,

he won't be able to finance any of his nasty little pleasures anymore. He'll be shunned in society, and believe me, to a man like Lord Roger, that's worse than having a knife stuck in your back." Bitterly Lynnette recalled how the Lord of Pennsworth had loved to dupe polite society into thinking him a respectable man, enjoying the favor of the elite, all the while preying on those weaker than himself, leading men like her father further and further into his debt with gambling vouchers and favors until they could refuse him nothing for fear of being ruined. And he'd forced them to turn a blind eye while he . . . Enough! Just thinking of what the man had done to her and her family was bound to send her into a killing rage. She drew a deep breath, calming herself.

Without money, Lord Roger could no longer wield the power he'd used to destroy innocent people. And to find himself in the very same prison where he'd forced so many others to go when they were no longer useful to him would be an apt revenge for what he'd done to her family. But for what he'd done to Sarah, there was no hell deep enough or hot enough to fry him in. "No. It isn't enough," she admitted finally. "When this is done and the last of his ships is ours, I'll have to go to London and flush him out."

"Ye can't be serious!" he cried in alarm. "Even if ye weren't recognized fer who ye used ta be, someone for sure'd know ye fer who ye've become!"

"I'll have to take that chance. Nothing less will satisfy me." And with that, Harry knew, there would be no arguing. He'd seen that look of finality on his lassie's face before.

A knock on the door brought about a round of scorching curses from the occupant of the richly appointed chamber. Roughly shoving the parlormaid who'd been on his lap onto the floor and motioning her to leave, Lord Roger of Pennsworth responded by yelling, "Damn you, I said I was not to be disturbed! What do you want?"

While her lord was thus occupied, the woman picked herself off the floor, surreptitiously rubbing a bruised derriere. She took the opportunity to escape through the servants' entrance, grateful that she would not now have to service her employer until later that day. Better yet, he might forget all about his plans for her. That bastard. Though he blackmailed

n his service (a common occurrence
rvants, who would not stay any other
n fun at his expense when she could.
paid well by an unknown employer to spy
—and occasionally do more . . . She enjoyed the
great deal, as seeing the man's fearful reaction to
ubtle terrors she arranged on her employer's orders was
ne of her only pleasures. Still, if he wasn't holding the key
to her brother's freedom in his hands, she'd have taken her
chances and left without a reference years ago. But he'd
caught the boy stealing, and threatened to send him straight to
Newgate if she didn't cooperate with his wishes. She couldn't
let that happen, and so her life had become little more than
slavery, a fate many had suffered under the earl's hands. But
now the messenger would feel some of that wrath, and she
could take the chance to flee. Better him than her, thought the
girl as she made her way quickly down the servants' stairs.

The unfortunate bearer of bad tidings got a better grip on
his battered hat and sucked in his breath. "Milord, I have news
you will want to hear immediately," he shouted anxiously
through the closed door. Futilely he hoped the man would send
him away instead of ordering him to tell what he knew. The
lord in question had a bad reputation for blaming the messenger for the faults of the ones who paid him to relate their
mistakes. But he heard the command to enter. He did so, feeling as though he'd been invited into the devil's own study.

Lord Roger listened to the news with rising fury. That bitch
of a pirate had escaped his trap! He couldn't believe it. Captain
Thorne had seen through his plan to ambush her ship. The
warships he'd had to beg and plead for to accompany his vessel nearly two months ago had lost sight of her ship after
scoring but slight damage on the *Maiden's Revenge.* He'd
called in all his favors with the Admiralty just to get those
damned ships, promising them the glory of capturing a notorious pirate and liberally greasing their palms to get them to
agree to his scheme. Thorne had made a laughingstock of them
all with her effortless evasion. Damn those incompetent fools!

Roger thought quickly. With her uncanny knowledge of his
intimate affairs, Captain Thorne would realize quickly that the
ship he'd sent out with the naval escort had been a decoy. Had
she discovered the real ship? The *Invincible* had had a rich

cargo weighing her down when she sailed a few we
the decoy. Damn it to hell! He was forced to conclu
the demon-spawned bitch had in all likelihood scutt
as she had so many others of his line. He knew he could
afford to lose any more. His finances, tied up in the heretof
profitable venture of shipping, were all but panned out. Back
ers were leery of him and his run of incredibly bad luck, preferring to employ other companies to trade their goods,
companies that weren't being systematically looted and plun-
dered.

All this despite his carefully planned traps. But that was
not the worst of it. The worst was that Pennsworth could not
even put a face to the name of the pirate who was doing all
the damage. All he knew was that a female pirate—incredible
as it seemed to all he knew about the weaker sex—had repeatedly attacked his ships with perfect success, and was about
to beggar him.

He knew that he was a man with many enemies, even enjoyed the knowledge to some extent, but he had no idea who
this one could be. The problem with ruining so many people's
lives, he mused, was that it made the list of one's possible
enemies damnably long. He could think of several men off the
top of his head who would like to see him fall from the ped-
estal of financial stability he had long rested on, but none who
would be likely to hire a pirate, male or female, to do it for
him.

No, the bitch must be acting on her own. None of his victims, specifically chosen for their weak natures and large fortunes, would be the type to think up such a determined and
effective revenge. The trouble was, none of the women he'd
toyed with in the past—the ones he'd left alive, at any rate,
he thought with remembered pleasure—could have been this
pirate, either. The rumors had told of a tremendous woman, a
giantess, really, who could bash men's skulls in with a single
blow. Nay, women like that were not Lord Roger's favored
breed, he thought with a shudder. He liked them soft and innocent; helpless to do aught but his will.

An image came to him suddenly from the past, an image
of a large-eyed skinny girl about sixteen years of age. He
remembered that the silly wench had held a gun to him, forcing him to interrupt the rape of her sister and flee. Could that

gawky child be his nemesis? With a snort, Roger dismissed the notion out of hand. The chit had been tiny, frail, spirited though she'd been in her sister's defense. And with the death of her father soon after, she'd been left penniless. No doubt in the more than seven years that had gone by since the incident, the girl had died in the slums of London, victim of disease or violence as well as his own harsh treatment.

Nay, he was looking for someone more formidable than a mere child, perhaps not even someone out for specific vengeance for anything he had done. It was possible, after all, that this monstrous female had simply been attacking his vessels because of the great wealth they represented. Perhaps the woman had access to his plans through a leak in his security, and was using the person with the information to take him for all he was worth.

Well, it mattered not who the bitch was. He was going to make her pay, and pay but good. This Captain Thorne was about to meet her equal, and when she did, there would be the devil's retribution.

No more would his dreams be haunted by visions of huge women, some with faces that he recognized as those whose lives he'd callously destroyed, others faceless but horribly menacing, all crowding around him and screaming for his blood, as they had ever since the pirate had begun to target him. He hadn't had a peaceful night's rest since the first reports had begun to trickle in seven years ago that his ships were being marked for plundering by a woman. Lord Roger felt hunted all the time, which, if he had known it, was exactly how Lynnette wanted him to feel. He was tormented by his inability to place his enemy.

And then there were the little reminders: anonymous, chilling gifts left on his doorsteps in the darkest hours of the night, notes in an unknown hand found in the most surprising locations, warning of retribution to come. Worst were the little anomalies he would come home to occasionally, like misplaced items and rearranged furniture that were meant to let him know his security had been breached. At first he'd thought he was going mad, after the third time he'd come home to find the arrangement of family portraits in his gallery had been changed. But his own portrait was gone, and the chill of that message had sent him sleepless to his chambers many nights.

Lord Roger didn't doubt for a second that the author of these
anonymous messages was the same person who was systematically destroying his business. Even if he hadn't noticed
the pattern of terrorism, the notes he'd found assured him he
was being ruined out of vengeance.

He'd beefed up his defenses, hiring a small army of guards
to watch over his town house at night and himself when he
went abroad—discreetly, of course. There was no sense in
advertising his dilemma to all and sundry. News that he was
being stalked by an unknown enemy would not be good for
his reputation or his business. There was no one he could
appeal to for aid. He was a virtual prisoner.

But not anymore. Never again would he awake sweating
and terrified by these dreams of *women*. By annihilating the
pirate whore, he would put an end to this living nightmare that
had become his life in recent years. The constant paranoia that
had made him a shell of the man he once was would end with
her death. His hands would stop shaking, his nerves quiet, and
he could finally relax. He would no longer feel the constant
need to be on guard. Yes, the whore would die.

A plan began to form in his mind. Pennsworth knew that
implementing it would send him even deeper into debt, but he
did not care. It would be worth it to get this pirate out of his
life. Afterward he could rebuild his fortunes easily, for as the
man who had captured the infamous Captain Thorne, confidence in his business acumen and efficiency would be at an
all-time high. Quickly he penned a broadsheet raising the
bounty on Thorne's head to twice the previous amount, adding, in florid language, the assurance that she could and would
be caught. He'd have a servant take the missive to the printer
who had made out the "wanted" posters for him previously.

By tomorrow night the new bounty for Captain Thorne's
head would have been circulated all across the city. It was a
good way to convince potential backers that he was a worthy
risk, by proving he was serious about cracking down on piracy, and also by showing that he still supposedly had the
money to pay for her capture. Then he called in his man of
business, ordering him to outfit the last of his ships for a trap.
Despite the balding man's frantic protestations about the risk
and the cost, Roger was sure that this time he would not fail,
and he was willing to bet everything he owned to prove it. No

woman would ever best him! He was far too cunning and skilled in the tricks of deceit and cruelty to be beaten at his own game. Nay, Roger thought. He'd use false rumor to flush the pirate out and send her to her grave. And he planned to let the rumors that were the backbone of his scheme abound.

Tales would fly of a ship carrying her weight in gold, not to mention hosting her careful, concerned owner. Lord Roger would let it be known that he was aboard personally to make sure no heathen pirate scum dared molest his shipping, though of course he would do no such thing. (Ships of any sort made him horribly seasick.) The greedy wench would not be able to resist the double lure that gold *and* his supposed presence would provide. After all, the last time he'd had it bruited about that he was on board, it had brought the bitch on the run, and he had nearly caught her. This time there would be no "nearly."

CHAPTER FOURTEEN

CAPTAIN AND crew of the *Maiden's Revenge* returned triumphant to their little island. Celebration was the order of the evening, and the rum flowed as freely as the curses. Men could be seen prancing about in outrageous garb, for plunder taken from Lord Roger's vessel included fine outfits of embroidered silk and heavy velvet, which now strained at the seams to fit the bulky muscles of the buccaneers who'd commandeered them. There were also huge black wigs of real human hair that were presently hanging askew on drunken pirates' pates. One or two of the crew could even be seen parading up and down the beach in women's clothing, yards and yards of billowing fabric trailing ridiculously behind them as they staggered across the sand in a bizarre imitation of the gentlewomen their costumes had been intended for.

All those who occupied the beach were having an uproariously good time. Even the laconic Omar was holding court by one of the huge bonfires that blazed on the coral-colored sands, a bottle of sweet rum in one hand and an absurd hat with a shower of peacock feathers attached to it adorning his head. Men crowded about him as he described his prowess in the battle just past with wild gesticulations and loud yells. It was unusual to see the surly pirate so voluble, especially about such a small fight as the merchant ship had provided, but Lynnette had seen the amount of alcohol he'd consumed since disembarking this evening, so she was not much surprised.

She surveyed her men, finding them to be well satisfied. Many had raised a toast to their leader this night, praising her for her uncanny ability to find them booty, her skill in leading them in and out of a fight unscathed. With two prizes in as many months under their belts, the *Maiden*'s crew was more than pleased; they were ecstatic at their good fortune to have Captain Thorne as their leader.

But Lynnette could not join in their jubilant feelings. She was troubled by other, more disquieting emotions. On their way back to No-name Island they had stopped for news on St. Eustatius—news of the ransom demand for Captain Bradley. All unwilling, the pirate queen had found herself wishing that there would be no news to hear. She had not wanted word to arrive that Simon Richards had come to collect his partner and was awaiting information on when and where to make the exchange, as per her instructions. But word *had* come.

Hugging her oversized frock coat closer to her body as if to ward off a chill, Lynnette moved nearer to one of the bonfires. Despite the warm late summer night, she felt cold, cold to the bone, when she should have been relieved to have the troublesome captive out of her way. All along she had been praying for the ransom to come quickly, to rid her of the man who had constantly disturbed her thoughts since he'd arrived so explosively into her life. But now that she knew that tomorrow she would have to release him, would probably never see the silver-eyed rogue again this side of heaven, she felt unaccountably distressed.

Likely if Captain Bradley knew he was about to be set free, she castigated herself, he would not be experiencing the same irrational reaction as she. Nay, he was more likely to howl his joy to the heavens at being well rid of his captor. She was being stupid, she knew, to regret the fact that the merchant who had so turned her life around would soon be but a memory, but she couldn't repress the feelings that washed over her.

Knowing her grim expression was hiding absolutely nothing from her men, Lynnette stood up and took her leave, insisting—despite loud and vociferous protests from her drunken sailors—that she was too exhausted by the day's events to enjoy their revels. Though disappointed, they let her go, but not before giving her their loud-voiced praises and several hearty slaps on the back that came perilously close to knocking the slim buccaneer right off her feet. Harry, eyes narrowed speculatively, merely wished her a pleasant night before turning back to his game of dice. But she saw that he had perceived her unrest. It was comforting to know that she had such loyal men at her back to support her, but she knew that though they might wish to help, there was nothing anyone could do for her present dilemma.

As she walked cat-footed along the shell-lined path and up to her room, Lynnette cursed herself with each step for being a fool. Hot wax dripped on her fingers as she lit a candle and set it on the nightstand, but the pain did nothing to distract her anguished thoughts from their wayward direction. Whether she liked it or not, visions of her last encounter with the peacock were emblazoned on her memory, and she knew with hopeless certainty that she would never forget that time.

She was not recalling their duel, however, but what had come after it. Even more so than before, Daniel had managed to arouse her body that day to a fever pitch with his tormenting kisses and skillful caresses. She had wanted the culmination of their lovemaking so badly, she'd shaken with frustrated desire for hours after storming out of his room. He'd made her feel things never before imagined. The taste of him, the warm masculine smell, still lingered in her memory as a reminder of what could have been.

It was too dangerous to think that way. Bad enough he'd defeated her in a fair fight. The fact that he'd done so where no one else had been able to come close still amazed her. It made him even more of a threat to her, mind and body. Before he had won, she could still tell herself that he was no match for her, and therefore not a real worry. But now she was forced to acknowledge that he was her equal, possibly even more of a danger to her than she could be to him. Yet at the same time as she feared the power he wielded over her emotions, she admitted to herself that somehow, it only made him all the

more attractive. A man she couldn't control was definitely
more of a challenge than one she could . . .

Damn it! She should be crowing her latest victory over
Lord Roger to the sky, not brooding unhappily over a man
who was, after all, nothing more than a prisoner! She wished
she could still blame Daniel for influencing her mind in this
uncomfortable manner, but she knew to do so would be lying
to herself. He was no sorcerer, as she'd accused him of being
when she had stormed out of his quarters two full days ago.
He was just a man: a damnably handsome, too-virile-for-his-
own-good man, true; but still a man like all others she'd encountered, and she'd do well to remember that. Only his effect
on her senses was different.

Merely thinking of his heated kisses brought a rosy blush
to her creamy cheeks, and recalling his touch . . . ! Coils of
heat spiraled through her at the mere thought, causing a hot
ache to form low in her belly. It was unbearable. But it wasn't
just his arousing influence on her body that caused Lynnette
to sink to her bed in deep depression. If it had only been his
lean, rangy form that fascinated her, she could have dealt with
her unsuitable feelings. But it was his smile, his quick wit, his
determined nature, and his bizarre, unwarranted chivalrous behavior that caused her heart to squeeze painfully at the idea
of the merchant leaving forever.

The pirate was aware that she had not done anything to
cause Daniel to desire her as he seemed to. In fact, she knew
that by rights he should be spitting at the very mention of her
name. But he did want her; there was no way for him to hide
it. And he had seemed to enjoy their talks during the time they
had spent alone on the island . . .

What was she thinking? A dangerous idea had entered her
mind; one that she hesitated to admit she'd been entertaining.
But even as she realized it, the thought grew within her,
drowning out all others until she was forced to examine it.
What if she simply gave in to her urges? her traitorous brain
whispered. What if she were to go into the room across the
hall and announce to its occupant that she wanted to make
love with him until neither of them had the strength to move
a finger, let alone lift a sword? What if she were to tell him
that she wanted to taste every square inch of his skin, to join
heated flesh to flesh until there could be no separation . . .

She was crazy. She knew she was completely and utterly insane, but the pirate queen couldn't stop herself from entertaining images of lying down with the man who obsessed her every waking thought and finally fulfilling all of their frustrated desires. As the wild scheme unfolded in her thoughts, it began to make more and more sense. Or perhaps she was merely rationalizing the idea to herself until it seemed lucid. Whatever. She couldn't control the path her thoughts were taking any more than she could push back the raging waters of a tidal wave. Excitement pulsed in her veins as she considered the options. If she hadn't known that she'd not touched a drop of alcohol this evening, Lynnette would have sworn that she was drunk. Still . . .

Making love with the merchant, she reasoned, could no longer pose a threat to her plans, not when Bradley would be ransomed the very next day. She would not have to fear his effect on her emotions when he would no longer be around to stimulate them. The temptation he presented by his mere proximity would not be a factor. Once he was gone from her island and her life, she could go on as though they had never met. She'd feared that prolonged contact with Daniel would cause her to soften, become distracted. But this was just for one night. One all-too-short night.

There was another factor that had been plaguing her. Lynnette secretly feared that leaving all the desires and frustrations that lay between herself and her captive permanently unresolved would cause her to brood endlessly. Captain Thorne was not a woman who liked to leave loose ends behind, and increasingly, she had begun to feel that if Daniel were to go before the scene was played out between them, she would be left with too many unanswered questions. Like how it would feel to experience the culmination of their passion; to lie beside him and truly discover all there was to be learned in his arms . . .

She *hated* regrets, and knew with absolute certainty that if she allowed her bewitching prisoner to leave the island without further contact, she would never see the end of them. And that, she rationalized, would be far more detrimental to her revenge than anything else. Stifling a feeling that she was betraying her sister in some vital way, she told herself wildly that what she was about to do would *further* the cause of vengeance, not hinder it. Her mind was made up.

Only one more doubt remained. How was the unpredictable Captain Bradley going to react to her abrupt change of heart . . . ?

Daniel stared blindly at the sheet of foolscap that had just been slipped under his door. The rustling of the parchment, as well as the unlatching of the lock, had jolted his attention from the beach below where the pirates were roistering to the fact that he was not alone in the villa. He'd heard no footsteps to indicate otherwise, but the proof was here in his hand. Having read the note once over, he seemed unable to take in the meaning of the words it contained. He forced his eyes to focus on the bold handwriting.

> *Sorry about the locked door—had to go out "pillaging and plundering" on short notice and didn't want to take the chance of your making an abrupt departure.*

The words fairly oozed wry sarcasm, and Daniel had to smile, imagining the captain's mocking voice as she wrote them. It was pure Thorne. But that wasn't what was so startling about the message. It was the next short sentence that was causing his blood to heat at the same time as his mind had difficulty reconciling the words with their author.

> *Come to my chambers at midnight. L.*

Daniel had received notes akin to this one before. Notes from women who wanted a great deal more than just his opinion on the weather. He looked back with fond remembrance on no few occasions when he'd received such missives and responded to them. But this one—nay, he must be putting his own overhopeful interpretation on what was probably simply an innocent summons. Most likely she'd had word of his ransom. Perhaps even now Simon was waiting to take him back to England. The thought caused him a momentary and totally inexplicable pang, but his curiosity pushed it aside. Thorne wanted to see him. Soon. He estimated that midnight was less than half an hour away.

Before he could get carried away in fantasies that perhaps

the wench had changed her mind about allowing him to pleasure them both, he squelched the train of thought. The summons *had* to be about the ransom. Lynnette had never shown
any true signs of softening toward him before, and their last
meeting had been no different. Anger and recriminations were
more the pirate's style than midnight trysts. Yet she had never
invited him to her rooms for any reason before, and he doubted
very much that they were her first choice of location for a
business meeting with him. The sight of her gigantic bed
looming darkly in the bedchamber would be extremely distracting to two people with that much stifled attraction sizzling
between them . . . At least, Daniel hoped it would be.

CHAPTER FIFTEEN

WHEN HE judged that enough time had gone by, Daniel
impatiently stepped out of his room and crossed the
hall. He gave a quiet knock at the pirate's door, half expecting
there would be no response. But after only a brief hesitation,
he heard the soft command to enter. He obeyed, crossing the
antechamber to the place where the voice had originated.

What he saw there was enough to stop him dead in his
tracks, mouth agape.

Lynnette, dressed only in a clinging, sheer white shift, outlined by soft lamplight and unbelievably gorgeous, stood by
the open window of her bedroom. A slow breeze lifted tendrils
of the red-gold hair that had escaped the braid lying across
her chest and blew them softly across her heart-shaped face.
Her emerald-green eyes glittered in the warm glow of the oil
lamp, and her cheeks flushed becomingly against her golden
skin. The sweet firm swell of her breasts was outlined by a
small ruffle of lace at the neckline of the gown, drawing the
eyes to the shadowed cleft between them. He had never before
seen her in such feminine garb, found the sight profoundly
stimulating. Irresistibly, he looked lower. The light was par-
tially behind her, and the thin cotton shift hid nothing from
his devouring gaze, not the tender indentation of her tiny
waist, not the soft flare of her rounded hips, nor the incredibly

long, slim legs. She was absolutely stunning, a siren with the power to steal a man's very soul.

Some cerebral part of his mind registered the fact that the light, gauzy garment had probably not been worn in some time, for it was slightly wrinkled and smelled of the lavender commonly used to store clothes and keep them fresh. The fragrance was intensely erotic as it wafted to his flaring nostrils. He fancied that he could also smell the deeper, more womanly scent of the pirate herself, musky and sensually mysterious. With an effort, Daniel raised his gaze back to hers.

What he saw there in her deep green eyes told him that there would be no talk of ransom tonight, if her attire had not already confirmed that fact for him. Her gaze was steady, intent, but there was more to it than that. The walls the slim buccaneer had so stubbornly erected against him were gone. She looked vulnerable and open for the first time since he had met her. Acceptance of what was to happen between them was writ clearly on her luminous features. But she also looked frightened and strangely determined, as though breaking down the barriers between them had been an untold effort on her part. He saw the way her fingers clenched nervously in the folds of fabric at the sides of her gown, and felt a surge of emotion flood through him; not purely lust—though surely that element was present in full force—but something nameless and far more tender. Just for tonight, she would trust him. And there was no way in hell that Daniel Robert Bradley was going to abuse such a precious gift.

Wordlessly, he moved toward her and she stood firm, though he could sense that she was trembling a little with the urge to flee. He took her cold hand in his strong, warm one, and kissed her long, slim fingers with the lightest brush of a kiss. Even so, he felt her jump at the caress. He stared into her eyes, willing the beautiful pirate woman to see that he treasured her surrender, would not take advantage of it. She seemed to understand, her hand in his squeezing almost imperceptibly, her other hand reaching out tentatively to touch his cheek. Neither was willing to speak, for both feared that words would break the fragile spell that bound them.

He could feel the sword calluses that padded her fingertips as she stroked them against his stubble-roughened face, tracing the line of his jaw to his chin and then sliding upward to explore the corner of his chiseled mouth. He smiled, letting her feel the change of his expression, feel the wonder of standing in his arms and basking in his presence.

But Lynnette was still afraid, afraid that he would continue, afraid that he wouldn't. Daniel was being so gentle tonight, unlike his behavior during their previous wild encounters. Somehow he had sensed she needed time to adjust to the idea of what she was about to do, wanted to move slowly instead of race madly into these uncharted waters. Knowing that he was so acutely attuned to her needs warmed her all over, reassuring her that she had not made a mistake in inviting the intriguing merchant captain to her bed. Her fear began to fade, replaced by a feeling of awed wonder.

Daniel could feel the change in her, the relaxation of tensed muscles, though all that bound him to her was their joined hands. She was ready to take things one step further. With one sinewy arm, he gently pulled her closer. She came without protest. Then he raised his other hand to cup her face as she had his, feeling the delicate strength of her jaw with his fingertips, the determined chin, his touch gradually moving to stroke her nape. His steady silver gaze never left hers as he drew her in for a kiss of aching tenderness.

His warm, firm lips molded hers in a worshiping caress, feeling like lush velvet to her sensitive nerves. Desire warmed to life within her, singing dizzily in her veins and traveling the entire length of her body, from her curling toes to her tingling scalp. She could feel his palm like a brand on the back of her neck, rubbing, massaging the tension from her body. Lynnette kissed him back, fear all but forgotten by now.

His tongue traced the lush curve of her bottom lip, creating all sorts of heavenly sensations down her spine. Opening her mouth at the softly insistent urging of his lips and tongue, she felt her knees weaken dangerously when he slipped into her willing mouth. Their tongues mated leisurely, savoring the erotic dance like the finest wine. Daniel curved his arm around her waist to hold her closer, letting her now-warm hand go in the process. She brought both hands up to his face, cupping it between them to prevent him from breaking the seal of their lips, as if the thought of abandoning the sweet manna of her mouth had occurred to him. He felt as though the touch were a lifeline, and he would drown if he could not drink in the heady taste of her.

Stroking the straight line of her back, he intensified the kiss, no longer satisfied with the slow pace of their lovemaking. Thrusting deeper into her honeyed mouth, he made her whimper with surprised delight, and soon she was matching his movements with her own tongue. He thought he would burn up, she was so hot and wanton in his arms. Holding back until Lynnette was ready was going to test the very limits of his control. The merchant walked his pirate lover backward until they reached the massive bed, then urged her onto it, following at her side. She showed no coy reluctance, only protesting the separation of their lips with a hand on the back of his neck to pull him back to her.

Lynnette had never felt so good, so *right* in her whole life. Briefly, she recalled her dream, and instead of frightening her, recollection made her want to see it realized more than ever. But she had been naked then. Not stopping to think, she reached to pull off the shift, but Daniel's hand on hers prevented her. "Not yet," he murmured against her mouth. "We have time." But they didn't have time, she thought hazily. Tonight was their only chance for happiness in each other's arms. The thought swept her with mingled regret and desire. It had to be now, and she wanted their coming together with a need that was unstoppable.

"Then you take yours off," she suggested huskily. And more shyly, she admitted, "I—I want to see you."

Wordlessly, he did as she asked, pulling his shirt over his head in one fluid motion. She sighed with pleasure, running her fingers across the sleek, muscled surface of his chest. It was so wide, she marveled. And so strong. Leaning over, she gave his collarbone a hesitant peck, darting a look in his direction to see how he would react. He responded by kissing the breath out of her. She lay back, content to let him do what he would, to take control just this one time. Lynnette was no longer afraid. He wouldn't hurt her, she knew. She watched him watch her, seeing the hot light enter his tarnished silver eyes, turning them to slate and burning her with their fire. She sucked in a breath of pure anticipation.

He bent, kissing her eyes closed, then spreading feathery touches across her nose, cheeks, chin, and finally lips, stopping only briefly there before continuing on to slide his hot mouth down the side of her neck, the sensations making her shiver with pleasure. He drew a line with his tongue up to her ear, blowing softly into the perfect, shell-like swirls. Involuntarily, a soft *mmmh* of desire escaped her when he began to kiss the sensitive spot behind her ear. He continued to torment her there until she gasped and pulled him up to thank him for the pleasure with a searing kiss. Daniel slid his body over smoothly to make contact more comfortable, pressing against her side from shoulder to knee, feeling her lissome curves burn their contours into his flesh.

God, she was beautiful. Through tangled black lashes he gazed at her luscious form. He doubted he would ever tire of seeing the gorgeous pirate queen this way, so warm and wanton, eagerly awaiting his touch. He didn't know why Lynnette had chosen to end their torment tonight, but he, for one, was not about to question his good fortune.

He had a sudden urge to see her glorious hair unbound from its braid, his to touch and admire. He took up the end of the wrist-thick rope, removing the ribbon and running his fingers through the silky strands until the shiny mass spread like a coppery mantle across the white sheets. He sucked in his breath at the vision she presented. He had never seen the pirate captain with her hair loose before, and he found the sight strangely moving. She looked like a mermaid with her long tresses trailing across the pillows.

So close above her, loosening her hair with an intent expression of concentration and desire on his face, Daniel was even more handsome than she'd thought it possible for a man to be, the pirate thought with a rush of longing. Those silver eyes so clear and beautiful, the planes and angles of his sculptured face caressed lovingly by the light from the lamp, the large muscles of his arms and chest delineated finely. She wanted to run her hands over all those hard curves and angles. Well, why not? Tonight was the night to fulfill all her fantasies, for there would not be another chance, not in a lifetime of wanting. Suddenly fierce, the pirate wrapped her arms around his back, her hands racing over his strong, lean frame and lips kissing every inch of his face frenetically, until Daniel laughingly put a stop to her wildness by claiming her mouth again.

He thought she was trying to suck the very soul from his body with her brazenness, she was abruptly so passionate. The buccaneer writhed against him with a poignant desperation, as though she were trying to climb inside his skin. There was an odd sort of sentiment in her actions, as though with her body Lynnette was trying to tell him something she couldn't say in words. He couldn't guess what it might be. Wryly, he thought, *So much for going slow,* before he responded to her frantic lovemaking in kind.

Leaving her lips, his own traveled down her throat to the small indent where her pulse beat rapidly, darting his tongue out in time with the rush of blood under her skin, then moving on to tickle the sensitive point where her neck met her shoulders. Lynnette tugged her gown down so that he could travel lower. Daniel glanced into her eyes, seeing only dazed urgency, no hesitation. With deft movements he untied the tiny ribbons that held the shift closed, kissing every inch of flesh he bared. The garment fell open, revealing breasts that were round and firm and lovely, like cream with peach nipples. Nay, he decided, tasting one with the barest flick of his tongue, they were more like ripe cherries.

Lynnette gasped, feeling his touch like a fiery brand on her breasts, arching her body upward to follow him when he made as if to pull away. She felt as if she would die if he didn't continue his sweet torment.

Luckily, he had no intention of stopping, doubted that he *could* stop even if all the pirates on the island were to burst into the room with swords drawn. He cupped the satiny mounds in his hands, loving the way they fit in his palms as though made specifically for his touch. His tongue returned to tease and tantalize, flicking across the hard tips, laving and suckling until she was moaning with fevered desire. Lifting the twin globes in his hands, he buried his face between them, muffling a groan in her silky flesh. God, but he wanted this woman!

She felt the rasp of his beard stubble against her exquisitely sensitive skin as he pulled her shift lower and lower with his teeth, sending shivers of delight radiating to all points of her body, but especially between her thighs. She was hot all over, but in that secret portion of her anatomy, the flames burned brightest. She wanted him to touch her there, but Daniel was taking his own sweet time, laving the undersides of her breasts and spreading leisurely kisses down her sides. It would have tickled if it wasn't so arousing to have him send his teeth and lips across her ribs. His glossy raven hair teased her stomach, and his hands slid her cotton gown even lower, until it rested on the swell of her hips.

Daniel paused in his explorations to look at her once more. "Lord," he breathed reverently, "you are *so* lovely." She blushed, looking away, but he would not let her turn her face. "You are, you know. Quite the most beautiful woman I've ever seen."

Privately Lynnette thought Daniel was far more beautiful than she, if there was such a word as beauty applicable to men. Handsome didn't quite fit. Sensual, she decided. Sensual was the best way to describe Captain Bradley's looks. But adjectives fled her mind when he began kissing her stomach. Oooh, that was really wonderful. She squirmed, making husky little love sounds in the back of her throat when his hands came down to stroke her abdomen and moved to her hips. Such hard, strong hands, yet so gentle as they caressed her body . . .

He stroked her thighs and calves, sliding a hand beneath her shift to trace his way back up from the hem, which rested at her shins. She gasped when he ran the tip of one finger across the delicate flesh behind one knee and up the back of her thigh, quivering with ever-heating passion. He reached higher, tugging the material along with him and stroking the sensitive insides of her firm thighs, ever nearer to the epicenter of her desire. Yet she lay still, her hands only stroking his hard-muscled shoulders and chest, waiting breathlessly for him to touch her *there*.

He moved slowly, tormenting her with feather-light caresses that brushed the downy hair hiding her femininity, until all of Lynnette's concentration became centered on his touch, his fingers, the aching torture of wondering *when* he was going to relieve her mounting tension. Just when she thought she could stand no more, he would move closer, the tip of his finger just grazing her damp nether lips, only to back away before the touch could satisfy.

"Please!" she gasped, too far gone to care that she was begging. And her plea worked. Swiftly sliding two long fin-

gers deep into her wet, hot passage, he caught her pleasured
moan in his mouth simultaneously. She felt as if someone had
just poured water on a hot iron, sending clouds of hot, relief-
filled steam into the air. She rocked against him, wanting more
of the same, blindly seeking the source of the erotic feelings
coursing through her body.

God, he thought as he listened to the sound of his own
blood roaring in his ears, she's so tight, so hot for me! He
wanted to rip her gown off and thrust into her right then and
there, but he knew they would both receive more satisfaction
if he held himself back. Shaking perceptibly and breathing
hard, Daniel rested his forehead against the pirate's, trying to
regain control. It wasn't easy with her sighing and whimpering
so erotically in his ear and his fingers deep inside her wet
sheath. She arched her hips demandingly, and he responded
by thrusting his fingers slowly in and out of her body, deepening and quickening the motion as he sensed her about to
climax.

Lynnette was sure she was going to die, and equally sure
that there was no better way to go than *this*. He was stroking
deep inside her, his fingers working and fondling in such a
way that she couldn't even think of anything but him. And
when his thumb began to rub sensuously against the hard little
button that was deeply hidden in petals of hot, swollen flesh,
she thought she would scream from the ecstasy of it. Waves
of pleasure engulfed her like a stormy tide, pulling her under
and taking her to some nameless destination. The feeling was
building, building fast. Almost, she was afraid of the power
of her desire, afraid of what would happen at the culmination,
but Daniel's whispered encouragement, voice dark and sexy
as he urged her to let go, let it happen, sent her over the edge
in spite of her fear. With a cry, she stiffened, the waves crashing over her and sending her mind into oblivion as her body
arched and bucked against the stroking hand that controlled
its pleasure.

Daniel felt her climax, felt the clenching of inner muscles
as she spasmed, and watched the pirate's enraptured expression with his breath suspended in his lungs. She was beautiful,
eyes closed tight and mouth in a soundless O of ecstasy, abandoned wholly to hedonistic pleasure, savage in her passionate
delight. The sight sent a rush of blood to his already stiff groin.

He groaned, weeks of frustrated desire making him unable to hold back any longer.

He withdrew his fingers, hardly hearing her disappointed murmur of protest, quickly pulling the rumpled shift down her hips and off, throwing it heedlessly to the floor, shedding his own boots and breeches just as quickly. He settled himself between her spread legs, feeling the cradle of her thighs surrounding him, welcoming him. He braced himself with an elbow on either side of the pirate's head, his mouth seeking hers for a hot kiss that she returned dazedly, still sated with pleasure. Then with one quick motion, Daniel thrust his aching shaft deep inside her warm, wet passage while his tongue plunged into her mouth. He felt something stretch, give way beneath the onslaught, and for a second his dizzy brain refused to recognize it for what it was. Then—

"Damnation!" He stopped cold, looking down with bewildered shock at the woman whose virginity he'd just callously, brutally taken. She'd tensed beneath him, was watching his face with wariness, but, he saw with deep relief, she didn't seem to be in any serious pain. "Why?" he asked quietly, a world of questions in that one simple word, a load of self-hatred and guilt swamping him. God in heaven, he'd never suspected anything like this! "Why didn't you tell me?"

She smiled wryly, remaining motionless under him. "Would you have believed me if I told you the truth?"

Probably not. Starting to pull away from her, though doing so was harder than anything he'd ever done when overwhelming passion still raged unchecked in his body, he asked tensely, "Have I hurt you?"

She wrapped her long, strong legs around his hips to keep him where he was, pulling his head down to hers to whisper sensually, "You'll only hurt me if you stop now."

In fact, it *had* hurt, but the slight pain when he'd pushed inside her body was nothing to a woman who had been knocked around by storm and foe as often as Lynnette Blackthorne had. It was more the surprise of the sensation of his thick, hard shaft entering her unplumbed depths that had caused her to stiffen. But already the ache was fading, replaced by a warm feeling of fullness and a deeper, slower echo of her previous pleasure. She could feel him throbbing within her, and each pulse sent a frisson of desire throughout her body as she adjusted to the newness. She was sure that only if he *remained* inside her could she recapture those stunning new feelings, and she was discovering she had quite a taste for lovemaking. There was no way she was going to let a momentary flash of discomfort prevent their long-awaited joining!

Captain Thorne always got her way, thought Daniel with a touch of humor as her legs locked tighter in a viselike grip around him. Those long limbs of hers were strong as well as sexy! It was a damn good thing that their wills on this matter coincided, because he wasn't *entirely* sure that he could break away from her demanding hold even if he wanted to. Luckily he would not have to find out. Shock at discovering that his pirate queen had been a virgin was overcome by pure, hard-driving lust as she pulled him deeper into her tight sheath, arching her pelvis against his. Everything was forgotten except the feel of her sweet body beneath his, her gasp of pleasure as he thrust—carefully, this time—even further into her body. And, oh, she felt so good, so right as she took him into her, not allowing him to hold back from filling her with every inch of his hardness.

He tried to be gentle, but Lynnette would have none of it, holding to him with arms and legs, urging him on with hot words until he lost all semblance of control. Amazingly for one so recently deflowered, she matched his passion, and Daniel could hear her harsh breath coming in strangled little gasps from her lips, her body eagerly meeting his long, slow thrusts and demanding more. He kissed her throat, her ear, moving finally back to her lips to match the rhythm of his body with his tongue, surging in and out of her warm, honeyed wetness.

Lynnette was on fire, Daniel's first plunging movements having brought back to life all the ecstasy he'd sated so thoroughly with his skillful fingers earlier. More quickly than she'd imagined possible, she felt the exquisite sensations building again, stoked by her lover's powerful body, the feel of him crushing her into the soft feather mattress with his welcome weight, his chest rubbing against her sensitive nipples, his hips grinding against her own. God, it was everything she'd ever dreamed—more than she'd dreamed possible! All lingering aches fled before the onslaught of passion, making her gasp and cry out against Daniel's mouth when he picked up the pace. They were perfectly matched, his rhythm conjoined to hers. He thrust and she arched to meet him, she moaned and he caught the sound with his kiss. They moved in a world of their own, all thoughts of past and future obliterated. There was only *now*, to be grasped with both hands and taken for all it was worth.

She couldn't think. The sensation was so overwhelming she felt she would fall off the edge of some tremendous cliff any second and not even care if she fell. And then she *was* falling, screaming in ecstasy as she climaxed, the feeling bursting inside her with such incredible intensity that she forgot to breathe for a moment, simply letting her body *feel*.

Daniel experienced her orgasm from the most intimate position possible, her legs tightening about his waist forcefully, her sweet passage clenching around him, making him groan with rapturous pleasure, pulling him over the edge with her. Plunging compulsively into her welcoming sheath, he arrived in bliss only seconds behind his pirate lover, pulsing his seed into her body in hot spurts that caused her to moan with surprised delight. Smaller explosions of pleasure continued to ripple through their bodies like aftershocks from an earthquake until finally they collapsed in each other's arms, utterly spent.

The two, pirate and merchant, jailer and prisoner, lay together in sated silence for a long time. Finally Lynnette murmured, deep content belying her petulant words, "I didn't even get to *see* it." She indicated what she was talking about with a glance at where their bodies were still joined together. Daniel merely chuckled, rolling them both over to ease her of the burden of his weight while remaining inside her.

"I assure you," he whispered seductively in her ear, "you'll get to see it before I'm through with you. More, I hope you'll want to touch it as well, many times in the years to come."

Years to come? What was he talking about? Lynnette realized that he didn't know about the ransom, didn't know that tonight would be the first and last time they'd ever lie together. Her conscience informed her that she ought to tell Daniel, but she couldn't bear to spoil the relaxed mood between them. Still, his words puzzled her. Surely he realized that at best, there could be only weeks before his ransom was paid and she had to let him go. A thrill of suspicion went through her, ruining the mood despite her attempts to maintain it. "What do you mean, 'years?'" she asked warily, struggling to sit up, disappointedly feeling him disengage from her.

Ignoring her sudden tension as if he hadn't even noticed it, Daniel crossed his arms lazily behind his head and answered blithely, "Why, when we're married, of course."

"What!" she gasped in uttermost shock. "Married! But—" Momentarily speechless, Lynnette merely stared at him. Then, she said, "Have you gone *completely* mad?"

"Well, it *is* the next logical step," he replied imperturbably. "Or, actually, it should have been the one previous to this." He indicated the rumpled bedclothes and their naked bodies, no longer entwined.

Sudden realization dawned, and helplessly, the pirate began to laugh.

Not a single, smothered snort or politely choked-back snicker. These were deep, ringing peals that shook her body with mirth. She flopped back on the bed, fairly giggling with the uncontrollable spurt of humor. The bell-like sounds filled up the room, and still she continued to chuckle.

Daniel waited. Trying to rein in his patience, he allowed what he assumed was sufficient time for Lynnette to regain control of herself.

She nearly fell off the bed, "ha-ha-ing" and "ho-ho-ing" until her sides began to ache. She clutched them in a vain effort to hold her guts in. And still she continued to laugh.

Patience wore thin rather quickly, he discovered.

The pirate was gasping for breath, her chortles sounding choked. Yet every time he thought she was winding down, fresh spurts of amusement made her double over again.

It wasn't *that* funny! Patience gave up the game, losing heavily to a rush of dark anger as the merchant realized Lynnette was not simply using mirth to hide her stunned reaction to his proposal. She really *was* mocking him. He cut through a spate of hysterical laughter to say coldly, "I meant it in all seriousness, Lynnette."

At the sound of her name on his lips, the slim buccaneer managed to sober long enough to sputter, "I—I'm sure you did." She shook her head helplessly, more laughter interrupting her. "Just b-because we—you think you—Oh, Jesu!" She lost it again.

Now he was really furious. Having the woman one had just proposed to convulse with hilarity was not exactly flattering to a man's ego. The sound of her chuckles began to grate on his nerves, badly. "Will you *stop*!" he yelled at the top of his lungs, instantly cutting off any further outbreaks. Lynnette stared at him in shock for the second time that night, but, he mused with satisfaction, it was doubtful *this* silence would be a prelude to any more scornful levity. His deep baritone cut sharply through the suddenly tomblike atmosphere. "I take that to mean your answer is no."

"Of course it's no, you idiot! Why would I marry you, simply because we were together? Perhaps you consider my recent virginity to be cause, but *I* don't!" Her tone was incredulous. She couldn't believe the peacock had said anything so utterly foolish. What was she supposed to do, give up everything in her life—her quest, her home, her very freedom? And all that merely because of the loss of a bit of flesh she'd never taken note of before anyway? The mere idea was ridiculous!

"I do indeed consider it cause to marry," he responded grimly. "Laying aside for the nonce the fact that I've ruined you for marriage to any other man, which you do not appear to care overmuch about, have you considered the possible consequences of our lovemaking? As we speak, my seed may be taking root in your womb."

Even as he said the words, a jolt of unexpected pleasure swept through him. Just thinking of a child, a son or daughter with his dark hair and Lynnette's green eyes, a beautiful, perfect infant brought into being by their actions this night, sent a thrill of unexplainable joy into Captain Bradley's heart.

It had shocked him as much or possibly more than the pirate to hear his own mouth open and the word "marriage" tumble out. Although he felt a tremendous guilt at having unwittingly deflowered Captain Thorne, marrying the wench by way of restitution had not *consciously* occurred to him. But the more he thought about it, the less strange the idea of wedding an infamous buccaneer seemed.

Wedding her meant that he would have an unlimited length of time to plumb the mystery of her outrageous character and actions, while gaining the unreserved use of her lush body. And, yes, if he were honest with himself, marriage to the elusive pirate would give him a hold on her, a way to keep her by his side. Daniel was aware that his time on No-name Island was nearly up, and had been regarding his upcoming release with mingled relief and sorrow. Part of him desperately needed to get away from the woman who tormented him with her baffling combination of ferocity and vulnerability, yet an even stronger, less rational part knew that never in his life would he meet another woman who could claim such a strong grip on him, mind and body. Nay, there'd never be another woman who could challenge him with wit and steel like Captain Thorne, and he was sure beyond any doubts that he would never be able to forget his time with her.

Although he knew quite well it was madness, Daniel thought that perhaps consigning himself to a lifetime with an unpredictable pirate for his wife was the best idea he'd had in years.

But Lynnette was staring down at her belly, hands clasped over it as though she could already feel life growing inside. And her expression, in the split second before she covered it with fierce determination, was horrified. Even before Daniel heard her reply, he knew its content. Captain Thorne would never agree to wed him. Deep down, he'd known her answer from the instant he'd offered his unorthodox proposal, but her changed attitude this night had given him cause to hope that perhaps she was softening toward him, was beginning to feel something more than mere lust for his body. Bitterly, he reflected that he should have realized her show of trust and openness was an anomaly, not to be seen or enjoyed more than once. The pirate was fiercely independent, cold, and determined to follow a course that he couldn't understand or accept. Still, when she said with deadly calm, "If that should happen, I will deal with the matter myself," rage overcame any lingering tenderness he might have been harboring toward her despite her cutting rejection.

"Think you you can handle *everything* alone, dear Captain?" he sneered harshly. "Think you I will be content to be your stud horse, summoned to bed you and then put out to pasture while you continue to do as you will, casually ruining people's lives and walking away?" His tone was angry, incredulous, his eyes glowing with an inhuman light. "And do you truly think that I could sit back and allow you to bear my child, if there should be one, as a bastard, raising it amidst a bunch of filthy gutter rats?"

A bit frightened despite herself by the absolute rage in Bradley's voice, but not about to let him intimidate her, Lynnette yelled back just as loudly. "Just what do you think you could do about it, *Peacock*?" she asked scathingly. "How would you propose to stop me? You have no control over what I choose to do!"

"Do I not?" he rasped, looming over her so that she had the sudden urge to cover her nakedness and flee, but instead glared up at him with mute defiance. Still, she was unprepared for his devouring, punishing kiss when it came. Swooping like a hawk, he caught her lips in a fierce lock, pushing her back down on the bed with the force of his anger.

For a moment, stunned paralysis numbed the pirate's reactions, but within seconds she'd recovered the wits to battle against Bradley's bruising assault. He was heavy, but she was wily and well trained in the art of throwing a bigger opponent. In a whirlwind of flailing arms and legs, Lynnette snarled and ripped her mouth free of his. "You'll pay for that, Peacock!" she growled, rearing back and freeing an arm to sock him in the chin. The joy of hand-to-hand combat rushed through her veins dizzily, warming her to the struggle.

Daniel felt the crunching impact of her doubled fist against his face, and though it rocked him back and sent a jolt of pain through his entire head, he was so furious that the blow provided no deterrent to his dark purpose. He threw one heavy leg over her thrashing limbs in an attempt to still them and protect the delicate portions of his anatomy that she was trying her damnedest to pulverize at the same time. He whispered, close to her face, "Bite me, and I'll bite you right back," just before his lips descended for another brutal kiss.

Lynnette realized that her struggles were exciting him when she felt his throbbing hardness brush her naked, squirming thighs. Daniel was not the only one feeling sexual excitement, she admitted candidly to herself. Battle euphoria was fast transforming itself into a different kind of passion, just as ferocious, but less destructive. The sensation of his hard-muscled body lying heavily atop her own, his quick breathing, their nudity, and her newly awakened sensuality all combined to send a heated message to her brain.

But he was far angrier than she; that Captain Thorne saw immediately. It was hard, she found, to hold a grudge against a man whose instincts were so gentlemanly, even if they were not at all applicable to the situation at hand. Of course, the idea of wedding Captain Bradley was absurd, out of the question for a woman with a mission like hers; yet, she realized belatedly, she ought to have been mature enough to deflect that line of thought from his head without being quite so insulting. It was just that it had been such a surprise! She felt an urge to laugh again at the peacock's unexpected and unwarranted chivalry, but masterfully, Lynnette clamped down on it. She couldn't have managed a sound in any case, what with Daniel's lips mashing her own against her teeth. Feeling a bit more sympathy, she guessed that, had Bradley been so totally rude to her, she would have responded far more aggressively to his outburst than merely kissing him!

Thinking so, Lynnette allowed him to capture her wrists with only token resistance, continuing to struggle simply because she, to tell the truth, was enjoying the fight. Aye, she was still angry, but not mad enough to distract her from wanting him. And what better way to diffuse some of that emotion than by physical expression? There was only one thing, she'd just discovered, that was better than a good fight . . .

Daniel was thrown into confusion when Lynnette, caught fast in his hold and panting, suddenly grinned ferally and raised her head to kiss him with as much fire and force as he had recently kissed her. But in her steamy caress he felt little anger, only lots of white-hot desire. As the heady feeling of her tongue in his mouth penetrated the red haze of his fury, he felt a glimmer of admiration well up in his heart. She might not want to marry him; yet he supposed that didn't really surprise him. Thorne was too wild, too free and unpredictable, to consider surrendering her unusual way of life merely because a night spent in a man's arms had cost her her virginity, and he ought to have realized that.

Besides, what could he possibly offer Lynnette that could convince her to give up her chosen path? He doubted that simply saying, "Leave behind your marauding ways, and I'll make you the wife of a merchant," would make much of an impression to a woman whose fortune surely dwarfed his own several times over. Nor would the rather lonely, dull life of a ship captain's wife be likely to appeal to one accustomed to taking command of her own ship *and* her own destiny as Captain Thorne was. Nay, she was not about to concede anything of the sort.

But she *was* about to surrender her body, to a man who was beginning to feel very grateful for even that concession, for he knew that no other man had been granted as much as he was being offered with such hot, ready passion. And, to his mind at least, the gift of the pirate's body was nothing to turn one's nose up at. He would be a fool to deny them both out of anger when he could be enjoying what she was so wantonly presenting instead.

Not that he had completely forgiven her—he was not even close to that stage. That she obviously considered his place and say in her life to be negligible still rankled and made him want to shake the unlikely buccaneer until her gleaming white teeth rattled. Still, the demanding pressure of his mouth softened slightly as he felt her move sinuously under him, the feel of her satiny skin brushing his sending a wash of dark desire to dissipate all thoughts from his mind.

Furious energy not at all abated, differences still presenting an insurmountable chasm between any meeting of their minds, captor and captive used their bodies to mate with animal passion, hungry mouths locked and limbs intertwined. Over and over they rolled, each trying to gain the upper hand, Lynnette's hair flying in all directions and impeding their sight. Heat flared between them, and the pirate moaned in rising anticipation when Daniel came to rest on top of her, breathing heavily and grinning at his advantage. She could feel his throbbing shaft poised at the slick entrance of her femininity.

Before he could guess her intent, she thrust her hips upward hard and felt him plunge inside, heard him emit a grunt of surprised delight. Holding tight to him, she threw herself over with all her strength, landing with a smack on Daniel's chest, straddling him. Now it was her turn to grin in triumph, until he said, "If this is what losing a fight with you is like, remind me to lose more often!"

He was right, she realized. This was a battle two could win. Yet she was unwilling to let him take over from there, though she knew he had more experience in the art of giving pleasure than she. Feeling the slim hips beneath her thighs as she sat on him, hearing his sharp inhalation when she experimentally rocked her hips forward, sent a rush of power coursing through her veins, making her almost light-headed. Lynnette tried a few more motions, gauging their effectiveness in groans and gasps. Pleasure swamped her as she discovered that she could take just as much as she wanted of him, rising slowly up and feeling him just a few inches inside her body, or slamming down suddenly so that his entire hard length impaled her. She worked her body feverishly, whimpering in delight, lost to everything but the feel of the man she rode.

Finally, Daniel couldn't stand any more. *She* might not realize just how arousing her little experiments were, but his groin was telling him that if he didn't do something about them, he'd not be accountable for the result. Grasping her rounded hips in his big hands, staring up at her to watch her reaction through curtains of rose-gold hair, he pushed up into her tight sheath, mindful that she was probably still sore. Her eyes widened, glazed with passion and gleaming emerald in the soft lamplight, contrasting with the skeins of reddish hair that filtered light like leaves in an autumn forest.

When she made to pull teasingly away, a bit displeased that he sought to take control, he held her firm upon him, showing her the way of it, till she caught his rhythm, anger and playfulness both forgotten in the surge of raw desire that came with his slow, steady thrusts. He was so deep inside her, filling her in a way that made her wonder how she'd lasted so many years empty before this night, when only now did she realize what it meant to be fulfilled. It was not long before she felt the pleasure cresting in breathless surges that matched the increasing pace of Daniel's deep, hard thrusts. Her back arched, her breasts rose and fell in time with her gasping breath and the sliding, upward shoves that raised her toward climax. Letting her heavy hair fall forward, she turned her head to meet the gaze of the man who had shown her ecstasy undreamed of.

His silver eyes burned with a hunger that matched her own, and she saw that he was feeling the same sensations as she, riding the crest with her, unafraid to let it take them where it would. The heat was intensifying, the motion of his hips creating an unbearable friction in her wet depths, a friction she built on by slamming down to meet every upward arc. They were like dry tinder, rubbing together, moaning and crying out as they sought to reach their mutual goal.

The flames blazed into brilliant life suddenly, exploding in both with a shower of aching, incredible fulfillment. Lynnette screamed his name, arching herself backward in a paroxysm of release until her forehead fairly touched Daniel's knees. Simultaneously, she felt him stiffen, his shaft throbbing with spurting seed, his cry hoarse on his lips.

She collapsed atop him in a limp mass of limbs and hair and sweaty skin, too spent to move. Daniel could barely raise his shaking arms enough to curve them around her back and stroke the damp red-gold tendrils from her peaceful face.

Uncaring that the sheets were trapped beneath them, and that the night was turning cool, they slept the sleep of the truly, completely worn out.

CHAPTER SIXTEEN

*D*ANIEL AWOKE very, very slowly. A feeling of content-ment deeper than anything he'd ever felt before had taken root in his bones, and waking up was the last thing he wanted to do. He was afraid if he opened his eyes, last night's emotions and its singular events would fade into the realm of dreams and fantasies. But it seemed he was not to have a choice. Someone was shaking his shoulder. Daniel cracked open his eyes, only to recoil in horror, seeing what appeared to be the face of a gargoyle bare inches from his own.

As his bleary eyes began to focus, he saw that what had roused him was not, in fact, a demon—though judging solely by looks he wasn't far wrong. Omar the pirate stood looming over the bed, Daniel's clothing in one hand and a menacing scowl on his craggy features.

Bewildered and still sleep-fuzzed, he shook his head and glanced wildly around. The sea of sparkling white bedding was empty. No Lynnette. She was nowhere in sight. He also realized that he was stark naked, without even a sheet to cover his rangy frame. During the long, passion-filled night, they must have kicked all the covers off the gargantuan bed.

What the hell was the ugly pirate doing here? And where was his captain? A bit embarrassed and more than a little bemused, Daniel snatched the proffered clothing, dragging on his breeches hurriedly. Did Lynnette want *everyone* to know what they had been doing last evening? And then it hit him. The reason for Omar's presence and his mistress's absence was obvious. She did not intend to see him again.

"Where is she?" he demanded, pulling on his boots with vicious yanks and shoving inky strands of hair back from his eyes. "Where is Captain Thorne?"

As usual with the surly buccaneer, there was no reply. He merely jerked his thumb toward the open doorway, indicating that the prisoner should precede him outside. But Captain Bradley had had enough of following orders. He was furious, more so than ever before in his life.

"Goddamn it, I said, where *is* she?" When Omar continued to stare mutely, his opaque eyes giving away nothing, Daniel felt the killing rage well up inside him. By all the saints, enough was enough! With a bloodcurdling yell, he went for the pirate's throat, catching the man off guard and slamming him against the wall with enough force to knock the breath out of him. "Tell me where your mistress is," he said for the last time, voice low and deadly as he bit off each word, "or I'll wring your filthy, scrawny neck like a chicken's."

But even as he spoke those words he could hear the sounds of others rushing to Omar's aid. Before he could do more than spin about to face his attackers, they were upon him in a flurry of flying fists and brutal kicks. He fought the pirates wildly, furiously, but there were simply too many to defeat. A hamlike fist connected with his chin and he felt himself rocking back, losing consciousness. As darkness overtook his eyes, Daniel suffered one last agonizing realization: his beautiful, treacherous sea witch had betrayed him yet again . . .

Waking up in darkened holds with a splitting headache was beginning to be a habit with him, Daniel thought with sour humor some time later. Gingerly, he brought a hand up to test the swelling bruise on his chin, wincing at the pain his own touch brought. Bare seconds after the pain came the rage at the one who had caused it. Captain Thorne. As sure as if she'd punched him herself, the pirate queen was responsible. No matter that the deliverer of the stinging bruise had been one of her men; the message was clear.

He had vastly underestimated the extent of her coldness. The fact that she'd casually sent him a wake-up crew of angry buccaneers made that much plain. The men had *not* been pleased to find him in their leader's bed. Omar's black glare had confirmed his guess that Lynnette's men were highly protective of her welfare, and did not appreciate him lying with her one bit.

He could guess as well where he was being taken. Simon must have shown up finally with his ransom, and now the dirty profiteers were on their way to make the exchange.

Many of last night's questions were answered by this latest action of Lynnette's. That look of regret in her eyes, brief as it had been. The very act of giving herself to him. Her seeming surrender to the undeniable forces that bound them together. What a farce, he thought savagely. She had never meant their passion to last beyond one all-too-short night of ecstasy. And he'd played the fool nicely for her, Daniel realized furiously. No wonder she'd laughed so hard when he'd—he forced himself to think it, even through waves of humiliation—when he'd asked her to marry him.

God, what a fool he'd been, to think their lovemaking had meant anything to the pirate, as it had to him. Nay, she was a coldhearted bitch, through and through. The loss of her maidenhood meant nothing to her, nor did the man she'd lost it with. Not even the incredible, once-in-a-lifetime fire that raged between them had deterred her from her purpose. She had no qualms about taking what she wanted, and no trouble letting him go afterward.

Strangely, it was that last part that caused him most pain. Lynnette *would* be free, and she cared not at all whose heart she trampled to stay that way.

Daniel was wrong. Lynnette *did* care. As she stood at the cabin window staring blindly at the white-capped waves before her, the captain of the *Maiden's Revenge* felt worse than she'd felt in years. Her shame was overwhelming. Her men had told her of the struggle the merchant had put up this morning when they'd come to fetch him. It had taken five men to subdue Captain Bradley long enough to get him aboard. Obviously, he'd not been at all happy with her actions.

Too, her men had not been overly gentle with him, she

thought with a shrinking feeling of remorse. She ought to have realized the sort of animosity they would feel toward the merchant, but, to tell the truth, she had not considered it until later. She saw only now that her crew, always protective of her safety, would certainly consider Bradley a danger. Hadn't she treated him differently from the start? Only a blind man wouldn't have seen the tension that stretched between herself and her prisoner. No wonder the pirates had surmised that all had not gone smoothly there during the dark hours when she'd ordered Omar to fetch Daniel from her chamber the next morning *and* told the other men to wait in the hall in case of trouble.

She was a rank coward, she berated herself harshly. To send Omar to waken Captain Bradley just because she was afraid of the accusation she'd see in his eyes if she told him herself about the ransom was unforgivable. But worse was the knowledge that he had certainly guessed by now her purpose last night. She would be too vulnerable by far if she let him see her in her weakness. For the fact was, she could not have let him go without tasting of the pleasures he offered, without *living* for that moment in his strong arms before she returned to her cold, harsh world of revenge. Facing him, knowing he held that powerful hold over her, would have been impossible.

But the worst part, she judged, was not the shame over how she'd treated her captive, nor the feeling of utter cowardice that had caused her to retreat and allow her men to deal with the merchant today. It was her complete miscalculation of her reaction to his lovemaking.

All her brave, reckless estimations about how coolly she would be able to continue on after lying with Daniel, her hopes that she could simply go on with her task and forget all about the silver-eyed rogue who'd taught her the meaning of desire, she knew now to be delusions. She would never forget. And tasting just once of passion would never be enough. Now that she knew the pleasure that came with making love with her captivating prisoner, her life would never be the same.

She'd stayed awake long after their last bout of lovemaking had sent the exhausted Daniel to his rest. As dawn was creeping over the horizon, she'd stared at the man who'd shown her how much she still had to learn about living, watching his handsome features relaxed in sleep, and knowing she would have to give him up. Nothing had ever hurt so much as that realization. Her heart cried, *No! Don't ever let him leave you!*, and she had wildly in that moment imagined herself defying all sense and reason and forcing him to stay by her side, fighting off anyone who would gainsay her.

But she knew that was impossible. Captain Bradley was not the sort of man who would tamely let any woman—especially a pirate who had taken his ship and held him to ransom—dictate to him forever. And she was not the sort to try. Lynnette had enough respect for Daniel to know that he was no captive bird to be caged away at a whim. He was too proud, too commanding and vital for that. He would break free of her chains, hating her for trying to trap him. As she would hate herself for her weakness in trying to keep him.

Lynnette was well aware how detrimental the merchant was to her resolve. He made her want to forget all thoughts of vengeance and spend every second of her time reveling in the pleasures of their bodies and minds. Gazing down at his sleeping countenance, the slim pirate had marveled that this man could have such a hold on her. It frightened her to think of the paths her mind was wandering; away from duty and blood ties, away from sworn vows, toward some unimaginable future and dreams of peace—and love. *Fool!* she screamed mentally. *Those things are not for you!* Any chance at love and happiness she'd ever had had been brutally torn from her one violent night in London seven years ago.

Nay, this was the way it had to be. And thinking it over again now, in the morning's light, changed nothing. The deed was done; Daniel would not forgive her now even should she swallow her pride and beg for his understanding. Turning away from the bright vision of endless aquamarine ocean at her window, the pirate queen slowly paced the musty dimness of the cabin. She did not reemerge until they reached their destination just off the coast of Tortuga a day later.

When Simon Richards caught his first glimpse of the lady pirate, standing stiffly at the rail of her own ship not fifty feet from his, he could not prevent uttering a low whistle. Contrary to rumor, the wench was not a hideous hag—the very opposite, in fact. But he felt no rush of desire at the sight of her exquisitely perfect beauty. She was, he thought wonderingly,

the coldest human being he'd ever seen. His first glance told
him unequivocally that this lady was hard as stone and about
as forgiving; not his type at all. Nay, Simon liked his women
soft and warm and friendly, as completely different from this
icy marble sculpture of a female-in-breeches as he could imagine.

She met his gaze with cutting emerald eyes, nodded slightly
in recognition of his leadership. As the ships drifted closer, he
saw the stark lines of tension drawn on her white face, the
determined way she straightened her spine. And here he'd
been intending to rib his partner no end for getting captured
by a mere woman. Captain Richards decided all at once that
poking fun at his best friend would *not* be a good idea. A
good, stiff drink and a commiserating, compassionate ear for
his partner's troubles would be far more appropriate, for now
he could understand how such a freak happenstance as the one
that had befallen Daniel could occur. All that he needed to see
was written for him in the intense, burning green eyes of Captain Thorne.

Just then he caught sight of his friend being led topside by
two brawny-looking seamen. Simon sighed in relief, pleased
that Bradley looked to be in good health, if a bit shabby
around the edges. He needed a shave and a change of attire
rather badly, Captain Richards thought fondly, but otherwise,
he saw, the man was probably *more* fit than last he'd seen
him, darkly tanned and hard-muscled. The wonders of the Caribbean climate, he mused, or was it something else entirely?
Even the most dull-witted could not fail to take note of the
way both Daniel and Captain Thorne stiffened when they
caught sight of one another.

Daniel moved slowly and purposefully along with his guard
toward the railing where Lynnette and her men stood, hands
resting with deceptive casualness on cutlasses and pistol butts,
facing the crew of the merchantman. The ships were made fast
to one another, a narrow channel of space all that separated
them. The two buccaneers assigned as Daniel's guard halted
him ten paces behind the group with a rough hand at each
elbow. The moment had come. He heard Lynnette speak, her
voice pitched to carry over the rising wind.

"The money."

He saw Simon across the narrow strip of water, saw him reach down to his belt for a fat leather pouch and toss it to the pirate, who caught it deftly. He heard his partner call for his release, felt the hands at his arms fall away. Anger, already simmering hotly in his veins, boiled to new life. The pirate would not even look at him as he strode forward. The men surrounding her gave way so that he could approach. For one endless moment he stared at her averted face, burning her flawless profile into his memory. He wanted to hurt her for the hurt she had caused him, to inflict just the tiniest portion of the agonies she had made him feel back on her. He wondered if that was even possible. As far as he could tell, Captain Thorne *had* no finer feelings; just cold, hard determination and white-hot passion with nothing in between.

When he spoke, it was for her ears only, and what he said was not pleasant. "I hope that gold can warm your bed as well as I did," he whispered darkly, his lips so close to her ear that she could feel his hot breath teasing her sensitive flesh, causing her to shiver involuntarily. "I do believe," he said silkily, "that's the highest price anyone has ever paid to a whore for her services. I *almost* believe it was worth it."

And before Lynnette could respond to that, he leapt the channel between the ships in one graceful vaulting motion. As he stormed across the wooden deck, heading straight for Simon's cabin, Daniel did not once look back.

If he had, he might have seen the glimmer of tears sparkling on Lynnette's black lashes in the instant before she hastily brushed them aside and turned back to her men. In a voice that quavered slightly, Captain Thorne ordered the pirates to release the grappling hooks and set sail.

Simon followed his brooding partner inside the cabin. *He* had not missed the hint of tears in the pirate queen's eyes, and his curiosity was overwhelming.

"Care to tell me what happened between you and that virago back there?" he asked his friend's broad back innocently.

"No!" Daniel didn't bother to turn around.

Simon slapped an arm around Daniel's shoulders sympathetically. "Well, 'tis all over now," he said soothingly.

" 'Tis *not* over. This is only the beginning." He spun about to face his friend, silver eyes burning unnaturally. "We're not going home just yet."

"What do you mean? She's got the money, the ship, everything. If we want to keep the company from bankruptcy, we have to return to England immediately and repair whatever of our financial damages we can from there."

"I have a better idea," Daniel said blackly. "We're going to get back what we lost from that heathen pirate directly." He reached behind his confused friend and closed the door as he began to outline his plan.

The latch clicked shut with a rather ominous snap, sounding, if only she'd been aware of it, the end to Captain Thorne's days of freedom.

CHAPTER SEVENTEEN

*L*YNNETTE DEARLY wished André would just shut up. As she stared into the murky depths of her fifth tankard of ale, she realized that if her sometime companion did *not* stop babbling into her ear about God-only-knew-what escapade, she was liable to belt him one. Hard. She took a deep breath to calm herself and deliberately loosened her white-knuckled grip on the dented pewter tankard set before her. It wasn't André's fault she was irritable and moody, she supposed, and punching the man would hardly be reasonable. *Satisfying,* yes, but politic, no. It was just that, right now, the last thing she wanted to hear was another of her fellow buccaneer's long, detailed accounts of his latest wenching experience. Especially not now that she had a far clearer idea of what he was so explicitly describing.

Damn! Was there no peace and solitude to be had on this entire stinking pit of an island? The only reason she'd even made port on Tortuga after yesterday's ransom exchange was that her ship and her crew both needed reprovisioning. If not for the fact that No-name Island could not supply all their needs, both of foodstuffs and otherwise, Lynnette would vastly have preferred returning to the quietude of her home base so that she could have a chance to think about all of the unsettling events of the past several weeks. The raucous atmosphere to be found at the ramshackle den of iniquity a past owner had, with uncertain wit, named the *Rising Gorge* was certainly not the place for reflection.

She looked about incuriously. This was the best of the taverns Tortuga had to offer. Which meant only that the rushes strewn about the packed dirt floor had been changed during this century, and the ale and spirits approached the realm of drinkable. The clientele wasn't much, however. Greasy men with coarse manners sprawled about the wooden trestle tables, their female counterparts circulating the tables sloshing foam from tankards as they tried—or didn't try—to evade the outstretched arms that grabbed at their flesh. The occasional mug was hurled good-naturedly across the room, but the patrons had long since learned to duck them without much fanfare.

". . . and the biggest teats you ever saw." André's enraptured voice intruded into her survey of the smoke-filled room. Out of habit, she had not neglected to give a thought to defenses in her choice of seating. Both she and the French captain, by unspoken agreement, had chosen a table close to the rear exit, positioning themselves with backs against the wall so that no one could surprise them. This was no more than ordinary precaution—anyone who'd survived as long as they had knew there was never a time when a person in their profession could afford to allow their guard to slip.

In Lynnette's case this was especially true. A woman who carried a sword and whose record of prizes far outweighed most male pirates' was an easy target for envy and outraged sensibilities. How many times had she heard men call her unnatural, or worse, a witch? Some even covertly made the sign against evil when she passed. She was well aware how easy it would be for a group of them with too much rum in their bellies to take it into their heads to rid the Brotherhood of its too-daring sister. She didn't much relish the thought of having a knife thrust between her shoulder blades one dark night.

By all the saints, she wearied of this life! The constant strain on ever-wary nerves, the fight to retain her men's respect, to hold a position of power in a hostile, cruel world of cutthroats, was more than she could bear sometimes. Not to mention the strength it took to hold on to her vow of revenge, to never rest until she had gained it.

And now this wholly unacceptable fascination she'd developed for her former captive. His parting words still rang in her mind, brutal, yet with a barb of truth that cut her to the bone. Whore, he'd called her. And perhaps she was one of those unfeeling women, for surely she'd used him to gain his money, then let him go without a word of parting.

But coin had not been her motive for inviting him into her bed, a bed no man had ever shared with her before . . . Lynnette cut the thought off ruthlessly. Already Daniel's effect on her had caused the pirate to indulge in ale far more heavily than was her wont, by tormenting her with memories of passion-darkened silver eyes that stole into her very soul and stirred it with unwanted and unfamiliar emotions. The remembered sound of his deep voice husky with desire, the rumble of his laughter on those few occasions when they'd got along, his quick and easy smile, and even his slow anger were magnificent to behold. And she never more would. Though she knew it was dangerous to dull her wits in this fashion, she reached again for the stale, warm brew and gulped repeatedly until she'd drained the tankard.

All in vain, she knew, for no amount of liquor would help her forget the man she'd taken by force into her life, and who had then neatly taken over *hers*. All the pirate's emotions, thoughts, and actions had been changed because of Captain Bradley, and she cursed him for it bitterly, even as her treacherous body, warmed by the spirits she'd imbibed, ached for him with renewed longing.

". . . and the things she could do with her mouth! Ah, what a night that— *Chérie,* you are not listening!" Bellairs's drunken, smiling face creased into a befuddled frown as he realized his audience of one might as well have been an audience of none. "I am *trying,*" he slurred with great emphasis, "to tell you about the most incredible night of my life, and you do not even care! You are a coldhearted woman, *chérie.*"

André's tone was light, teasing, but his words struck a chord with the pirate queen that was anything but. He called her cold. Daniel thought her cold as well, she knew. Scowling blackly, she grabbed another tankard from a passing barmaid, and prepared a verbal sally that would toast the annoying Frenchman's ears to a cinder.

He beat her to it, his expression lighting almost comically in sudden comprehension. "I have it!" he cried. "I have just figured out why Captain Thorne is such dull sport tonight," he announced loudly to the tavern at large. Several heads turned curiously to hear what he would say, sailors being a gossipy lot, and Captain Thorne a ready subject of interest.

Lynnette hissed warningly at her tactless friend, having the uneasy premonition that his pronouncement would have a great deal to do with her erstwhile captive. But André, with the skill of an accomplished tale-spinner, allowed the anticipation in the room to grow just the right amount, sublimely unaware of how close he was coming to permanent bodily harm. He leaned back in his chair comfortably while Lynnette debated whether or not the cutlass was the correct weapon with which to shut someone's mouth.

"Well, boys, you surely recall that our friend the estimable Captain Thorne," and he waved to indicate the pirate queen's rigid features, "has just concluded a rather profitable business venture." The pirates roared with laughter to hear a ransom transaction described so delicately. "What you may not know, but what I have from several highly reliable sources, is that the trade involved some extremely well-put-together goods." Again, more laughter, and this time some ribald comments as well.

Lynnette's face flamed with rage and humiliation. She would kill André for this! Make filet of Frenchman! Throw his liver to the sharks whilst he still lived to watch! Her hand reached under the table for her sword hilt before she stopped herself. She couldn't slay the man just for embarrassing her, much as she was tempted in her present state of mind. But she would not, could not, forgive him for this. Before anger could overcome her in spite of her resolution, the pirate abruptly stood and headed for the rear exit, stiffly ignoring the waves of mirth her reaction created. She couldn't stay here and listen to this a moment longer!

Behind her, she could hear André saying gaily, "I think, my comrades, that she is missing him. Why—just look at her racing to leave. She is overcome with *amour*!"

Lynnette stepped out the back door and walked into an alley filled with darkness, stinking refuse, and more. Shouts and laughter from the tavern followed her out, and she cringed inwardly, knowing she was the butt of their humor. The pirate was unaware, unusually, of any potential danger, the closeness of the fetid night air in the narrow space between buildings and the greater than normal quantity of ale she had consumed causing her to be off her guard. She would later curse both conditions heartily.

With only a slight scraping noise for warning, she felt her sword being pulled from its scabbard and away. She spun, suddenly alert, and felt a rush of heady adrenaline replace her drunken fog as she glared into the pitch-black alley. Her attacker—no, attackers (she counted four)—were mere bulky shadows lurking just behind her, close by the doorway. As she watched, another emerged at the mouth of the alley, blocking the only means of escape.

They must have been waiting here for her all evening, she thought swiftly. Were they thieves? Nay, this attack was no crime of opportunity, and no ordinary thief could have known ahead of time about the money she was carrying in a secret sash about her waist. These men wanted more than coin, from the lowering look of them. Had her nemesis finally chosen to fight back by sending hired thugs to kill her, or were these simply unfriendly members of the Brethren come out to teach her a lesson in humility? She dismissed the latter idea immediately. If anything had been planned, everyone in the tavern would have known about it, for secrets were hard to keep in buccaneer haunts. She would have sensed from their faces that something was afoot. Nay, it had to be Lord Roger.

Well, they'd not have much to report back to the bastard, she vowed, snarling silently in fury. They'd not be *coming* back, except perhaps in shrouds, if she had aught to say about it. Despite the fact that they'd gotten her cutlass, she was far from unarmed. Besides the lethal dagger sheathed in its boot holder, her body itself had been trained for use as a weapon. Five burly men against one woman with a knife was not normally good odds, but Lynnette was not the average female, and she had the advantage of fury with her. Her chances for survival were not good, she was aware, but she wasn't going to go down without taking at least three of the curs with her.

The men rushed her, nightmare shadows in the dark reaching to drag her to hell. Thorne's hand was going for her dagger even as the first one neared, roaring like the demon he seemed. He carried no weapon but his meaty paws. In the split second while she twisted out of the way of his wild swing and whipped her knife free, she wondered why. Fists could kill, certainly, but they weren't the weapons of choice for assassins. A knife in the dark or a garrote would be quicker and quieter.

The others, also strangely unarmed, ranged themselves around her, joining the first, trying to form a circle and cut off her retreat. She had no choice but to put her back against the wall and face them, escape through the tavern door having been denied her in the first instant of the ambush. And it was a good place for an ambush, the pirate thought, wryly giving the thugs their due. No room for evasive maneuvers, only one way out into the streets—and that blocked by an ape of a man the size of a mizzenmast. It was fight straight or nothing, and Lynnette wasn't about to hand her life up meekly to a bunch of hired filth.

They circled her warily, milling about restlessly after the first encounter had failed. Why weren't they attacking, damn them? "Come on, then!" she yelled into the night, voice hoarse with fear and anger in equal measure. The noise leaking from the tavern assured her a shout for help would go unheard, and even if anyone *had* heard, it was debatable whether they'd intervene. André, she guessed, had probably taken that doxy he'd been eyeing upstairs as soon as he'd finished regaling the others with tales of her doings, and anyone else in the *Rising Gorge* was as likely to help out her assailants as herself. The Brethren were not the most loving family of which one could be a member.

The men remained still, more menacing somehow in their immobility than they would have been if they'd attacked in a melee. At least then she could have fought, rather than be forced to stand and wait. "Come on, you cowards, fight! 'Tis what you came to do!" She slashed furiously with her dagger at the nearest man. He leapt back, then, growling at having retreated from a mere woman, moved forward purposefully. It served as a signal for the others.

Ah, now! she thought. Now they come. Lynnette kicked the first to reach her with a powerful roundabout that connected solidly with his solar plexus. He grunted heavily, stumbling back and doubling over. The next she slashed wickedly, missing her intended target as he twisted, but opening a deep wound in the flesh of his shoulder instead. The man howled as he was temporarily disabled. But the man she'd kicked was straightening, murder in his face.

One down, and not for long, either, by the looks of it. Four more yet to deal with. But now they were angry and closing in. Lynnette felt the rough wall scratching her back through her thin linen shirt. Cold sweat beaded on her temples and upper lip. The second man reached for her with outstretched meaty hands, a grin on his broad face at her obvious dilemma. She felt like a trapped fox with the hunting dogs yapping at her heels. And like a cornered animal, she lashed out with all she had, dagger whipping viciously at her foe. The thug drew back quickly, but not fast enough, grin fading to a snarl of rage at the blood dripping from his wounded hand.

"Not one of you can take me!" cried the pirate queen with triumph in her voice. These were patently inept brutes, she thought, giddy hope warring with confusion. They just stood there, reluctant to attack, when clearly if they rushed her, the fight would be over in seconds. She might have a chance yet!

"Then we'll take ye all together!" growled the one she'd cut first, the one who appeared to be the leader of this motley bunch. Lynnette's chance flew out the window as he gestured to the others to come at her. Why on earth had she given them the idea with her rash words?

A hand grabbed her upper arm before she could react, spinning her away from the sheltering wall and into a circle of hostile faces. She ripped her arm free, lashing out with boot and knife and doing a good deal of damage, but not enough. No matter what she did, the bastards kept coming at her! She turned round and round in wild circles, trying to protect all sides from attack.

She could hear her own breath coming in harsh pants, the occasional grunt or hiss of pain from one of the thugs, but all in all, it was an eerily silent struggle. These were surely the oddest ruffians she'd ever encountered. This was no random attack—they had an agenda, of that she was quite sure. To take her back alive to Lord Roger? Possible, but why should he want her alive when he would gain relief from attack on his shipping by her death? No matter, she'd rather die than be brought to that scum in chains.

She knew she could not last long this way, not without

sword or pistol. Against three men, even armed as she was with just a dagger, Lynnette might have prevailed, but five was simply too many. She'd learned to fight with her body, to use the leverage of her opponent's weight against him, and to inflict deadly injuries with her fists and feet, but in a crowded alley, with so many to fight, these skills were nearly useless. To turn her attention to really taking one or two men down would be to leave herself open to too many others.

Out of the corner of her eye, the pirate caught a flash of movement and sent a brutal kick to the aggressor's head. He shrieked in agony, hit the ground hard, but now the leader was on her, the look of a grudge in his eyes. Recognizing that he was more dangerous than the others, she focused her full attention on him as he stepped closer menacingly.

This was a mistake. Even as she judged the best angle to strike at him, great muscled arms came about her in a crushing vise from behind. Lynnette yelled with rage and disbelief, realizing her arms were pinioned to her sides quite hopelessly. The leader came forward, grim wrath on his face, hugging his injured arm close to his side. Just as grimly, the pirate used her captor's solid weight for balance in a sudden move, heaving back with raised legs to drive into the man's stomach in a kick strong as a mule's. The plan was to disable the one in front of her and break free of the one behind, but she was successful in only one part of her twofold goal. With a great whoosh of outrushing air, the leader crashed to the ground. But the one holding her, whose hot breath scorched the back of her neck and whose beefy arms were crushing her ribs, let up not a whit, barely staggered by her backward lunge.

Lynnette thrashed wildly and rained curses on the thugs' heads, but to her horror, could not get free no matter what she did. She tried every trick she'd learned in seven years of dangerous living, but the sheer strength of her captor withstood it all, and she could not catch her breath from the squeezing he was giving her lungs with his massive grip. Then she saw the one she'd dropped gain his feet again, and felt a heavy dread pervade her senses. To have it all come down to this . . . Lord Roger would win, after all.

The bleeding ruffian faced her, watching her struggles impassively for a moment. Then he turned to the others, who were obviously awaiting his orders, and wheezed, "Ta hell wi' not 'urting the bitch!"

The last thing the pirate queen saw was a huge fist streaking toward her jaw. Then a flash of blinding light and agony— and a long slow fall into utter blackness.

CHAPTER EIGHTEEN

ANIEL SAT in the well-appointed cabin's wing-backed chair, staring at his handiwork. Upon the wide four-poster bed lay the spread-eagle, nude form of Captain Thorne, unconscious and vulnerable as he'd never seen that fierce virago before. She lay above the covers, wrists and ankles tied with silk scarves to the bedposts. She looked young, innocent, even defenseless. The sight bothered him inordinately, considering it was his doing that she was in the position in the first place. He scowled, brooding darkly on his own conflicting feelings. His plan had worked out better than he could have hoped; he had the pirate at his mercy, and yet his sense of victory was not complete.

Not for the first time, he wondered what he'd gotten himself into by assaying to take revenge on the pirate queen. To be sure, his rage at her had not abated one whit, but now it was commingled with feelings of uncertainty and, if he wanted to be brutally honest with himself, remorse. He was not at all sure that his planned punishment for her was quite just, albeit it was splendidly biblical in nature. She was, after all, a female, and chivalry demanded he protect all women from those who would do to them exactly the sort of things he planned to do to Lynnette.

Yet, Captain Bradley reminded himself with a renewed sense of furious indignation, the laws of chivalry had been created to serve women who were gently bred and defenseless, two things Captain Thorne definitely was *not*. The code of honor he'd lived his life by had never prepared him for a woman like the pirate now lying before him. She was, he decided, feeling a tiny bit more justified, outside all the rules, and that by her own choice. So why, then, did he feel such anger at the woman, and at the same time, still experience guilt at seeing her trussed up and naked on his bed?

And that was not even the worst of Daniel's wretched confusion. Nay, the worst was the unbridled lust he could not prevent from thickening his shaft and sending blood racing through his veins at the sight of her bared body, positioned so that no aspect of her lovely, stunning femininity was denied his hot gaze.

He felt another stab of remorse, looking down at her and remembering how his men had brought her aboard ship, her body limp, limbs drooping across the third mate's cradling arms. Too, he recalled the outrageous shock of fear he'd experienced at seeing her that way, desperately afraid something had gone wrong and she'd been killed. He'd given orders that she was not to be injured, damn it! As soon as Daniel assured himself that Lynnette wasn't seriously hurt, he'd set the men who'd brought her to him to trembling with his vicious tongue-lashing.

Indeed, Daniel's wrath had barely eased when they explained they'd had no choice, displaying their injuries, which ranged from mild to one—the self-same third mate's—that would require weeks of recuperation before he could resume full duties. The strain of carrying the pirate showed in his white face, but he gravely took responsibility for all the men's actions, having been the commander of the expedition. He described in great detail the tremendous fight the pirate had put up. If they'd been speaking of any other woman, Captain Bradley would have believed his men were greatly exaggerating the struggle they'd suffered, but he knew Lynnette all too well and he was hardly surprised by their tale. He said little to the men, merely ordered them to find the ship's surgeon, and afterward their hammocks. Then he took the unconscious woman into his arms and carried her belowdecks.

Two shocks greeted Daniel simultaneously when he removed her ruined shirt and her breeches. The first was fast becoming familiar to him: a deep and instantaneous rush of heat to his groin at the sight of her magnificent, breathtaking nudity. The second was far more unexpected. About the pirate's slim waist was strapped a strangely fashioned belt—a money belt, he realized, elation warring with a sense of irony in his mind. He might well be gaining far more than personal

vengeance tonight, he thought as he stripped it from her un-
resisting form. Their roles were well and truly reversed. Now
he held the captive, now *he* commandeered the property . . .
but he was no remorseless pirate. Nay, he only took what he
was owed.

He would leave her the golden chain that still gleamed upon
her slender neck, and if that was as much because it stirred
his blood to see her clad in it and naught else as because the
necklace was a part of Captain Thorne she rarely removed,
well, that was his own business. Turning from her quickly, he
opened the separate pouches of the belt, which were made so
that coins would not clink together and reveal what was meant
to be hidden, and dumped the contents onto the desk bolted
to the floor of the cabin.

His breath caught as gold winked at him from the mahogany surface of the desk, shining dully in the lamplight. More
gold than he'd ever seen together in one place at one time.
Quickly, Daniel counted up his findings. An astounding fortune in Spanish doubloons had girded her willowy form—
enough, he judged, to reimburse himself and his partner for
the loss of the *Empire* as well as for the ransom.

Triumph filled Daniel as he continued to stare at the heavy
coins. This would set them back in business, indeed! But why
was the woman carrying so much coin at one time? He knew
for a fact that the crew of the *Maiden* had already been given
their share of the booty from the sale of his ship and his person, and no matter that captains always received the greatest
share of the profits from their missions, this was more than
her takings from that particular venture could have been. But
then, the buccaneers had taken another vessel recently, hadn't
they? Could the gold represent the spoils from that new act of
piracy?

Well, whatever the answer, he'd have plenty of time to
wrest it from his prisoner in the coming weeks, he thought
with a great deal of satisfaction. Her capture had been a better
scheme than even he had dreamed! Thinking about the
money—wealth that represented months of frustration and
fury on his part—hardened his heart against the pitiful sight
of the woman lying pale and helpless upon his bed. She'd
shown no such tender feelings of remorse for him in the past,
and surely, with the life she'd lived, she'd not expect to be

treated like a lady once caught by one who had suffered at her hands. Nay, Lynnette herself would laugh at him for his squeamishness.

Recalling the last time she'd laughed at him, Daniel's resolve hardened to granite, all conflict dissolving. He would proceed according to the plan he'd apprised Simon of, and nothing could stop him, not even his partner's disapproval. The man had certainly been surprised when his silver-eyed friend outlined the remorseless plot. And when Simon had seen Lynnette's inert body being carried up the gangplank, he'd turned to his friend with questioning eyes.

"You're sure you want to do this?"

"Aye. We agreed upon it, didn't we?" Bradley's voice, despite his will to keep it firm, was the tiniest bit uncertain as he watched the sailors coming toward them.

"Yes, but, well—it just doesn't seem quite the thing to do, even to a pirate, you know."

"To one who has quite possibly ruined our hopes of success in the future? I couldn't disagree more. I think this is *exactly* the thing to do. Besides," he continued, sending his partner an admonitory glance, "you agreed not to interfere."

Simon thought his friend was probably overstating the case; it was nearly certain that with a lot of hard work and a great deal of persuasive talking to the investors back home, the Bradley-Richards Trading Company would remain in business a while longer. "I remember what we agreed upon, and I have no plans to renege, but I don't have to like it." Then, with a hint of mirth to dispel the tension, he added, "But it doesn't seem quite fair that while I have to pilot the ship this voyage, you get to enjoy the comforts of the captain's cabin—*and* of the lady who'll share it."

Daniel had paid little heed to this attempt at witticism at the time; now, he reflected with smug satisfaction, Simon would discover that his partner was not the only one to enjoy the outcome of their little kidnapping foray. Indeed, Daniel was quite sure the other man would lose all reticence about keeping their prized captive once he found out what the wench had been carrying on her person.

He allowed himself the luxury of examining his captive. "His captive"—the words had a savor on his tongue that he relished. Revenge would indeed be sweet, if the vision before him was any indication.

Lynnette was a glorious sight, rosy nipples hard in the chill night air, sweet curves bared for his hungry gaze, gold links and emeralds glittering against the creamy skin of her throat, coppery hair tumbled in fiery skeins about her shoulders, every inch a pagan goddess. Sweet Jesu, it had been less than two days since he'd seen her thus, yet he felt like a man deprived for years of his heart's desire. She looked like Diana, the virgin goddess of the hunt, impossibly pure and innocent. And his mind was set to sully that untamed heart.

He reminded himself again of her callous, cold nature, as unlike her warm and sweet appearance as night from day. Captain Thorne was no angel of grace, but a bloodthirsty, cruel, amoral pirate. She had no gentle side, no human emotions at all, only a driving ambition and an unswerving will that enabled her to ruthlessly cut down anything or anyone in her path and never look back. The crimes she had perpetrated against him, piracy and kidnapping being the very least of them, would not go unpunished, Daniel vowed.

As he watched her coming around, moaning softly and tossing her head on the pillow, his expression was dispassionate. Lynnette had gotten what she deserved, and he was going to enjoy every moment of his revenge. If it killed him.

Lynnette knew something was wrong, but the dark mists shrouding her mind would not let her focus on just what it was. Little things came to her attention like unconnected pieces of a stubborn puzzle. A thick strand of hair was caught in her mouth. But hadn't she put it up this morning? She couldn't recall taking it down again. Her arms ached dully, as did her jaw. Goose bumps rose on her flesh from a chill breeze. And the bed did not seem to be quite steady, which was odd, because she couldn't remember going to bed in the first place, on land *or* at sea. Aye, something was definitely wrong.

Part of her thought it might be best to let the darkness take her again, for a niggling sense of doom was crawling through her veins. It told her that waking would be far more unpleasant than the swirling oblivion gradually receding from her brain like a slow ebb tide. But the fearful unease was growing in her, and ingrained reaction told the pirate that danger left unfaced was likelier to be fatal than that which was met head-on.

The feeling of wrongness solidified as she became aware of being watched. Her body surged suddenly with adrenaline as she came fully awake, and she came out of her confusion with a start and an upward jerk of her head.

Except that her body was supposed to follow. Certainly, she'd intended to sit up, but her limbs could not respond to her commands. A sharp pain in her arms as she wrenched against resistance caused her to gasp. Her eyes flew open, seeing only a dark expanse of wooden ceiling and tangled skeins of hair before she whipped her head to the side to see what was wrong with her arms. Lynnette could just see her wrist out of the corner of her eye, bound with something white and silky to the massive bedpost of an unfamiliar bed. Momentarily uncomprehending, she checked the other side and found the same was true there also. *Symmetrical*, she thought muzzily, then wondered whether her legs were the same. She tried moving them, but they too were held fast. Fear gripping her, she raised herself up as best she could to look. That was when she discovered she was completely nude.

And that was when she discovered why; for there, sitting calmly in the chair at the foot of the bed, with his legs crossed negligently at the ankle and an unreadable expression on his chiseled features, was Captain Daniel Robert Bradley.

All that had befallen her since leaving the tavern in a drunken huff came back to her in a rush, events falling into place with an almost audible click; the attack in the alley, her desperate fight, the meaty fist heading for her jaw.

Captain Thorne began to curse as if her life depended on it.

Daniel waited patiently, face impassive, for the wild explosive struggles, the torrent of vile threats, oaths, promises of violence, and other sundry abuses against his person to wind down. He moved not a muscle. And finally, even Lynnette's vast store of obscenities was exhausted, as were her strained reserves of energy. She fell back against the mattress, realizing fighting against her bonds was useless, for Bradley had tied them too well.

She was panting, furious at what he had done to her and

at how neatly he'd been able to do it. She couldn't believe
he'd dared to humiliate her this way, to strip her and keep her
tied to his bed like some whore! Well, he'd pay. Sure as the
sun rose in the east, he'd pay for this insult! She might have
expected this sort of treatment from her enemy, Lord Roger;
but from the peacock?

Indeed, she'd thought it was her nemesis who'd ambushed
her, had been nearly sure it could only be that bastard Pennsworth. But it seemed she'd once again underestimated her erstwhile captive. Lynnette cast a glare his way, and what she saw
on Daniel's face chilled her. Gone was the laughing, open
expression she'd been accustomed to seeing him wear. Now
he was absolutely cold, dispassionate, a stranger—nay, an enemy.

Damn the drinks she'd so thoughtlessly quaffed tonight,
and damn herself for allowing her mind to wander when she
knew full well danger stalked her day and night! The fact that
she hadn't even considered Captain Bradley might come after
her for what she'd done to him was proof of her carelessness
of late. She'd been so busy feeling miserable about seeing the
last of him that she hadn't even thought she might *not* have.
And that was the height of stupidity, as Lynnette reckoned it.
She knew him well enough to know he didn't take insult passively, didn't take anything passively, not captivity, not any
of her many challenges to him, and certainly not their lovemaking. She cut *that* thought off immediately. Lovemaking
was definitely not what Bradley had in mind this time.

But what then? What *were* his plans for her now? Lynnette
took account of what little she knew of her situation. She was
aboard a ship, that much she could immediately tell, as well
as that it had already left harbor, for the rocking of the vessel
beneath her had the peculiar rolling motion that only the open
sea could engender. She was naked, a captive, completely
helpless for the moment to the uncertain desires of a man who
had much to hate her for. And she was afraid.

Slowly, she lifted her head to stare into Daniel's glowing
silver eyes. "What do you intend to do now?" she asked, her
tone as firm and dispassionate as she could make it with rage
and fear racing through her veins.

His eyes flicked down the length of her body slowly, insultingly. His gaze was a deliberately crude appraisal of her

figure that made the pirate feel the nakedness of her flesh even more vividly, if possible, than before. She was reminded of the expression she had seen once on the face of a slave-buyer at an auction in Jamaica, the man looking at the terrified woman he was considering as if she were a prime piece of horseflesh he wasn't sure whether to ride or put to stud.

It was as if all the easy conversations they'd shared, all the moments of camaraderie, even the brief but uncommon sense of communion between them when they'd made love had never occurred. Ever since she had met the man, Lynnette had felt a strange connection with him, as though she could almost guess how he would feel about an issue, or react to something she said. He'd seemed to feel the same connection. It was as if they instinctively *knew* each other, would never be strangers. But now when she looked at Daniel, she saw that he had shut himself to her, had closed off any trace of familiarity and would take no account of their past except to use it against her in his revenge.

She nearly cringed when he moved to sit by her side on the bed so she could see him better. Belatedly, she realized that he was going to answer her question. "Oh, I'll do naught more to you than you deserve, and take no more than you owe," he drawled lazily, a slight smile twisting his sculpted lips. One finger traced its way along the curved length of her side. Her concentration was pulled unwillingly to focus on the motion of his hand when he began to draw slow circles on her hip, even as he rubbed his jaw with the other hand in mock thoughtfulness. "Well, shall we count up the debts you owe me, one by one?" Daniel asked politely. He didn't wait for a response.

As she stared in horror at the cold, cruel stranger Captain Bradley had become, he ticked off items on his fingers. "First, you took my ship and cost myself and my partner a great deal in ransom money. However, we have just been recompensed for that inconvenience," and he nodded significantly at her bare waist.

With a mental curse, Lynnette recalled the money belt she'd been carrying with her tonight. She'd been intending to commission a few structural improvements she'd designed for the *Maiden* before their final encounter with Pennsworth, as well as pay for the supplies they needed to set out again, using the spoils of several recent ventures. She'd planned to deposit the rest of the gold into one of her already hefty bank accounts. Now, it hardly mattered. Never having been one to deny the obvious, no matter how unpleasant it was, the pirate accepted the seriousness of her situation immediately.

She'd been caught; not by Lord Roger as she'd originally thought, but she had no doubt that this would hardly prove better for her. The peacock was capable, obviously, of greater deviousness and vengeance than she'd guessed. If she wanted to get out of this predicament whole and sane, she must never underestimate him again. If he had forgotten so easily the attraction between them, the compelling, unnameable force that had caught them upon her island, then she must endeavor to do the same. Her heart told her that would not be simple. Even now, she admitted, some ridiculous part of her still thrilled at the sight of him, just as, equally, she feared him as never before . . .

But he was still talking. "And then there are the months of captivity to consider," he mused silkily, his hot hand now sliding casually up and down her thigh. "Oh, yes, I definitely must get something back for that." He smiled at her and she shivered, feeling his hand on her leg like a red-hot brand, frightening her and heating her blood at the same time. "Since you cannot give me back *my* lost time, you'll simply have to give me the next few months of *yours*. The voyage to London, give or take several weeks, should suffice."

Lynnette could no longer hold her tongue at this, little as she wanted to give him the satisfaction of hearing her helpless outrage. "London! Absolutely *not*!" she cried before she thought of how much she might be giving away. " 'Tis exactly the opposite direction from where I need to go!" Then she bit her lip, becoming aware as his sharp gaze pierced her suddenly that she'd shared more than she wanted to about her future plans.

"Besides," she finished lamely, trying to cover her loose-tongued words, "there's a hefty price upon my head should the authorities find me in London. My face is printed on notices of piracy all over the wharves."

"No one asked you your opinion on the direction of this vessel, mistress," he replied cruelly, stressing the last word in a way the pirate didn't like. Inwardly, he was more than intrigued by her slip. So the pirate queen had another venture in mind already. From her tone, he judged that this was a most important mission to her. Well, she would just have to miss her date with destiny. He could wait a bit to discover just what she'd intended, however. Right now he had other things on his mind.

"As for the possibility of your capture, I must say that is really none of my concern. In fact," he pondered aloud, "giving you over to the authorities might be a good idea, now that you mention it. I will have to think on the matter more fully before I make my decision." He saw the rage deepen on her face and relished every moment of her helpless fury. He had no intention of handing her over to the magistrate for punishment, for, angry as he might be, he considered his revenge a private matter. Not for anything in the world would he sentence the pirate queen to the degradation and torture of Newgate prison. The very thought of it made him physically ill. But she was not to know that.

"I might, however, be persuaded," he drawled, "to help you go free once we reach England if you are, shall we say, *cooperative* during your stay aboard the *Triumph*. I daresay you'll have a far better chance of eluding the hangman's noose if you please me than if you don't."

Lynnette simply stared at him, shocked and appalled. Never had she dreamed his hatred went so deep, or that he would demand such a price to mollify it. Renewed anger welled up in her as the import of his words sank in. "I'll not whore for you!" she hissed. "Not even if it means my death to deny you!"

"Then you'll just have to take your chances with my clemency, will you not?" he replied evenly.

"You would not do it," she gasped on a mere breath of air. In truth, she felt no such conviction. Her mind raced. If he took her to London, handed her over for hanging, there would be no escape for her. She would die, and Lord Roger would go free. "Not when I'm so close to the end," she whispered, unaware of speaking aloud. She'd always known a pirate's death was a possibility, had accepted that risk, but she had never considered that it might happen before she could complete her revenge. Unless she could escape Daniel and his nefarious plans for her, she would miss the rendezvous, miss her chance to take that last ship that would finally ruin her enemy. Nay, she must find a way to get out of this, and do it fast, before her crew scattered, her chance was lost, and Pennsworth could begin to recoup his losses.

Daniel heard her last words, though they were spoken so softly he had to strain for the sound. "Close to the end of what?" he questioned sharply. Lynnette's eyes snapped up to meet his, luminous emerald orbs filled with defiant fury. He knew she would not speak further even before she spat the foul curse at him, for he sensed she'd nearly revealed something vital. He guessed, acutely attuned to her mind as always, that her cryptic words had much to do with the purpose that was driving her, the cause of her reckless behavior. Though she guarded her secrets well, he knew beyond a doubt that something more than money had driven her to take up the sword. After all, she'd barely blinked when he'd told her he'd taken her gold.

"If you tell me what you meant," he coaxed, "it might make things easier on you."

She didn't believe him for a second. First it was whore for him, now it was tell her secrets. She'd rather take the consequences, damn it all! She was no quivering maiden to be affrighted by mere threats! She was Captain Thorne, and she'd dealt with men of his ilk before. She felt her anger returning to clothe her like a suit of armor, squelching her fear beneath a wave of indignation and confidence. She'd find a way to escape.

"Go to hell," she snapped, voice firm and strong once again. "Do your worst and be done already. I grow weary of your blathering, *Peacock*." The name was a purposeful insult, showing all of her disdain. As a further declaration of unconcern, the pirate turned her head away to stare at the wall. It was a brave show coming from a woman who was tied naked to her enemy's bed. Inwardly, she still trembled with fear, but she swore she'd never let the cur see it.

Lynnette cared not a whit that, in truth, Bradley had as much right to take her prisoner and humiliate her as she'd had to do the same to him. She felt not an iota of respect for him for besting her—no mean feat, surely—and refused to concede anything but that she hated him for this torture he was putting her through. Then his hand began to stroke her inner thigh, and she sucked in her breath, stiffening. What was the bastard up to now?

"But, my dear, you have not even heard the 'worst' as you call it; your last debt to me," he replied smoothly. His hand continued its intimate caress.

What other debt? She owed him nothing more. The torment of his warm hands on her body must surely be just another way of taking vengeance for his enforced stay on No-name. She flung her head about to spear him with a burning glare. "Is it to be rape, then?" she rasped through gritted teeth.

"Hardly, my lovely Captain Thorne. I doubt very much that I shall have to resort to anything so crude as that." He looked purposely at her pebbled nipples, straining and ripe.

And to her everlasting shame, she knew it was true. Her mind might despise him all it willed, but her traitorous body could not forget the rapture he had brought her, the ache only he could satisfy. She'd known just once would never be enough in his arms, and now the truth of her weakness seared her to the core. She'd been wrong to ever take him to her bed, wrong to think she could taste just once of passion and then walk away from it forever. Though Daniel had become a stranger to her mind, her body knew his all too well, and it wanted to succumb to the magic of his touch, even as she knew to do so would be playing right into his hands. He would possess her in a way that no one else had ever been able to, would take her freedom by seducing her into willing submission more surely than if he'd simply forced himself on her. And she was not at all sure that she could stop him.

"I never did such to you!" she cried.

"Did you not, sweet Captain?" he sneered.

"Never!"

"That is not the way I recall it, I'm afraid. Indeed, it seems to me you tormented me with your ripe curves and hot kisses almost constantly. I hardly had a moment's respite from the teasing of your voluptuous body. I see no reason why you should not also suffer the same frustration." The tone of his voice was decidedly smug, for this was the best part of the revenge he had planned, certainly the part he most looked forward to.

The pirate forced a disdainful smile. " 'Twill never happen, Peacock! I care naught for your touch," she bluffed. "You are

arrogant in the extreme if you think otherwise." Bravely, she
ignored the fingertips brushing her exposed inner thighs. "Put
whatever labels on the deed you will, but 'twill be rape, for
you disgust me!" She wished she were not lying, for she would
rather suffer her sister's fate than surrender to passion with
this man who wanted only her destruction. But even the sight
of his handsome face caused her heart to beat faster, her blood
to race in her veins with anticipation. His touch was too much
for her weak control to abide.

"Shall we discover the truth of that, Lynnette?" he whispered seductively. He leaned close, and she tensed.

"You'll regret this!" she hissed as his warm sweet breath
teased her lips.

"Oh, I don't think so." With their lips an inch apart, he
whispered, "You will remain this way at my convenience, naked in my bed, ready to serve my needs, *mistress*." And as
she gasped out a denial, his mouth came down hard on hers,
punishing, devouring.

Daniel might be a granite-willed stranger to her now, a
frightening tormentor, but his kiss was achingly familiar,
scorching her with waves of pleasure even as she fought to
resist. She struggled furiously, straining at her bonds and trying desperately to tear her mouth free of his drugging lips, but
his hands cupping her cheeks held her head still, and the strong
silk of her ties would not loosen a whit. She moaned in fury
and despair as dark desire clouded her senses and sent her
reeling into a realm of pure sensation. Daniel released her lips,
slightly out of breath, to murmur close to her ear, "I think you
are a liar, my sweet. Your body betrays you."

"You bastard!" she hissed. Lynnette's helplessness crashed
down on her like a hurricane. No matter what he did to her,
she realized he would always have command over her body,
and the knowledge crushed her. Always she had prided herself
on being no man's slave, on taking command of every aspect
of her life. But now she was captive to another—captive to a
silver-eyed devil with power over her destiny *and* her soul.
And he wanted it all. He was forcing her to give it to him,
with his lips, his tongue, his hands. A single caress and she
was undone, no matter that his touch was rough and angry.
Indeed, the very urgency and fury in his body matched her
own wild, uncompromising passion.

They had always communicated better with their bodies than their words. All Daniel's frustration, anger, and desire went into his kiss, along with another unrecognized, unnamed emotion stronger than these. He was met with Lynnette's rage, fear, and ardor, her own desperate longing joining them all together as she fought both against him and herself, losing both battles. Daniel didn't know it, but he had hit upon the worst punishment possible—for himself *and* his prisoner.

As his fingertips slid their way up and down the sensitive insides of her arms, Lynnette moaned softly. He was undoing her, picking apart her defenses one by one with a magic she couldn't comprehend. His voice seduced, his lips coaxed, and his warm, strong hands drew out responses to his lovemaking she hadn't known she was capable of. With her eyes closed to counter the stirring sight of his dark head bent to suckle at her breasts, her mind turned fanciful. Her lover was still Daniel, but he was not angry, not now. Instead he loved her with all the sweetness and tender emotion that was lacking in her life, his mouth soothing and exciting at the same time as it laved and sucked on her throbbing nipples. His palms ran the length of her body, setting all the fine hairs rising with their warm possession. His linen shirt was raspy and soft at the same time as it brushed her silken skin, and his raven-black hair sweeping her face and neck was like the wings of a butterfly, teasing and delightful. Unknowing, the pirate arched to meet her captor's dreamlike seduction, harsh words and deeds forgotten in the splendor of his loving.

Daniel's husky voice became the center of her world, whispering encouragement and spicy love words to guide her untrained body, so newly awakened, to deepest ecstasy. Her flesh responded to his touch, not her own will, as he stroked and caressed every part of her from her toes to her hair. When he closed his wet, warm mouth around her biggest toe, she nearly fainted from the highly unexpected pleasure. And when he ran his seeking tongue along the length of her leg from ankle to thigh, she thought she would surely not outlive the experience. But it was when his invading mouth closed hungrily over the aching core of her desire that she knew she had truly died and gone to heaven.

Like a skilled violinist, he wrung every note on the scale of passion from her, playing upon her sleek body until she was mindless and shuddering. He ignored the incoherent mutters of protest over his intimate fondling, for even as she gasped at the shock of his tongue tasting and swirling around her pleasure bud, she arched her hips hungrily to meet the touch. And then she couldn't speak at all, for her body was pulsing and roiling with the inexplicable sensations he was creating.

And when she would have reached the peak, he smiled tenderly against her thigh and eased the magic of his touch, left her gasping and wanting. Meeting her glazed emerald eyes sincerely, he murmured, "You don't want this, sweet." He paused, watching her flushed face register first confusion, then dawning understanding. "That *was* what you said, wasn't it, sweet Captain? I believe your exact words were: 'I care naught for your touch.' Tell me that was just a lie."

No! she wanted to scream, whether in denial of her own words or of his conscienceless torture she didn't know. The fantasy ended abruptly. Here was no besotted lover but, instead, a very determined man. Determined to make her beg, that is. Her aching, unsated body urged her to surrender, to admit that she'd lied, that she could no more deny her need for him than hold back a tidal wave with a leaky bucket. But her spirit damned him to the lowest circle of hell for what he did to her, for the ruthless way he was carrying out his revenge. Somehow, she managed to keep her lips closed against the words of admission that would both set her free and make her the veriest slave, even as his fingers parted her swollen, damp folds and his mouth came down to devour hers.

She tasted herself, musky and exciting against her tongue. She tasted him, warm and mysterious and probing, promising a whole world of new, sensual pleasures for her delectation. Her adventurous spirit called to her to accept Daniel's challenge, to explore with him the delights of lovemaking and forget everything but the passions of the flesh. She wanted him inside her, wanted his hard male flesh penetrating her softness, giving her everything a man could give a woman. But she would not beg for it. Not aloud. Silently, she arched her body to meet his, pressing bare skin against cloth, wishing her hands were free to disrobe him. The need to feel his bare, supple flesh against her own was nearly unbearable.

She strained against her bonds again, hating her helplessness, her inability to touch him. If she were free . . . ah, then she'd show him how dangerous it was to play games with a pirate! If she were free, she'd give him a taste of his own torment, ferreting out all the places that pleasured him most and using the knowledge mercilessly. She wanted to pull that dark head down for a kiss that would leave him mindless with passion. She wanted to run her palms down over his flanks, his belly, across his rampant maleness, stroking him until he begged for consummation. But her silken ties would not give. She moaned in frustration and rising desire. Her helplessness only fired her passion, for her own need, put together with the expert teasing of his caresses, were an explosive combination.

Again and again he brought her to the pinnacle, always knowing just when to stop, to let her down without appeasing the raging hunger in her blood. She wanted to cry, she wanted to give in to his whispered demands that she admit his touch was like no other, that she craved him, needed him, would die if she couldn't have the ecstasy of his body filling hers. Stubbornly, she clamped her mouth shut against those traitorous urges, allowing only strangled moans of frustrated pleasure to escape her lips.

Daniel eased apart from Lynnette as he felt her body begin to shudder yet again with the first ripples of climax.

"Admit you crave my touch, Lynnette. Tell me you want me, and I shall take you beyond the bounds of reason with me. Just say the word, my sweet . . ."

"Nay!" she panted, her desire having nothing, to her mind, to do with her pride. He *knew* the extent to which she wanted him. She wouldn't admit it aloud.

Daniel drove his fingers deep inside her in punishment. She let out a smothered scream of ecstasy. "I want to hear you say what we both know, love: that you are no unwilling partner."

"Nay," she moaned again. "Never!" It was too much to be borne, this attack both mental and physical. She couldn't think, struggled through blinding passion to retain control enough not to betray herself to him wholly, even as her wanton flesh blazed where he touched it. *At least,* some remote corner of her mind screamed, *don't give him this! He may control your body, but he cannot make you say it!*

It became all she could do to hold on to the hypocrisy that called their wild mating rape. Again, he urged her confession, voice dark and beguiling in her ear, and again she refused, the pleasure he was bringing her making it nearly impossible to speak. Heaven waited a second away, needing but a single touch to send her spiraling up to it, when Daniel tore his mouth from hers with a pained groan.

Abruptly, he pulled away from her and rolled to his side. She gasped with shock, feeling as if she'd been dashed with icy water. The pirate could only stare up at her captor, waves of intense feeling crashing through her body.

"Never," he panted softly, his tone managing to sound incredibly distant from a mere foot away, "let it be said that I forced an unwilling woman."

CHAPTER NINETEEN

*L*YNNETTE WAS waiting. She had been waiting for what seemed like forever, but what was, in reality, little more than the hour since she'd woken up. There was a certain urgency to the matter beyond simple boredom. She was afraid that if someone did not come to attend her needs, and come quickly, she was going to disgrace herself.

Not that she ever wanted to see that filthy stinking cowardly excuse for a merchant ever again. She'd rather die than reveal the embarrassing state she was in—nay, that he'd *put* her in! The man was sadistic, fiendish . . . a monster! Where was he, anyway? Did he intend for her to languish here in torment until she either starved or burst from a too-full bladder? Or worse, after last night's fiasco and his all-too-apparent anger over her refusal to surrender, did he plan to send someone else to see to her? As much as the idea of being humiliated by Daniel turned her stomach, the thought of anyone else—even a cabin boy—seeing her in this disgustingly helpless state made her feel even sicker.

And what if he abandoned her to the mercies of his crew? Or turned her over to the authorities for the piracy she was most definitely guilty of? She thought, nay, she *hoped* he'd not be capable of such cruelty. However, she reminded herself with a chill of fear, she had no way of knowing. Daniel was not the man she'd thought he was; he'd proven that amply last night.

Last night. She winced, remembering. Her near-complete surrender to him yesterday had been the most demoralizing event in Lynnette's young life. At first, after he'd left, she'd wished she could just crawl away and lick the emotional wounds he'd inflicted. Devastation and humiliation had welled up to crush her with their weight. The ease with which he had torn down her defenses, made her into a whimpering, needy slave to passion, revealed just how vulnerable she really was. Her hard-won control was a joke, a fiction. She was not strong. She couldn't even resist her own body's lust.

Lynnette had felt as if, in the course of one night, Daniel had managed to eradicate her whole existence as a free woman, a woman capable of taking command of a ship full of hard-bitten sailors and turning them into some of the most successful pirates in the Caribbean. He'd showed her how simple it was for him to make her exactly as he wanted her, to make her feel things she didn't want, to make her respond to his caresses like a trained animal. Now she was nothing more than the women she'd always scorned, helpless creatures who depended on men to see to their every need. Perhaps she'd been fooling herself to think she ever *had* been more.

But as she'd stared at the planking above her head sleeplessly, the pirate's feelings had gradually changed. The determination for which she was famous returned to steel her spine. Why was she so angry at herself? True, she'd been weak, but that indisputable fact she shoved into the back of her mind for now. She couldn't change what had already happened. But she also couldn't allow one instance of weakness to destroy her. She must remember that, until she'd met Captain Bradley, nothing had ever stopped her from pursuing her vengeance and leading her life as she chose.

Reluctantly, she'd conceded that he was by far the toughest opponent she'd ever come across. But that little fact did nothing to endear the man to her. The way he used his strength, his power over her, was despicable. Her methods might be ruthless, she thought righteously, but *his* were downright dirty. Certainly nothing she'd ever done to the merchant merited his treatment of her last night! A deep indignation had welled up inside her, rapidly replacing her despair. *She* wasn't at fault

here, Daniel was! It was *he* who had trussed her up and used
her like a whore! Memories of the casual way he'd played
with her had caused rage to build inside, deep and black and
ready to explode.

Snarling with fury, she'd yanked and tugged at her bonds,
wrenching her shoulders and hips but getting no further than
before in her attempts to win free. Finally, exhausted, she'd
contented herself with cursing his name loudly enough for the
whole crew to hear. And she was sure they *had* heard, for an
absolute and unusual silence reigned over the ship until she at
last fell asleep, words that no lady should know still tumbling
hoarsely from her lips.

This morning Lynnette was still angry. And getting more
so by the minute. Anger was bracing, far better than cringing
weakness. The pirate vowed that she would never experience
such soul-deep shame again, and that meant never allowing
him to use her again as he had. But how was she to stop it
from happening? she asked herself. He meant to use his power
over her body, to torture her with his teasing until she gave
in to his demands and admitted her desire for him. Even then
she doubted that Daniel would let her be. Something in his
eyes told her he would be satisfied with nothing less than total
possession. Never one to delude herself, Lynnette had no
doubts that when next the rogue came to torment her, try as
she might, she would not be able to make her flesh agree with
her mind in its disgust of him. Not when every time she caught
a glimpse of him her heart skipped a beat. Not while the memory of his incredible lovemaking was still impossible to ban-
ish.

She had to escape. It was the only way both to get back to
the business she had left unfinished when she was abducted,
and to prevent becoming hopelessly entangled in Daniel's dangerous web of passion and revenge. That, however, was easier
said than done. On a ship in the middle of the open sea, an
opportunity might not present itself for weeks. Unless she
could steal a boat, and do it at a time when the ship passed
close enough to shore to make the attempt feasible, she could
not hope to get free. Already, she knew, they were well out
to sea, and there was a good chance she wouldn't make it,
superb sailor that she was, to land before she grew too weak
from exposure to sun and sea to sail her craft. And before all

that could happen, she had to find a way to get free of her bonds.

She would have to wait and seize her opportunities as they arose. Until then she must be strong, for Lynnette absolutely refused to let Daniel gain victory over her.

Lost in resolute musing, the pirate did not notice the quiet entrance of her captor until he stood directly in her line of sight. When she did, she was instantly glad of the sheet he'd callously tossed over her on his way out the night before. Even decently covered up to her neck, Lynnette felt his scorching gaze burning her with its intensity. She read nothing of his thoughts on his closed features, but she was sure he could see her sudden tension, hear her accelerated heartbeat in the unnatural silence. For a long moment, neither spoke.

Finally, Lynnette couldn't bear it any longer. "Back to maul me again, Peacock?" she sneered. "I would expect no better from an overbred, undermannered cad like you, to tie a woman up and force her to accept your disgusting pawing—"

"Actually," he interrupted her ranting mildly, "I thought you might want something to eat." For the first time, Lynnette noticed the tray he carried.

"And how am I supposed to eat, with my hands tied?" she growled, not pacified in the least by his polite tone or the food he brought. Though she was relieved he apparently didn't intend to continue what he'd started yesterday just yet, she was wary of whatever new tricks he might have in store for her. But he merely set the tray down beside the bed and reached over to free her wrists and ankles. Thankfully, he didn't linger over the task. She sat up stiffly and took the embroidered sheet with her. She felt very naked despite the wadded cloth she quickly wrapped around her.

No longer was she the captor, with the security of knowing that she could do as she pleased with her prisoner, of knowing she was on home ground and had allies to back her up. Now Daniel had all the advantages of ship, crew, and strength, while she possessed nothing but her wits and courage. For a moment, she felt uncomfortably aware of the fact that she was now going through exactly what *he* had, but she brushed off all feelings of sympathy with a mental reminder that this was exactly how Captain Bradley had engineered his revenge. An eye for an eye, and damn the consequences.

But some of the unforeseen consequences of being held captive and tied up were becoming rather uncomfortable, her bladder reminded her urgently. With all her might, the pirate resisted the urge to squirm. Daniel, perceptive as usual, guessed anyway, smiling as he removed himself from the bed. Pausing for a leisurely look at Lynnette's scantily clad form without even a hint of compunction about his perusal, he murmured, "I think you'll find what you need behind the screen."

"Aren't you going to leave the room?" she asked incredulously.

"I don't trust you left to your own devices, my dear," he replied. "You're far too resourceful to set at liberty just yet. You'll simply have to tolerate my presence, I'm afraid."

The pirate felt rage well up again, but she refused to rise to his bait. If she argued, she'd get nowhere, she could see that clearly. This was just one more abasement to suffer. "Rotten *merchant*," she muttered, giving up the battle. She really *had* to go . . . Lynnette felt sure she heard the sound of a snicker as she stalked, bright red from head to toe, behind the discreet privacy screen.

Her business quickly done, the pirate was not half so quick to come out from her safe hiding place. She was fuming, enraged that the merchant had put her through such a degradation. Bad enough he made her prance about nearly naked in his cabin for his pleasure, she thought. Now he forced her to shame herself by admitting her base bodily needs. And this, she reminded herself furiously, wasn't the first time he'd made her silently acknowledge her "needs."

She was going to murder the man. She really was. Just as soon as she worked up the courage to emerge from behind the painted screen. But then she thought of Daniel waiting just on the other side of the thin wooden barrier, smirking because he knew she was too cowardly to face him, and that did the trick right enough. She took a deep breath and prepared to face her new nemesis. If she didn't, she knew he would just come and fetch her, heedless of any shreds of modesty or dignity she might have left.

Daniel watched her coming toward him, smiling just a bit too sweetly for a woman in her situation. His own expression grew wary, but by the time his instincts had stopped howling at the sight of her full, rounded breasts barely confined by the sheet, her narrow waist and her curvaceous hips draped in its folds, all framed by the halo of her long, shiny autumn-hued hair, and *started* howling that he should watch out, it was far too late. The pirate walked right up to her captor, looking like every man's wildest, most exotic fantasy, and punched him solidly in the gut.

That felt *tremendously* good. So she hit him again. This time the blow connected with his jaw, snapping his head back when he would have doubled over from the first swing. This one felt even better, and she brought her fist up a third time, intending to pay the swine back for all the humiliation she'd suffered at his hands since he'd abducted.her. But before she could do more than pull her arm back in preparation, he'd grabbed her wrist with blinding speed, his grip nearly hard enough to snap the bones. She gasped in shock, for he'd moved so quickly she hadn't even seen him reach for her.

Reflexively, she twisted, her body going into combat maneuvers before her brain had a chance to catch up. He still had hold of her wrist, but now the grip was across her shoulder. She heaved, her intention being to throw her opponent over her shoulder to land in a heap on the floor. It was a trick that had always worked in the past, leverage and surprise giving her the advantage over a stronger foe. However, nothing happened this time. Nothing at all. Daniel didn't go flying past her ear with a satisfying cry of shock, nor did he crash with a thud at her feet.

Thinking she must have gotten the angle of her throw wrong, she grasped his arm more tightly and heaved once more. No good. She tried a third time, unwilling to give up when the reward of seeing Captain Bradley lying stunned before her was so great. She was vaguely aware that the movement was throwing her posterior into contact with a certain section of his anatomy that her mind refused to name, but again there were no gratifying results.

Sanity returned slowly, telling her this fight was utterly ridiculous, for not only was Daniel stronger and heavier than she, the outcome was irrelevant. She couldn't do anything about her predicament right now even if she managed to get by the merchant and escape the cabin. She'd known that at the beginning. All she'd wanted was to knock the man down a peg—literally. And she couldn't even do that. He was too

quick and too well trained to be felled by such a simple maneuver. Instead all she'd wound up doing was shoving her rear
against him. If it weren't so embarrassing, she might have
laughed at the absurdity of it all.

Then his arm came around her waist, and any fleeting moment of levity fled at once. The feel of his steely grasp around
her, warm hair-roughened flesh sliding across her silky skin,
brought Lynnette up short as she was about to attempt breaking free. Her sheet had slipped to the ground unnoticed in the
struggle and the sensation of clothed, hard-muscled male
pressed up against her nude, vulnerable body was shocking.
His arm tightened, drawing her closer and closer until she was
flush with him, naked back to linen-clad chest. And broadcloth
breeches. And the hard heat beneath them. She dropped his
other arm, which she'd been holding in a death grip a moment
before, as if it scalded her. His palm came to rest gently on
her shoulder. Lynnette felt a slow burn start to smolder deep
in her belly.

"Your efforts," he began with a chuckle, "are much appreciated, but I think we both know it's futile."

Lynnette blushed crimson, for he illustrated what he meant
about "appreciation" with a rather unsubtle nudge of his pelvis
against her buttocks. His breath was hot against her neck, and
his lips brushed her skin just below the ear. She had to fight
not to shudder with unbidden pleasure. Oh, how she hated
him! He made her blush and tremble like a schoolroom chit,
instead of the hardened pirate she was. He rendered her helpless so skillfully, so effortlessly, with his words, his touch, his
very presence. He made her very real efforts to fight him off
seem no more than a child's romp, telling her with his amusement how ineffectual he considered her struggles. He made
her whimper in delight when she should be screaming in fury.
Nothing in her experience had taught her how to handle a man
like Daniel.

It didn't matter. He would not control her! she vowed. No
mere merchant had the right to reduce her to this, handsome
and cunning as the devil or no. Lynnette could not allow him
to take over her senses this way. Somehow, she had to get out
of this clinch, and fast, before her unseemly reaction to his
nearness became apparent. And contempt was the only weapon
she possessed right now.

"Oh, excellent, Peacock," she sneered with far more bravado than she felt. Her spine stiffened until she stood ramrod straight in his grasp. "Is this more of your oh-so chivalrous treatment, then? Indeed, I thought sure you'd had enough of rapine and coercion last night."

Stung by her bitter words and by the reminder of his own less-than-gentlemanly behavior the previous evening, he shoved her away from him abruptly.

"Damn you, wench," Daniel muttered under his breath. With her cold disdain, she made him feel like an aging roué chasing chambermaids around tables, when he knew damn well she was no hapless victim but an obstinate vixen who chose, out of pride, to deny them both.

He'd hoped that with his little demonstration last night he might convince the pirate to admit his effect on her senses; hoped that she would give up the pretense of being forced and simply enjoy the pleasures he could give her. He'd wanted to make her confess that she needed him, if not on a deep, emotional level, then at least bodily. Before the night had ended in frustration and unfulfilled desires for both of them, he'd been forced to admit his hope had been pure fantasy. She'd shown him her will could not be overwhelmed by any act of his, pleasurable though it might be. He'd left her at last with cruel words to cover the vast disappointment and hurt he felt at her rejection.

Lynnette would never give herself to him freely, not as a captive, not when she still hated him for kidnapping her and holding her prisoner. Last night had proved to him that, in their battle of wills, she was the stronger. He might have the upper hand, but without her consent and her willing participation, their lovemaking, far from being sweet, tasted like ashes in his mouth. His revenge had no savor, either. He stared broodingly down at the pirate queen who watched him warily, the cover once again wrapped securely about her slender frame.

"Eat your breakfast," he commanded abruptly, turning away from her.

Lynnette wondered at his sudden change of topic, but decided it was not wise to taunt her captor further at the moment and went along with it. Her tactic had worked; he'd let her go. Let his mood shifts be his own business! Besides, she *was* extremely hungry, not having eaten since early yesterday. And if she wanted to keep Daniel at bay, she would need her strength.

She sat down on the bed and dug into the cold, congealing ship's fare. He said nothing, merely watched her with a disturbingly direct gaze until she became too self-conscious to eat another bite.

What was he doing now? Why was he staring at her so? He didn't seem disposed to make further assaults on her person today, and she thanked heaven for that, even as a small part of her mind couldn't help wondering why not. Indeed, Daniel seemed quite reserved, cold and commanding and inscrutable. Had he changed his mind about holding her prisoner? Would he let her go, or at least allow her to dress? Not knowing what went on in the merchant's head was making her extremely nervous. She wanted to bolt, but knew it was useless. She wanted to scream at him to stop staring at her so, as if he could strip her of her soul as easily as he'd stripped her of clothing.

She set the tray down carefully on a desk by the bed. "What now," she asked mockingly, "the rack?"

He just glared at her sardonically in response, one brow quirked as if he were considering it.

"This can't go on," she said simply. Honestly. She tried to face him squarely, not an easy task considering the distinct disadvantage of having to hold the sheet tightly to her chest. To her surprise, he agreed.

"No, it can't." He sighed, not looking directly at her. He wanted to tell her he'd changed his mind, that he could not bear to treat her again as he had last night, for in hurting her, he had hurt himself. But he knew he would say nothing. Lynnette would only laugh if he confessed his second thoughts about this revenge he'd engineered. He couldn't bear her scorn, couldn't bear to open himself again to her contempt. Instead he told her nothing besides the obvious. "We're far enough out at sea now to make escape impossible, as you'll surely be wise enough to realize. And I cannot in good conscience keep you bound any longer.

"But be that as it may, the situation hasn't changed." He looked keenly into her eyes now, angry determination clearly writ in his own. "You're still a prisoner, until you choose to change that. You know what you have to do."

"Give in to your disgusting, lecherous demands, I suppose," she growled, but the effort was halfhearted at best. Lynnette simply didn't feel like fighting anymore. After spending the better part of the night resisting every advance he made, physical as well as mental persuasion included, she was exhausted and relieved just to have the liberty of her body. The rest would have to come later, for he was right, she couldn't escape right now. Before she could make any serious attempt, she'd have to scout out the ship, find out who was on watch at what hours, and who was lax in his duties. Innumerable other details swarmed her mind as she looked fiercely up at him, not the least of which was how to get out from under his watchful eye long enough to prepare the rest of her plans.

"I'll take that as a 'no,' " he replied dryly.

"Damned right, Peacock. I'll never be your lightskirt willingly."

"Somehow, I knew you'd say that." Daniel smiled with self-mockery. "Well, then, what say you to a bargain, Captain?"

Pulling the sheet more closely about her, she glanced suspiciously at her nemesis. "What sort of bargain do you propose, Captain?"

"A simple exchange is all. I will allow you the same freedoms you allowed me on the island if you will agree to cooperate and cause no troubles."

"It's not so simple as you would have it sound, Bradley, and you know it. Things have changed since those days on No-name, and there's no sense denying it." Lynnette took a deep breath. "For one thing, what happens when we get to London?" She didn't wait for his answer. "And what of the rest of the journey? I will not have as much freedom on this vessel as you did when I held you on the island. Will I have my own cabin?" she dared.

"Nay," he said without hesitation, answering her last question first. "You are correct. Things *have* changed, and some of those things are to my liking, Captain Thorne. Your presence in my bed being uppermost. That point is not negotiable."

"I've told you I'll not whore for you!"

He leaned close, lips a brush away from hers. "Perhaps

you'd prefer to bed down with the boatswain?" he drawled. "This is, after all, a working ship with a full crew complement. Where do you think you could be safer than right here?"

Lynnette bit down an angry comment to the effect that an alligator pit might look nice compared with her treatment at his hands, wisely realizing that the blasted rogue was right. She knew sailors—did she ever!—and while she might despise Captain Bradley, at least he was an evil she knew. An evil she was drawn to . . . Quickly, she cut that thought off before it could bring up more stirring memories. "If I remain here, I shall expect you not to force yourself on me again," she announced imperiously.

Daniel's lip curled with amusement at her audacity as he nodded solemnly. "I shall not, as you say, *force* you to lie with me again, though it is debatable whether force ever entered into our dealings together." She had no right to demand *anything* at this point, but rather than tell her so, in the interest of peace, he held his tongue.

The pirate didn't know what to make of his seemingly easy acquiescence. Unfortunately, she knew that she had nothing at all with which to bargain, and any concessions Daniel might make were purely for his own reasons. She had no choice but to take his apparent about-face on faith, though she had the suspicion that he'd been just as unsatisfied by their erotic hostilities as she had, and had decided to change his tactics with her. She would remain wary.

Daniel had agreed not to use force to win her to his bed, but he doubted that would prove necessary, Lynnette's legendary stubbornness notwithstanding. He knew full well that with the two of them inhabiting so small a space as his cabin, within weeks they'd be sharing everything a man and a woman could share. Including their secrets, he thought, which brought him to the next article of treaty he wanted to impress on his captive pirate queen.

Daniel began removing weapons from his sea chest as he considered how best to phrase his next demand. He collected anything that might conceivably be used in an escape attempt, as well as anything the virago could use to throw, stab, or bludgeon him with. Finally, hands full of sharp objects, he turned to face Lynnette, who was standing defensively by the side of the hated bed. "To answer your other question, what will happen to you when we get to London is also a matter of how well you cooperate." Seeing her open her mouth to spit out the familiar protest, he quickly went on. "What I require is information, Captain. To be precise, information about yourself."

"What do you want to know?" she asked warily, her earlier thoughts about his damnable curiosity making dread spiral through her insides.

"I want to know why it's so important to you that you go back to your ship, your men, your piratical ways. 'Tis plain as day you were meant for better than that, and you know it." Unknowingly, a trace of longing mixed with admiration entered Daniel's voice.

Stricken, Lynnette stood very still for a moment. The merchant meant to drag her deepest secrets from her, to strip her bare of the defenses she'd erected so successfully and maintained for so many years. He would render her helpless! She took immediate refuge in sarcasm. "Is that right?" she scoffed. "What is it about me that gives you the idea that I don't fit the part of buccaneer? The lack of a sword? But no, I seem to recall carrying one openly about me with some regularity. It must be that I don't have a ship, nor take prizes by the strength of my wits and my arms. Strange, then, that I seem to have acquired so much booty and such a shocking reputation as a corsair." Lynnette dripped scorn. "I really must apply myself to setting the gossips straight, since they have maligned me so cruelly." She smiled with utmost mockery.

Daniel fumed inwardly, wanting to shake her until her teeth shook, until she was forced to drop the façade of composure she carried so well, but he spoke calmly enough. "Excuse my mistake, milady. My wits must have gone wandering to think you could ever be more than a lowly thief upon the high seas."

It was Thorne's turn to fume. "Lowly, is it?" she growled, advancing on the merchant menacingly. "I'll show you lowly . . ."

"I wouldn't," he warned silkily. "It would be no great effort to have you back in your former position—with the former understanding back in place as well."

She stopped cold, visibly getting a hold on herself as she realized she was being baited. Mastering herself, she said coolly, "Your terms are unacceptable. I shall tell you nothing."

"Why ever not?" he asked, just the right amount of innocence and taunting in his countenance. "If you've nothing to hide, surely a little explanation will do no harm. You can explain your unaccountable passion for piracy, satisfy my urge to understand it, and provide yourself with your liberty at the same time, so what possible reason could you have for your persistent silence?"

"Bastard!" Lynnette hissed. It would be easy to tell him about the rendezvous she had planned with Pennsworth's ship of the line, but not so simple to explain why it was so necessary that she take *that* ship in particular. And if she did tell him she was planning an attack, might not that information lead him to learn more about her? Nay, it was too risky, even if it would make her plight aboard the *Triumph* less difficult. She'd tell Daniel nothing. He had far too close a hold on her, body and soul, already. Her secrets were her own to guard, whatever reasons he might have for wanting them.

Unbidden, her sister's pale face, eyes wild and hopeless, bruises staining her porcelain cheek, swam before her eyes and she reeled with the force of memory swamping her. She squeezed her eyes closed, trying to shut out the vision. *Sarah,* she thought despairingly, *I swore I'd avenge you, and I shall, no matter what the cost! No damned peacock of a merchant can ever stop me from fulfilling my duty to you, my sister.*

When she opened her eyes, Daniel was staring keenly at her, concern etched on his brow. "Are you quite well, Captain?" he asked quietly. She stiffened, furious that she had allowed him to see even that much of her inner thoughts.

Her spine rigidly straight, she took up a cocky stance. "I guess you'll just have to hang me when we reach England, then, won't you?" If she wasn't flown halfway to China by then in whatever craft she could manage to steal.

"Obstinate wench! You really don't know what's good for you, do you?" he raged. "If you'd give even a goddamned inch—"

"What then?" she interrupted just as heatedly. "Would it truly improve my lot? I'd still be half a world away from where I need to be, in a place where I'm not safe from the authorities, my enemies, and certainly not from you!"

His voice low, almost inaudible, Daniel murmured, "You

would be safe, Lynnette. Do you truly think I would allow anyone to harm you?"

Lynnette was struck to the heart by his softly spoken words. She knew what Daniel wanted of her with a sudden clarity that shocked her. He asked that she put her trust in him and allow him access to her secrets, her problems, and her heart. In return, she thought with amazement, he actually wanted to protect her! It was the strangest idea she could imagine, and she merely stared at him for a long moment, suspicion and bewilderment warring for mastery on her lovely features.

How, she asked herself, could she possibly benefit from such an act of naïveté? No man had ever offered her anything save heartache and grief. No man had ever wanted to share her burdens, and she didn't believe that was what Daniel was after, either, though some secret part of her being yearned to trust his sincerity. She laughed bitterly. "You would protect me? Oh, that's rich. Let me tell you something, Captain. You know absolutely *nothing* about what you're dealing with here—and knowing would do nothing to help you *or* me."

"Then there is nothing more to say," he ground out. "Tomorrow you shall have the liberty of the ship, but I suggest you start giving thought to our destination, and how you wish to arrive—with chains or without." With that, Daniel slammed out of the room. He ignored the crash of the pewter plate that hit the door only instants after he locked it behind himself.

CHAPTER TWENTY

*L*YNNETTE EASED herself slowly into a chair after the merchant had gone. She felt shaky all over. *Damn him to the lowest tier of hell!* she thought while fury and the strangest urge to cry warred inside her. Looking around dully, she took thought to finding some clothing. She did not find her own breeches and shirt, since Daniel had taken the bloody, torn clothes to be cleaned and mended, but she felt no compunction about raiding Bradley's chests for something suitable.

Dressed a few minutes later in an oversized white linen shirt and breeches that could have held two of her, feeling

slightly ridiculous but nonetheless relieved to be decently covered, Lynnette paced the tiny yet cozy space. In the course of
her agitated perambulations, she found a scarf that she knotted
about her waist to keep the breeches from falling off her body
and a leather vest that, though far too big for her, felt oddly
comfortable. It had a nice smell to it, she thought. Then she
realized why. It was Daniel's scent that enveloped the buttery
black leather, and her along with it. She flushed hotly, almost
tearing the garment off her body before she determined not to
be silly. It kept her covered, and the more she hid her curves
on this bloody ship, the better she would fare.

Besides, she had far more important things to worry about
just now than whether an article of clothing had a scent to it
or not. Like Daniel's damnable, incessant questions. Why did
he want to know so much about her, anyway? she fumed.
Knowledge, it was said, was power, but what kind of power
could he be looking to gain over her—besides the obvious, of
course? Unbidden, the memory of Daniel's ill-timed proposal
came back to her. If he wanted power, she thought slowly,
puzzling it out, then it was in order to hold on to her in some
way. Everything he had done so far, it occurred to Lynnette,
had been in order to understand her, to get closer to the center
of her. In fact, she realized, he'd had an almost unnatural interest in her doings from the start, far beyond what the ordinary captive would want to know of his jailer.

Why? Did he plan to use his knowledge to possess her?
she wondered. It was a common trait in men, this need to
possess everything in sight, she thought cynically. So why did
the thought of Captain Bradley's knowing her innermost heart
cause such a strange flutter in her gut? Surely, she had no
need of this man! If he wanted a hold on her, there could be
no good reason for it, no matter what the rogue might say.

Still, Lynnette wondered. Nothing she'd seen of Captain
Bradley made her think he was an evil man. He had never
truly abused her; instead he had merely used her own weaknesses against her, and while she might hate him for that, she
knew he could have no power over her that she did not give
him. But there was no help for it. She could not pretend, even
to herself, that she was unaffected by Daniel. The truth was
quite to the contrary. She was tempted by him in a way that
nothing had ever tempted her before.

She wanted to surrender and let herself trust him, believe in him, let him keep her safe. The pirate had a sudden image of herself standing at the top of a tall cliff, and Daniel at the bottom urging her to jump, to fall into his arms. She imagined letting herself drop off into empty space, having faith that he would catch her. Her stomach spasmed into a tight knot of fear. She could not do it. She just couldn't! Her breath caught in her throat in a choked-off sob.

She had to plan her escape. If she could not surrender, the pirate must be free of this unbearable, tearing captivity, be free of Daniel before he broke her heart. Yes! She would leave him, walk away from the heartache he promised and return to the life she had known. Vengeance would once again be foremost in her mind. It was easier to stomach than this pain.

Feeling suddenly revitalized as her blood started to circulate again, Lynnette began to plot with a vengeance. First she double-checked the cabin for any item that might be of use to her, though she was sure Daniel had been quite thorough when he removed all such helpful little niceties. She found nothing of use. No matter, she told herself stoutly. She would find a way to escape.

After all, they would have to stop to take on fresh water and supplies in a few weeks, when they reached the Canary Islands. If she hadn't found a way off this accursed ship before that time, she would surely find a way to elude her guards when they docked. From there, she knew, it would not be difficult to find passage on a ship bound for Tortuga or one of the other nearby islands. Aye, she would have wasted weeks, perhaps missed this chance to strike at Lord Roger but, she consoled herself, she would always have another chance to ruin the bastard. Revenge would just take a little longer if he managed to make a success of his last desperate trading mission, rather than the spectacular failure she'd planned for it. She only hoped Harry and the others would be on No-name when she returned.

They wouldn't likely be coming after her, she knew, for all that they were loyal men. No one knew just what had happened to her, for her abductors had shanghaied her in the dark of night. There would be no clues for Harry and her crew to follow even if they chose to mount a search. And the pirates were practical men. Even should they discover her whereabouts by some

chance, they might decide to leave her to accomplish her own
rescue. Captain Thorne knew that she could not expect them
to plan a dangerous rescue that might lead them directly into
waters patrolled by English men-of-war—not when they could
simply elect a new captain and sail in search of more booty.
Harry would argue, she thought fondly, but even he could not
prevail against a healthy dose of buccaneer greed.

Nay, she thought, she would just have to work her way
back to familiar waters, whether she escaped in the Canaries,
or if she was forced to wait till they reached London. But once
in London . . . the pirate's mind began to race.

Wait a moment—why return to the Caribbean at all when
her nemesis was right there within her grasp? She knew quite
well the fiend hid himself away in a heavily defended mansion
right in the heart of town. After all, over the years, she'd sent
several agents to that mansion to do . . . errands . . . for her.
She had spies in that house, knew its location and the habits
of its master. If she could get inside . . . the master would not
have long to live. Lynnette allowed herself to indulge in a
fantasy of coming face-to-face with Lord Roger of Pennsworth
after all these years. He would tremble before her wrath, plead
for his wretched life, but she would show mercy only to the
extent that the bullet she put in him would go straight for his
black heart. She wouldn't torture him as he'd tortured Sarah.
But she would kill him just as dead.

God, how she wanted to do it! She'd waited this long because she wanted him to suffer ruination both financial *and* in
the eyes of society before she came for him. She'd wanted
him to suffer the same way his many victims had suffered
over the years. Yet, in the guise of Captain Thorne, Lynnette
had already taken every ship he owned bar one. Perhaps it was
time, finally, to move on to the next phase. But how could it
be done? The man lived in a veritable fortress, guarded by a
small army of men since she'd begun her campaign of terror
seven years ago. He lived in fear, Lynnette knew, thanks to
the tricks her spy was paid to play on him, and the knowledge
gave her no small satisfaction. But he also lived securely, according to the information the unfortunate girl had given her.

How could she manage to negotiate her way through his
defenses alone? Even with the detailed information the parlormaid could give her regarding the mansion's layout, the

pirate had no way to breach his security precautions. If only her men could be there to help her! She had money in several hefty accounts stashed away with her London bankers, so finances were not a problem. But she needed men she trusted to help her with her plans . . . Damn it all!

Anything was possible, if only she could get off this blasted ship! Tomorrow, if Daniel held to his word and allowed her abovedecks, she could think about this further. She needed the reassurance of the feel of a fresh breeze on her face and the sight of the sea below her if she was to formulate a good, solid plan. She wasn't going anywhere for a while, she knew. There was time.

Daniel stood with Simon upon the deck in the evening breeze. He watched the sun slowly sinking into the vastness of the ocean, heart feeling as heavy as that immense fiery orb. The two men stared at the quiet beauty of the vista before them for a while, until Simon finally broke the silence.

"From the grim look on your face, my friend, I gather that all does not go well belowdecks." He spoke hesitantly, not wanting to pry into what was so clearly a sensitive matter for his friend.

Daniel sighed. "Nay, it does not. The wench is more stubborn than even I had anticipated. She refuses to surrender— though she knows that it is what we both desire most!" Frustration laced his voice, and he ran an agitated hand through his heavy raven hair.

Simon, aware of what his companion had planned for their pirate captive, just shook his head sympathetically. "Women," he muttered. "Who can understand 'em?"

"I understand Thorne all too well," Daniel replied, surprising his longtime friend. "She is as unbending as steel, and yet I sense a great need within her, a deep womanly instinct to be loved and protected, which she fights more strongly than she does me." He sighed again. "This battle we fight is more about whether she can trust me or not than whether or not she can forgive me for abducting her."

Captain Richards just stared, mouth agape, at the man he'd thought he knew. *Daniel,* claiming to understand what went on in a woman's mind? For that matter, Daniel, *caring* what went on in a woman's mind? Where was the cynical man who believed most women were grasping, greedy creatures with little more in their heads than their newest lover or the expensive gewgaws they might glean from him? "My dear Captain," he laughed, "I believe you are in love with that red-haired virago!"

Daniel scowled furiously, but kept his voice even, knowing that to show emotion would make him look like a stuttering fool. "Love her! Have your wits gone wandering? Surely you know me better than that. God's truth, I would hardly allow myself to fall for a woman who owns more weaponry than *I* do!"

"Indeed?" Simon didn't sound convinced.

"Indeed!" snapped Bradley. "If I know the witch's mind well, 'tis because I was forced to spend so much time with her upon that cursed isle of hers. What I feel for her is no more than lust, pure and simple." Privately, he wondered if that were true. Surely mere lust could never be this powerful. He shook off the unwelcome thought, made uncomfortable by the very notion that his obsession encompassed more than simple bodily desires. More to himself than so his friend could hear, he added, "She is a fire in my blood, a challenge I cannot allow to pass me by."

Wisely turning the topic, Simon murmured, "But if she won't surrender, what will you do?"

Daniel grimaced. "I have already given her leave to move about the ship, beginning tomorrow. It would be well if you informed the crew that she will be among them, as well as warn them that she is off-limits to them. I don't want her molested," he finished tightly.

"Why this sudden change of heart, Daniel? It seems a bit unusual to let a prisoner roam about on deck, especially when that prisoner is as comely as Captain Thorne, and dangerous to boot."

"Have no fear, my friend. I haven't gone soft in my old age, if that's what you're thinking. 'Tis part of my plan to win the woman's confidence, to get her to trust me."

"And when we reach England? Will you give her over to the authorities for her crimes?"

"Nay!" Daniel growled harshly, then realized his vehemence was telling. He lowered his voice, trying to still the sudden clenching of his gut at the thought of Lynnette dragged off to hang at Tyburn. "Nay. I intend to keep her with me, whatever means I have to use to persuade the vixen."

Simon shrugged and clapped his partner on the back. There was nothing more he could do to help his friend. Bradley would have to work through this obsession on his own. Simon just hoped that it would pass before the other man did something he'd regret, if he hadn't already. He didn't understand Daniel's overweening desire for this pirate wench. Oh, she was comely, no man with eyes could deny that, but her beauty wasn't what had his partner tied up in knots. Women nearly as beautiful as the pirate queen threw themselves at the handsome, dark-haired captain all the time.

Well, it was surely not his business to know what made this wench so special to his friend, and he suspected any effort he might make to find out would send Daniel into fits of jealousy. Simon fought a smile. He might deny it if he liked, but all the symptoms were there. Daniel was in love. Simon only prayed, for his friend's sake, that Mistress Thorne was caught in those same coils.

CHAPTER TWENTY-ONE

WHEN DANIEL entered the cabin later that evening, he more than half expected to find Lynnette crouching behind the door, ready to clobber him with whatever was handy. To his surprise, he found her sitting quietly in a wing chair by the room's only window—a leaded-glass affair that allowed more light than scenery to penetrate—reading one of his books. The sight of her dressed in his clothing, with her shimmering red-gold hair braided loosely and falling across her breast, struck him, as her presence always did, and he helplessly felt his anger with her dissipate. The outfit was ludicrously large on her, but Daniel felt not a bit like laughing when he saw the pirate lift her head at his entrance. She was beautiful. He did not want to fight with her again so soon, so he decided to tread cautiously. Sharing a cabin with his prickly

pirate queen could prove quite a stimulating experience. At
least, he hoped it would.

"Hello," he said softly. She hesitated before replying, as if
his civility were spoken in a foreign tongue. Then she relaxed.

"Hello yourself, Captain," she allowed ungraciously.

He closed the door behind him, locking it with a key he
drew from a cord about his neck beneath his shirt. Seeming
to ignore the pirate, Daniel moved about the room dousing
lanterns. In truth, he was very much aware of her, from the
delicately arousing floral scent of her skin, to the nervous tension clenching her slender fingers into tight fists in her lap.
Well, he thought, hiding a smile, it wouldn't hurt her any to
sit and stew a while, wondering what came next. It was a
sensation he'd become all too familiar with during his weeks
as her prisoner. Turnabout was fair play, after all.

Lynnette perched uncomfortably at the edge of the chair,
watching him warily. Did he intend to carry on where they'd
left off yesterday? Well, he'd best think again if that were the
case! She braced herself for a fight, but none came. Daniel
merely continued settling himself in for the night, paying no
attention to his captive whatsoever. It was not an accustomed
situation for Lynnette, who could hardly remember being ignored in her life. Hated, despised, cursed, quite often; but ignored, never! And now this merchant was calmly disrobing
right before her eyes!

When he sat down on the bed and began to remove his
boots, she grew flustered, bolted out of her chair and paced
the length of the cabin. She sat down again agitatedly. Daniel
calmly untied the laces on his shirt, then pulled it over his
head in one fluid motion, baring his beautiful, tanned expanse
of chest. She swallowed.

"What are you doing!" It came out in a croak.

He feigned surprise. "Why, Captain, whatever do you
think? I'm getting ready for bed, as anyone can plainly see."

He hadn't slept in the room last night, having left her to
her own devices after his despicable treatment. Of course, this
was his cabin. He would want to sleep in it now that hostilities
supposedly had ceased between them. He'd said as much earlier, but somehow the reality of the sticky situation hadn't
penetrated until now.

She scowled. "I realize that, Bradley. I just don't see why

you have to strip to sleep." She steadfastly ignored the fact that she herself often slept in the nude, finding it far less confining than smothering under a layer of twisted fabric.

He paused, his hands at his waistband. "Are you afraid you'll see something you like?" he taunted. A slow smile spread over his face as he realized the source of her hostility.

"I've already seen everything you have, you rogue!" She regretted the words as soon as they were out of her mouth, not wanting to remind him of their passionate lovemaking. *She* didn't want to remember, either.

"Ah, then you *know* you'll like it." So much for not starting another argument with the pirate, he thought in amusement. This was just too good to pass up.

"You arrogant peacock!" she stormed. "You have *nothing* that I might want!"

"Then you won't mind if I take my clothes off, will you?" he returned smugly.

Lynnette threw herself back in her chair with a noise suspiciously like a raspberry. She tried to look anywhere but where her captor stood, nonchalantly baring himself to the world. He had no shame, she fumed inwardly, staring at the wall intently. She wouldn't watch the spectacle he was making of himself. She had a sense of modesty, even if *he* didn't! Despite her righteous resolve, her peripheral vision picked up movement to her left, and she couldn't help glancing over. It was reflex, she told herself crossly. Nothing more. It could not possibly have anything to do with the magnificent form slowly denuding itself right before her cursedly interested eyes.

Her gaze traveled slowly from the low-slung breeches he was easing off his hips, down to the muscular thighs the fabric encased so lovingly, skittered over the bulge at his groin quickly, memories of what that portion of his anatomy could stir within her making her face heat. Damnation! She was actually blushing! She couldn't remember the last time she'd done anything as ridiculously insipid as blushing at the sight of a naked man. She scowled to cover her chagrin, sweeping her gaze back to his face to see if he'd noticed. Daniel was looking at her sardonically. The ghost of a grin crossed his finely sculpted, sensuous lips. He'd noticed. She quickly looked away, too flustered for a moment to meet his unspoken challenge.

Curse the rogue! She drummed her fingertips agitatedly against the arm of the chair, stopped herself quickly as she realized she was betraying her nervousness with the action. He knew he was discomfiting her. Knew, and was enjoying every moment. If she turned her back like an outraged maiden, he would only laugh at her, claim another victory in their war of wills. Well, she decided suddenly, full of temper and recklessness, he'd won too many of these battles of late, and it was time she began to reclaim some ground.

Her emerald eyes sparked with challenge and she swept them up over his lean frame appraisingly, knowing he was still watching her. The look she gave him was exactly the type that made women feel naked whenever a man bestowed it on one of them, and it was the same one he'd given her several times in the past. Crossing her arms negligently, she studied him languidly, as though he were a prize stallion she was considering putting to stud. Not part of his anatomy escaped her attention. Not his wide, muscle-banded chest, bronzed and gleaming dully in the light of the single lantern left shining by his bedside. Not his long, straight legs, rock hard and perfectly delineated by the breeches he still hadn't fully removed. She knew he was prolonging the process of disrobing in order to disturb her. She hoped to disturb him instead.

She drew her gaze reluctantly up to his face to see how she was doing, felt a shock as she saw that his slight smile had become a full-fledged, completely masculine grin of appreciation. The rogue was enjoying her perusal! Daniel was entirely unfazed, seeming to relish her insulting appraisal. He was completely arrogant, had not a shred of modesty in his body. Of course, she thought with a rush of heat, he had nothing to be ashamed *about*, and a great deal to flaunt. With an incredible effort of will, Lynnette forced herself not to look away from the amusement she saw in his silver eyes.

Instead, she quirked a brow at him, daring him to continue disrobing under her apparently unimpressed gaze. She felt hot all over, but she knew it wasn't from embarrassment. At some point in the last few minutes, she'd gone beyond that stage with Daniel. Nay, what she felt was pure, unadulterated lust. But she'd be damned if she'd let him know that.

Daniel, on the other hand, had no way of hiding what her emerald-eyed perusal was doing to his body. It would be more than obvious from ten feet away, let alone the much shorter distance between the merchant and his captive pirate. And it would soon become even more apparent, when he removed his breeches the rest of the way. Already, they clung to his slim hips by the barest margin of decency. However, he did not mind in the least that she saw his desire. He wanted her to see it, wanted her to feel it even more.

Yet he knew that tonight was not the night for anything more than mere looking. Lynnette was suspicious enough of their truce. If they made love tonight, no matter that it would certainly be by mutual consent, she likely would use it as an excuse to withdraw even further from him, to distrust him irrevocably. He wouldn't take that chance yet, much as his randy, impatient body demanded that he tumble the pirate queen willy-nilly and make her scream with ecstasy.

Daniel was not above a little teasing, however, no matter how sensitive he might be to his captive's uncertain emotional state. He pushed down the breeches another inch, holding the pirate queen's eyes all the while. One last downward shove and the game was up. The pants landed on the floor with a soft sigh of fabric, and he wore nothing beneath them.

The pirate had her first good, long look at his rampant maleness since that long-ago day when she'd spied on the merchant bathing in her private pool, and the sight sent a rush of shocked desire shuddering through her body. He was magnificent! Lynnette sucked in her breath, and her gaze faltered before she sternly brought herself under control. She wanted to squirm in the chair, do *something* to release the tension and heat gathered abruptly in her gut. She forced herself to remain still, swallowing down a lump of desire big as a cannonball. Daniel laughed suddenly, shaking his head at her stubbornness. With a shrug, he turned his back on her and climbed into bed.

When the sheet covered him decently, Lynnette went limp with relief, then was flooded with anger just as suddenly. Damn him for putting her through such discomfort, and then laughing about it! When he spoke, she was thankful to be able to answer him with the proper sharpness.

"Come to bed, sweetheart," he coaxed.

"Like bloody hell I will, you arrogant peacock!" she spat.

"There's plenty of room." He patted the mattress at his side invitingly. "I'll slide over."

"Hah!" she scoffed. "Right onto me, I'm sure."

"If you'd like," he murmured, grinning that maddening grin.

"No, thank you! I'd rather bed down with a pig!"

"I believe that can be arranged, my dear Captain. There's one on board at the moment, though I doubt he'd be as pleased to have you join him as I would."

"Oh!" she gasped, too furious to speak. This was beyond anything. The pirate's fist curled tight and she fought the urge to smash him one right in his arrogant, smirking face. She'd only invite his ire—and his touch—if she lost control. Fuming, she crossed her arms and slouched down in the chair.

Daniel sighed, apparently tired of teasing her. "Honestly, love, you've quite exhausted me with your stubbornness. I've promised not to maul you," he said sarcastically, "and even if I wanted to, I doubt I could be any threat to you at the moment. I'm too tired." He yawned theatrically to illustrate his point.

It was a bold-faced lie, and they both knew it. The sheet stretched taut over his lean hips did nothing to hide his desire. He was no more helpless than a wolf in a sheep pen. "Besides," he continued, "where else would you sleep? I happen to know that the chair you occupy so gracefully is absolutely abominable for sleeping. You'll wake up with your neck permanently bent at an angle. Isn't that pushing the limits of defiance a tad far when you might sleep comfortably *and* unmolested in a bed?" he pointed out.

Lynnette envisioned curling up next to the merchant on the wide luxurious bed, and knew in her heart that if he did not make a move to touch *her*, she would reach out and touch *him*. Her body thrummed with unfulfilled desire, and she realized there was no way she could be that close to him and not do something to precipitate their lovemaking. It was a sobering thought, and not one she intended to let her captor be privy to. "I'll sleep on the floor," she steamed with forced anger.

Daniel sighed, tossed her a cover and a pillow. "Better you than me, I suppose."

Catching the bedding, Lynnette went to work silently and

efficiently making up a bed for herself as far away from the merchant as possible in the little room. She lay down in a huff, telling herself she'd slept on worse in her lifetime and trying to ignore the disgruntled voice in her head that told her *he* should have taken the floor, while she slept in comfort on the feather mattress. Hah, she sneered at the voice. When was the last time a man had offered her a courtesy like that? Never. Daniel was no better than the rest, no better than he should be. The floorboards creaked under her ear like malicious laughter. She beat her pillow, imaging with some pleasure that it was the handsome face of her captor.

Daniel doused the lamp, lay back comfortably for a while. He heard the pirate shift restlessly, uncomfortably. He grinned into the night. She was so stubborn! She rustled again. Laughter tingeing his voice, he tried one last time. "Sure you don't want to share the bed?"

"Shut *up,* Peacock!"

Chuckling, he did as he was bid.

CHAPTER TWENTY-TWO

*T*HE *Triumph's* crewmen were still wary around Lynnette after several days of getting used to her presence on deck. The pirate had done nothing to encourage them to be otherwise, keeping to herself and spending most of her time staring out to sea or reading one of the several books she'd found in the captain's cabin. Though she carried no weapon— not, of course, by choice—the men had heard from their mates of the vicious fight she'd put up on Tortuga. Her reputation as a corsair as well as the third mate's slowly healing wounds kept the men on their toes around her. Still, though they did not approach her, Lynnette saw their leering glances, heard their mumbled comments, comments that boded ill for her.

Besides being a young, attractive female on a ship full of men, she was personally responsible for injuring no few of those men. On top of all that, she was a pirate, natural enemy to honest sailors. She could tell the men didn't know quite what to make of her, but they didn't want her aboard. Lyn-

nette's weather eye for trouble told her it was only a matter
of time before their resentment flared, unless she acted to de-
fuse the situation. She was grudgingly grateful for the watchful
eye Daniel kept on her whenever she appeared on deck, for
she knew how easy it would be for a group of the rough sailors
to take it into their heads to attack her.

She had no plans to reconcile with Daniel, knew it was far
better for her own sanity that she remain distant from him both
mentally and physically. However, as a tactician, she knew
that for her own safety the tension among the crew had to be
dealt with before something ugly occurred. After all, she was
no pampered female, no gently reared lady considered off-
limits to common seamen, but a prisoner. As matters stood,
the only thing between her and the "attentions" of the sailors
was Captain Richards's command and Captain Bradley's
glare.

Lynnette was not reassured. Though she knew Daniel did
not want her harmed by his men, and Captain Richards would
enforce Daniel's wishes out of respect for his friend, she didn't
like the insecurity of her position. Unused as she was to de-
pending on men to protect her, she decided she ought to try
to mollify the men of the *Triumph*. She didn't consider the
effect her efforts might have on her captor. ·

Willie Jennings was practicing his knife-throwing. Since he'd
been wounded by that unnatural female his arm was stiff and
his aim was off. He scowled, squinting at the mast he was
trying to hit, though his glare was more for the wench who'd
injured him than the innocent wood. He let fly with the first
of his three matched throwing-knives, cursing as he missed
the target painted on the mast and embedded the dagger in the
deck beside it instead. He tried again, but this time as he drew
back his arm, his sore shoulder cramped and the knife went
flying off backward. He clutched the shoulder, swearing even
more foully.

That same knife whizzed past his ear a moment later with
a suddenness that stunned him. It thwacked into the mast dead
center of the target and buried itself three full inches. He gaped
at the quivering blade dumbly for a moment, amazed by the
accuracy of the throw, before he spun around to see who had
been so callous about whipping it past his head. When he saw

who it was, he paled, then turned red with fury.

Lynnette, standing ten paces behind the man with her hands on her slim hips, smiled brilliantly at the sailor she'd wounded. If she was to pacify the crew, she deemed it best to start with the one who had most reason to hate her. "You might try loosening up that stance a bit and dropping your shoulder before you let fly," she said mildly.

Willie swallowed the furious retort in his throat, aware that they were not alone on the deck. Had they been . . . well, things would be a great deal different, he judged. He scowled harder, as aware of the beauty of the woman before him as he was of what she could do. "Thank ye," he sneered, sounding anything but thankful, "but I'll not be needing any advice from the likes o' ye."

Lynnette allowed her smile to grow as she retrieved the knife from the mast. "No, I don't suppose you do," she conceded. "I imagine it's not your skill that is at fault, but your wound." She paused for a moment. "No hard feelings about that, I hope." Once again, she turned up the volume on her smile as she held the blade out to the mate.

No hard feelings . . . Was the wench daft? He eyed her incredulously. Was that a spark of mischief in her eyes? Why, he'd wrap her little smile around her head, he would . . . if it weren't so damn fetching. Willie found his anger and suspicion draining helplessly away in the face of the pirate's gorgeous smile and conciliating stance. "Sure," he heard himself say. "No hard feelings."

"Fancy a match, then?" she challenged, a light of good sportsmanship in her eyes.

"Aye, I s'pose I do."

"All right then." Lynnette grasped the knife he handed her and took up a stance before the mast.

Daniel was alerted that something was going on by the sudden commotion amidships. He noted that the rest of the vessel was empty of anyone who wasn't absolutely needed at their duties. Those who remained were craning their necks to see around the crowd on that deck. *Lynnette,* he thought immediately. What else would cause such an uproar on his normally calm ship? He moved swiftly to intercept whatever disaster was occurring, fear for her almost overwhelming him.

He found the pirate in a circle of his men, laughing uproariously and waving a knife in her hand with the air of someone who is giving a speech.

"This knife," she said, smiling, "is a good example of its type; it's well balanced, slim bladed, and the hilt is heavier than the blade." She nodded to Jennings, its owner, who beamed. "That gives it its spin, allows it to land with its point toward the target more easily." She twirled it expertly between her fingers, then flung it hard to land in the center of the target. The men whistled and cheered appreciatively.

"However, it's only as good as its wielder. Here," she said, offering another of the set of blades to a blushing young man, "you try it." Egged on by his mates, he grabbed the dagger and tossed it as hard as he could at the mast. It hit hilt-first and bounced away, to the amusement of his comrades. "I'll show you how it's done." She grinned, and the young man eagerly let her position him in the correct stance.

Daniel suspected his compliance had more to do with wanting to be near the gorgeous, outrageously dressed female than any real desire to learn the art of knife-throwing, but he was too amazed by the transformation his men had undergone to do anything but stare. Why, only this morning they'd been eyeing the wench as though she might be carrying plague, and now she was jesting and gaming with them like the best of friends.

Very quickly, he discovered that he didn't like this change of attitude one bit. He wanted to be the only one to enjoy Lynnette's favors, and now, it seemed, he was the only one excluded from her camaraderie. The pirate had fairly ignored him for the last several days, treating him with scornful civility and avoiding him whenever possible. Now she was fraternizing with his men when she wouldn't so much as give him the time of day.

Even Simon stood nearby, occasionally offering up an amused comment when one of his men made a particularly bad throw. He was also tacitly reminding them of his authority; letting them know he was watching and there was to be no mischief involving their pirate captive. Daniel knew that consciously, but he couldn't stop himself from gritting his teeth against a surge of jealousy when Lynnette bestowed a blinding smile on Simon for complimenting her skill.

Before he knew precisely what he meant to do, Captain

Bradley was striding into the center of the group of sailors, expression thunderous. The men fell silent when he came among them, intimidated by the fierce glare he swept across them all. "What's this I see?" he asked with silken menace, his soft voice more frightening than the loudest shout. "Have you all nothing better to do than stand about tossing daggers with my prisoner? A prisoner, I might add, who is *not* supposed to be handling weapons?"

The sailors were silent, none of them wanting to defend their actions in the face of their employer's obvious fury. Lynnette, however, glared right back at him, stiff-backed. "I'm sure it's terribly dangerous for me to be holding a dagger," she sneered. "Why, I might manage to kill each and every one of you with this tiny little blade and sail the ship back to Tortuga all by myself." Her derisive tone sharpened even further. "Certainly the danger I represent is so great that you must deny me and these men our amusements, innocent though they are."

"Nothing about you is innocent, Captain Thorne," he replied just as tartly, "and I feel no shame in admitting that the sight of you wielding a weapon is quite enough to concern me."

"Is it?" She smiled recklessly, twirling the last of the knives between her fingers menacingly. Suddenly she pointed it directly at him, standing ready to throw. The hush around them deepened as the whole crew stilled. "I'm flattered to know you don't underestimate me," she continued calmly, as though she were not holding her captor at bay with only a dagger to aid her and a crew of men willing to take her down the moment she let fly.

Daniel too was still, though he betrayed no sign of nervousness. In a tone that matched the pirate's for casualness, he replied, "How could I? You are constantly reminding me of your deadliness."

Lynnette began to seriously regret her actions. It was madness to goad Bradley in this manner, especially when she had no hope of carrying through on her threat. She was well aware that Simon stood behind her, hand on the hilt of his sword. If she made to throw, he would not hesitate to cut her down. Her act of defiance would get her nowhere, except an early and unpleasant demise. And she wanted to live.

She also knew that this was one man she could never dream of killing. The sight of Daniel, proud and nonchalant at the wrong end of her blade, reminded her of another time he had been in that position, on the deck of his captured ship. He was brave and beautiful beyond words, and she despairingly admitted to herself that she could not harm him.

Still, she would rather die than throw down her weapon in front of all these witnesses. "You'll do well to remember that in future," she snarled, and slung the dagger past his head to drown in the sea. The sailors sighed with relief to a man, all except Willie, who said, "Hey," in a rather forlorn tone as his knife slipped beneath the waves. Simon removed his hand from his cutlass, but kept his eyes on the pirate warily. The immediate threat was over, but tension still crowded the air on deck as everyone waited to see how Captain Bradley would react.

Daniel remained perfectly still for a moment longer. He hadn't even flinched when the knife swept by him. It was as if he'd known the pirate would not make good on her ill-advised threat. Then he smiled. "Oh, I'll remember," he said softly. "I'll remember everything about this day, Captain Thorne." And before she could blink, he'd caught her by the arm and flung her ungently over his shoulder.

Lynnette squawked angrily and struggled to free herself from the undignified position, but he was striding across the deck, his shoulder in her stomach knocking the breath out of her and making it difficult to fight. Still, she got in a few good kicks and punches before he finally set her on her feet in his cabin. "That's the second time you've carried me thus against my will, Peacock," she hissed. "I assure you it will be the last!"

"I would to God it were!" he yelled back, his temper finally breaking. "Think you I enjoy having to bend you to my will in this manner, Lynnette? I do not, I tell you! But until you mend your ways and cease flaunting yourself before my crew, I shall do as I see fit with you!"

"*Flaunting* myself?" she screeched indignantly. "I did no such thing! I was merely trying to amuse myself when you had to barrel in like a spoilsport and ruin it."

Daniel ignored her defense. "Of course you were flaunting yourself," he retorted hotly. "What do you call smiling and flirting with all of my men and engaging in games with the lowest of them? I know you were not merely trying to stave off boredom, since you have purposely ignored *my* overtures of friendship these last several days!" He stopped suddenly, aware of how jealous he sounded.

Lynnette was quick to pick up on his slip. "I see," she said. "All of this righteous indignation is really because you're angry I spent time with your crew when I would not with you." She laughed bitterly. "Perhaps that's because I have less reason to hate them than I do you, Bradley."

"You do not hate me," he whispered, coming face-to-face with her. Their angry breaths mingled in the small space between them. "You *wish* you hated me, but you cannot." His lips were a mere breath away from hers.

She whitened as the truth of that statement crashed in on her. The pirate flinched back, staring wildly around for escape, but Daniel surrounded her with his presence, and she could see naught else but him. "Nay," she gasped. "I do hate you. I do—"

"You don't." His lips descended on hers in a possessive rush, sending shock waves of pleasure and fear through her body. Instinctively, Lynnette responded to the fear, slapping his face as hard as she could and spinning away from him before he could react. Backed into a corner of the room, she glared defiantly at her captor.

Daniel's silver eyes darkened as her hand print spread across his cheek like an unfurling crimson flag. He stood quite still, though his breathing was quick and savage. The pirate felt fear race through her veins. Surely now she'd gone too far, surely now he would hit her as he had not done so far. . . . But Daniel only smiled again. "That proves it, I believe," he said. "No woman can hate the man she slaps like that." And he turned and walked out of the room, leaving Lynnette to gape at his back as he disappeared into the passageway.

Weeks later, shuddering with cold and drenched to the skin, Daniel made his way to his cabin blinded with exhaustion. All he wanted was to strip off his wet clothes and wrap a warm blanket around his shivering body. They'd fought the sudden storm for thirty-six hours, thankfully managing to ride it out without too much damage, but there'd been moments when he thought they'd never make it. Bed sounded good, he thought foggily as he stumbled to his door. Very good. Especially with a certain red-haired virago to warm it for him. Though they slept apart, the very thought of the pirate who shared his cabin was always enough to heat him all over.

When Daniel stomped in, shedding water like a seal and bringing a draft of cold air into the cabin, Lynnette was in high dudgeon. For hours she'd been thinking of her ship, left behind with her men and her booty. She'd brooded over her missed opportunity to catch Lord Roger until she was ready to tear her hair out. And she'd brooded about the man whose actions had cost her all of these things.

She'd been locked in this dreary room for more than three days, since just before they'd docked for supplies in the Canaries. During their short day in port, Lynnette had been frantic to get out, to jump ship while they were near dry land. Unfortunately, once locked inside the cabin, there was no way out, even for a notorious pirate. She'd scraped her fingers raw trying to pry the door open. She'd even tried to break the three-inch-thick leaded glass of the cabin's single window with a chair. No luck, and now no chair to sit on, unless you wanted to count the splinters. She'd screeched for help, even attempted to poke a hole in the deck above her with a length of broken chair leg. It was hopeless, and she'd been forced to watch helplessly through the hazy stubborn glass as the busy port town receded in the *Triumph*'s wake.

Then the storm had broken directly after they'd left the islands, trapping her inside yet another two days. Daniel hadn't even had time to let her out for a breather between their stopover and the gale's enforced captivity. She didn't dare light a lantern belowdecks with the winds so high, for the danger of fire was a terrifying prospect at sea. The cabin, which had seemed spacious and rather luxurious to her at first, seemed to shrink with every passing hour she was forced to spend within its walls.

All day and throughout the night, she had tossed on the swells helplessly, lying on the bolted-down bed because nothing else in the cabin was as steady. At first she'd tried to occupy herself with plans for escape.

If she was lucky, Harry would have managed to hold the *Maiden*'s crew together in her absence, and she would be able to get word to them when she finally managed to slip her leash. Probably, Harry had assumed command of the ship, as per the contingency plan they'd discussed long ago. He would have had little trouble gaining the crew's vote for captain after he'd proved such a capable second in command these last seven years. But would they come after her?

They'd agreed (Harry reluctantly) that it was best not to waste too much time and effort searching for the captain should she vanish. Lynnette knew that should she turn up missing, it would probably be because she'd been killed. At the time, she'd been sure that nothing less than death could drag her away from her ship and her revenge. She had not counted on Daniel Bradley.

The merchant might still have her arrested when they reached England's shores. Though he'd not said anything about it recently, she knew her refusal to share her secrets might cost her her freedom if Daniel decided to follow through on his revenge. She'd avoided him, avoided the decision for as long as she could. Soon now, the pirate knew, she would have to decide what to do. Escape from aboard ship was a dim possibility with the way she was guarded and kept locked away. It seemed inevitable now that her next stop would be England.

But if she was forced to go to London, and assuming Daniel let her go when they made port (a big assumption, she knew), could she enlist the aid of her sailors if she decided to go after Lord Roger immediately? If she sent word to Harry to gather the men for a little raiding party into the heart of England's capital city, the only booty being the corpse of one wretched middle-aged man, would they come? Many of the men, English expatriates of long standing, would not be too eager to journey back to the place they'd left behind when they'd become outlaws. Would they, for her sake, risk capture and hanging to help her complete her revenge? Harry would, she knew. He'd lay down his life for her. But the others . . . It was impossible to tell. And it would be months before she could expect them to arrive back in England, if they arrived at all. She'd have to go to ground until then, or return to Caribbean waters to recruit their assistance. As the ship tossed feverishly, Lynnette turned these thoughts over and over in her mind.

She'd have to wait and see what the next weeks brought.

Right now, there was nothing she could do. Harry wouldn't come for her until he had word, and she couldn't save herself from her captivity. The thought of her helplessness clenched up Lynnette's insides, as did the storm raging outside. On nights like this, she was accustomed to being at the helm, out battling the elements and glorying in the raw power of an angry Mother Nature. Now all she could do was sit and brood.

At last she retreated to the comfort of the wine bottle that had been left behind for her. Three quarters of the way through it, she couldn't tell anymore if the ship was swaying or if she was.

While she waited impatiently (and tipsily) she amused herself by singing sea chanteys and bawdy pirate ditties. Her slightly out-of-tune contralto echoed back at her from the walls and mocked her. That activity paled quickly, so she took up her new favorite occupation—cursing Daniel. That contented her for a long while, but then her thoughts of him turned from anger to another sort of passion, and she was left in an even more foul mood than before. Eventually she gave up and tried unsuccessfully to sleep.

Now she sat up as he entered the room, still half-drunk and very, very annoyed. "I suppose you'll want the bed back," she grouched, sliding off it resentfully.

Daniel hadn't the strength to reply at length. He threw off his oilskin, removed his boots, and sat down on the disputed bed. "Yes," he answered. He'd noticed her waspish tone, but for once chose to ignore it.

Lynnette flopped down heavily on her impromptu pallet, making sure her reluctance was noticed. "Oh, that's just grand," she sniped. "You've dripped water all over the floor. I'll have to sleep on soaked bedding because of your carelessness."

Rousing somewhat, Daniel glanced blearily at his captive. The pirate wasn't one to act the shrew, and she certainly did not whine, despite her frequent struggles for freedom, so her carping struck him as strange. He didn't like it. "If you hadn't noticed, madam, there *is* a storm going on outside. It's hardly likely that after nearly two days fighting it, I'd manage to stay dry."

"And that's another thing, damn it," replied the irate Lynnette. "You promised not to lock me in, and you broke your promise! What kind of man cares so little for his word of honor?"

Daniel almost rose to the bait. Considering his exhaustion, however, and noting the mostly empty wine bottle by his bed, he decided not to. He smiled into her semiglazed eyes. "As a gentleman," he said mildly, "I am required to see to your safety no matter what I may have promised. Locking you in was the best way to ensure you remained safe. Surely you would not want me to go against all the laws of chivalry?" Seeing her struggle with about a dozen hot retorts, he went on before she could get any of them out. "As for the wet floor, there is something very simple you can do to avoid it, you know." He yawned casually, covering a grin behind his hand.

Lynnette spluttered. She turned red, her mouth opening and closing like a fish in her chagrin, and then she let loose a torrent of abuse upon his head. As the words flowed over him, Daniel felt some of his exhaustion dissipate. Lynnette always refreshed him, he thought, beginning to chuckle. Soon he was laughing out loud, and her curses grew more virulent. His laughter seemed only to upset her more, but he couldn't help it. The harder she wished him to perdition, the harder he laughed. Finally the pirate couldn't stand it anymore.

She threw her pillow at him.

Daniel howled louder as the fluffy missile hit him square in the face. "Stop it, you buffoon," she raged, but her words had no effect. He was curled up in a paroxysm of mirth, clutching his belly. Lynnette saw red and unthinkingly attacked. With a soft *oomph,* she landed on top of him, fists flailing. "Stop laughing at me, damn it!" she yelled. Daniel didn't—couldn't—comply, but he grabbed her around the waist and swung them both over so that he was straddling her. He grinned down into her furious face. All traces of his exhaustion fled.

"I knew that sooner or later you'd come to my bed," he joked, "but I had no idea you would do it in so dramatic a manner as to literally *pounce* on me."

"I didn't! I wasn't! I'd never—" Then she realized he was teasing. Their fight began to take on a ludicrous cast in her mind, as it obviously had in Daniel's from the start. "Well," she said sheepishly, smiling back up at him, "it was rather a melodramatic act on my part."

"But highly appreciated, I assure you, Captain," he said, lightly rubbing his hips against hers to make his meaning clear. Lynnette's smile faded a little, yet she still felt a wild playfulness inside her.

"Then you can do me a favor in return, Bradley," she murmured sweetly, "and get *off* me!" She heaved mightily, intending to surprise him and fling him off the bed. The dratted man didn't so much as budge.

"But I like it here, sweeting," he crooned. "It's so"—he stared pointedly at her breasts, crushed beneath his chest—"soft." And then he was too busy defending himself from her mock blows to come up with any more witticisms.

They brawled like street urchins, shrieking and laughing as merchant and captive forgot themselves completely in the fun. Daniel tickled Lynnette mercilessly, discovering that she was exquisitely sensitive to this new torture. Lynnette squirmed and writhed to escape his clever fingers, laughingly pleading for quarter, then when he gave it, using their gasping pause to sneak-attack him. They rolled over and over, each struggling in jest for mastery of the other. Lynnette locked him in a clever hold, her strong legs pinning his arms by his sides, her loosened hair blinding him to all but her wicked grin. "Give up, Peacock?" she chortled.

Daniel smiled back lazily, sensually. "Why should I, sweet? I'm right where I want to be." Indeed, lying pinned flat on his back with the pirate on top of him was fine with him. His eyes traveled across her delectable figure appreciatively.

Lynnette blushed, her mirth warming into more tender emotion. Then, embarrassed suddenly, she grabbed a pillow from behind his head in a lightning-quick move and stuffed it down on his beautiful face. Daniel roared with mock outrage. Before she knew it, Captain Thorne was flying through the air to land softly in a pile of discarded pillow ammunition. Just as quickly, he climbed back on top of the pirate. Her mouth formed a surprised O before she dissolved into giggles.

"So, wench," Daniel growled playfully from atop her, "you want more, do you? I'll give you more!" Suddenly Lynnette became aware of the rigid hardness between them, pressing hungrily into the sweet vee between her legs. "More," indeed. Her eyes darkened. Daniel's glowed silver, moonlit and deliciously frightening. The mood grew serious, sensuous, as was bound to happen. They both recognized it simultaneously, though neither gave sign.

Strangely, Daniel did not want to destroy the innocent pleasure they'd been sharing, to betray Lynnette by turning what had surely been one of her first carefree moments in years into something infinitely more complicated, if also infinitely more pleasurable. So he said with forced sternness, "I should not squirm so, madam, did I not wish to invite trouble." Lynnette was still playfully nipping at him and striving to shake him off, though she knew the fight was over.

She quieted, hearing the warning behind the teasing threat. Oh, there was danger here, no doubt. But it didn't come from the possibility of violence, nor from the strength in the tightly packed musculature of the man above her. It came instead from the treacherous unfolding of something deep and sweet inside her own belly, something fragile that had closed up its petals long ago and hidden itself so far inside her she had not known it still existed. It was returning now, however; returning strongly and so tenderly she felt she might dissolve into nothingness and light if she succumbed. The pirate stayed still for a long, long moment.

Afterward, Lynnette would swear some imp of mischief had entered her, for suddenly, a tiny light sparked in her eyes, and staring steadily into the merchant's eyes, she did what she had been warned against. She squirmed, ever so slightly, beneath Daniel's tensed body.

Their lips met instantly in an aching, tender kiss that excluded all the world and brought them together so closely they felt their spirits meld. If either sighed, neither knew, for everything was swept away beneath the power of that kiss. Sight, sound, smell: gone; all that was left was the wine-sweet taste and the blessed sensation of contact with each other.

Lynnette was stripping Daniel of his clothes before she even realized what she did. His wet shirt landed in the corner with a splat neither noticed. Her shirt, damp too from wrestling with him, came off just as quickly. Then they were skin to skin, oblivious to the dampness of the bed, hands racing over each others' bodies. It was a frantic, yet strangely gentle coming together. Neither could get enough of the other. Lynnette refused to break their kiss, even as they slid down farther on the bed together. She was wrapped around him so tightly she couldn't tell where she ended and he began. Daniel was no different. He held her to him compulsively, engulfing her beneath him, yet he took care not to handle her too roughly. They clung like monkeys, each completely swept away with need for the other.

Neither could say when or how they divested each other of their breeches, only that they were suddenly free of binding, and that their passion spiraled out of control. Fire burned low in her belly. Her legs spread of their own accord and Daniel was inside her, deep and hard and perfect. They joined like two halves of a whole, going still for a moment in awe as they felt themselves completed. Then the erotic dance began; fierce, tender, wild lovemaking beyond anything either could imagine. Her fulfillment was his own—they spiked, cried out, fell together into the abyss.

They lay still connected for stunned minutes, until the power of the pleasure-storm and the stress of the physical one overcame them, and they slept.

Daniel was awoken rudely sometime later that night when an arm whacked him across the face. *Uh-oh,* he thought, *here comes the regret.* But when he turned to face Lynnette, he saw she was still fast asleep. Her face was screwed up in an expression of pain or fear, he could not tell which in the dim light of the cabin. A nightmare, he guessed, immediately trying to soothe her in the circle of his arms. But she grew more restive beneath his tender stroking, not less. Her arms and legs flailed, her expression grew more tense. She began to mumble and thrash. Concerned, he gently shook her, trying to wake the pirate out of whatever horror gripped her.

She would not wake, and her struggles with the invisible opponent grew fiercer. Daniel began to grow alarmed. He'd seen people caught in nightmares before, but this somehow seemed worse. Lynnette was shaking her head, trying to speak, grabbing the empty air as though it were her enemy. Tears slipped from under her closed lids. Daniel tried again to shake her awake, calling her name at first softly, then with growing fright. She seemed not to hear him at all. He held her arms close to him and pinned her thrashing legs beneath one heavy thigh, afraid she might do herself harm. It seemed to make her even more angry, even more frightened, but he still feared the damage she might do herself and held on grimly.

The nightmare went on for several more tense moments, in which he shook her and called her name to no avail. Then suddenly she stiffened, and the word she'd been struggling to speak finally came out in a piercing, shattering wail. *"No!"*

Lynnette collapsed against Daniel's chest, ice cold and barely breathing.

Silence reigned in the aftermath of that scream. Daniel held her close. He knew she was awake now, though she hadn't yet opened her eyes. Then the trembling started. She turned her face against his chest and her whole body shook, freezing cold. He simply held her within the warm embrace of his arms and asked nothing while she rode out the tremors. Though her face was still wet, now that the pirate was awake she shed no tears.

CHAPTER TWENTY-THREE

*I*MAGES STAINED red with blood and black with fear flooded the pirate's mind and replayed themselves behind her closed eyes as she recalled the dream—as unbearably real tonight as it had been each time it ripped through Lynnette's slumber these last seven years. The events of the terrible night that had destroyed her innocence, the night that had taken her sister's very life, recurred again and again to Lynnette while she slept, dragging her cruelly through dark realms of horror and nightmare. Curled tight against Daniel's side and shivering uncontrollably, still half caught in the shadow world, Lynnette was forced to remember once again that which she longed only to forget.

She was back again in her father's town house on the outskirts of London's fashionable Pall Mall district, a girl of sixteen, afraid and completely helpless to control the events around her. Lynnette saw her father, head nodding from drink, slowly slide from his chair in the cold parlor they could no longer afford to heat. He collapsed unconscious on the bare floor, stripped now of the rich oriental rugs that had once carpeted it. She saw the two men who frightened her so much

lounging at their ease on the remaining furniture, saw how
they looked at her and her young sister, Sarah, barely fourteen
but already so beautiful she made the gawky sixteen-year-old
Lynnette fade into the shadows whenever they shared a room.

The men were inebriated, too, but not nearly to the extent
that Papa was . . . And the elder of them, she knew, the one
whose sheer menacing *presence* frightened her far more than
the younger one's callous brutality, had engineered things tonight to make it so. He'd gotten what he wanted of the sodden
Lord Blackthorne—his shipping business, his cash, his properties, everything he owned—except, of course, the man's innocent young daughters. He'd been saving them for last.

Lord Roger, Earl of Pennsworth, had been cultivating Lord
Blackthorne's acquaintance for several months now, ever since
the death of the middle-aged baron's beloved wife had sent
him into a grief-stricken decline—a decline beneath which he
would not allow his daughters to help him or to share his
sorrow. Pennsworth used their casual acquaintance from the
shipping trade to get close to Lynnette's father, encouraging
the distraught man to pleasures that would help him forget . . .
or so he said.

Lynnette suspected Lord Roger's professed philanthropic
intent even from the start, but her father refused to listen to
her. Claiming the sight of his girls was too painful a reminder
of their mother, he'd turned from Lynnette and her sister and
shut them out as he took to drinking and heavy gambling, all
at the urging of Lord Roger. Together they frequented gaming
hells and unsavory drinking establishments by the dozen, dis-
porting themselves like much younger men and generally engaging in every form of dissipation available to an English
gentleman with money to burn.

Except that Lord Blackthorne, whose ancestral estates were
modest, did not have money to burn.

From what she could gather, Pennsworth made a habit of
taking under his wing those who, for one reason or another,
had less force of will than himself. The men, young and old,
would get in over their heads, falling into ruin and owing
money to all and sundry; most especially to Lord Roger himself. She didn't know if he enjoyed taking their money or their
dignity more, but she suspected that the wealthy earl relished
the sport of ruining other men even more than he liked raking

in the spoils of their years of hard work. She'd sensed right away when Roger had befriended her father that the bereaved baron would end up becoming merely the earl's latest victim.

Lynnette's fears came true all too soon. Her father lost heavily at the card tables and gaming hells, and creditors began knocking at their door, threatening to take away everything they owned. Stunned with grief for her dear mother in her own right, unable to take in the changes that had disrupted her comfortable life, she'd not known how to respond to those angry men. Nothing in her gently bred upbringing had prepared her to deal with such unpleasantness. The house was stripped of valuables while she stood by helplessly. Before she knew it, the servants had all left, for there was no money to pay them. The investors who financed the baron's sailing ventures repossessed most of Lord Blackthorne's ships as they rotted in their slips at the Pool of London. Just one vessel, a fine sloop out on a trade run at the time of the repossession, escaped being sold at auction.

Blackthorne would give no orders, so his captains left him one by one, only the loyal Harry, a longtime family friend, remaining to present Lynnette a sympathetic ear. But even he was powerless to help; he could only watch as his old friend let fall apart all he had worked these many years to build.

Lynnette's father had made the unusual step of going into trade many years earlier in order to augment his family's fortunes, thereby joining the ranks of a small number of aristocrats like Lord Roger who dabbled in matters of finance. He'd had a good head for business, and enjoyed being the owner of a shipping venture. He'd even taken his dear wife and their two young daughters on short voyages with him, a fact that delighted his elder daughter, but that sent his wife and younger child running to the rail, green with sickness. Those had been grand days of closeness and laughter, days that had ended far too abruptly when Lady Blackthorne took ill and died suddenly of the influenza. With his wife went every spark of life in Lord Blackthorne's body, and as time passed and his grief didn't abate, his daughters even began to fear for his sanity.

Sarah and Lynnette had watched their father drown in dissipation, watched Lord Roger and his cronies lure him deeper into debt and despair, but it had been when the men started bringing their drinking and gaming home that the girls began to fear for their own safety. With no servants left to cater to them, her father's companions insisted that his daughters serve them, Lord Roger especially taking pleasure in ordering them about and leering at the frightened girls.

Lynnette and Sarah both tried in vain to gain their father's help, to make him see his so-called friends intended no good for him or for his children, but the baron was too deep in his cups and in his sorrow to notice anything amiss. After all, he raged when they approached him, his daughters should help the old man in his troubles, shouldn't they? Did they think themselves too good to play hostesses to his associates, who were only trying to cheer him up? Not knowing what else to do, and frightened by the unreasonable, angry stranger their father had become, the girls had obeyed, counting themselves lucky to escape unscathed at the end of each evening the baron's guests spent reveling at his house.

But *this* night things were getting out of hand, and even innocent Sarah knew it. With their father passed out and unlikely to stir to their aid, the last restraints were removed from Lord Roger and his hulking, ill-mannered compatriot, the only ones present tonight. They were free now to turn their attention to their host's nubile daughters. Especially, they focused on the beautiful younger sibling, a delicate, rosy beauty of extraordinary promise. In her simple hoop skirts and modest bodice with only a lacy chemisette to save it from total plainness, the fourteen-year-old was nevertheless a vision of loveliness men could not help ogling.

Lynnette, on the other hand, was still all planes and angles, elbows and knees, not having grown yet into her womanly beauty. Her mother had told her she took after her maternal grandmother, who'd taken uncommonly long to bloom out of an awkward adolescence. Lynnette had never cared about her appearance, preferring tree-climbing to mirror-gazing any day. But now she wished she had more of her sister's beauty, so that she might distract Sarah's tormentors away from the petrified girl.

Sarah threw helpless glances of entreaty toward her elder sister as she poured yet more wine at the behest of the drunken men. Roger's companion, a young nobleman whose name Lynnette didn't know but whose slack-lipped, lustful look sent shivers of dread down her spine, laughed as Sarah bent over his glass, grabbing her about the waist in a sudden movement. He pulled her onto his lap and began kissing her. Sarah tried to cry out, but her scream was muffled by the man's mouth. Adrenaline surged through Lynnette and she ran toward Sarah's side. She didn't know what she could do to stop a man twice her size, but, to save her sister, she was ready for any sort of violence.

Before she even got there, a heavy arm caught her around the throat and brought her to a choking halt. Roger's hated voice, familiar from many nights of watching him destroy her father, came clearly to her ear. "Would you spoil our young friend's fun, little girl? Or is it that you wish to take your sister's place?" His hot, stinking tongue swiped her neck in a long, slow lick that left Lynnette gagging. "You're not nearly as comely as she is, of course," he continued cruelly, "but you'll do in a pinch. In fact, I think you'll suffice quite nicely for our inebriated young lord, while *I* taste the sweeter charms of little Sarah."

And then he was pulling the young man bodily off Sarah and ordering him to hold Lynnette while he claimed seniority. The sodden man protested feebly, but Roger had such a strong hold on both his mind and his purse that he did as he was told, subduing the fiercely struggling older sister while Lord Roger advanced on the younger.

Caught fast and unable to help, hardly able to fend off the brutal man's hands from her own body, Lynnette burned with powerless fury to help her sister. She tried again and again to scream at Roger to stop, but her mouth was covered by the young lord's big, sweaty hand. She clawed and bit the man who held her while Roger forced her sister down on the embroidered divan and pushed her skirts up. Lord Blackthorne remained sprawled grotesquely motionless nearby on the floorboards, out cold and no help to his offspring in their desperate need.

What happened next was a blur in Lynnette's memory and in her dream. She twisted violently and managed to pull her mouth away from the paw that covered it. Screaming at the top of her lungs, she somehow fought free of her drunken captor and ran for the door. From the corner of her eye she saw Sarah's expression—hysterical, disbelieving that her only sister and lifelong protector was running out on her when she

needed her most. Lynnette registered Sarah's hurt and her terror, but she didn't stop running until she reached her father's
library and burst through the doors. He kept a brace of dueling
pistols here for show, didn't he? Yes, there they were. In a
blink she had their unfamiliar weight in her hands and had
started back to save her sister.

Halfway there she realized a fact that turned her stomach
to cold lead. The pistols were not kept loaded! It took long
nightmarish minutes, both then and in her sleeping recollection, to recall Harry's lessons on pistolry. She'd begged for
the lessons in her usual tomboy style, and Harry, with her
indulgent parents' permission, had given them one day shortly
after her fifteenth birthday, never dreaming to what desperate
purpose she would put his teaching. With shaking fingers, she
managed to load the awkward flintlocks, dropping the shot
several times in the lengthy process. What was happening to
Sarah while she delayed she could not imagine, didn't *want*
to imagine.

Lynnette ran back to the parlor as fast as she could, but it
seemed to take forever, as though, as she ran, the corridor
grew longer apace with her footsteps. She knew she had to
get back to Sarah, but the pistols were so heavy in her
hands. . . . At last she reached the door, only to be brought up
short by a sight that was burned ever after into her memory.
Lord Roger was pulling away from Sarah, who lay limp now
on the divan, bleeding from several blows to her face and from
between her splayed legs. He collapsed next to her and the
young man rose eagerly to take his place.

Lynnette went blind with rage, raising the pistol, squeezing
the stiff trigger mechanism. As the red faded from her eyes
and the roar of the pistol differentiated itself from the roar of
blood in her ears, she saw the man go down, half his face torn
away.

Roger turned toward her with a growl of surprised rage,
and Lynnette, feeling as though a stranger had inhabited her
body, leaving her feeling oddly calm, outside of herself, raised
the second pistol with a steady hand. "You're not as comely
as your friend," she said in a deathly, disembodied voice, "but
you'll do quite nicely to share his fate." She cocked the pistol,
but Lord Roger, pale now and suddenly sober, began backing
away, babbling frantically in his fear. "Now, now, little girl,

we were only having a bit of fun . . . No harm done, just put down the gun . . ."

As he spoke he backed farther into the shadows, toward the promise of escape in a French door leading to the garden. Lynnette didn't notice how close he was to fleeing safely, she merely sighted coldly down the barrel, ready, squeezing the trigger slowly . . . But with a lunge Roger made it to the door, thrust it open and dove outside, Lynnette's last shot harmlessly splitting the wood of the frame where his head had been an instant before.

She wanted to go after him to finish the job, but even now the blazing rage that had possessed her was fading, leaving her gray and in shock, weakening her knees so that she fell hard to the floor, unable to support herself. With only Sarah's safety in mind now, she crawled to her sister's side, reaching out an icy hand stained black with gunpowder to brush back the red-gold curtain of hair from Sarah's bruised face. The trusting green eyes remained closed. "Sarah," she whispered hoarsely. "Sarah, dearest, come back to me. Wake up." Sarah did not respond, and Lynnette grew frightened all over again.

Had the shock of the vicious assault been too much for her fragile, sweet sibling? Sarah had always been so delicate, so ethereal and innocent. Perhaps she did not want to return to a world that could treat her so horribly. "Sarah!" Lynnette repeated, fear making her tone sharper. "Please, darling," she pleaded, "wake up!"

For a moment Sarah's pure, jewel-like eyes fluttered open and focused on Lynnette's identical ones. She tried to smile, seeing the worry in her big sister's face and wanting to alleviate it, but she was *so* tired . . . Her eyes slid slowly closed again as she lost consciousness.

It was then that Lynnette saw the blood staining Sarah's hair and neck, and realized one of the blows Roger had dealt had been serious, indeed. She felt along the side of Sarah's head, finding a lump above her ear the size of a duck egg, rapidly growing and bleeding freely. Frantically, Lynnette gathered her sister in her arms, crooning to her senselessly, telling her over and over that she would be all right, that Lynnette would never let anyone hurt her again, would always take care of her. With a mighty effort, she picked her sibling up, not even knowing where she was going but sure she had to get Sarah away from this place of horror.

The stunned sixteen-year-old carried her sister across the bloody floor, stepping without a thought over the man she'd killed; stepping over her unconscious father the same way. He had not stirred once during the whole ghastly assault.

Lynnette bore her dear burden up two flights of steps and into the bedroom Sarah had decorated in frills and lace—decor Lynnette had always despised and had teased her about in better times. She tenderly laid Sarah down on the pink-satin-covered bed, soaked a kerchief with water and bathed all the wounds she could find on the slender, abused body. She awkwardly bandaged the gash on the side of Sarah's head, but could not entirely stop the bleeding. No matter what she did, Sarah would not wake, and Lynnette, deep in shock herself, finally gave up the attempt and laid herself down next to her sister, arms wrapped protectively around her. She rocked her that way deep into the night.

When she'd woken at dawn, Sarah had felt cold to her, so Lynnette fetched a coverlet and laid it over both of them. She spoke softly to her sister, telling her how sorry she was that she'd failed so miserably to protect her, begging her forgiveness, telling her how much she loved her. She talked for hours, tears running down her cheeks, her voice a tight rasp of emotion as she promised she would not let the ones who had done this to Sarah go unpunished. She hugged her sister, kissed her, stroked her cold cheek as their mother once had done.

It was a long time before she knew Sarah was dead. When at last Lynnette admitted the truth to herself, a howl of denial, of rage and pain and loss beyond bearing, was ripped from her throat in the single word, "No!"

That word always ended the dream for her, waking Lynnette with a shock of rawness in her throat and a refreshed memory of the pain that never left her heart. Awake and trembling in Daniel's protective arms, Lynnette inevitably recalled the events of the rest of that day.

Finally she had left Sarah, wandering dazed back downstairs to the scene of the appalling chaos last night. There she'd found her father just stirring, looking around himself in bewilderment, blearily demanding an explanation from her for the dead man lying on his parlor floor and the overturned furniture. Lynnette had walked right by the blustering, befuddled man she'd once called her papa, picked up one of the pistols discarded on the bare floorboards, and kept on going out the door Lord Roger had used in his cowardly flight the night before. She'd known in that moment that she would never go unarmed again.

Without knowing how she got there, Lynnette had found herself on Harry's doorstep that evening, unable to account for the missing hours of the day and unable to speak when the worried sailor anxiously inquired what was wrong, his face wrinkling in consternation at her bloody attire and haggard, drawn countenance. She'd collapsed in his arms, and Harry had cared for her as tenderly as a mother hen with but one chick. When finally she slept in the tidy, utilitarian flat Harry kept near the wharves, he'd gone back to the baron's town house to investigate, fearing the worst. What he'd found made him redefine the meaning of "worst."

Upstairs he'd discovered Sarah's pitiful corpse, laid out neatly as Lynnette had left it. Downstairs he'd found two more bodies. A strange young man with his face blown away lay next to Lord Blackthorne, also dead of a gunshot wound to the head. Next to the baron's body Harry had found the note that begged forgiveness for his many failures to his daughters. He'd returned home then, shocked at what he'd seen and fearing Lynnette would go mad from the horror of her experience. But she'd been sane, awake and sitting up in bed when he returned. She was able to relate the tale of the night's events to her old companion, and listened gravely when he told her of her father's apparent suicide. However, when Harry gently handed the suicide note to Lynnette, she crushed the parchment in her hand unread and threw it into the fire.

It was then that she told Harry of her plan for revenge. There was still one ship left belonging to her father, and possession of it now fell to her. Harry would teach her to sail it, teach her to fight and to command men as he had done all of his own life. She would not take no for an answer, and the loyal sailor, dismayed at the sudden change in the sunny-natured girl he'd dandled on his knee and taught to tie sailor's knots from the age of three, could not refuse her the vengeance she so needed to reclaim her soul.

Seven years and more she'd pursued that revenge, praying every single day that Lord Roger felt half the anguish he'd caused her family.

"Do you want to tell me about it?" Daniel asked softly. Lynnette didn't respond immediately. "That was no ordinary nightmare," he pressed gently, worry evident in his tone. "Might you not find relief in sharing the memory?"

Lynnette wanted to tell him. It surprised her just how much she needed to share this, to let the words tumble out of her and into the dark night from within the safe circle of Captain Bradley's arms. She had never told anyone about these episodes; never told anyone about this dream that took over her sleep and left her shaking and pale and afraid. It was strange to share her terrors, even inadvertently, with another person. It was strange too to wake up with that someone being there to hold her and whisper reassurance. Strange, but not unpleasant.

She drew in great gulping breaths, still trying to slow her heart down. Her face was buried against Daniel's strong, solid chest and she listened for a while to the steady beat of his heart. Her own heart told her to trust this man, to tell him everything, but she dared not listen to it. The dream had reminded her of why she didn't dare believe in any man, no matter how genuine he seemed. *They all fail you in the end,* she thought bitterly. Her father had claimed to love her, and look what good it had done. This man did not even claim so much, was no blood relation, either.

Despite the incredible loving they'd shared just hours ago, despite the blossoming feeling of tenderness and trust she'd glimpsed so briefly, she could never open her heart to Daniel. She knew that now. The dream had been a reminder of all that could never be, and a call to remember her duty to her slain sister. She would have to deny Daniel that which he sought so avidly.

Her decision, which she'd agonized over earlier, was made. She would refuse him, and take whatever consequences he dealt out. If he wanted to have her arrested when they reached London, so be it. Though she knew the grim reality of the punishment for piracy, Captain Thorne refused to change her mind. She'd rather swing in irons at Graves Point as a warning to honest sailors than betray her cause.

"Nay," she said softly, her terror-roughened voice so muted he had to tilt his head closer to hers to hear it. "I do not remember what I dreamt," she lied. "I am sorry I woke you." She tried to slide from his arms and turn away, but Daniel would not allow it. She gave up without a struggle; after all, she did not truly want to leave the merchant's embrace just yet.

Daniel made no comment, though his disappointment was crushing. He knew the pirate lied, just as surely as he knew he could not force the truth from her. He only wished she could trust him enough to share whatever troubled her so greatly that the memory of it sent her screaming out of a deep sleep. As he held her gently against his chest, it occurred to him that perhaps trust went both ways. Maybe if he confided his own dark secrets to her, she would come to believe in him and return the favor. He opened his mouth to speak.

"Lynnette, I want to tell you something I have never shared with anyone in my life. Only Simon knows the truth, and that is simply because he was there to witness some of it. I have never willingly shared this information with another soul. But perhaps you will feel more comfortable divulging your secrets to me if you know more about mine."

Before she could reply, before she could beg him not to make her vulnerable with such a gift of himself, he had begun, and the pirate discovered she wanted more than anything to listen to him.

"You know I joined the navy as a youth. What you do *not* know is that I didn't join by choice. I was abducted one night from my bed and brought aboard my first ship unconscious, not commissioned as an officer."

"I know you said you worked your way through the ranks," she dared to interrupt, distracted momentarily from her own dark memories by her interest in her lover's past. "But I thought you simply meant the ranks of the officers. Surely you don't mean—"

"I do mean. I began my career in His Majesty's illustrious service as a lowly cabin boy." Despite herself, Lynnette choked down a surprised laugh at the thought of proud, strong Captain Bradley hauling slops and mending officers' linens as

a sixteen-year-old cabin boy. She spared a thought for poor
Davie of her own crew.

"I don't understand," she admitted. "I've never heard of a
nobleman's son being taken by the press-gangs. How did it
happen to you?" She spoke quietly, the hushed darkness of
the cabin inviting whispered confidences.

" 'Twas not by chance, I assure you." She heard the first
traces of bitterness creep into his warm, deep baritone. "My
half brother arranged the abduction in order to get me out of
the way. He wanted to inherit my father's earldom."

"Why shouldn't he inherit, if he was the elder?" Lynnette
wanted to know. "Was he your mother's son and not your
father's?"

"He was my father's son, though no father ever had such
a curse for a child as did mine. He was disinherited and disowned when I was still a boy. It took an act of Parliament to
cancel my brother's claim to the estates, but my father was
willing to go through the whole lengthy process in order to
get quit once and for all of his misbegotten son.

"I only knew parts of the story, for no one wanted to speak
of it. Mostly I heard the whispers of the servants about his
foul treatment of them, and of others in the county we lived
in. Young girls were his victims mostly, though there were
rumors of other, even worse deeds. He used to take delight in
tormenting me as well when I was a lad, though he was much
older and could not excuse his deeds as youthful pranks. I
think even then he meant to kill me—why, I'll never understand.

"When I was very young he took me fishing out on the
ornamental lake behind the house, and he capsized the boat
purposely, leaving me to drown. Thank God the gamekeeper
saw the boat go over and rescued me in time. My half brother
couldn't weasel his way out of *that* deed the way he'd done
so many others; not when there'd been a reliable witness. I
didn't fully comprehend what had happened then, but I knew
my brother despised me. It was about that time my father cut
him out of his will and sent him from home.

"By the time I was old enough to understand the nature of
my father's quarrel with my brother, it was too late for me to
protect myself from his viciousness. He had already arranged
to have me kidnapped so that he might gain back what he'd

lost through his own wretched deeds. My father became ill—possibly because the shock of my disappearance was more than he could bear.

"When I was eventually able, much later, to make my way back to England and gather news of my family, I found out just how devious my half brother had been. My father, growing weaker by the day and fearing me dead, had changed his will again, leaving everything—title, estates, and all—to my brother. He had no choice but to do so—it was his duty to ensure his legacy would be passed on. He passed away soon after the changes were finalized.

"I am convinced to this day that my father would not have changed the entail without some cunning machination on my half brother's part, but there was nothing I could do. The will was ironclad, my brother reinstated as the elder son. There was nothing for me but to continue my career in the navy, a career that by then I had grown to appreciate. But I will never forgive him for what he took from me—my father's last years, my youth, my trust in my fellow man." An earldom.

Lynnette lay still for a long while, silently digesting this. Apparently she wasn't the only one whose family had disappointed her. She wasn't the only one with pain in her past. Daniel too had known hurt, struggle, betrayal; though perhaps not on the same level as hers. She knew his revelation was designed to bring about her own—he'd admitted as much—and she wanted more than ever to comply with his wishes. Yet even as she opened her mouth to confess what burdened her so deeply, she knew she would not be able to speak.

She told herself that there were simply no words to describe what had happened the night of Sarah's death. Wasn't it bad enough that she'd had to live with the memory of the incident these last seven years—was she now supposed to talk about it, too? It would only make the pain more real, she rationalized, growing angry with Daniel's tender method of prying into her secrets. But deep in her heart, she knew the real reason she would never speak of that night was her own deep sense of shame.

She was, in truth, afraid to tell him what had happened—afraid of what he would surely think of her. How could she make him understand her inexcusable failure to stop the situation that evening from escalating? What if Daniel blamed her for not protecting her sister better? Lynnette would forever remember the look on Sarah's face when she'd run out the door; that look of betrayal and accusation. If only she'd not taken so long loading the pistols! If only she'd thought of another way to stop the men . . . If only she had offered to take Sarah's place and saved her that awful violation. Daniel would surely turn from her in disgust if he knew the truth of her failure, and she could not bear his scorn.

So the pirate did the only thing she could do to protect herself from further hurt. She lashed out. "Poor Captain Bradley," she sneered deliberately. "Left out in the cold to fend for himself while his brother takes all. The classic younger son's tale. I suppose now you'll be blaming me all over again for ruining your fragile hopes for future wealth with your little shipping empire."

Daniel was stung to the quick by Lynnette's sudden viciousness. He jerked up on the bed, pulling away from her as if from a viper. "Is that what you think?" he managed past the lump of hurt anger in his throat. "Think you I shared this with you only to make you the story's villain?"

"I cannot imagine why else you would bore me with your pitiful woes," she retorted, hating herself more than she'd thought possible, but committed now to her course. She rooted around for her shirt and drew it on hastily when she found it, abandoning the tousled bed and retreating with a semblance of hauteur to the pallet in the corner.

"If you don't mind, I would appreciate no further revelations tonight, Peacock. I'm very tired." And she yawned deliberately. Insultingly. She lay down on the cold pallet in the dark, knowing Daniel couldn't see the hot flush of shame that suffused her cheeks at her deliberate cruelty. There was no other way, she consoled herself. Sarah could not be avenged until Lynnette was free of this strange obsession with the merchant. She must excise him from her heart, no matter how viciously it hurt.

Daniel stared unseeing into the dark at the lumpy shadow he knew contained Lynnette's bed in exile, feeling as if he'd been kicked in the teeth. Damn the wench! She made love so sweetly, gave of her body unstintingly, then turned around and not only refused to give her heart, but ripped his out, as well. He couldn't take it anymore! Again and again he'd done his best to be patient, understanding, caring. He'd told her things he'd not shared with anyone before. He'd offered her his support and his . . . his what?

His love. He had offered her *marriage,* for Christ's sake. He should have known then that what he felt was love; it was the only explanation for his rash proposal. He'd probably loved her from the instant he saw her standing so challengingly, looking so maddeningly beautiful, across the deck of his captured frigate months ago. Daniel could no longer deny his heart's truth. He was passionately, deeply, and insanely in love with the pirate queen. He knew he would die for her if she asked it. He would devote his every waking moment to her happiness, could do nothing less for her sake.

And she scorned his every offer. She didn't want his love, his chivalry, his confidences. All she wanted was to get away, get back to whatever demons drove her, whatever fateful mission compelled her to be so cold and callous.

He would have to let her go, he knew now. As he lay quietly in the tense hush that had fallen between them, Daniel knew with total certainty that everything had changed with this new revelation of his love for Lynnette. He had to give her what she wanted, and what she wanted was *not* him.

When he spoke again, the words were not the angry ones Lynnette had expected. "You win, Lynnette," Daniel said heavily. "I no longer care to fight this battle between us. Keep your secrets if they are so important to you. You need have no fear of what awaits you in London. I will not alert the authorities to your presence. If you wish it I will even arrange transport for you back to Tortuga or wherever you wish. You will be free," he finished, "since that is your greatest desire."

Daniel pulled on his breeches and left the cabin without another word, the door closing with solemn finality behind him.

For a long time afterward, the pirate lay still, stunned by the resignation she'd heard in Daniel's voice, and stunned too by how much it hurt to hear him say the words she'd been trying to wrest from him for so long. She'd wanted him to leave her alone, to stop prying and invading her privacy. She'd wanted him to set her free. She'd wanted to *win.* Now she was getting what she wanted, so why did she feel she'd just lost the greatest prize of her life?

CHAPTER TWENTY-FOUR

*L*YNNETTE HIKED the hood of her voluminous gray wool cloak closer about her face to ward off the chill. It had been so long since she'd been in a climate requiring a wrap that the cold and damp of London's ubiquitous fog seemed to seep into her very marrow. Or perhaps it was the chilly parting she'd experienced with Daniel just minutes ago on the deck of the *Triumph*. She didn't like to think of it.

They'd shared few words in the weeks since their last wrenching argument, when Daniel had agreed to let her go. He'd kept his word, she had to admit. The moment the ship docked at the mouth of the Thames, Daniel had appeared from wherever he'd been hiding to avoid her during the last weeks of their journey, carrying a cloak, a purse of coins (which she'd refused), and a few curt words of parting. She'd also politely refused his offer to arrange passage for her back to the West Indies, preferring to have no further contact with the merchant and not wanting him to guess her future plans.

He'd taken her refusals in silence, merely facing her across the stretch of wood planking, the hard planes of his features revealing nothing, his silver eyes blank polished mirrors as he gazed solemnly at her. In them the pirate read only her own regrets, the sadness that threatened to choke her at parting from him forever. *Forever.* God, how that one tiny word had the power to wound her very soul. Lynnette couldn't begin to fathom the idea that she would never see Daniel again.

She wanted to tell him how sorry she was; sorry for everything she'd done and everything she'd refused to do, but when she opened her mouth to speak, no words emerged. She wanted to kiss him one last time, to press her lips against his and communicate her remorse physically, but the distance between them had never seemed less bridgeable, and she'd let the moment pass. In the end Lynnette had left without a word or a gesture to indicate her feelings, just turned away and ran down the gangplank, to be swallowed up heartbeats later in the enveloping mist.

She'd never turned around to see the shaking hand Daniel extended after her.

Now the pirate forced her attention to turn elsewhere in the interest of self-preservation. The wharves of London town were no place to lose oneself in reminiscence, she chided herself as a ragged drunkard lurched across her path. Apparently some things never changed. The stench, for instance. Blue Ruin fairly reeked from the man's pores. And that was not the only scent in the air. Though it was far too foggy to see more than a few feet in any direction, Lynnette could smell the myriad odors of London close around her: rotting fish, fresh slops, coal smoke, meat pies being sold from a cart on the corner, and several other inventive stinks that seemed to come from oddly shimmering puddles at her feet.

Lynnette was grateful for the sturdy boots and breeches donated—grudgingly, she was sure—by some half-grown member of the *Triumph*'s crew. It would have been a good deal less safe to wander the area in women's attire than to do so anonymously garbed as a stripling sailor. Still, the pirate wasn't worried for her safety, now that she was free of Daniel's grasp. She had a knife (given her by Willie Jennings as a remembrance) and her wits about her. London, though certainly bigger than her island haunts of the last several years, was no different, albeit she recalled few landmarks from her younger days. All might look unfamiliar after seven years' absence, but Captain Thorne knew how to deal with the dock area of any port city she came across. Or thought she did.

Out of nowhere a hand shot out and grabbed her shoulder from behind, dragging her into the shadows of a fetid alleyway she'd been about to bypass in search of temporary lodging.

"And where d'ye think ye were goin', lassie?" a threatening voice growled.

Could it be?

"Harry!" Lynnette spun around, unable to believe her dear friend was standing mere inches from her. "What . . . I don't . . . How did you *find* me?" she sputtered, sheathing the blade she'd instinctively bared when she was grabbed.

"Well, now, be that any way ta greet yer ever-loyal first mate, lassie? When 'e set out after ye through storm an' sea, leavin' behind 'im not one single tavern standin' when they wouldn't give up word o' yer where'bouts?" Harry laughed heartily, hugging Lynnette tightly in his bandy arms, too re- lieved at having found her to take note of the astonishing fact that she didn't pull away from his touch but clung to him for comfort instead.

"Thank God you're here," the pirate murmured. "Did you manage to convince any of the crew to follow you?" She wasn't too hopeful of an affirmative response.

"*Any* of 'em? Sure and they're *all* 'ere, lassie! Ye didn' think Captain Thorne could go missin' without all her crew is up in arms on th' instant, threatenin' ta tear apart th' ship of any man jack could be hidin' her?! Not hardly! Th' men're all hidin' out in th' inns an' taverns hereabouts, watchin' an' waitin' fer yer arrival. We gave th' *Maiden* a new coat o' paint an' a new name fer th' nonce. She's jest up th' ways on Thames, waitin' fer ye ta come back ta 'er." At Lynnette's wondering look, the mate explained further.

"Once we found out who'd taken ye, we raced ta get our- selves aboard th' *Maiden* an' come after ye. We tried ta catch ye on th' open seas, ta capture th' ship, but th' blasted tub evaded us all th' way. We'd not 'ave gotten 'ere afore ye, save that th' storm that caught ye an' delayed ye so long outside th' Canaries barely brushed us. We knew we'd passed ye, an' decided ta await ye 'ere, rather'n take th' chance o' missin' ye on open water. We figured whatever damage 'e done ye by then was done." Harry squinted, looking his captain up and down. " 'E didn' hurt ye none, did 'e?"

Lynnette was forced to admit he had not.

"Good. I rather liked th' pup. Be a pure shame if'n I 'ad ta skewer 'im." Harry held up a wickedly sharp dirk in illus- tration. His jesting words belied the deadly serious tone with which he uttered them. Lynnette had no doubt Daniel wouldn't have survived mistreating her with Harry as her avenger. It was a great comfort.

"But how did you find out what had happened to me?" Lynnette asked in confusion. She'd never imagined Harry and the men could've come to her rescue so quickly, arriving *ahead* of her, no less. She ought to have had more faith in her stalwart crew, she realized now. Their loyalty ran far deeper than she'd ever guessed. The knowledge warmed Captain Thorne's scarred pirate heart considerably.

"When ye didn' show up ta meet me an' commission th'

work on th' *Maiden* in th' mornin' like we planned, I figured
somethin' 'ad gone awry. Ye never miss an appointment, so
I went lookin' fer ye. That braggart Cap'n Bellairs said as
how he'd seen ye leavin' th' *Gorge* late that evenin', but no
one could place ye any time after. Coupla wharf rats said
they'd seen a group o' men carryin' somethin' they shouldn'
aboard a frigate, so I checked up on whose ships 'ad been in
that part o' port, an' who'd left in an 'urry durin' th' night.
Sure enough, our prettyboy's ship was th' only one took off
that night, so I knew jest what'd happened. Went fer a little
revenge of 'is own, did 'e?" Harry hugged her close again for
comfort.

"Did he ever. Listen," the pirate said, looking up and down
the alley warily, "this isn't the place for catching up. Who
knows what ears might be listening, or who might be interested in a couple of rogues with a price on their heads?" She
grinned cockily. "Why don't you take me to wherever the men
have set up shop, and I'll tell you what I've got planned. With
them as well as you at my back, what I have in mind will go
far more smoothly than ever I'd hoped." Taking the wiry
sailor's arm, she urged him on.

Harry grinned wryly. It seemed a few weeks as a prisoner
aboard the merchant's vessel had indeed done his indomitable
captain no harm. She was her old commanding self, plotting
and scheming again within minutes of landing her feet on dry
land. It was grand to have her back!

Simon was worried about Daniel. He just wasn't his old self
anymore. In the two months since they'd returned home to
London, his partner had changed dramatically. Gone was the
ambitious, affably outgoing man Captain Richards had come
to know over the years, replaced with a brooding stranger who
drank to excess and stayed out doing God-knew-what until all
hours. While not neglecting their shared business interests,
Daniel seemed to have lost his joy in the work; not even the
ship they'd been able to buy with the pirate's gold to replace
the *Empire* had sparked Captain Bradley's interest.

At first Simon had calmed his worries with the thought that
perhaps it was merely the end of the trading season that had
got his partner so down. Neither man could sail again until
the spring, for the weather and their delays in putting together

a new cargo, caused by the time taken up delivering Daniel's ransom, had forced them to wait the winter out. Yet as time passed and Daniel remained sapped of all joy, Simon knew he could not lay his friend's continuing unhappiness on their business difficulties.

He watched in concern as the dark-haired man threw himself into raucous amusements, frequenting as many as ten parties a night among London's elite society, drowning himself in brandy and flirting with every woman who crossed his path. Despite the frenetic activity, Simon had never seen Daniel having *less* fun. And though the blond ship's captain hated to admit his closest friend had been brought low by a woman, he knew Daniel's fierce discontent must be the fault of the gorgeous pirate, who, though long gone from his life, had left an indelible impression on Captain Bradley's heart.

Daniel had weathered the gossip about his captivity at the hands of a woman well. Simon had tried to keep the story quiet for his friend's sake, but with both of them gone so unexpectedly, Simon taking the *Triumph* out after Daniel's *Empire* so soon, word had inevitably leaked out about Captain Bradley's capture. They'd decided to keep the story of Daniel's revenge on the pirate secret, both for Daniel's privacy and because they had no decent explanation for why they'd let such a notorious criminal go free, when by rights they ought to have her proudly displayed in irons for the world to see.

Though some of the *ton* whispered about the scandal and told third-hand stories of the hideous giantess who'd taken one of their number prisoner, few laughed at Daniel's predicament. Too many had heard of Captain Thorne's exploits to mock a man caught in her toils. Just look what she'd done to Pennsworth's shipping, for instance . . . Word had it that the earl had doubled the price on her head, and had new plans for her capture. It just showed what happened when a member of the peerage tried his hand at lowly matters of trade. Why, a man's whole fortune could be imperiled that way.

It was all well and good for a younger son to soil his hands in business, but for a peer to invest so heavily in the trades . . . it was scandalous. But then, so was Pennsworth. He never quite crossed the boundaries of good taste—at least not in public, and not when involved with anyone important enough that the scandal would get him thrown off the guest lists of the most prestigious families. But he was rumored to have a darker side, one he was careful to disguise behind a bland smile and a pocketful of ready blunt. His vendetta against the lady buccaneer was a well-publicized affair—one of many for the wealthy earl with the slightly unsavory reputation. And now Bradley was involved. The gossips were all agog.

Many had tried to wrest titillating information about the infamous, outrageous pirate queen from Captain Bradley, but he'd been quite frustratingly closemouthed on the subject. Too traumatized by the experience, some said. Too worn out, others, less charitable, snickered. Who knew what the wench had made him do while awaiting the ransom delivery . . .

Still, Daniel's transition back into the fold had been relatively smooth, for he was uniformly known as a charming rake, and though only a younger son with an uncertain financial future, he came of an impeccable background. Not marriage material for the best families, certainly, sniffed the sticklers of propriety, but welcome nonetheless for an evening's entertainment. Some baronet or squire would be lucky to have him for a son-in-law. It was simply too bad about the older brother. A shame he'd inherited the title instead of the far more suitable and vastly better liked Daniel.

Daniel was becoming *too* well liked by some of the ladies, thought Simon as they rode together in a rented hackney to Lord and Lady Hinkley's ball. If he wasn't careful with his attentions, some cunning mama would have him trussed up and waiting on the altar for her horse-faced simpering daughter before he could blink. It was just lucky the main Season was over, and most of the hopeful debutantes had retired back to the countryside for a wholesome winter of plum puddings and warm toddies by the Yule log before setting out again next spring to catch a husband in town. Those that remained were the most die-hard city sophisticates, the ones who knew how to play flirtation's game without losing their hearts.

"Don't you think you're going at the brandy a little too heavily for this early in the evening?" Simon asked, eyeing the silver flask his partner was tipping up to his mouth with disdain. "The way you've been going lately, it's amazing you can still get up to dance as many dances as you do."

Daniel bit down on an ungracious reply, knowing his old

friend was simply looking out for his welfare. "Have to drink, my friend." He smiled sardonically. Bitterness welled up in his spirit as he thought how empty his existence had become since Captain Thorne had walked out on him two months ago. Nothing was the same since they'd parted. When he'd set out for adventure and profit aboard the *Empire* just months ago, he'd had no idea what was in store for him. His whole life had changed when Lynnette had fired on his ship, and not for the better. Since their tumultuous relationship and its wrenching end, there was no savor in any of Daniel's old activities, no joy in his heart or hope for the future. Instead, he threw himself madly into a whirl a of social activities, hoping to drown out the voice in his head that told him his love was gone for good; a love he couldn't live without.

He'd frequented more balls and routs in the last weeks than in his whole life previously. He'd danced with more insipid women, roistered with more sottish young men, and guzzled more fine vintages than he cared to remember. And sometimes, it even worked. He could go whole minutes now without thinking of Lynnette. "Drinking is the only thing that makes these dull affairs and even duller women bearable." He held the flask out to Simon, who, after staring thoughtfully for a minute, took a swig and handed it back.

Daniel didn't offer him any more of the potent liquor. He'd need all the false courage he could get to stand being surrounded by a roomful of England's most beautiful, available women. Because they might be beautiful, they might be willing, but they were not *her*.

Across the width of the Hinkleys' crowded ballroom an hour later, Daniel spied the most beautiful woman he'd ever seen in his life.

In the crystalline refracted light of the chandeliers, she glowed with a fire that dimmed the features of every other woman in the room into obscurity. Her glittering jewels and gown caught the light, but it was her blinding smile that stunned every man present—including Daniel. Her gracefully erect posture and practiced, languid mannerisms marked her as among the most exquisitely well-bred of ladies. But *this* woman was no lady.

He knew this woman. And he knew the man whose arm

she clung to so tightly. The double blow staggered the merchant, who was already none too steady on his feet. Fortunately, the curvaceous brunette at his side held him steady.

It couldn't be! he thought, shocked. But it was. Despite the elaborate ball gown and intricately coiffed hair, there could be no mistaking his pirate queen. She even wore the famous cuff of emeralds and gold links about her slender throat, the colors set off to perfection by the gold watered-silk gown with embroidered leaves of maple-red and moss-green on the overskirt. He knew that tiny waist, cinched even smaller than usual by the corset and ribboned stomacher she wore. He knew those magnificent breasts, framed by the lace of a fine lawn chemisette and thrust up tantalizingly by the shockingly low square neckline of the gown. He knew the slender shoulders, clothed in a pleated waterfall of the burnished gold silk, which spread down her straight back to the hem of her gown and her delicate, satin-slippered feet—feet he was more used to seeing encased in leather jackboots. He knew the heavy rose-gold mass of her hair, left unpowdered but upswept in an intricate design with green gems and ribbons decorating its shiny waves. He knew everything about the woman—intimately. Captain Thorne had never looked more lovely.

There was no mistaking his brother, either. Lord Roger, earl of Pennsworth, was a familiar demon to Captain Bradley. In his plum velvet evening jacket, embroidered satin vest, matching knee breeches, and the diamond-buckled, red-heeled shoes he favored, Roger looked quite the distinguished older gentleman to Lynnette's wide-eyed young miss. His hold on the beautiful, deceitful pirate was proprietary—quite maddeningly so.

Daniel's first instinct was to go looking for Simon to make the other man verify the astonishing sight. Captain Richards had gone home half an hour before, however, preferring not to remain and watch Daniel's continuing descent into drunkenness and dissipation. Daniel only wished he could blame the sight before his amazed eyes on liquor, but he knew the explanation, however bizarre, could not be that simple. How he managed to shake off the curious, clinging woman at his side and make his way over to the hellish pair he never afterward remembered. But suddenly he stood before the two people responsible for the greatest moments of pain in his life. One he wanted to kill. The other he wanted to kiss.

CHAPTER TWENTY-FIVE

$\mathcal{L}$YNNETTE GRITTED her teeth behind a dazzling smile, ferociously subduing the urge to rend the hand resting firmly on her elbow into tiny, bloody shreds. God, this was harder to bear than she'd thought—and she didn't mean just the corset! Lord knew she'd never expected to wear such a torture device again, but the agony of her constricted lungs was nothing compared to the pressure of the tight grip she held on her temper. Her plan called for calm and cunning, but if she'd had her choice, the pirate would have drawn the pistol hidden beneath her weighty skirts and shot Lord Roger here and now in the Hinkleys' grand ballroom.

She'd tried other ways to get at Pennsworth in the two months since she and her men had rendezvoused in London, but the man was just too damn wily for them to catch on his home territory, and shooting him dead on the street wouldn't satisfy her need to confront the man before he died. She'd wanted a simple nighttime break-in, accomplished with the aid of her sailors and then brought to its deadly conclusion by her alone. But unfortunately, though her spy in the Mayfair town house provided information on its layout gladly, the disgruntled parlormaid could do nothing about the armed guards who patrolled its grounds night and day.

Had it not been so much to ask, Lynnette would have begged her men for aid in laying siege to the mansion, but she wouldn't risk their safety here on hostile ground. At sea, they had an even chance against any opponent, but here in the heart of England's capital, the chance of capture was too great to make a frontal assault on a peer of the realm in his own home. Lynnette was forced to rethink her plans. Again, it was the discontented maid who gave her the idea.

Lord Roger's finances were in ruins, so the girl had confirmed when approached again by the agents of her "mysterious employer." He was desperate for any quick means of regaining his wealth, for the creditors were breathing heavily down his neck now. He'd risked all on refitting a ship to go after his pirate tormentor, and he needed cash badly, though from the way he spent you'd never know it. He'd even been heard to mutter (said the maid with malicious glee) that he'd marry the ugliest woman in Europe, had she a fortune to recommend her. What he'd do with the girl after the wedding was better left unsaid, as his two previous marriages could attest.

Neither countess of Pennsworth had survived long enough to enjoy the privileges of the position. One young unfortunate had tripped coming down her husband's grand staircase only months following the wedding, while the other, wed soon thereafter to the earl, died of an unnamed stomach complaint after but a year of marriage. His atrocites to women had by no means been limited to poor Sarah, the pirate learned.

But it gave her an idea. If she couldn't get close to him by underhanded means . . . why should she not simply stroll right up to the bastard and do what she desired right out in the open? There was a certain ironic rightness about the plan, the erstwhile Lady Blackthorne judged. Pennsworth lived to prey on society. Let one of their number now prey on *him*! Posing as his favorite sort of victim, she would instead lead the earl into a deadly trap of her own. There was little chance he'd recognize the pitiful, frightened young girl she'd been when they last met seven years ago in the woman Lynnette was today. If he did remember her . . .

Well, now, the pirate thought with relish, he'd not be alive long enough to share the news of her identity. Leaving herself open to exposure with this plan was risky, but she felt it was a risk she was more than willing to take, since it kept her men reasonably far out of danger. The part she planned for them in her final act of revenge was small. They would only have to provide backup, in effect becoming her means of accomplishing a clean escape after the deed was done.

Much as Captain Thorne craved Lord Roger's demise, this was one ship she did *not* intend to go down with. She'd no intention of suffering punishment, capital or otherwise, in the course of accomplishing her mission of revenge. No, Lynnette wanted to live to enjoy the fruits of her long labors. After all she'd lost in pursuing Pennsworth's comeuppance, it was not part of her plan to get caught so close to the end.

Which was why she was standing, smiling witlessly, in a

stranger's glittering ballroom, and wearing a gown that, while it *looked* exquisite, *felt* like bloody hell. It was why she was allowing the man she hated like bitter poison to paw her while she simpered winningly up at him. Let him think she was no more than brainless marriage meat.

Let him believe all her lies, please, God. She'd endure anything these next few hours, just so long as she could get him out into the dark gardens by midnight. Her men would be waiting in the shadows, keeping the way cleared for her hasty escape once she'd done what she'd come to do.

It hadn't been easy to work her way in here. It had taken nearly the full two months just to worm her way into the elite, closed society of the *ton,* coming up with a believable false identity (she certainly couldn't use her own if she wanted to keep Pennsworth in the dark!), making the right discreet connections, greasing the right palms. Luckily, money was not an issue for the successful pirate, who had been depositing fantastic sums from her untouched share of the *Maiden*'s booty into the trusty hands of her London bankers for years.

She'd also made a few rather useful connections with several members of the Admiralty who wished their complicity with pirates and smugglers to remain unheard of. Since most governmental posts, including those in the Admiralty, were filled by members of the aristocracy, Lynnette had been able to wrangle invitations, under her assumed identity, to several social events where the earl of Pennsworth intended to show himself. This was her third such *soireé*, and the first time she'd caught sight of her quarry. The "chance" encounter with Lord Roger had gone even better than she'd hoped.

As the Comtesse de Beaucort—young, extremely wealthy and frivolous widow of an older French comte—Lynnette was welcomed with open arms by the winter-weary London socialites. And welcomed, as well, by Lord Roger, who'd sniffed out her wealth and her availability—not to mention her beauty—within the first moments of their meeting. He'd stayed close by her side all evening, charming her with witticisms that made the pirate want to ram a belaying pin down his gullet. The pig. When he had the advantage, he felt not the slightest compunction about raping and killing where he chose, but put him under society's watchful eye, with a woman who had something he needed, and he was all obsequiousness and fawning attentions. It made her want to vomit. Instead, she turned up the intensity of her smile.

Even a practiced villain of Roger's ilk wasn't immune to that smile. Lynnette began to enjoy the vision in her mind of the bastard's face when she steered him out into the gardens— all the while making him think it was his own idea, of course. He would come outside expecting one thing, but he'd *get* quite another! Nothing could go wrong with this plan—it was perfect, poetic justice. The man who had delighted in preying on society for so long would at last be brought down, in its very midst, by his own ambitions.

As the hand at her elbow closed rather too tightly on her flesh, Lynnette looked up sharply to see what had disturbed Pennsworth. And discovered that something could indeed go wrong with her scheme. *Had* gone wrong. Her world tilted and what little air she'd been able to wrest past the corset and into her lungs abruptly *whooshed* out.

Daniel was here, and he was heading right for her!

Trust the peacock to run in such rarefied circles as those preferred by her noble prey! He could ruin everything, and not just by exposing her. The mere sight of him, so elegant in severe black evening garb, so handsome and masculine that he stood out like a wolf among sheep in this crowd of useless leeches, sent the pirate's wits wandering helplessly, like the ninny she was pretending to be.

She glanced wildly around, but there was nowhere to escape from the tall, ferociously scowling merchant bearing swiftly down on them. She would have to brave it out. Lynnette didn't think she could do it. For the first time in her life, she felt her knees grow weak and her head spin. She was *not* going to faint, damn it, much though it would help get her out of this horrendous situation. The pirate dragged a breath into her tortured lungs, trying desperately to paste a bland, pleasantly interested expression on her face as Daniel approached. *Will he expose me?* she wondered, anxious dread spiraling out of control in her belly.

But when he spoke, his first words were not directed toward Lynnette. Indeed, he fairly ignored the buccaneer in favor of the man she stood with.

After exchanging a curt, almost insulting bow with the earl, Daniel adopted a carelessly offensive tone. "I haven't seen you

out and about much lately, Pennsworth. No innocents to strip
of their inheritances these days among the halls of the *ton*? Or
is that why you're here tonight?" He quirked a brow inso-
lently.

"I'm overwhelmed to see you back safely from your latest
endeavor, *brother*," the earl replied in a tone that plainly gave
his statement the lie. "Not too much the worse for your mis-
adventure with the lady brigand?" Roger sneered contemptuously. He looked his half brother up and down with disdain,
taking in the modest, tasteful evening attire, Daniel's unfash-
ionable lack of a wig.

"It seems she left you fairly well intact—all but your wits,
that is, and they were ever wanting." He laughed mirthlessly.
Both men seemed to take the tone of the conversation in stride,
as though each time they met it was the same, and they expected no more than the animosity that flared so easily between them.

Brother? Lord Roger was Daniel's *brother?* Lynnette felt
even closer to passing out than before for a moment, reeling
a bit in Pennsworth's grip, before all the information finally
coalesced. Of course! It all made sense. Though they looked
nothing alike, everything Daniel had told her about his half
brother fit in with what she knew of Lord Roger's character.
And Daniel never *had* shared the name with her in all the time
they'd been together . . .

Thank God she'd never told Daniel what he wanted to
know, the pirate thought with a rush of dizzy relief. She'd
been right, after all, to stubbornly keep her mouth shut, though
it had cost her such a heavy price in the loss of the merchant's
affections. Despite the hostility that was palpable between the
two, Lynnette couldn't believe Daniel would have remained
sanguine if she'd announced she meant to kill the man's only
brother.

Coming from a family where her sibling had been her main
comfort and dearest friend, the pirate could not comprehend
estrangement among brothers such as existed between Pennsworth and Bradley, even with all the merchant had told her of
their troubled relationship. The two might be nothing alike—
for which she thanked heaven—but surely the merchant could
not countenance his brother's slaying, as just an act as it would

be. Or could he? Daniel *had* told her of Roger's many crimes against him and their father . . .

What would Daniel do now if she finally confided in him? Would he help her or would he try to stop her? His aid would be most welcome in this mission, but if he refused or, God forbid, if he tried to stop her, she couldn't afford the complications the ensuing ruckus would certainly bring. Her position here was insecure enough. Nay, she decided. She could not bring the merchant into this matter of her personal vengeance. Yet she also knew that if he'd hated her before, he would want to kill her when he saw her behave with the pretense of amorous interest in Lord Roger her scheme called for. Lynnette felt sick.

The one man whose regard she cared for clearly despised her now, and in a moment would detest her utterly. She would have lost him irrevocably to the mission that drove her so mercilessly. Despairing, she looked lingeringly one final time at Daniel before she drove him away again. He was magnificent, putting all other men in the room to shame with his loose-limbed, feral grace and his sensuously sculpted features, even with such rage on his face as she saw glaring back at her. She could not plead for understanding, not even with her eyes, but she could say good-bye to this man who'd meant more to her than any other. She regretted his loss in ways she could never have imagined. It was one more debt, Lynnette thought darkly, to add to her burgeoning account against the despicable earl of Pennsworth. She trembled with the need to finish it.

"Are you ill, my dear?" Roger queried solicitously, noticing her sudden paleness and how shaky she was on her feet. Lynnette managed a watery smile and a shake of her head. "I am well," she murmured in her faint French accent. "The heat, is all . . ." She snapped open her delicately painted fan and waved it briskly before her face, not so incidentally hiding her expression from both men.

"But you haven't introduced me to your friend," Daniel said smoothly, looking, as he spoke to his brother, polite and for all the world as if he'd never seen her before. He saved his darkling glares for her alone, not allowing Roger or anyone else to see the intense emotions she sensed beneath the surface. His aplomb was admirable, Lynnette thought distantly. She'd do well to imitate it and stop gaping like a fish before, fan or no, Roger caught wind of her distress.

"Ah, yes." Pennsworth slid a proprietary arm about Lynnette's waist—causing her to repress a shudder of revulsion as she recalled the last time he'd held her thus—and pulled her forward proudly. He wanted to show off this prize before the brother who had always garnered the lion's share of feminine admiration, while he was forced to take Daniel's leavings, title and estates or no. "Lady de Beaucort, may I present my half brother, *Mr.* Daniel Bradley." Roger could not help stressing Daniel's lack of title, for it was a source of much glee to him. "The comtesse de Beaucort is a widow gracing us with her presence in London for the winter while renovations are completed on her château in the Loire Valley."

He parroted the story she'd given him perfectly, Lynnette thought with faint humor. She pulled herself together and gave Daniel the tiny curtsy due his "inferior" station. Daniel took her hand in his, bending over it with perfect etiquette. The kiss he placed on its back, however, was anything but the proscribed peck. It burned right into her flesh. "Charmed, I'm sure, *Capitaine*," she murmured through locked jaws, trying to sound bored and impatient. Christ, she had to get out of here! She couldn't stand between these two men much longer, torn between hatred for one and desire for the other.

"Your accent is very good," Daniel said mildly, the words lazy and steeped in irony despite his blazing anger. Indeed, the *faux* French accent was undetectable from a real one, for which she could thank the several French members of her crew. The merchant's fierce anger, masked, but still detectable to the pirate through the extraordinary emotional connection they shared, told her unequivocally that he would demand answers from her, would not allow her to put him off.

"*Merci,*" she replied with a curtness that was not at all feigned. Then Lynnette turned a winsome smile upon her contemptible escort. "Roger, dear, it is *so* dull and stuffy in here." She looked pointedly at Captain Bradley, suggesting the source of the problem with her haughty glance. "Will you be so kind as to escort me to the refreshment tables, my lord?" And she cut Daniel direct with a single turn of her slim shoulder, behaving as if he were the dreariest man she'd ever met. Roger smirked at his half brother, immeasurably pleased at having had the good fortune to encounter the rare lady with the taste to prefer him over his handsome younger sibling. Triumphantly, he led his comtesse off.

Daniel, incredulous at her bold performance and brassy defiance, watched the pirate flounce off on his half brother's arm. He needed a drink—badly.

Lynnette heartily wished for a drink to calm her nerves. Midnight was swiftly approaching, and the pirate had managed to steal just a moment alone to pull her wits together before she had to swing back into action. She stood in a shadowed alcove by the balcony doors leading to the gardens, ostensibly waiting for Lord Roger to return with her wrap and take her for a turn about Lady Hinkley's extraordinarily well landscaped grounds. It would take Pennsworth quite a few minutes to reach her side once more, with the crush by the cloakroom and his many acquaintances in the gathering. As she took several deep breaths, praying for a cool head in this most important of all encounters, Lynnette saw Daniel searching the crowd for her again, determination writ large on his striking features. She shrank farther into the alcove, using a lush potted palm as a shield against his sharp gaze. Luckily, his glance swept past her hiding place without stopping.

She'd done a fair job of avoiding the confrontation he so obviously wanted all night, though she'd been forced to duck into the ladies' retiring room so often she was sure people were beginning to think she had a medical condition. When that tactic failed, she'd turned her back on him more than once, an insult of the highest order in polite society. In such company as filled the sparkling ballroom tonight, word was beginning to get around that the gorgeous French countess had taken a dislike for the young merchant. He could not, she knew, approach her again without causing a scandal—though she doubted he cared about a little bad manners when she was perpetrating an enormous deception on this august assemblage simply by passing herself off as one of their number.

It felt so odd to be again among people with so many rules concerning behavior, to remember those rules and the time not so very long ago when she'd been forced to abide by them. Lynnette had exchanged more idle chatter with the guests tonight than she could remember engaging in during the whole of the last seven rough-and-tumble years she'd been a pirate. These people seemed so strange to her, stilted and artificial, never saying what was on their minds . . . Then again, they didn't kill each other over sixpence or a nasty insult, either, as buccaneers were known to do.

Lynnette had been too young to have had her own debutante season when she'd fled London at the age of sixteen, but she recalled her mother's lessons in manners and deportment vividly. A dyed-in-the-wool tomboy from her earliest years, Lynnette had despised her enforced lessons on dancing, etiquette, and posture—not to mention the dreaded watercolors she'd practiced so endlessly in that former life.

She'd thought these womanly occupations a useless waste of time, when what she really wanted was to go off and see the world, live the life of adventure as men were free to do. Yet now these polite skills served her well navigating the shark-infested waters of the *ton,* giving her the ability to smile and graciously make small talk, to dress properly and completely allay suspicion by comporting herself as if she had every right to be here. In another life, she would have. *Knowledge is never wasted,* Lynnette thought wryly. She only hoped this would be the last time she'd have to use her "social graces." If she could just accomplish her long-awaited mission as planned tonight, she'd happily retire back to— Her thoughts stumbled to a halt abruptly. Back to where? Back to *what*? The pirate realized she'd never really thought beyond her revenge.

She could always return to her cozy little house on No-name Island, Lynnette supposed, but she felt strangely uncomfortable with the notion. How could she go back to the villa when it held so many memories of her time with Daniel? His image in her mind haunted her already, when the *real* man wasn't doing the haunting for her, as he was tonight. Too, she'd never intended to continue on as a pirate after she'd destroyed Lord Roger. With her enemy finally disposed of, her reason for piracy disappeared, as well. Though she loved sailing, loved commanding men and facing adventure with every new dawn, the pirate did not enjoy plundering innocents, nor battle and its attendant loss of life. Still, she couldn't simply remain on No-name as a retired buccaneer even if she'd wanted to—it was too dangerous with all those who might try to drag her back into the fray, or turn her in for the reward on her capture.

She would have to leave and go somewhere she was completely unknown. And that might mean giving up the *Maiden's Revenge*. Just the thought of selling her beloved sloop caused a sharp pain in Captain Thorne's heart. Even if she sold the vessel to Harry and the others and could be sure the ship was in good hands, never seeing her again would be a constant wound to Lynnette's spirit. Even if she traveled abroad to fulfill her need for new experiences—and she had plenty of money to do it in style, not to mention the skills and training to take care of herself in any situation—she knew life would still seem empty and meaningless, for Daniel would not be there to share the wonders of each new discovery with her. Nothing was the same without Daniel.

The object of her longing loomed before her suddenly, startling the pirate out of her morose ruminations. Damn and blast it! She had to get rid of him right away! As much as she wanted to fling herself into his arms and cling to him forever, *now was not the time*.

"We need to talk," he said, leaving little room for argument.

What time was it? She craned her neck to see around his broad shoulder and look at the ornate clock on Lord Hinkley's mantel. It read nearly twelve already, and Lynnette could see Roger's dark head as he threaded his way through the crowd in her direction. Nay, now was *definitely* not the time. "Perhaps later, kind sir." She continued to pretend she didn't know the man, smiling falsely as though he were a bothersome swain she was refusing a dance. The merchant must be furious, but there was no time now to mollify his anger. Roger was halfway across the room, and might catch sight of them together at any moment.

Daniel felt his fists clench with the urge to grasp his lady pirate by the shoulders and shake her 'til she spilled her secrets. How dared she refuse him, and in such a callous manner? With one shout he could expose her for the outlaw she was, and still the wench dared to cut him as if he were the veriest coxcomb! He didn't know what she was doing here or why she'd singled out his hated half brother for her attentions, but he intended to find out, by God!

Had the two of them been in league all along? he wondered

with a sudden sinking suspicion in his gut. Was Lynnette just another in the long string of torments Roger had devised for his sibling over the years? But no. It was impossible. Even if Lynnette had been a woman whose services could be bought, and he knew she wasn't, Roger simply didn't have taste that good. Still, he seemed quite interested in her now—as, impossibly, Lynnette seemed equally interested in the forty-year-old earl. All night she'd stuck close to him while she ignored Daniel, laughing up into Roger's saturnine features, dancing with him, bestowing her blinding smile upon the wretch. Even now she was craning her neck to catch sight of him over his shoulder. None of it made any sense. As the earl approached, Lynnette's ermine-trimmed mantle over his arm, Daniel's arm shot out and he grasped her arm in an unbreakable grip. "We'll talk *now*, Lynnette."

"Unhand me this instant, Peacock," she hissed savagely, "or you'll regret it in ways you've never dreamed!"

"I'm willing to cause a scene," he replied matter-of-factly, gaze shrewd. "Are you?"

"You wouldn't."

"Oh, you'd better believe I would, sweetheart," Daniel growled. "So why don't you smile for the benefit of our audience," he continued, nodding politely at several avidly watching gossips, "and walk with me outside in the gardens, where you may explain your extraordinary appearance here tonight to my complete satisfaction." He knew he had her trapped.

Caught between a rock and the hard glare on Daniel's face, Lynnette knew she had no choice. Her erstwhile lover was furious—justifiably so after all she'd forced him to put up with—and now showing up in society with the brother he despised on her arm was simply too much for him to take lying down. He wanted a full explanation, but what could she tell him? Anything but the truth. And *anywhere* but the gardens! Her men would not mind taking the merchant in Pennsworth's stead, not one bit!

"All right," she conceded, glancing hastily about her for an alternative to the balcony doors nearby. She saw that Roger had not yet noticed them, had stopped instead to exchange pleasantries with a fellow guest. Damn it, her time was so short! If she didn't get him outside before one o'clock, her sailors had instructions to melt back into the shadows and give up the attempt. With bitter regret, the ever-practical pirate realized it was probably better to let them do so, for tonight at least.

They'd regroup later as planned, for she'd told the men that if she couldn't get Pennsworth outside by then, something would surely have gone wrong with her plan. She hadn't wanted the pirates lurking in the shrubbery until the party ended at dawn, increasing their risk of detection with every minute they lingered. Blast! She was so close. To give up tonight's attempt for this . . . But she couldn't deny Daniel his explanation.

Even if she'd wanted to ignore him—and she didn't, for he deserved better—he'd given her no choice but to grant him her undivided attention. He was just angry enough to do something rash if she didn't comply. "We'll talk," she agreed. "But not outside. It's far too cold," she temporized. "Come, follow me." Since his hand was still clamped like a vise around her forearm, it was easy to lead the tall, raven-haired merchant around the edges of the crowd to a side door exiting the ballroom.

"There must be an empty room somewhere around here," the pirate muttered as they found themselves in a dimly lit corridor. She could feel Daniel's hot, brandy-scented breath on her neck, feel his impatience as he crowded close behind her, and it sent all the little hairs at her nape standing on end. She squinted into the dark, trying to find a place to get this confrontation over with before she lost her nerve. The Hinkleys, while sparing no expense on the rooms guests were likely to see, obviously preferred more thrifty practices in the private areas of the house.

The first door they came to opened silently to reveal a darkened library. Unfortunately, it appeared to be occupied, and its two half-naked occupants, locked in a torrid embrace, did not seem to desire further company. Lynnette yanked the door shut hastily and moved on.

The next door they tried was a sitting room. The *three* occupants of this chamber appeared to have found their further company already, and were too busy with their astonishing activities to take any note of the interlopers. Lynnette closed that portal even more swiftly and came to the last door in the hallway. With hesitant fingers, she reached to turn the handle, and let out a sigh of relief to find the little accounting room revealed by a bare shaft of moonlight blessedly empty. She entered and Daniel followed close on her heels.

Turning to face him, she squared her shoulders. The sights they'd witnessed in the last two rooms had given Lynnette the slightly hysterical urge to laugh. Some of that humor remained in her tone when she spoke to the proud, outrageously attractive man silhouetted in the moon's silver light.

"I don't suppose you'll believe me if I tell you I came here to see you," she tried.

"Hardly." There was not one iota of matching humor in the merchant's clipped tone. "Especially not when I find you nestled cozily in my brother's embrace." Some of his emotions broke through the veneer of control he'd been struggling to maintain. "God, woman, haven't you bedeviled me enough for one lifetime? I thought I'd seen the last of you two months ago, and now I find you happily ensconced in the arms of my most hated enemy!" He took a deep breath. "I tell you things I've never told anyone before, and how do you repay me? By attaching yourself to the very man who tried to ruin my life. You of all people know how much we abhor each other!"

His tone stung, reducing all traces of Lynnette's levity to ashes. "I did not know Lord Roger was your brother until tonight, Daniel," she said quietly. She felt awful for the seeming betrayal, but, after all, their surnames *were* different, so how could she have known? Of course, Roger was known by his title, while Daniel used the family name. Still, it was incredible that in all of her researches into Lord Roger's background, she'd never given thought to the man's last name or relations. Yet it had seemed so unimportant when all she truly needed to know was where to come after him.

Her soft-voiced confession deflated Captain Bradley's anger somewhat, but it still didn't explain what the pirate was doing here, what convoluted scheme she had going—or why she hadn't stopped associating with Pennsworth the instant she'd discovered he was Daniel's half brother. "Now you know. I hope you will avoid him in future." He was not voicing a wish, but rather a stern command.

"I'm afraid I cannot make any such promises, Peacock," she said with deliberate hauteur. He'd find out soon enough that she'd no intention of ignoring Pennsworth, so she might as well admit it and deal immediately with the inevitable fire-storm her words would call up. Bracing for Daniel's anger, the pirate called up some of her own in defense. After all, who was he to tell her what to do? She'd never taken well to being ordered about, even when she happened to agree with the orders.

"I find Lord Roger's company quite pleasant, despite your reservations about his character." Lynnette nearly choked on the lie, but went on determinedly. "In fact, Peacock, I intend to be in his company whenever the desire takes me, and you can do nothing to stop me. You've no control over whom I choose to spend my time with," she finished coldly. "Now, if you'll excuse me, my presence is awaited outside—"

"I've no control?" he interrupted incredulously. "My dear Captain, do you seriously think to walk into *my* territory and drop a challenge like that in my lap? You must be jesting. This isn't some two-bit shantytown in the Indies, in case you hadn't noticed. You have no sovereignty here, my sweet, de-luded pirate queen, no right to give orders—or even expect to parade yourself brazenly about the Hinkleys' ballroom one more hour a free woman. Indeed, half the men present tonight have lost money to your acts of piracy and plunder. If I were to say one word . . ." He let the threat trail off.

"You'd never do it," she dared wildly. The pirate couldn't believe she was having this conversation now, while Roger awaited her in the ballroom, eager to be lead into her well-baited trap. She was ignoring her enemy in favor of the mer-chant, something she'd sworn never to do again. All of her attention was focused purely on Daniel and his words, his emotions, his sheer masculine allure overwhelming the tiny room. Nothing seemed more important than him.

"And why not?" he growled. "You've given me no reason to keep your secrets. No reason at all."

Lynnette looked up suddenly into his tarnished eyes, glow-ing with silver fire in the pale swatch of moonlight coming in the half-curtained window. "No reason?" she breathed, caught abruptly in the spell of his anger and his incredible, passionate magnetism. She swayed closer. "No reason?" she asked again, lips a breath from his. She meant only to distract him, but when those full, skillful lips came down angrily upon her own, Lynnette found herself the one distracted from all sense of purpose. God, he tasted so good—like brandy, like heat, like *man*. She'd missed him with an ache so deep she'd thought she'd die from it.

She hadn't allowed herself to think of Daniel these past months while she planned the final act of her vengeance. At least not during the days. But at night, lying awake with longing and regret in the cold comfort of her spacious rented apartments near St. James, his image took over every sleepless moment. She'd imagined their lovemaking a thousand times. Now, fantasy became reality as Lynnette had no choice but to give in to the untamed desires that were so much more powerful than her resolve. The time slipping by, her enemy awaiting her so close, the promises she'd made, all dissolved in the face of her blinding passion.

Daniel was no different. Every question he'd meant to ask flew out the window at the first touch of her lips, so sweet; sweeter still for the time since last they'd touched his own. He forgot his anger, his jealousy, his confusion at her presence here, and simply kissed her as he'd so longed to do these past months. His strong, lean hands came up to cup her cheeks and position her for his possession. His mouth opened on hers and his tongue swept inside to express all of his pent-up desire in one lightning-bolt kiss. Lynnette responded in kind, her hands sliding into his glossy raven hair to hold the contact of their lips while her knees threatened to give out on her for the second time that evening.

Daniel sensed her weakening and looped an arm about her tiny waist, damning all the clothes his pirate queen—usually so accessible in her garb of breeches and shirt—was swathed in from neck to ankles. His need to touch her, feel her nakedness against his own, burned hotter than ever before, even as his fury and despair were stronger. Without words, he showed her just how much she affected his senses, his emotions, his very spirit. Lynnette responded to the language of his kiss equally powerfully, expressing her own sorrow, regrets, and needs as she returned the touch of tongue and teeth and lips.

She needed him so! If only she could tell him everything, give him what he wanted, soothe the anger and the hurt she'd caused him. Well, the pirate thought with what little capacity for reason she had left, if she could offer nothing else, at least she could give him the surrender of her body. In truth, she couldn't *help* surrendering to him, though she knew, dimly, the folly of it, knew she was missing the chance to strike at her foe in order to be with Daniel. Overwhelming passion, far too long denied, would not let her make any other decision, and she clung to Daniel as to a lifeline.

Before she even knew what he was about, the merchant had, with one careless fling of his arm, swept clear the desk in the little accounts office they occupied. His other arm about her waist pulled her close to his body while he bent her back across the polished oak. A last coherent thought that now all three rooms in the hall were being put to licentious use made Lynnette smile against Daniel's mouth, before she was sent over the edge of rationality by his masterful touch.

She managed to get her hands beneath his coat and shirt to feel the heat of his well-muscled chest. The pirate groaned, impatient with their many layers of clothes. "I want you," she sobbed in frustration against the strong column of his neck. He nipped her ear sharply in response, his hands racing over her tight bodice to cup and shape the mounds beneath. His lean, muscular frame pressed her hard against the desk, and of their own accord, her legs, dangling over its edge, spread to cradle his lean hips between them.

"Don't make me wait," she begged, her hands at his waist now to unfasten the breeches that hid what she craved so badly. Daniel, in a frenzy of desire just as great as hers, pushed Lynnette's clumsy hands away and undid them himself, his erect, massive shaft springing free between their bodies. Lynnette swallowed hard, her body readying itself for his invasion with a rush of heated pleasure so intense it felt like pain. She cried out with excitement, her hands at his hips urging him on, and Daniel, unable to resist her passion, gave her what she wanted. One hand yanked up her skirts to bare her femininity for his possession, the other grasped his hardness and, finding her slick entrance readily, sent it pumping deep and hard inside.

He caught her scream of ecstasy in his mouth, caught all her cries and gasps thus as he moved atop her, feeling the incredible heat and wetness of her sheath surround him blissfully. His sudden possession, when they'd been fighting so heatedly just seconds before, sent shudders of desire rushing through Daniel's strong frame. Raising his head from the drug-

ging caress of her lips momentarily, he looked down at the
pirate, flushed and disheveled beneath his thrusting body, and
felt a surge of primal possession unlike anything he'd ever
known before. This woman, he vowed with each long, gliding
stroke, was *his*.

As he brought them both closer and closer to the edge of
mindless bliss, Daniel knew there could never be another like
this woman he loved—and he wanted her to feel just how
much he appreciated that. He reached down between their
straining bodies, beneath the rucked-up gold silk of her skirts,
and sent his fingers sliding in a rhythm over her pleasure bud
that sent her absolutely wild in his arms. She bucked, she bit,
she cried and gasped, and finally, when she couldn't bear the
intensity anymore, she climaxed in a paroxysm of pure sensation so incredible her toes curled and her fingernails bit into
the flesh of his back hard enough to draw blood.

Daniel, caught in her toils, could do nothing but follow her
into fulfillment.

It took a while, but when Lynnette could finally stop panting
and bring her mind back to earth from the celestial realms it
had been inhabiting, she knew it was long past one o'clock.
As she'd suspected, it was far too late now to pursue her vengeance tonight. If Pennsworth hadn't already given her up in
disgust, her men certainly had. She would have to do what
she could to control the damage her lapse of judgment had
caused. But what a pleasurable lapse!

The pirate slid a hand into Daniel's sweaty raven hair and
pulled his mouth down to hers for a tender, regretful kiss. She
wished she could always forget herself this way and simply
stay in his arms, but she knew it was impossible. Sarah still
waited, a hungry, suffering ghost, for her sister to give her
release in revenge. So Lynnette broke the kiss and squirmed
to get up from beneath the merchant, pulling her skirts back
into a semblance of order as she sat up on the desk.

She looked Daniel, who was still somewhat glazed over
with spent passion, right in the eye. "Now you know how
much I still want you—how much I need you, Peacock. But
know this, too. It changes nothing. I cannot discuss my plans
with you, and I cannot change them to suit your wishes. And
you aren't going to like it when you find out what I've got in

mind. In fact, you may very well want me dead when I've done what I came here to do.

"Believe me," she continued in a voice that shook with turbulent emotions, "I regret hurting you more than you will ever know, but I will not do anything to prevent its happening. I've made a vow I cannot break, no matter how I may feel. So let us end things here." And she slid down from the desk, simply leaving the room without even bothering to straighten her dishabille. Without waiting to hear what the stunned, incredulous merchant had to say in response to this astonishing speech.

For Daniel, recovering far more slowly from the incredible effects of their lovemaking, there was not much to say in any case. The cold, callous pirate queen had done it to him again: crushed his foolish heart beneath her heel and walked away without so much as a backward glance.

It was half-past one in the morning, and Lady de Beaucort still hadn't showed up for her agreed-upon walk in the gardens with Lord Roger, leaving the earl to scowl blackly as he held on to the silly bitch's cloak and waited, feeling foolish. If the comtesse weren't so ravishingly beautiful, and he weren't so damnably out-of-pocket just now, he'd have left the Hinkleys' rather dull affair to pursue his other less wholesome but far more pleasurable interests long ago.

The little French tart was a bit spirited for his tastes, but definitely rich enough to marry, as he'd done with the two other poor creatures he'd wed and then conveniently disposed of once he'd secured their fortunes for himself. Innately cautious, Pennsworth added a caveat to his line of thought: he'd marry the wench *if* she checked out. He'd have to make inquiries to ensure she was all she'd claimed to be before he pursued her in earnest. For some reason, Roger's well-honed suspicions had been bothering him about this woman, and the longer he stood waiting by the terrace for her to make an appearance, the greater his suspicions grew.

He didn't know why, but it seemed to him her smile had been just a little predatory, come to think of it. Of course, when she was nearby, using it on him, he couldn't think past the desire to kiss it right off her, but now, out of its immediate area of influence, the earl began to wonder. Where had she gone, and with whom? She'd been missing nearly an hour now. And why, he wondered, had the otherwise proper, well-mannered countess seemed so attached to him on first meeting that she'd agreed to his somewhat scandalous proposal to walk outside with him? Or had it been *her* idea to stroll the darkened gardens, so perfect a scene for seduction? He couldn't remember now.

Though he did not doubt his attractiveness for a moment, Lady de Beaucort's immediate, overwhelming flirtatiousness was enough to set Lord Roger's mind ill at ease. And then there was her strange behavior toward his benighted half brother. They'd acted like two wary dogs at the sight of each other, he recalled now, wondering how he could have failed to notice earlier. If the curvaceous comtesse hadn't been nestled in the curve of his arm at the time, and if he hadn't bristled with hostility at the sight of his handsome half brother, he probably would have realized sooner. Now that he reflected on their behavior, there was definitely something strange about it . . . Something in their conversation hadn't been quite right. Mentally, Pennsworth went over the exchange. He had it!

He'd introduced Daniel as *Mr.* Bradley. But she had responded by addressing him with the French term for "captain" How could she have known the merchant's title or business if they'd never met before? It was impossible. But if they'd been introduced previously, why would they pretend to be strangers unless they had something to hide? There was no doubt but that one or both had something up their sleeves. It was only a question of what.

Where could Captain Bradley have met the lovely Lady de Beaucort? Daniel had not been to France recently, that much his brother knew, for he kept careful tabs on the merchant, aware of everything he did—just in case he should ever need to get rid of him. But the countess said she had not left her native country until recently . . . Unless the mysterious beauty was a liar, a fraud. And if she *was* a fraud, she was probably in league with his tiresome little brother in some ridiculous scheme to do him harm, thought the earl with a swift flash of ire. The theory made too much sense to ignore.

Lord Roger supposed it wasn't really so surprising that Daniel was finally attempting to strike back at him after all the years the earl had spent bedeviling his younger half brother. And how like the little bastard to muddle it by coming up with such an obvious scheme! Why, it was laughable how little the stupid merchant knew about matters of deceit and dishonor. Perhaps he was relying on his little French moll to pull off their scheme—certainly the girl had proven herself a far better actress than her lover by managing to capture his attention so fully tonight.

But when could the two have met? And what could they have planned? The answers came to him in a rush. Where had Daniel been these past months but on the ship of the very pirate who'd plagued him for the last several years? The very *lady* pirate. A pirate, he recalled now, who wore a cuff of gold and emeralds around her neck rumored to be worth a king's ransom. He'd ogled the necklace earlier tonight with greed, never thinking it could be the key to unraveling the mystery of his faceless enemy. As he pieced together the information in his head, Roger felt a chill of fear slide down his spine. He knew what they wanted now that he knew who the bitch was. Without a doubt, they wanted him dead.

Though rumor said Captain Thorne was a hideous giantess, horrendously scarred and brutish, he dismissed the stories now that the pieces of this puzzle were coming together. Naturally his captains would tell tales of a monstrous wench, to make their losses to the bitch seem more excusable. Pennsworth felt foolish now for listening to their tales, for taking the rumors without a grain of salt. Indeed, in his fearful, feverish dreams, the lady pirate had always looked as he'd been told; a lumbering, faceless golem wielding a massive sword and crying for his blood. These nightmares had been enough to send him screaming into wakefulness countless times these past seven years. Lord Roger was suddenly furious as he relived his former fear. How could he have allowed himself to quiver in terror at the very thought of the bitch for so long? Well, never again would he cower before her!

It was almost too much to believe that the stunning, delicate lady he'd met tonight, who seemed so fragile and enticingly helpless, could truly be the same hellish banshee who'd hounded him for so long. But now that he knew . . . Of course the stupid bitch was still after him, and now she'd recruited Daniel in her efforts to destroy him. His brother, Roger was

sure, was quite a willing accomplice after all he'd done to the
sniveling fool over the years.

They thought themselves so clever, Pennsworth mused with
glee, but *he* would get the two of them before *they* could get
to him. A plan was even now coalescing in his brain—a brilliant plan that would catch them both! At last, he'd be rid of
the woman who haunted his nightmares, and with her he'd
destroy the brother he loathed. Things were looking up!

CHAPTER TWENTY-SIX

NOTHER DAY, another corset, and a far more wary Lynnette stood fanning herself in the stuffy confines of yet
another magnificent ballroom. Society, she'd learned to her
detriment last night, held more pitfalls than she'd anticipated—
pitfalls like a certain handsome merchant captain with the
power to set her resolve melting in a heartbeat. Tonight, she'd
vowed, would *not* end the same way as the last one had, no
matter what she had to do to prevent it.

A pleasant expression on her face, she chatted lightly with
the host and hostess, a comfortable-looking older couple
named Lord and Lady Barrett, in the receiving line. At the
moment, the pirate was describing the weather this time of
year in France with a glibness backed by no knowledge whatsoever. Captain Thorne, in fact, had never yet visited France,
though she thought it might be nice to go there someday when
this was all over. That was, if she managed to survive the
torture of languishing in society—a torment inflicted by the
necessity of following her prey into his home territory.

As she scanned the room, with its high, medallioned ceiling, mirror-polished marble floor, and cream-colored paneled
walls set with dozens of tall mirrors and sconces to catch and
reflect the light, she wondered if Pennsworth had gone to
ground, or if he would attend the gala as planned tonight. She
suspected he'd make his appearance at any moment, and she
intended to be ready for him.

Lynnette had seen no reason to change her plans for gaining
vengeance simply because she'd missed one opportunity. The

only thing she need do now to make the original scheme work was to "accidentally" come across the earl tonight, apologize for her abrupt departure the night before (caused, naturally, by the swift onset of a particularly nasty headache), and further their acquaintance with smiles and flirtatious charm. No complicated new plots were needed.

All she'd done, in fact, following her unnoticed disappearance from the Hinkleys' ball late last night after her passionate encounter with Daniel, was meet up with her sailors and tell them where to regroup to try the plot again. She hadn't explained the hitch, and they hadn't questioned it when she told them circumstances had made the attempt untenable. But tonight's effort, she grimly promised them—and herself—would suffer no such setbacks. This had to be the last try. Aside from everything else, she simply couldn't stand another day in a corset!

She'd learned earlier from her informant in Lord Roger's house about the parties for which he'd accepted invitations. After a quick reconnoitering of the grounds this afternoon, the pirate had discovered that Lord and Lady Barrett's home was even more suitable for an ambush than the Hinkleys' gardens had been, so she'd chosen it over the others for her much-delayed confrontation with the man who had destroyed everything she loved. As she scanned the crowd discreetly, she wondered when he would show up.

She wondered too if Daniel would make an appearance—and how she would react if he did.

Lord Roger, sixth earl of Pennsworth, nominally Viscount Margrave, as well as host to a number of lesser honorary titles, caught sight of the bitch who thought so foolishly to bring him down. She was stunning in a gown of midnight-blue satin with silver trimmings, but he cared little for her appearance, more interested in bringing the whore to heel. How dared she walk up to him bold as brass and play her games, expecting that he'd not figure her out! She'd underestimated him badly, and would pay dearly for her error.

It was pure luck she'd managed to do as much damage to him over the years as she had, he reasoned furiously. No doubt it was because he'd been forced to leave his shipping in the hands of underlings, not being a sailor himself. But had he been there . . . he'd have fixed this she-devil *permanently*! He didn't know why she plagued him, still hadn't been able to discern her quarrel with him, but it no longer mattered now that he had her in his sights. Her ridiculous scheme to destroy him would fail.

No mere woman, aided by his brother or not, could hope to successfully ruin *him*! Why, he'd invented the very game! But he was ready for her, Pennsworth thought with savage joy. Ready for her lover, his upstart half brother, as well. Both would suffer at his hand tonight, before he'd drawn out every last drop of pleasure possible from their anguish. Then they would die.

Lord Roger moved on into the ballroom, making himself conspicuous. He wanted the bitch to find him, after all. And before long he had what he wanted. With perfect charm, he managed to greet his fake comtesse, express sympathy for her sudden malady of last night, and allow her, as she thought, to twine him around her little finger. Before the hour was out, they had agreed to take the midnight stroll that had been interrupted the night before, merely exchanging one palatial set of gardens for another. He had her: hook, line, and sinker.

Daniel had followed Lynnette to the party—a feat that was easily accomplished. All he had to do was check his elder brother's social schedule, for he knew that wherever the earl showed himself this evening, the pirate was sure to be close by. He couldn't figure out why she so obviously wanted the bastard's company, but it was clear Lynnette had a most unseemly fascination with him. What was the attraction? Was it the titles, the lands? It made no sense! Captain Thorne was a wealthy woman herself, unless he missed his guess. So what could she possibly want with Pennsworth?

Her anguished words to him last night had been damnably cryptic, telling him no more than that he'd been right to suspect a deeper motive behind Lynnette's piracy all along. However, what that motive *was* and what it had to do with the corrupt, depraved earl of Pennsworth, Daniel was no closer than ever to figuring out. He knew he should leave it alone, for he didn't think he could stand another of her heartless rejections, but he simply could not walk away. He *had* to know what brought the sultry pirate queen into his domain.

He hadn't figured it out yet when, soon after he arrived and greeted Lord Barrett, who was an old friend of his father's, he saw the stunningly bejeweled and bedecked pirate slipping off with none other than Pennsworth by her side. Rudely excusing himself from the older man's company, Daniel compulsively followed the two as far as the edge of the room. He told himself he would go no farther, would have nothing more to do with the mysterious pirate and her inexplicable games. Certainly, he thought angrily, he would not stoop to spying on the woman!

No matter that he loved her, no matter that he felt deep in his marrow that she was in a world of trouble. She had told him not to interfere, and he wouldn't. Peering clandestinely at her and her companion through the glass did *not* count as interference. At least, he rationalized, he was not listening at the door!

Still, he couldn't help the knot that formed in his gut just knowing they were out there somewhere, doing god-only-knew-what. He could not see them yet, but he hoped they would come into view soon. If they didn't, he wasn't sure he could prevent himself from going after the two and knocking the stuffing out of his older brother when he found them. Glancing around to make sure no one had noticed his intent sentinel stance by the glass-paned doors, the merchant caught sight of a lingering footman and grabbed a drink from the man's tray. Lady Barrett surely did like her footmen brawny, he thought with a drop of amusement to lighten his dark mood. Not a one of them under six feet in height, and all picked especially to fill out their livery. No other qualifications were necessary, certainly not skill in serving. This one seemed especially brutish . . .

And then Daniel thought no more about servants or their ability to wear a uniform, for Lynnette and his half brother had come into view.

In the shadows of a box hedge, Lynnette leaned closer to Lord Roger, giving him an impressive view of her cleavage in the process. Harry and the others had orders to stay back in the cover of the foliage until it was done, and she knew they would not disobey, no matter how they might rib her later about her underhanded methods of getting to her nemesis. She didn't care about her silent audience at this moment, however. All of her attention was focused on her quarry.

She smiled, swaying closer as though for a kiss, and simultaneously slid a hand into the special pocket of her skirt, made for just such an occasion. Reaching through the slit material, she grabbed the pistol hidden in her pannier. While his eyes were still half-closed in anticipation, she brought the weapon up to his head and cocked it, the ominous click sounding loud in the nighttime stillness. To her surprise, Roger's lids remained at half-mast and he betrayed no satisfying expression of shock—or fear.

"I was wondering when you'd get to that—before or after you'd let me kiss you," he murmured in loverlike tones, as though the false mood of intimacy hadn't been broken. "Too bad it's now. I would have enjoyed tasting the lips of so notorious a pirate." At her swift intake of breath, he chuckled nastily. "Of course I figured it out, you stupid bitch," he laughed. "I've known since last night."

Lynnette thought quickly, waving one hand behind her back at the pirates hidden in the bushes, signalling them to stay back. She was sure she'd heard a rustle among the men stationed there when Roger hadn't reacted with sufficient fear. They could tell something had gone wrong, but before they came to her aid, she needed to know what that something was. If the bastard was telling the truth—and there was no reason to think otherwise, considering his cool reaction to the flintlock pointed directly at his head—then he must have something else up his sleeve. He wouldn't walk into her trap without planning something of his own to counteract it. She knew she wouldn't like whatever it was.

Holding the gun steadily and staring her nemesis straight in the eye, she spoke as calmly as he. "If you know who I am, then you know as well what it is I want."

"Actually," he said with candor that was supposed to be disarming, and wasn't, "I've no idea what you want, Captain Thorne. Or what you've wanted these past several years, unless it be the obvious—all of my ships and cargo."

Lynnette realized with a sense of wonder that the man still hadn't put it all together. Had Sarah's death and her father's descent into misery meant nothing at all to the earl? Had everything he'd done to them been just another day's work to him? Apparently so, for though he'd guessed she was his pirate enemy, he still had not recalled the girl he'd left alive, the girl who'd held a pistol at his head this same way but in another life. How fearful she'd been then, how innocent!

Captain Thorne was neither of those things now. She was merely a vessel for revenge, full of rage and deadly purpose. She would never be so helpless again as she'd been that night in her father's home. "I want nothing less than your corpse at my feet," she spat, overcome with bitter memory. "You owe me that, and more."

His eyes widened, for something in her tone struck a chord in his memory. There'd been another girl once, with autumn hair and the same flat expression. She too had held a gun on him, forcing him to flee ignominiously. But it couldn't be! That girl had been all planes and angles, awkward youth in winter, waiting to bloom. This woman had definitely blossomed into the full flower of her beauty, but it was the same look of cold rage that suffused the delicate features he was beginning to recall from that long-ago night of drunken debauchery.

Of all those from his past to come back to haunt him, it was incredible that *she* would be the one who came so close to gaining revenge when so many others had failed. He'd imagined the pitiful, gawky young girl long dead in the cruel slums of London, a victim of poverty and abuse years since. Yet here she was, still coming for him as she had that night long ago. It was really too much melodrama! he thought merrily.

The earl was not at all worried about Captain Thorne's chances for success. Putting a face—especially such a sweet, delicate face—to his enemy had greatly restored Roger's shaken confidence. Pirate or no, she was merely a woman, and thus no match for him. She wasn't the terrifying monster he'd envisioned for so long, but instead a mere slip of a girl like so many others he'd broken. He knew how to deal with upstart females . . . oh, he did indeed. She would suffer dearly for her impertinence—and he would enjoy every minute of her pain. Excited, he decided to play with the wench before he ended it.

"Can it be little Lady Blackthorne I see before me?" he scoffed. "I'd thought you dead along with the rest of your family ages ago, and here you've been playing scofflaw and brigand this whole while. I should have guessed the truth ere now. You were ever the bloodthirsty wench." Lord Roger relished the whitening of the pirate's face in reaction to his cruel taunts.

"Tell me, sweetness, did you kill that worthless father of yours, or did he finally do the right thing and blow his own brains out? As I recall, you had quite a fondness for pistols then as now." He laughed heartily, ignoring the gun trained unerringly on him.

"Ah, you remember at last," she murmured, calm now that she was finally confronting this demon from her past. She ignored his taunt, though the mention of her father's death stiffened her spine a notch. "That's good, you bastard, because *I'll* never forget what you did to my sister—or my father. And now you'll die for it." She aimed the pistol carefully, seeing a double image in her mind of the night seven years ago when she'd done the same, superimposed over the actual act she performed now.

"But, my sweet, if you do that, there'll be two corpses for the magistrates to find come morning."

"You'll not bring me down with you, you scum!"

"I wasn't referring to you, dear Captain," he smirked, "but to my fool of a brother, standing by the window, playing voyeur. He hasn't seen your gun yet," Pennsworth added quickly, "and I suggest you not allow him to. It would be a shame for the last of my line to die without issue," he concluded with palpable mockery.

Lynnette could not resist a glance toward the light of the ballroom, though she knew it was risky to turn her back on the snake before her. Sure enough, she saw her lover's familiar silhouette framed in the doorway against the light of a thousand brilliant candles. From his angle, she realized, all he could see was the two of them, standing together in intimate conversation. Most of her form was blocked from his view by Roger's bulkier frame, including the hand that held the pistol. Daniel could have no way of knowing about the intense drama playing out between them.

"What are you suggesting?" she asked tightly.

"I'm suggesting, you upstart whore, that if you carry through on your pitiful threat to use the pistol you're holding,

Captain Bradley will not live through the night. You see the rather hirsute footman standing slightly behind him?" He waited while Lynnette confirmed that she did. "That man is in my employ, and he has orders to follow Bradley from the party tonight and kill him should anything happen to me."

What Pennsworth did not say was that the man had such orders regardless of the state of his master's health. Daniel would die tonight, as he should have long ago. This last defiance would be met with swift and deadly punishment. But the wench didn't need to know that.

He doubted his threat to her lover would stop a callous woman like the pirate queen—a woman with a belly full of hate because of what he'd done to her—from doing him harm with that gun she'd brought, but it would distract her long enough for him to catch her off guard and take it from her. Foolish of her, Pennsworth thought, to drag him out here alone where she was helpless after all her careful plans to destroy him. Women, he thought contemptuously, were ever careless and impatient when it came to important matters. It was a trait that had served his brand of cunning well.

"What do you want?" she asked hoarsely, Roger's threat having sapped her mouth of all moisture.

He realized he'd miscalculated when he heard the note of fear in her throaty voice. Ha! This was even better than he'd hoped! The wench was carrying a torch for his little brother. He could see he'd knocked the tar from the silly Blackthorne chit with his words. She seemed to visibly shrink with the mention of the danger to her, lover. He could definitely use this to his advantage!

"Why, what else but your cooperation?" Lord Roger laughed triumphantly. "You'll do exactly as I tell you, bitch, *when* I tell you, if you want him to live. And the first thing I'm telling you is to *drop that pistol!*" While Lynnette was still reeling from the power of the realization swamping her, Pennsworth whipped out his own pistol from inside his heavy, satin-lined jacket.

The pirate had just enough sense left in her to again surreptitiously signal her men to remain in place and not disclose their presence. *They* wouldn't care about a threat to Daniel's life, but *she* did. Lord, did she ever! For now, when she least wanted to admit it, when it was most dangerous to admit it, she had no choice but to give in to the truth.

No wonder she'd surrendered in to the magic of his touch so often when she'd known she shouldn't. No wonder she thought of him night and day, felt her heart flip in her chest each time she caught sight of him. No wonder she'd jeopardized her mission time and time again simply for the chance to be with him. It all came clear to her in a sudden flash of insight.

She loved Daniel. Loved him beyond all hope. Loved him more, she discovered with a crushing sense of shame, than the vengeance she'd sought for so long. She couldn't let him be harmed.

If she were willing to ignore Roger's threat, to let Daniel become another victim of the bastard's perfidy, she could still kill the earl now. Pennsworth would be dead with one shot, before he could pull the trigger on his own weapon, and she'd be over the garden wall and on the back of the horse brought for her by her men. And then Daniel would die, in Roger's last act of viciousness. She, on the other hand, would get away free, and Sarah's poor ghost would finally have the peace she sought. Except that Lynnette couldn't do it. Seven years of struggle were suddenly worth nothing. Because she knew that while she'd sacrificed everything else to this quest, she couldn't sacrifice Daniel.

Instead, she would probably die for him tonight, given what she knew all too well about Lord Roger. It was a price, she marveled, amazed at the strength given her by this newfound realization, that she was willing to pay. She just hoped that her sister would understand her decision. *Sarah,* she anguished, *I'm sorry. I cannot do this thing for you.*

"I will cooperate," she said softly. With infinite reluctance, she laid her flintlock down on a stone bench and turned to face her enemy with empty hands. "Just leave Captain Bradley out of this matter. It is none of his concern, after all. He knows nothing of what has passed between us. He thinks only what everyone else here believes—that you and I are conducting an affair."

Lord Roger chuckled again, a sound that sent chills up and down her flesh. "Then let us make sure he *continues* to believe that," he said smoothly, nodding to indicate the figure still frozen in the doorway. "Come here, wench."

Lynnette approached warily. "What do you want, you bastard?" she hissed.

"You." And he grasped her firmly about the waist. "Don't struggle, whore, or I'll make sure your lover suffers all the torments of hell before he dies." With that, his foul lips came down on her own, and it was all Lynnette could do not to vomit while he ravaged her mouth with his teeth and tongue.

Hearing more noise in the bushes, the pirate frantically signaled once again that her men were to do nothing. This nightmare would all be for naught if the pirates came forward and attacked her nemesis. Not only would they expose themselves to danger, but Daniel would most certainly pay the ultimate price. Lord Roger did not make idle threats, she knew.

At last he let her up for air. The pirate gagged and gulped for breath wretchedly. He ignored her difficulties, his hand closing bitingly around her arm. "Now, wench, you'll accompany me back across the room, past my pathetic little brother and the rest of the guests, with every appearance of coming willingly—eagerly in fact. You will wait with me politely for my coach, and enter it like the lady you most certainly are not. And then we will return to my abode and see about your punishment. I doubt you'll live past morning," he finished pleasantly.

Lynnette wanted to spit at him. She wanted to slice the victorious grin off his face with a dull knife. She did neither. Instead, she silently followed the urging of his arm and did exactly as he ordered.

Love, Captain Thorne thought faintly, really stank.

Daniel watched Lynnette glide past him on the arm of his half brother, a blank look on her face as she ignored him and swept on by in a wash of foaming midnight skirts and silver lace. He was in shock, feeling completely poleaxed. He'd just watched the woman kiss Lord Roger with a fiery passion he'd thought reserved solely for himself. The sight had hit him like the weight of St. Paul's Cathedral collapsing on him, crushing him utterly.

Somehow, despite the pirate's warnings that he wouldn't like what she'd come here to do, he still couldn't take it all

in. Jealously, hurt, anger, and despair all swam to the surface,
and blindly, he scooped up another drink from the burly footman in attendance. As he watched the two leave together for
what was clearly to be a night of amorous trysting, he drank
down several more glasses of wine in quick succession. Then
he went in search of something stronger.

Hours later, the merchant was none too steady on his feet,
but his emotions were not one whit dulled by his reckless
consumption of alcohol. He still felt as though the ground had
fallen out from under him, and people were beginning to notice his unfashionably foxed condition. Best he leave before
he offended anyone else, Daniel thought hazily. Liquor had
done no good anyhow. Nothing could help him now. Lynnette
had chosen his brother over himself. Heart aching more than
the headache he knew he'd have in a little while, Captain
Bradley made his excuses as best he could and walked out
into the cool November air.

A long line of coaches and hacks for rent lined the darkened
street, the horses patiently waiting for their late-night passen-
gers. None of the coachmen were in evidence. Daniel heard
the sound of voices and the rattle of dice from the stables
beside the house and understood. The drivers, he thought in-
differently, probably preferred awaiting their charges in the
warmth and companionship of the Barrett stables to freezing
with their animals in the street. Daniel walked on in a fog,
glad to be alone.

A muffled scuffle, a couple of thuds, and a grunt, quickly
stifled behind him, brought the former naval officer spinning
around in a reflexive crouch. What he saw made him wonder
what had been in old Lord Barrett's punch, for Omar the pirate's gargoyle face loomed out of the darkness at him with a
feral grin. The buccaneer stood over the inert body of the same
overgrown footman who'd served Daniel tonight.

As the stunned merchant looked on, Harry, Captain
Thorne's first mate, emerged from the darkness, followed one
by one by what appeared to be her full crew complement.
Daniel blinked for a moment, wondering what in heaven's
name was going on. Last he'd heard, the buccaneers were still
living it up on Tortuga, not prowling London's fashionable
districts! The brigands were an unlikely sight for Mayfair

in their spotty sailors' garb, bandoleers, and cutlasses, to be sure.

"What the devil . . . What have you done to that poor footman?" he began, but Harry cut him off.

"No time fer talkin' now, lad! My lassie's in trouble, no mistake, an' she needs yer aid." The older man grabbed the merchant's arm and urged him toward a rented hack. Before Daniel knew what he was about, the grizzled sailor pushed him inside, and one of the others leapt atop the vehicle. The coach had already rumbled into motion before he collected his wits enough to protest.

"Now listen here, fellow," he growled. "This is *London,* not some shantytown in the colonies, and I'm not about to let you kidnap me again!" He grabbed the other man by the lapels of his threadbare coat menacingly. "I've had about enough of you and your mistress and your warped games!"

"No, *ye* listen!" Harry shouted back, worry making him sharper than he'd ever sounded before. "This is no game, laddie! Ye don't know th' truth of it, but I'm 'ere ta tell ye, if ye'll but shut yer cake 'ole an' give me yer ear one blasted minute! My lassie's life is in danger!" That stopped Daniel cold, and sobered him considerably.

By the time he'd heard all the mate had to say, as the coach neared his half brother's strongly fortified mansion, Captain Bradley was soberer still—more sober than he could ever recall being before. And more frightened.

His heart was clenched tight by a giant fist of fear for the woman he'd come to love so deeply. He felt such a fool! While he'd been mooning over her backstabbing, Lynnette, rather than betraying him, had been sacrificing her life for his own. Was sacrificing it, if they weren't too late already, to the man who had raped and murdered her only sibling, who'd destroyed her father's life along with her own.

All this time he'd been misreading her, trying to understand the deeply scarred woman and being pushed aside instead by her cold refusals. He should have tried harder. After all Harry had just told him, every cruel action on the pirate's part was explained. His half brother was far more vicious than even Daniel had imagined. The man deserved to be shot down like the rabid dog he was, so he could never hurt another innocent as he'd hurt Lynnette.

No wonder the woman couldn't bear to discuss her past! It was a credit to her strength and resolution that she'd managed to remain sane after the incident, let alone come so far and pursue her vengeance to this bitter end. Now she was giving that vengeance up, he realized, because of her love for him. It was a gift from a magnificent, brave woman—one he had no time to treasure just yet, but that warmed his heart nonetheless.

Daniel couldn't believe he'd sat there passively while she was in mortal danger, drinking and sulking! He should have had more faith in her, should have known his pirate queen better than to take her actions with Pennsworth at face value! But there was no time now for regrets. Now was the time for action!

"The men are waiting for us by Pennsworth's house?" he asked tightly.

"Aye, lad. They'll be waitin' fer us. Ye have a plan ta git us in?" Harry's normally genial features were pinched with anxiety. He was good in support, but he'd known immediately when things had gone wrong in the gardens that he needed help from someone who could plan the daring raid that was their only hope of getting the captain back safely. Together with the rest of the *Maiden*'s crew, he'd huddled helplessly in the dark after their captain had fallen prisoner to Lord Roger, forced by her own command to watch the man degrade her, then lead her away to a fate worse than any hanging could possibly be.

The mate was unconcerned with his own safety or the possibility of capture, as were the others who'd gathered tensely in the shadows of the Barretts' leafy grounds to decide what to do. Still, it would do Captain Thorne no good to be captured *before* they could rescue her. They needed a tactician—someone who knew the area well, preferably—to help them carry it off, for Lynnette had deemed it impossible to make a straight-out attack on the earl's well-guarded manse. In the end it had been young Davie who'd come up with the solution.

"If the captain's so set on dyin' for the bloody peacock," he'd squawked with adolescent indignation, finding it hard to accept that his idol fancied another, "why don't we see if *he* feels the same 'bout *her*?"

Twenty pairs of pirate eyes had gleamed back at him with

conspiratorial agreement. Why not, indeed? Let the peacock prove his worth.

Daniel did *not* intend to disappoint these men, not when his beloved's life was on the line. He would kill his own brother without hesitation to save her. "Aye, I've a plan," he replied at last to the first mate. "I just pray we're not too late."

Harry silently seconded that prayer.

CHAPTER TWENTY-SEVEN

*T*HE CORPULENT watchman made a funny hiccuping sound and fell heavily to the ground outside the kitchen gate, victim of a sudden sharp blow to the head. Simultaneously, guards were toppling all around the grounds of Pennsworth's mansion, according to Captain Bradley's orders. With their beloved leader in such a bind, the pirates were more than willing to risk themselves to rescue her, unconcerned to a man for their own safety. Their leader felt the same. He'd give his life to get Lynnette back unharmed.

Daniel, seeing that no one had been alerted by the guard's hard meeting with the cobblestones, gestured Harry and two other handpicked men forward. They soon had the little door at the back of the house out of their way. The tattooed giant named Charlie simply lifted the heavy planks off their hinges and laid them quietly to one side of the courtyard leading to the kitchens and servants' quarters. They didn't want to wake the guards they knew remained in the house—or any of the staff, for that matter. One yell and the game would be up.

Lord Roger's mistreated maid had proven loquacious in giving her unknown benefactor information about the household routine and layout when Lynnette had come to her in disguise two months ago, bearing gold. She'd been more than happy to betray the secrets of the malicious sadist who held her in thrall, as long as her own involvement was kept concealed. Thus, Harry, privy to his captain's information all along, had been able to provide Daniel with the knowledge that Pennsworth employed several watchmen in the house as well as out.

The earl believed, with somewhat justified paranoia, that someone was after him, and so kept himself and his property under close guard. The number of the hired muscle varied, as did their location, but the rescuers were confident they could best the thugs indoors as easily as the ones they'd dispatched outside. It was the other information provided by the maid that worried all of the men.

Lord Roger's taste for the bizarre and the sadistic carried so far that the man had built himself a dungeon in the cellars of his town house for his nocturnal amusement. According to the disgusted young woman who had no choice but to serve the earl, his lordship brought girls down there quite often— and not all of them were willing to play his games. Of the contents of this dungeon, the maid refused to speak, other than to shake her head in pity for any woman trapped down there.

The men knew with dreadful certainty that this was where Pennsworth would be holding Lynnette. Would they get to her in time before Roger did her irreparable harm? Daniel wondered anxiously. Hours had gone by since the pirate had been forced, for his sake, to give herself into the man's hands.

If she was dead, the merchant swore, he would kill his brother personally, and feel no more remorse for the deed than for squashing an ant.

Lynnette was holding up better than she'd expected. At least the bastard had cut off her corset along with her dress, allowing her the occasional breath to accompany her grunts of pain and strangled curses. The shift and stockings he'd left her were torn in places where the whips had shredded the material, and her arms felt ready to come out of their sockets from the tightness of the manacles pulling her wrists to the ceiling of the dank, foul chamber. She'd been praying she'd not disgrace herself under Pennsworth's torture, and felt lucky that he'd decided to toy with her a while instead of getting right down to business.

It gave her the hope that Harry and her men might come for her before the earl pulled out one of the bigger knives resting on the sideboard full of terrifying instruments. She could tell that many of the tools had been used before, for they still bore the blood of the poor souls who'd come before her. The man was insane; far more malevolent and evil than even she'd guessed. This private hell of his was ample evidence of his madness. No man in his right mind would have a place like this in his home where the wine cellar ought to be!

The subterranean room had been created to resemble a medieval torture chamber, complete with dripping, mossy stone walls and rusty chains decorating the ceiling. Rats squeaked and rustled in the rushes scattered over the bare granite floor, while racks of monstrous antique iron implements lined the walls and rested on tables. The light was minimal, a flickering combination of smoking torches and lanterns that nevertheless served to illuminate the malice on her captor's face far better than she liked.

Please, lord, let me not succumb to my enemy! she prayed. If the pirates could not reach her, thought Captain Thorne, at least she should die with some dignity, not beg this monster for mercy.

Still, though the pirate queen had courage enough for ten men, the iron poker Lord Roger was heating in the sullen embers of the fire pit in the center of the round stone room looked pretty terrifying to her. Far worse than the cat-o'-nine-tails he'd been using off and on, between taunts and the disgusting, lascivious touch of his hands on her body. She'd been able to block those out with some success, though she could feel dribbles of blood soaking into her ruined shift from her back and thighs.

Each drop of her blood that slid down the pirate's sweaty spine was more fuel to feed the fires of her rage at this man. God, if only she could get free, she'd rip his lungs out, using his own tools of terror! She'd give him an hour of pain for every minute he'd caused her sister—and herself. She'd take gleeful pleasure in hearing the man beg and whimper for mercy—and ignore his pleas with even greater joy. Lynnette struggled in her bonds again, the urge to do mayhem overwhelming, but the chains stretching her onto her toes wouldn't budge.

Unlike Roger's thugs, several of whom she'd sent crashing to the ground before the bunch of them took hold of her and got her locked into the rusty manacles. She'd agreed to go with Pennsworth to save Daniel, but when Lynnette had seen the dungeon and realized his plan, she'd fought like a mad thing to avoid her fate. Only the brute force of Roger's many henchmen had overcome her in the end. It wasn't easy, she discovered, fighting in full ball regalia!

As Roger turned back to her, a twisted smile on his dissolute features and a hungry gleam in his black eyes, Lynnette spoke for the first time in hours. "Give it up," she rasped, lips and throat parched though she'd not yet given voice to her pain. "You'll get no satisfaction from me—you'll get nothing at all from me but my death, you fiend. I'll never beg or scream for your amusement."

"Then I'll just have to take your death, if that's all you'll yield, my sweet brigand. But I think I'll take my time at it, for it gives me pleasure just to watch you suffer. The screams and the pleas *will* come later, I assure you." She could see he was aroused by her pain, anticipating adding to it with sick amusement. He grinned, coming toward her with the poker held menacingly in his hand. Lynnette could not help focusing on the glowing tip fearfully, but she refused to show that fear. Instead, she gathered what little moisture was in her mouth and spat full in the villain's face.

With a roar of rage, Lord Roger pulled his hand back and slapped her viciously across the face. The pirate swung back in her chains, her head ringing and eyes watering so badly she could not see for a moment past the orange glow of the hot iron close to her face and the mad gleam in the eyes of her nemesis. When finally her eyes would focus again, she still could not believe what they were telling her. For there in the doorway, beyond her tormentor, stood Daniel. Behind him were ranged the burly forms of Harry, Charlie, and Omar, though her fond eyes lingered only on the merchant. He was still in his finely tailored evening clothes, and he leaned against the doorjamb with lazy, animal grace, his glossy raven hair loose and framing his sculpted features lovingly. He looked tall, elegant, and breathtakingly handsome.

Not to mention dangerous.

"Drop it, brother!" he ordered harshly.

Roger swiveled about, poker held up in defense. Who dared to interrupt his just and highly pleasurable punishment of the pirate wench? No one was allowed to witness the deeds he performed in this room! He caught sight of his half brother and the other three intruders at the entrance of the dungeon chamber tucked away at the bottom of the cellar stairs. The red glow of a few scattered torches showed that all four men were heavily armed with knives and pistols, and fresh blood stained the blades of two of the rough-looking men.

These, he guessed, eyes narrowing, must be some of the pirate's comrades, here to liberate their leader from his hands. They'd obviously teamed up with her lover, his darling little brother, thought the enraged earl. Well, they'd get her over his dead body! The whoring little bitch deserved her comeuppance after all the years she'd decimated his businesses and forced him to live in fear. No one would rob him of the pleasure of her slow death.

Roger knew the blood on the weapons must have come from his guards, and realized he couldn't count on them to come to his aid. He would have to deal with these scabby fools and their misguided leader on his own. He had only one ace up his sleeve—an old trick, but one that always worked, especially when the dolts on the receiving end were as softhearted as these obviously were. He brought the fire-iron up to the pirate's fair face, the implication clear in his stance. If the rescuers came closer, he would burn Lady Blackthorne's pretty green eyes out.

"Well, well. How charming." Lord Roger faced Daniel and addressed him in a relaxed tone that barely masked the brutal fury roiling inside him at this invasion of his territory. So the stupid wretches thought to break into his secure retreat and take back what he'd rightfully captured? Corner him in his own home like an animal? It was not to be borne! Hanging was too good for these lot. He'd make sure the pirates and their bitch leader received far worse, if and when he escaped with his prize. He'd have just one chance to get away. Later, for his final act of retribution, he would arrange another deadly little accident for his meddling brother—*this* time of the sort that could no fail.

"Once again, you didn't die like you were supposed to. I gather you found out about the footman before he could do his job?" Pennsworth *tsk*ed his tongue, shaking his head mournfully. His façade of urbanity sat ill with the florid color on his venal features and the veins standing out on his temples and neck.

"No doubt you're here now to play the eager young hero,

come to save his poor ladylove from the clutches of the terrible villain." Roger laughed aloud in mockery, seeming not the least disconcerted by the men waiting with drawn blades to kill him. Mania glittered in his eyes, along with bloodlust and a rabid cunning. "Haven't I seen this little play before?" He brought the iron bar even closer to Lynnette's face, so that she could feel the delicate skin of her cheek heat painfully.

"Very well," he sighed playfully. "I'll say my lines like a good penny actor." The earl made his voice deepen into a ringing, melodramatic baritone. "Come no closer, lest you wish your fancy-piece permanently scarred!" He teased Lynnette with the fiery tip, laughing madly, bringing it close to her eyes so that she was forced to close them, then to her lips, where the heat began to blister them. Involuntarily, she hissed. But she didn't want her men or Daniel to know the full extent of her pain, so she chose that moment to do a little acting of her own.

"Good evening, Peacock." She smiled wanly, drawing as far back from her enemy and his instrument of torment as she could. "So glad you could join us." Inwardly, her heart was singing. He'd come for her! She'd never thought to see Daniel come to her aid tonight or any other night, not after all the times she'd done her best to make him give up on her. She should have had more faith in this man who'd proven himself worthy of her trust again and again. So many times he'd held the power of life and death over her and never used it. Instead, he had tried to earn her trust, her belief in him. Now, finally, he had it.

She would never doubt him again. Never before had the pirate queen needed help to get out of a tight situation, but now that she did, it was wonderful to know she could count on the man who'd stolen her heart to be there. A part of her that had been tightly guarded for too many years finally came unknotted and allowed warmth and trust to blossom in its place. Just looking at the merchant, so dashing and vital as he raced to her rescue, facing down his own flesh and blood for her sake, made another surge of love well up in her breast. She hoped he could see her feelings in the look of gratitude she sent him, in contrast to her flippant words.

Daniel's heart constricted at the sight of Lynnette hanging in chains in her torn shift, blood and sweat staining the fabric in places, her hair wild and slipping from its former elegant coiffure. She looked terrible, but bravely held herself erect— no mean feat when the chains forced her to balance on her toes. Exhaustion and pain radiated from the slim buccaneer, despite her cocky demeanor. But her heart still shone in her eyes when she looked at him, confirming what the first mate had told him so recently. She loved him, though he didn't deserve it after what he'd believed about her and Lord Roger. He couldn't have been more wrong about the relationship. God, what had the bastard done to her?

"Are you all right, sweetheart?" he asked in a raw voice that told eloquently of his concern.

"Oh, fine. Just hanging around, waiting for you to show up." She tried a smile, but it turned into a wince when Roger growled and grabbed her hair, threatening her again with the poker as he kept a wary eye on Daniel and the others.

Daniel took a half step forward before he could stop himself. He ached for her, felt the overwhelming urge to take her in his arms and soothe away all the pain and horror, but would take no chances with a madman like Pennsworth holding her hostage. He could not bear to see his beloved pirate hurt.

"Enough talking, bitch! And you, *brother,* come no closer. I'm warning you for the last time!" Roger was no longer laughing. There were too many men out for his blood in this room, and nothing he could do but hold the woman as surety against their attack. Damn it, this wasn't how tonight, his moment of triumph, was supposed to end! He'd planned to take his time killing Captain Thorne, then proudly display her broken body before all, proving he'd made good on his promise to destroy the menace to his shipping and winning back his investors' confidence at the same time. He'd have been back on top in a matter of months, Roger convinced himself; wealthy and powerful and living high as he'd done since becoming earl of Pennsworth nearly twelve years ago.

No man, since his father's death, had ever gotten around his careful plans or prevented him from doing exactly as he liked; but with his damnable half brother, none of his plots or schemes ever seemed to go as planned. The man simply did not know when to die! Three times now he'd tried to kill the little bugger, and each time Bradley had survived. Well, in this case, fourth time would have to be the charm. The merchant's weakness for the woman would be his undoing.

"That iron will cool," Daniel returned, voice low and threatening. "I'm willing to wait. And know this: if you touch her, you'll die. I wouldn't mind that a bit, *brother*."

But Roger, realizing the truth of Daniel's statement, smiled nastily and withdrew his pistol again from inside his jacket, pointing it first at his half brother and the pirates, then at Lynnette. Adrenaline surged in him, giving him a boost of confidence. "I doubt *this* will cool," he smirked.

Trapped between the evil blackguard and his threats to hurt their captain, the loyal men who had come with Captain Bradley to rescue her could do nothing save helplessly watch the drama play out. Harry, standing directly behind the merchant in the doorway, clenched his hand impotently around his dirk. They'd come this far, sneaking through the dark streets of London, felling any number of guards to reach the secret little room beneath the house. Yet now they could only stand uselessly by and hold their breath. "*Do* somethin', lad!" he muttered, his own powerlessness and fear apparent in the impatient words.

Like what? Daniel wondered. He was caught fair and square in this delicate situation. Any move he made would jeopardize Lynnette's life, something he could not bear to contemplate. He'd have to bluff his way through this, and pray Lord Roger backed down before he himself was forced to do so.

"No, perhaps not," he conceded to the man with the pistol. "But you've only got one shot, brother. Kill her, and I'll tear you to pieces. These men here will be happy to help—and believe me, before they finish you'll suffer more pain than you've ever thought possible to endure." The men behind him fingered their blades avidly. "If you kill me, on the other hand, they'll still take you down the moment you're unarmed. Or"— he paused to drive his point home—"you can drop your weapon and take your chances with the pirates' mercy. It's your choice."

Roger's apoplectic refusal was couched in unmentionable terms, and Daniel shrugged. So much for bluffing.

"Then we seem to have reached an impasse. If you're waiting for your hired scum to save your worthless hide, 'twill be a long wait, indeed. They've all been taken care of. There's no way out for you, brother. A score of men surround the compound, and they don't take kindly to what you've done to their leader." To underscore that understatement, the pirates at Daniel's side snarled ominously.

Roger began to feel the pressure, as evidenced by the sweat beading at his temples. His poker had cooled, indeed, leaving him with only the flintlock between himself and the determined men he faced. Yet the grim reality of his situation still hadn't truly come home to him. He refused to believe his days of committing misdeeds with impunity were over, that his perfidy had finally come back around to haunt him and he must pay for what he'd done. After all he'd done to gain the earldom, all the years of plotting and deceit, Pennsworth thought recklessly, he couldn't lose it all to his brother and that whore of a pirate! Why, the very idea was laughable!

Nay, he decided, pulling himself together with a touch of the arrogance that had served him so well over the years, he didn't intend to lose his composure now . . . But perhaps he could make Daniel lose *his*. If so, perhaps he'd still have a chance to get out of this sticky situation . . . With careful calculation, Pennsworth chose the words he knew would anger his hated sibling most.

"You couldn't be more wrong, brother. I think I have you *exactly* where I want you," he bluffed. "Just as I always have. I've played you like a fiddle your whole life. As I played our father, when I made him believe you were dead after you 'joined' the navy." Gaining confidence as Daniel went still under the burden of his words, Lord Roger smugly delivered the coup de grâce. "I gave the old man the poison that killed him, you know; administered it drop by drop along with my lies."

Daniel felt blind rage sweep him, and took another step forward. Roger laughed again, encouraged, but Harry grabbed the back of Daniel's coat and held him back, afraid he would set Pennsworth off. Lynnette, the first mate saw, had drawn herself as far away from the earl as possible, and looked ready to take advantage of the slightest opportunity to strike at her enemy. But Roger still held the pistol steady at her temple.

"You never guessed? Oh, but of course, how could you? You were too busy fetching and carrying and bending over for the officers aboard His Majesty's finest warships. I'll bet you made quite a winsome cabin girl." Pennsworth smirked,

seeing the fury that suffused Daniel's face. If he goaded the
merchant beyond reason, he'd have a chance . . .

"Yes, I poisoned the old man. The bastard had the consti-
tution of an ox before I got to him, but I had to make it look
natural. Slow and sure, that's the way. It took months for him
to die, and by the end he was willing to believe just about
anything I told him. Except about you, naturally. He was stubbornly insistent on your good character, despite the lies I
spread. He never *once* took my side over yours." Jealously
was plain in the twisted expression on Roger's face.

Instead of goading Daniel, he was merely succeeding in
enraging himself further, but Pennsworth didn't notice his plan
had gone awry. He was too wrapped up now in his own bitter,
warped memories of their shared past. With each second he
grew angrier, recalling the old earl's marked preference for his
second son, and his own disinheritance as a young man. The
unforgiving old goat had even gone so far as to have him
disowned, so that the earldom might not pass to his firstborn.
It had taken some fancy maneuvering to undo that while the
man was dying!

"That's why I had to tell him you'd been killed—after
you'd run away to sea and abandoned him so shockingly. I
think thàt was the death blow to Father, when all the poison
in the world wouldn't kill him." Lord Roger laughed mirthlessly.

"You do know you'll not outlive the night, don't you,
brother?" Daniel said softly. He was more infuriated than he
could remember being in his life. Yet Harry's hand on his
back held him firmly to his purpose, making him act cautiously when he wanted to fling himself on his half brother
and pummel the vile bastard until there was nothing recogniz-
able left.

Lord Roger heard the deadly intent in Daniel's voice, and
for the first time that night felt fear. He'd acted with impunity
all his life, but now two of his victims had come to collect
at once, and the hatred in both was palpable. The woman he
could handle, he thought, but Bradley was another affair. Time
he took matters into his own hands.

"I'll take the bitch with me if you lay a hand on me, I
swear it! Don't test me!" he threatened. "Now, all of you, put
your weapons down if you don't want her dead." He jerked

Lynnette's head back with one hand tangled in her red-gold hair, the other prodding the gun up under her jaw.

Staring his handsome younger brother in the eye, Roger deliberately cocked the massive flintlock. His black eyes took on an unholy gleam. "And tell those others to leave," he said, nodding to the pirates backing the merchant up. "This is a matter for *family* to settle, don't you agree?"

Lynnette didn't agree. "If I'm to die," she said clearly, determined to have some say over her fate, "then I want *him* to come with me, Peacock." The teasing nickname was obviously a term of endearment now. "You'll do that for me, won't you?"

"You're not going to die," the merchant replied with firm reassurance. He would have to do as Pennsworth ordered, at least for now. The man was too far over the edge to push further. Reluctantly, Daniel put his weapons down and quietly ordered Harry and the others to leave. He would not, could not, risk her life.

Harry protested. "Now, lad, I can't be doin' that! Can't ye see me lassie needs me an' th' boys?"

"Do as he says, Harry." Lynnette backed up Daniel's order in a calm, resolute voice. "I never meant for you to be a part of this, old friend."

"But, lass—"

"*Now,* Harry." Even in chains she was a commanding woman. "That's an order. You too, Omar, Charlie. Daniel and I can handle this alone."

Looking agonized, the three loyal sailors backed cautiously out of the room. After a moment, their footsteps could be heard dragging slowly up the stairs.

Silence reigned for a long moment as the combatants were left to face each other. Black hatred was palpable in the hellish chamber, coming from all three within its walls. There would be death in here before they were done. It was only a matter of whose.

"What a touching display of loyalty," Roger sneered. Swiftly, he bent and retrieved Daniel's pistol from the rushes and cocked it. Now he had bullets enough for both of them, he thought gleefully, a weapon in both hands making him far more confident of his chances. He'd bluffed and won. "But it's so much more cozy without them.

"Of course, I'm sure those charming fellows are waiting for me just outside with the rest of their mates. It's lucky indeed there are more ways out of this place than one. I'll need them for my escape once you're both well and truly dead." His chuckle this time sounded like the mad cackle of a Bedlamite.

"Now, brother, you'll watch your precious whore die before I kill you, too." He directed the pistol's muzzle at the pirate with deadly accuracy.

Daniel had to do something, and fast. Yet when he spoke, his words were cool, taunting but controlled.

"Do you know why Father loved me best?" he asked softly. Hoping to draw Pennsworth's fire away from Lynnette, he chose his words carefully, knowing Roger's weakness when it came to his dead mother's good name. She was the only person he'd ever cared about, though the vain, selfish creature had done nothing to deserve it during her short lifetime. When, after her death, their father had remarried and begotten Daniel, Roger had never forgiven the man for the perceived betrayal of his precious mother, and had tried repeatedly to destroy the son who'd usurped his place, along with the stepmother who'd never treated him as well as her own child. It had been the young Roger's twisted way of showing love for the woman who'd spawned him.

"It's simple, really." The merchant smiled provocatively, going for the throat. "It's because you are an ugly, warped, homicidal toad of a man, and your mother was a round-heeled slut who spread her legs for every man in the county!"

Abruptly, the room erupted in chaos.

Roger, as Daniel had hoped, went berserk with rage and leapt toward his brother. Lynnette, however, had other plans for her foe, and had had enough of waiting patiently for him to finish trading insults with the peacock.

As Pennsworth swung the flintlock away from her head and lunged forward to meet Daniel, the pirate queen marshaled the last of her flagging energies in a final massive effort. Springing up as high as she could from her toes, Lynnette grabbed hold of the chains above the manacle cuffs holding her wrists, and, in a burst of strength, surged high into the air.

While her arms took her weight, she bent her strong legs up and out, flinging them around the neck of her nemesis as he turned his back on her. Roger choked as her long, muscled limbs closed in a vise around his throat, yanking him back and forcing him to shoot wildly into the air. Both pistols, harmlessly discharged, fell from his hands to clatter against the damp stones of the dungeon floor. Though he clawed and struggled, the mangled remains of vicious oaths tearing from his foaming lips, Lord Roger could not get free.

Through the smoky air, Lynnette caught Daniel's eye, the light of battle in her own. She was wild to kill Pennsworth now that he was finally within her grasp, could feel the strength of rage possess her limbs and send her blood singing through her veins. After all these years, at last she could end it! But she would not kill her beloved's brother if it were against Daniel's wishes.

In his steady silver gaze she saw permission for what she would do. As Roger dangled, blue-faced and gasping, from her unbreakable hold, Lynnette exchanged a long look of understanding with her beloved. Finally, he nodded wearily.

One twist and a loud crack, and the erstwhile earl of Pennsworth fell dead from the slackened grasp of her legs. Almost as limp, the pirate sagged in her bonds.

It was over.

CHAPTER TWENTY-EIGHT

"*R*EMIND ME not to make you angry when I'm within reach of those legs," Daniel said wearily, giving his pirate queen a faint, wry smile from across the dank little chamber.

"You won't make me angry, Peacock," she replied. "Besides, I've got other uses for my legs when you're near." Lynnette wriggled her eyebrows suggestively, though she looked anything but sexy in her bloodstained, exhausted state. "Now, will you *please* get over here and take these damn chains *off* me!"

Daniel walked over to the pirate, carefully sidestepping Pennsworth's corpse crumpled on the damp stones between them. Chains and all, he kissed her tenderly for a long moment.

To his surprise, Lynnette began to cry as soon as his lips left hers. Harsh, racking sobs shook her slender frame; obviously the tears of a woman who had not cried in far too long. Hurriedly, the merchant found the key and unlocked her manacles, gathering her gently into his arms as she sagged helplessly, all strength gone. He held the pirate tightly for a long time, pressing kisses to the top of her head, her cheeks, brow, nose, lips—wherever he could reach without letting go his possessive hold. Relief made him as weak as she.

"I hated hurting you, Daniel," she wept against his shoulder, face hidden in his thick hair. "I'm sorry—so sorry. If you only knew what he'd done to me . . . I wanted to tell you about it when you pressed me. But I just couldn't. I was ashamed to tell you at first, but then, when I learned he was your brother, I knew I had to pretend—"

He stopped the rushing torrent of words with another long, drugging kiss. "I know all about it, sweetheart," he soothed. "You don't have to explain. Harry told me everything on the way here—after he'd shaken some sense into me first. I'm sorry, too, darling, so very sorry for leaving you in such terrible danger. I was just too damn stupid to realize you'd never betray me."

"Never, Peacock," she sniffled. "I could never betray the man I love—even though there were times when I wanted to, times when I should have. Instead, I betrayed Sarah. I couldn't bear to lose you. I'm so ashamed of what I've done—and yet, I wouldn't change it, given the chance. I love you far too much."

Daniel felt happiness spread like a dawning sun through his body at her words. He'd guessed her feelings, but hearing his pirate queen say she loved him was a balm no mere conjecture could match for potency. Yet her eyes were still shadowed with remorse, and he hastened to soothe her anguished heart.

"God, Lynn, how could you be ashamed? You did more for your sister's sake than any sixteen-year-old girl could be expected to do—hell, more than any man of *any* age could have done! I'm sure Sarah understands that, and her spirit is resting now. You've fulfilled your promise. And you've still got me, too, my sweet buccaneer."

Lynnette looked doubtfully up into his eyes, lifting her weary head from its resting place on his shoulder to verify the truth of his words in his steady silver gaze. She was unable to believe she hadn't let her sister down, nor had she succeeded in alienating her former captive. It was too ingrained in the pirate to feel guilt and shame. Daniel brushed her tangled hair back from her forehead, gently shifting her to face him completely, careful to avoid the welts on the pirate's sore back, so that he could look her fully in the eye.

"Sarah understands," he repeated firmly, "because she loves you. As *I* love you. You are the bravest, strongest, most beautiful woman I've ever known, Captain Thorne. My life hasn't been the same since you charged into it, but I'll never regret that you did. You *are* my life." Daniel's deep voice was husky with emotion, and his big hand trembled on her cheek as he brushed away her tears with the lightest of feather touches.

The last traces of pain and bitter memory seemed to vanish from around Lynnette's heart. He was right; at least in as much as she had indeed finally succeeded in fulfilling her bloody vow to her slain sister. As the realization that she'd accomplished her mission at long last swept through her, the pirate felt a sense of poignant relief suffuse her soul. Vengeance was a thing of the past now, all hatred having spilled out of her body in the instant her enemy breathed his last.

She felt light, free as never before. And she had Daniel to thank for it. Without him there could be no meaning to any of it. He'd made life after revenge more than a hazy, dreamlike concept—he'd made it something to wish for and look forward to. He'd given her feelings she'd never thought to feel, given her a pillar of strength to lean on. In truth, he'd allowed her to become more than just a vessel for an avenging spirit; he'd made her a woman under the guidance of his loving, physically *and* spiritually. Despite all she had done to deny him, he'd remained with her to the end. She didn't deserve such happiness—but she wasn't about to give it up when it was offered. The brigand in her planned to guard this booty jealously, indeed!

"And you are the best man I've ever known, Peacock," she replied, smiling through her tears. "The *only* man for me." Lynnette placed a tremulous hand over his heart to feel the steady reassurance of its beating. She felt fortunate beyond words, and wanted to share the sudden buoyancy in her soul. "Besides," she teased, "who else could I find to best me with a sword?"

They laughed together, then took each other's lips again in a kiss of overwhelming, tender passion.

A little while later, Lynnette broke the contact of their mouths, her emerald eyes shining in the torchlight. "We'd better tell Harry and the boys that we're all right before they get it into their heads to mutiny and burst in here regardless of orders. This isn't exactly how I want them to catch us." She grinned, indicating the hand Daniel was resting high up on her thigh. "It's bad for morale, don't you know."

Daniel removed his hand with infinite reluctance and helped the pirate to rise stiffly from the damp stone floor. He was very careful of her injuries, but Lynnette herself seemed to shrug them off, only keeping her arm around his waist for the pleasure of it. Both were thankful to be leaving the horrid little chamber and the lifeless body of its malevolent creator far behind.

"Don't tell me Harry's going to be the maid of honor at our wedding," he teased as they headed for the stairs.

Lynnette did *not* laugh at the mention of the word "wedding" this time. Instead, she merely said, "Bite your tongue, man! Harry would as soon dance a reel with a blue whale. Nay, I was thinking maybe Omar would better suit—"

Daniel captured her smiling lips with his own.

"Though Davie might look comelier in the dress . . ." she gasped when she could breathe again.

In answer, the merchant simply kissed her again. He'd kiss her until the end of time if he had to. It was the best way he knew to shut the pirate up.

EPILOGUE

TWO BLACK-HAIRED, green-eyed children played happily upon the pink sands of a protected cove, building a fantastic castle by the shore. The sound of clashing steel rang out nearby from beyond a screen of lushly flowering foliage, along with shouts and peppery curses.

"Mother and Daddy are at it again," sighed the little girl to her twin brother.

"They're *always* at it," replied her brother with a world-weariness that belied his mere seven years of age.

"Well, you know how they love to duel whenever we make port on Peacock's Paradise," said the girl, referring to the idyllic little utopia once known only as the pirate refuge No-name Island.

"Yeah," the boy agreed. "Maybe all that sailin' around gives 'em cabin fever, like they say we get when we're cooped up belowdecks in a storm." He nodded sagely. "Grown-ups just don't like to admit it when they're bored." Listening intently for a moment to the sound of the rapiers clanging and the laughter ringing out even louder, he dimpled. "It sounds like it's gonna be a long match. Let's go watch."

"I'm betting on Mother," the impish little girl cried, then dashed off to the main harbor where the duel was taking place.

"No fair," cried her twin, racing after her. "You had Mother last time!"

"Yes, but *Daddy* won last time!" Giggling, they caught hands and splashed through the surf to see the combatants fight. Their parents were always in their glory when they battled each other for mastery.

Indeed the two, merchant and ex-pirate, husband and wife, successful shipping magnates now, enjoyed their winters on Peacock's, as the paradisiacal island was known for short. It was a break from the hard work and monotony of sailing the West Indies trade—a trade that, with the aid of Lynnette's hoarded pirate stake, had made them, along with their partner, Simon Richards, very wealthy, indeed.

They'd had enough money to buy back, many times over, the notes held on Pennsworth Abbey and the other properties attendant with the earldom that now fell to Daniel, though both were uncomfortable under the mantle of the title worn for so long by their mutual enemy. They kept the properties in trust for their children, Sarah and Alexander (named for Lynnette's sister and Daniel's father respectively), who had no such negative memories of the estates or their former owner. Though they lived part of the year in London's Mayfair, just off fashionable Park Lane, neither had much desire to venture out into society. They would reserve that honor for their children, when they grew up enough to decide how they wished to amuse themselves.

On the high seas, however, where both were most comfortable, and where they co-commanded a fleet of fast ships, Daniel and Lynnette reigned supreme, for no one ever thought to plunder their vessels.

Indeed, the company had had an unblemished record of business since its third owner stepped in to help run the show. Rumor had it several former pirates were among the men she'd brought to their crews, and the man she'd made head of security for the outfit was a grizzled old salt with more cunning than a school of barracuda.

Rumor also whispered (though the woman herself modestly denied the tale, claiming she was just a plain, respectable matron) that this third owner had once, in her heyday, outfought the best brigands in the Caribbean and earn herself the title "pirate queen." Legend warned she was as likely to run up the Jolly Roger and take any potential attackers captive as *they* were to harm *her*. No one, however, was willing to test this rumor for truth.

As the modest, respectable matron lunged forward across the sparkling hot sand and neatly disarmed her laughing, handsome husband, her own smile was bright with loving anticipation. This duel, she knew, would end as had their first. With a kiss.

Survey

⌒

TELL US WHAT YOU THINK AND YOU COULD WIN

A YEAR OF ROMANCE!
(That's 12 books!)

Fill out the survey below, send it back to us, and you'll be eligible
to win a year's worth of romance novels. That's one book a month
for a year—from St. Martin's Paperbacks.

Name _____

Street Address _____

City, State, Zip Code _____

Email address _____

1. How many romance books have you bought in the last year?
   (Check one.)
   __0-3
   __4-7
   __8-12
   __13-20
   __20 or more

2. Where do you MOST often buy books? *(limit to two choices)*
   __Independent bookstore
   __Chain stores *(Please specify)*
     __Barnes and Noble
     __B. Dalton
     __Books-a-Million
     __Borders
     __Crown
     __Lauriat's
     __Media Play
     __Waldenbooks
   __Supermarket
   __Department store *(Please specify)*
     __Caldor
     __Target
     __Kmart
     __Walmart
   __Pharmacy/Drug store
   __Warehouse Club
   __Airport

3. Which of the following promotions would MOST influence your
   decision to purchase a ROMANCE paperback? *(Check one.)*
     __Discount coupon

___Free preview of the first chapter
___Second book at half price
___Contribution to charity
___Sweepstakes or contest

4. Which promotions would LEAST influence your decision to purchase a ROMANCE book? (Check one.)
    ___Discount coupon
    ___Free preview of the first chapter
    ___Second book at half price
    ___Contribution to charity
    ___Sweepstakes or contest

5. When a new ROMANCE paperback is released, what is MOST influential in your finding out about the book and in helping you to decide to buy the book? (Check one.)
    ___TV advertisement
    ___Radio advertisement
    ___Print advertising in newspaper or magazine
    ___Book review in newspaper or magazine
    ___Author interview in newspaper or magazine
    ___Author interview on radio
    ___Author appearance on TV
    ___Personal appearance by author at bookstore
    ___In-store publicity (poster, flyer, floor display, etc.)
    ___Online promotion (author feature, banner advertising, giveaway)
    ___Word of Mouth
    ___Other (please specify)_____

6. Have you ever purchased a book online?
    ___Yes
    ___No

7. Have you visited our website?
    ___Yes
    ___No

8. Would you visit our website in the future to find out about new releases or author interviews?
    ___Yes
    ___No

9. What publication do you read most?
    ___Newspapers *(check one)*
        ___*USA Today*
        ___*New York Times*
        ___Your local newspaper
    ___Magazines *(check one)*

      __*People*
      __*Entertainment Weekly*
      __Women's magazine *(Please specify:_____)*
      __*Romantic Times*
      __Romance newsletters

10. What type of TV program do you watch most? *(Check one.)*
    __Morning News Programs (ie. "Today Show")
      (Please specify:_____)
    __Afternoon Talk Shows (ie. "Oprah")
      (Please specify: _____)
    __All news (such as CNN)
    __Soap operas   *(Please specify: _____)*
    __Lifetime cable station
    __E! cable station
    __Evening magazine programs (ie. "Entertainment Tonight")
      (Please specify: _____)
    __Your local news

11. What radio stations do you listen to most? *(Check one.)*
      __Talk Radio
      __Easy Listening/Classical
      __Top 40
      __Country
      __Rock
      __Lite rock/Adult contemporary
      __CBS radio network
      __National Public Radio
      __WESTWOOD ONE radio network

12. What time of day do you listen to the radio MOST?
      __6am-10am
      __10am-noon
      __Noon-4pm
      __4pm-7pm
      __7pm-10pm
      __10pm-midnight
      __Midnight-6am

13. Would you like to receive email announcing new releases and special promotions?
      __Yes
      __No

14. Would you like to receive postcards announcing new releases and special promotions?
      __Yes
      __No

15. Who is your favorite romance author? _____

WIN A YEAR OF ROMANCE FROM SMP
(That's 12 Books!)
No Purchase Necessary

OFFICIAL RULES

1. To Enter: Complete the Official Entry Form and Survey and mail it to: Win a Year of Romance from SMP Sweepstakes, c/o St. Martin's Paperbacks, 175 Fifth Avenue, Suite 1615, New York, NY 10010-7848, Attention JP. For a copy of the Official Entry Form and Survey, send a self-addressed, stamped envelope to: Entry Form/Survey, c/o St. Martin's Paperbacks at the address stated above. Entries with the completed surveys must be received by February 1, 2000 (February 22, 2000 for entry forms requested by mail). Limit one entry per person. No mechanically reproduced or illegible entries accepted. Not responsible for lost, misdirected, mutilated or late entries.

2. Random Drawing. Winner will be determined in a random drawing to be held on or about March 1, 2000 from all eligible entries received. Odds of winning depend on the number of eligible entries received. Potential winner will be notified by mail on or about March 22, 2000 and will be asked to execute and return an Affidavit of Eligibility/Release/Prize Acceptance Form within fourteen (14) days of attempted notification. Non-compliance within this time may result in disqualification and the selection of an alternate winner. Return of any prize/prize notification as undeliverable will result in disqualification and an alternate winner will be selected.

3. Prize and approximate Retail Value: Winner will receive a copy of a different romance novel each month from April 2000 through March 2001. Approximate retail value $84.00 (U.S. dollars).

4. Eligibility. Open to U.S. and Canadian residents (excluding residents of the province of Quebec) who are 18 at the time of entry. Employees of St. Martin's and its parent, affiliates and subsidiaries, its and their directors, officers and agents, and their immediate families or those living in the same household, are ineligible to enter. Potential Canadian winners will be required to correctly answer a time-limited arithmetic skill question by mail. Void in Puerto Rico and wherever else prohibited by law.

5. General Conditions: Winner is responsible for all federal, state and local taxes. No substitution or cash redemption of prize permitted by winner. Prize is not transferable. Acceptance of prize constitutes permission to use the winner's name, photograph and likeness for purposes of advertising and promotion without additional compensation or permission, unless prohibited by law.

6. All entries become the property of sponsor, and will not be returned. By participating in this sweepstakes, entrants agree to be bound by these official rules and the decision of the judges, which are final in all respects.

7. For the name of the winner, available after March 22, 2000, send by May 1, 2000 a stamped, self-addressed envelope to Winner's List, Win a Year of Romance from SMP Sweepstakes, St. Martin's Paperbacks, 175 Fifth Avenue, Suite 1615, New York, NY 10010-7848, Attention JP.